NEW FLESH

THE NEW FLESH

Tales of Shapeshifters and Strange Transformations

edited by
MARK MORRIS

BRITISH LIBRARY

This collection first published in 2026 by
The British Library
96 Euston Road
London NW1 2DB
bl.uk

1 3 5 7 9 10 8 6 4 2

Represented in the EU by Authorised Rep Compliance Ltd., Ground Floor, 71 Lower Baggot Street, Dublin, D02 P593, Ireland. arccompliance.com

Cataloguing in Publication Data
A catalogue record for this publication is available from the British Library

ISBN 978 0 7123 6915 2
e-ISBN 978 0 7123 6285 6

Frontispiece illustration by Mag Ruhig. Illustrations on pages 6, 14 and 320 from the *Monstrorum Historia* of Vlyssis Aldrouandi (Ulisse Aldrovandi), 1642.
Cover design by Mauricio Villamayor with illustration by Mag Ruhig.
Text design and typesetting by Tetragon, London
Printed in England by CPI Group (UK) Ltd, Croydon, CR0 4YY

MIX
Paper | Supporting responsible forestry
FSC® C013604
FSC www.fsc.org

CONTENTS

INTRODUCTION 7

A NOTE FROM THE PUBLISHER 15

Transformation MARY SHELLEY 17

A Pastoral Horror ARTHUR CONAN DOYLE 39

Mr Meldrum's Mania JOHN METCALFE 61

The Black Hare FLAVIA RICHARDSON 99

The Beautiful People CHARLES BEAUMONT 109

Furry Night JOAN AIKEN 133

Royal Jelly ROALD DAHL 151

Temple of the Fox JAMES WADE 185

David's Worm BRIAN LUMLEY 203

Strange Roots DAVID CASE 215

Arbor Day MARY DANBY 257

The Jaguar Hunter LUCIUS SHEPARD 275

The Girl on the Suicide Bridge JOHNNY MAINS 307

INTRODUCTION

Long live the new flesh.
VIDEODROME

To explore the theme of transformation in fiction in just a few pages is an impossible task. Transformation has been central to storytelling for as long as stories have been told. It is present in the oldest existing examples of literature, such as the *Epic of Gilgamesh* (*c*.2100–1200 BCE), Homer's *Iliad* (*c*.670–650 BCE), and, perhaps most significantly, in Ovid's *Metamorphoses* (8 CE), the latter a work so inspirational that its effects still resonate in fiction today.

Transformation is a common theme in international folklore and fairy tales, and even in the Bible: Lot's wife is turned into a pillar of salt when she looks back at the destruction of Sodom (Genesis 19), and Jesus's first miracle is to turn water into wine (John 2: 1–12). Indeed, it is such a ubiquitous plot device, more often than not used to symbolize additional themes—such as personal growth, human duality, fear of mortality and/or the unknown—that it is central to many of the stories involving more defined and recognizable tropes of weird fiction, such as werewolves, vampires, ghosts, witches and even, you could argue, that more modern weird fiction character, the superhero.

Pretty much every story of the weird with transformation as its theme can be placed into one of five categories. These are:

1. Human into Beast (or into a different kind of human)
2. Beast into Human
3. Human into Object

4. Object into Human
5. Object into Different Object.

The first category is perhaps the most common, and to return to Homer and his peers, is a device we see employed time and again in Greek mythology. To give just a few of many examples, we have Zeus transforming King Lycaon into a wolf as punishment for killing and cooking his son, Nyctimus; we have Ares turning Alectryon into a rooster for failing him in a task; we have Demeter transforming Ascalabus into a lizard, and King Lyncus into a lynx, both again as a form of punishment; we have Athena transforming Arachne into a spider as punishment for Arachne's hubris in claiming to have weaving skills superior to the goddess's; and we have Artemis transforming Actaeon into a stag for spying on her as she bathed.

This first category is also most prevalent in world folklore. In British and Irish folklore, for example, witches are noted for their ability to change into various animals, particularly hares, and in the Irish myth of Aoife, she turns her stepchildren into swans to be rid of them. In Norse mythology, Loki takes the form of various animals, including a horse and a bear, and Freyja, who owns a cloak of falcon feathers that enables her to transform into a falcon, changes her protégé Óttar into a boar in order to hide him. In Filipino mythology, the aswang is a creature that can take a multitude of forms—bat, boar, cat, dog—to stalk its prey. And Creole cultures, from Canada and North America to the Caribbean, abound with tales of shapeshifting creatures, which are not dissimilar to werewolves, called the *loup-garou*, or *rougarou*.

A vast number and variety of modern stories, too, involve humans transforming into beasts, or into different kinds of humans. Some well-known examples include fairy tales such as *Beauty and the Beast* (1740) and *The Frog-Prince* (1812); *Strange Case of Dr Jekyll and Mr*

Hyde by Robert Louis Stevenson (1886), where the beast is not an animal, but a manifestation of the reputable Dr Jekyll's baser instincts; *Metamorphosis* by Franz Kafka (1915); and the seven-book Harry Potter series by J. K. Rowling (1997–2007), in which some characters, known as "animagi", have the ability to transform into specific animals at will.

As can be seen from the above examples, the reasons why humans become animals (or otherwise beast-like) in fiction are many and varied—in Greek mythology the transformation was often meted out as punishment, whereas in later examples, such as *Strange Case of Dr Jekyll and Mr Hyde*, or in the case of various Marvel superheroes, such as Spiderman or the Incredible Hulk, the changes occurred as a result of scientific mishap or misdemeanour.

Perhaps because animals are generally seen as "lesser" beings than humans, in category 2 stories—Beasts into Humans—transformations are rarely meted out as punishments, but instead are often credited with more sinister motives. In Celtic mythology, the selkie—a seal that can remove its skin to become human—is often depicted as undergoing a transformation in order to procure a human mate. Though these stories, romantic as they are, often end in tragedy, selkies are relatively benign when compared to water spirits such as kelpies, which emerge from lochs and rivers in the form of horses or women to ensnare and kill lone travellers, or the *each-uisge*, an even more vicious form of water-horse spirit, which drowns its victims before devouring them.

Chinese, Japanese and Korean mythology seethes with stories about animals with the ability to take on human form. Most common are tales of dangerous fox spirits, which, in the guise of beautiful women, entice male victims. The Korean *kumiho*, for example, has nine tails, and in order to fulfil her desire to be a human, uses her beauty to seduce men and devour their hearts. The TV series *The Terror:*

Infamy (2019) featured as its antagonist a *bakemono*, a shapeshifting creature with evil intent, which most commonly took on the guise of a desirable woman.

In some stories, animals, rather than having evil intent, are granted human form as a reward. In Indian mythology, a cobra who undergoes one hundred years of penance may be blessed by Lord Shiva to become a shapeshifter capable of assuming human form, and gifted with an abnormally long life.

In category 3 stories—Human into Object—the transformation is almost always enforced as a punishment, or is seen as the result of dark magic. Stories associated with standing stones are prime examples of this. The Na Fir Bhrèige stones, also known as The False Men, which are situated close to Loch nam Madadh in North Uist, Scotland, are said to be three men from Skye who were turned into stone by a witch as punishment for deserting their wives. The Rollright Stones on the Oxfordshire and Warwickshire border in England were once reputedly a king and his army, who were transformed into stone by a witch, who herself then transformed into an elder tree—which, if cut, will break the spell, restoring the stones to life. And the three thousand-plus Carnac Stones near the south coast of Brittany in France are said to be a Roman legion who were petrified while fleeing by none other than Merlin himself.

For a rare exception to the almost universally held notion that transformation from human into object is a bad thing, we must delve once again into the treasure trove that is Ovid's *Metamorphoses*. Here we find the tale of Baucis and Philemon, a poor and elderly couple, who, as a reward from the gods for their kindness and hospitality to Zeus and Hermes, are transformed at the moment of their deaths into a pair of entwined trees.

Category 4 stories—Object into Human—are few and far between, though there are some prominent examples, both ancient and modern.

Returning to Greek mythology, one task given to Jason was to sow dragon's teeth, which then grew and transformed into fierce warriors. In a memorable sequence from the 1963 film *Jason and the Argonauts*, the dragon became the many-headed Hydra, and its teeth begat the "children of the Hydra", animated, armed skeletons, brilliantly realized by special effects genius Ray Harryhausen. In other stories from Greek mythology, Deucalion and his wife Pyrrha repopulated the world after a devastating flood by casting stones which transformed into people—Deucalion's becoming men, and Pyrrha's becoming women. And the sculptor Pygmalion fell in love with Galatea, his perfect ivory statue, which was then transformed into a living woman by the goddess Aphrodite.

Statues and puppets coming to life have been used to creepy effect in many a story of the weird, though perhaps the most famous example, and one in which the wooden puppet ultimately transforms into a flesh and blood human, is *The Adventures of Pinocchio* (1883) by Italian author Carlo Collodi. This novel, too, features a category 1 sequence, whereby as a result of their laziness, Pinocchio and his friend Candlewick are transformed into donkeys in the Land of Toys.

Perhaps one of the most audacious examples of an Object into Human transformation can be seen in season five of the popular supernatural drama series *Buffy the Vampire Slayer* (1997–2003). In episode one of series five, regular viewers were baffled to discover that Buffy suddenly had a younger sister called Dawn, who had never appeared in the show before. Even more bafflingly, the regular cast acted as though Dawn had always been part of their lives, and even Dawn herself seemed oblivious to the fact that she had appeared out of nowhere. It is not until episode five of the same season that Buffy finally discovers Dawn's true nature, when she is informed by a dying monk that her sister is a mystical ball of energy known as "the Key", which can unlock the barriers between all dimensions. To prevent "the Key" falling into the hands of a hell-goddess called Glory, the monks transformed it into human form, gave it the memories of a teenage girl, altered the memories of everyone else associated with Dawn so that they would accept her presence without question, and then put it—in the form of a younger sister—under the Slayer's protection. Buffy subsequently keeps the truth from Dawn until episode thirteen, whereupon Dawn then has to deal with the terrible revelation that her entire life as she remembers it is a lie. It's powerful stuff, that in the guise of a frothy teen show, deals with themes of identity, loss, memory and perception.

The final category—Object into Object—most commonly features transformations that are part of a wider story, and which are usually achieved via magic or some other miraculous practice, such as the pumpkin being turned into a carriage in the fairy tale "Cinderella" (1697). More often than not, these transformations are arbitrary and used as little more than convenient plot devices, one example being a block of salt which transforms into a mountain to thwart a giant in the Norwegian folk tale "The Master Maid" (1864; first English translation 1889). More commonly, particularly in modern children's fiction, the transformative properties of objects are used to disguise their true nature. Examples of this are the four mythical treasures—spear, sword, stone and cauldron—in Alan Garner's *Elidor* (1965), which change into innocuous pieces of junk when brought into the real world, and Percy Jackson's sword Anaklusmos in the *Percy Jackson* book series by Rick Riordan (2005–present), which conveniently transforms into a ballpoint pen when not in use.

The stories I have selected for this anthology, which range from 1831 to 2014, examine transformation in all its many and varied forms. There are "body swap" stories here; stories of possession; stories involving witchcraft, curses, genetic manipulation and scientific misconduct.

Within these pages you'll find folk horror, science fiction, magical realism, and perhaps even one or two tales that make you laugh, or bring a tear to your eye.

Most importantly of all, though, these are all stories about that most fundamental aspect of human existence: *change*.

MARK MORRIS, 2026

MARK MORRIS is, in the words of Clive Barker, "one of the finest horror writers at work today", as well as an award-winning editor of haunting anthologies, including the "ABC of Horror" series published by Flame Tree Press (2020–). His horror novels include *That Which Stands Outside* (2024) and *Bad Things Happen Here* (2026), while his scriptwriting credits include audio adaptations of the 1971 film *The Blood on Satan's Claw* and the M. R. James ghost story "A View from a Hill" (each of which won a New York Festival Radio Award). Morris has received two British Fantasy Awards, along with multiple nominations for the Bram Stoker, and Shirley Jackson, Awards. Beyond horror, Mark has written novelizations for *Doctor Who* and other popular franchises.

A NOTE FROM THE PUBLISHER

The original short stories reprinted in the British Library Tales of the Weird series were written and published in a period ranging across the nineteenth and twentieth centuries. There are many elements of these stories which continue to entertain modern readers; however, in some cases there are also uses of language, instances of stereotyping and some attitudes expressed by narrators or characters which may not be endorsed by the publishing standards of today. We acknowledge therefore that some elements in the stories selected for reprinting may continue to make uncomfortable reading for some of our audience. With this series British Library Publishing aims to offer a new readership a chance to read some of the rare material of the British Library's collections in an affordable paperback format, to enjoy their merits and to look back into the worlds of the past two centuries as portrayed by their writers. It is not possible to separate these stories from the history of their writing and therefore the following stories are presented as they were originally published with three edits to the text, and minor edits made for consistency of style and sense. We welcome feedback from our readers, which can be sent to the following address:

British Library Publishing
The British Library
96 Euston Road
London, NW1 2DB
United Kingdom

1831

TRANSFORMATION

Mary Shelley

Born Mary Wollstonecraft Godwin on 30 August 1797, Mary Shelley is of course best known for writing the novel *Frankenstein; or, The Modern Prometheus*, which was published in January 1818 when she was just twenty years old. Her early life was difficult—her mother died from complications of childbirth when Mary was eleven days old, and her father's publishing company struggled to make a profit, which meant that the family was often in debt. Always a keen reader—often, as a child, at her mother's graveside—young Mary published her first poem *Mounseer Nongtongpaw* in 1808, and in June 1814, she ran off to Europe with her father's student, the aristocrat Percy Bysshe Shelley, and soon became pregnant. The couple married in 1816, and during their tumultuous relationship had four children, only one of whom, Percy Florence, born in 1819, lived to adulthood.

In July 1822, Percy Bysshe Shelley died in a sailing accident at the age of 29, leaving Mary to bring up their son on her own. She supported the two of them for the rest of her life through her writing, and through promoting her husband's work. After *Frankenstein* she wrote several more novels: *Valperga; or, the Life and Adventures of Castruccio, Prince of Lucca* (1823), *The Last Man* (1826), *The Fortunes of Perkin Warbeck, a Romance* (1830), *Lodore* (1835) and *Falkner* (1837), along with travel diaries, magazine articles and short stories like "Transformation", which was one of several Gothic tales published in the British literary annual *The Keepsake*.

First published in 1831, "Transformation" is one of the earliest examples of that subgenre of "shapeshifter" fiction, the "body swap" story. Later examples include *The Master Mind of Mars* by Edgar Rice Burroughs (1928), *Laughing Gas* by P. G. Wodehouse (1936), the H. P. Lovecraft tales "The Shadow Out of Time" (1936) and "The Thing on the Doorstep" (1937), and *Freaky Friday* by Mary Rodgers (1972). In "Transformation", the protagonist Guido is portrayed as a reckless and profligate man, determined to live a life of pleasure—a character perhaps inspired by Mary's late husband? Certainly, it has been suggested that the story could have been influenced by Mary and Percy Bysshe Shelley's mutual friend Lord Byron, whose unfinished drama *The Deformed Transformed* (1824) explored similar themes to "Transformation", and was transcribed by Mary Shelley in 1822/23.

Forthwith this frame of mine was wrench'd
  With a woful agony,
Which forced me to begin my tale,
  And then it set me free.

Since then, at an uncertain hour,
  That agony returns;
And till my ghastly tale is told
  This heart within me burns.

COLERIDGE'S ANCIENT MARINER

I have heard it said, that, when any strange, supernatural, and necromantic adventure has occurred to a human being, that being, however desirous he may be to conceal the same, feels at certain periods torn up as it were by an intellectual earthquake, and is forced to bare the inner depths of his spirit to another. I am a witness of the truth of this. I have dearly sworn to myself never to reveal to human ears the horrors to which I once, in excess of fiendly pride, delivered myself over. The holy man who heard my confession, and reconciled me to the church, is dead. None knows that once—

Why should it not be thus? Why tell a tale of impious tempting of Providence, and soul-subduing humiliation? Why? answer me, ye who are wise in the secrets of human nature! I only know that so it is; and in spite of strong resolve—of a pride that too much masters me—of shame, and even of fear, so to render myself odious to my species—I must speak.

Genoa! my birth-place—proud city! looking upon the blue waves of the Mediterranean sea—dost thou remember me in my boyhood, when thy cliffs and promontories, thy bright sky and gay vineyards, were my world? Happy time! when to the young heart the narrow-bounded universe, which leaves, by its very limitation, free scope to the imagination, enchains our physical energies, and, sole period in our lives, innocence and enjoyment are united. Yet, who can look back to childhood, and not remember its sorrows and its harrowing fears? I was born with the most imperious, haughty, tameless spirit, with which ever mortal was gifted. I quailed before my father only; and he, generous and noble, but capricious and tyrannical, at once fostered and checked the wild impetuosity of my character, making obedience necessary, but inspiring no respect for the motives which guided his commands. To be a man, free, independent; or, in better words, insolent and domineering, was the hope and prayer of my rebel heart.

My father had one friend, a wealthy Genoese noble, who in a political tumult was suddenly sentenced to banishment, and his property confiscated. The Marchese Torella went into exile alone. Like my father, he was a widower: he had one child, the almost infant Juliet, who was left under my father's guardianship. I should certainly have been an unkind master to the lovely girl, but that I was forced by my position to become her protector. A variety of childish incidents all tended to one point,—to make Juliet see in me a rock of refuge; I in her, one, who must perish through the soft sensibility of her nature too rudely visited, but for my guardian care. We grew up together. The opening rose in May was not more sweet than this dear girl. An irradiation of beauty was spread over her face. Her form, her step, her voice—my heart weeps even now, to think of all of relying, gentle, loving, and pure, that was enshrined in that celestial tenement. When I was eleven and Juliet eight years of age, a cousin of mine, much older than either—he seemed to us a man—took great notice of my playmate; he called her his bride, and asked her to marry him. She refused, and he insisted, drawing her unwillingly towards him. With the countenance and emotions of a maniac I threw myself on him—I strove to draw his sword—I clung to his neck with the ferocious resolve to strangle him: he was obliged to call for assistance to disengage himself from me. On that night I led Juliet to the chapel of our house: I made her touch the sacred relics—I harrowed her child's heart, and profaned her child's lips with an oath, that she would be mine, and mine only.

Well, those days passed away. Torella returned in a few years, and became wealthier and more prosperous than ever. When I was seventeen, my father died; he had been magnificent to prodigality; Torella rejoiced that my minority would afford an opportunity for repairing my fortunes. Juliet and I had been affianced beside my father's deathbed—Torella was to be a second parent to me.

I desired to see the world, and I was indulged. I went to Florence, to Rome, to Naples; thence I passed to Toulon, and at length reached, what had long been the bourne of my wishes, Paris. There was wild work in Paris then. The poor king, Charles the Sixth, now sane, now mad, now a monarch, now an abject slave, was the very mockery of humanity. The queen, the dauphin, the Duke of Burgundy, alternately friends and foes—now meeting in prodigal feasts, now shedding blood in rivalry—were blind to the miserable state of their country, and the dangers that impended over it, and gave themselves wholly up to dissolute enjoyment or savage strife. My character still followed me. I was arrogant and self-willed; I loved display, and above all, I threw all control far from me. Who could control me in Paris? My young friends were eager to foster passions which furnished them with pleasures. I was deemed handsome—I was master of every knightly accomplishment. I was disconnected with any political party. I grew a favourite with all: my presumption and arrogance was pardoned in one so young: I became a spoiled child. Who could control me? not the letters and advice of Torella—only strong necessity visiting me in the abhorred shape of an empty purse. But there were means to refill this void. Acre after acre, estate after estate, I sold. My dress, my jewels, my horses and their caparisons, were almost unrivalled in gorgeous Paris, while the lands of my inheritance passed into possession of others.

The Duke of Orleans was waylaid and murdered by the Duke of Burgundy. Fear and terror possessed all Paris. The dauphin and the queen shut themselves up; every pleasure was suspended. I grew weary of this state of things, and my heart yearned for my boyhood's haunts. I was nearly a beggar, yet still I would go there, claim my bride, and rebuild my fortunes. A few happy ventures as a merchant would make me rich again. Nevertheless, I would not return in humble guise. My last act was to dispose of my remaining estate near Albaro for half its worth, for ready money. Then I despatched all kinds of artificers, arras, furniture of regal splendour, to fit up the last relic of my inheritance, my palace in Genoa. I lingered a little longer yet, ashamed at the part of the prodigal returned, which I feared I should play. I sent my horses. One matchless Spanish jennet I despatched to my promised bride; its caparisons flamed with jewels and cloth of gold. In every part I caused to be entwined the initials of Juliet and her Guido. My present found favour in hers and in her father's eyes.

Still to return a proclaimed spendthrift, the mark of impertinent wonder, perhaps of scorn, and to encounter singly the reproaches or taunts of my fellow-citizens, was no alluring prospect. As a shield between me and censure, I invited some few of the most reckless of my comrades to accompany me: thus I went armed against the world, hiding a rankling feeling, half fear and half penitence, by bravado and an insolent display of satisfied vanity.

I arrived in Genoa. I trod the pavement of my ancestral palace. My proud step was no interpreter of my heart, for I deeply felt that, though surrounded by every luxury, I was a beggar. The first step I took in claiming Juliet must widely declare me such. I read contempt or pity in the looks of all. I fancied, so apt is conscience to imagine what it deserves, that rich and poor, young and old, all regarded me with derision. Torella came not near me. No wonder that my second father should expect a son's deference from me in waiting first on him. But, galled and stung by a sense of my follies and demerit, I strove to throw the blame on others. We kept nightly orgies in Palazzo Carega. To sleepless, riotous nights, followed listless, supine mornings. At the Ave Maria we showed our dainty persons in the streets, scoffing at the sober citizens, casting insolent glances on the shrinking women. Juliet was not among them—no, no; if she had been there, shame would have driven me away, if love had not brought me to her feet.

I grew tired of this. Suddenly I paid the Marchese a visit. He was at his villa, one among the many which deck the suburb of San Pietro d'Arena. It was the month of May—a month of May in that garden of the world—the blossoms of the fruit trees were fading among thick, green foliage; the vines were shooting forth; the ground strewed with the fallen olive blooms; the fire-fly was in the myrtle hedge; heaven and earth wore a mantle of surpassing beauty. Torella welcomed me kindly, though seriously; and even his shade of displeasure soon wore away. Some resemblance to my father—some look and tone of youthful ingenuousness, lurking still in spite of my misdeeds, softened the good old man's heart. He sent for his daughter—he presented me to her as her betrothed. The chamber became hallowed by a holy light as she entered. Hers was that cherub look, those large, soft eyes, full dimpled cheeks, and mouth of infantine sweetness, that expresses the rare union of happiness and love. Admiration first possessed me; she is mine! was the second proud emotion, and my lips curled with haughty triumph. I had not been the *enfant gâté* of the beauties of France not to have learnt the art of pleasing the soft heart of woman. If towards men I was overbearing, the deference I paid to them was the more in contrast. I commenced my courtship by the display of a thousand gallantries to Juliet, who, vowed to me from infancy, had never admitted the devotion of others; and who, though accustomed to expressions of admiration, was uninitiated in the language of lovers.

For a few days all went well. Torella never alluded to extravagance; he treated me as a favourite son. But the time came, as we discussed the preliminaries to my union with his daughter, when his fair face of things should be overcast. A contract had been drawn up in my father's lifetime. I had rendered this, in fact, void, by having squandered the whole of the wealth which was to have been shared by Juliet and myself. Torella, in consequence, chose to consider this bond as cancelled, and proposed another, in which, though the wealth he bestowed was immeasurably increased, there were so many restrictions as to the mode of spending it, that I, who saw independence only in free career being given to my own imperious will, taunted him as taking advantage of my situation, and refused utterly to subscribe to his conditions. The old man mildly strove to recall me to reason. Roused pride became the tyrant of my thought: I listened with indignation—I repelled him with disdain.

"Juliet, thou art mine! Did we not interchange vows in our innocent childhood? are we not one in the sight of God? and shall thy cold-hearted, cold-blooded father divide us? Be generous, my love, be just; take not away a gift, last treasure of thy Guido—retract not thy vows—let us defy the world, and setting at nought the calculations of age, find in our mutual affection a refuge from every ill."

Fiend I must have been, with such sophistry to endeavour to poison that sanctuary of holy thought and tender love. Juliet shrank from me affrighted. Her father was the best and kindest of men, and she strove to show me how, in obeying him, every good would follow. He would receive my tardy submission with warm affection; and generous pardon would follow my repentance. Profitless words for a young and gentle daughter to use to a man accustomed to make his will, law; and to feel in his own heart a despot so terrible and stern, that he could yield obedience to nought save his own imperious desires! My resentment grew with resistance; my wild companions were ready to add fuel to the flame. We laid a plan to carry off Juliet. At first it appeared to be crowned with success. Midway, on our return, we were overtaken by the agonized father and his attendants. A conflict ensued. Before the city guard came to decide the victory in favour of our antagonists, two of Torella's servitors were dangerously wounded.

This portion of my history weighs most heavily with me. Changed man as I am, I abhor myself in the recollection. May none who hear this tale ever have felt as I. A horse driven to fury by a rider armed with barbed spurs, was not more a slave than I, to the violent tyranny of my temper. A fiend possessed my soul, irritating it to madness. I felt the voice of conscience within me; but if I yielded to it for a brief interval, it was only to be a moment after torn, as by a whirlwind, away—borne along on the stream of desperate rage—the plaything of the storms engendered by pride. I was imprisoned, and, at the instance of Torella, set free. Again I returned to carry off both him and his child to France; which hapless country, then preyed on by freebooters and gangs of lawless soldiery, offered a grateful refuge to a criminal like me. Our plots were discovered. I was sentenced to banishment; and, as my debts were already enormous, my remaining property was put in the hands of commissioners for their payment. Torella again offered his mediation, requiring only my promise not to renew my abortive attempts on himself and his daughter. I spurned his offers, and fancied that I triumphed when I was thrust out from Genoa, a solitary and penniless exile. My companions were gone: they had been dismissed the city some weeks before, and were already in France. I was alone—friendless; with nor sword at my side, nor ducat in my purse.

I wandered along the sea-shore, a whirlwind of passion possessing and tearing my soul. It was as if a live coal had been set burning in my breast. At first I meditated on what *I should do*. I would join a band of freebooters. Revenge!—the word seemed balm to me:—I hugged it—caressed it—till, like a serpent, it stung me. Then again I would abjure and despise Genoa, that little corner of the world. I would return to Paris, where so many of my friends swarmed; where my services would be eagerly accepted; where I would carve out fortune with my sword, and might, through success, make my paltry birth-place, and the false Torella, rue the day when they drove me, a new Coriolanus, from her walls. I would return to Paris—thus, on foot—a beggar—and present myself in my poverty to those I had formerly entertained sumptuously? There was gall in the mere thought of it.

The reality of things began to dawn upon my mind, bringing despair in its train. For several months I had been a prisoner: the evils of my dungeon had whipped my soul to madness, but they had subdued my corporeal frame. I was weak and wan. Torella had used a thousand artifices to administer to my comfort; I had detected and scorned them all—and I reaped the harvest of my obduracy. What was to be done?—Should I crouch before my foe, and sue for forgiveness?—Die rather ten thousand deaths!—Never should they obtain that victory! Hate—I swore eternal hate! Hate from whom?—to whom?—From a wandering outcast—to a mighty noble. I and my feelings were nothing to them: already had they forgotten one so unworthy. And Juliet!—her angel-face and sylphlike form gleamed among the clouds of my despair with vain beauty; for I had lost her—the glory and flower of the world! Another will call her his!—that smile of paradise will bless another!

Even now my heart fails within me when I recur to this rout of grim-visaged ideas. Now subdued almost to tears, now raving in my agony, still I wandered along the rocky shore, which grew at each step wilder and more desolate. Hanging rocks and hoar precipices overlooked the tideless ocean; black caverns yawned; and for ever, among the seaworn recesses, murmured and dashed the unfruitful waters. Now my way was almost barred by an abrupt promontory, now rendered nearly impracticable by fragments fallen from the cliff. Evening was at hand, when, seaward, arose, as if on the waving of a wizard's wand, a murky web of clouds, blotting the late azure sky, and darkening and disturbing the till now placid deep. The clouds had strange fantastic shapes; and they changed, and mingled, and seemed to be driven about by a mighty spell. The waves raised their white crests; the thunder first muttered, then roared from across the waste of waters, which took a deep purple dye, flecked with foam. The spot where I stood, looked, on one side, to the wide-spread ocean; on the other, it was barred by a rugged promontory. Round this cape suddenly came, driven by the wind, a vessel. In vain the mariners tried to force a path for her to the open sea—the gale drove her on the rocks. It will perish!—all on board will perish!—Would I were among them! And to my young heart the idea of death came for the first time blended with that of joy. It was an awful sight to behold that vessel struggling with her fate. Hardly could I discern the sailors, but I heard them. It was soon all over!—A rock, just covered by the tossing waves, and so unperceived, lay in wait for its prey. A crash of thunder broke over my head at the moment that, with a frightful shock, the skiff dashed upon her unseen enemy. In a brief space of time she went to pieces. There I stood in safety; and there were my fellow-creatures, battling, how hopelessly, with annihilation. Methought I saw them struggling—too truly did I hear their shrieks, conquering the barking surges in their shrill agony. The dark breakers threw hither and thither the fragments of the wreck: soon it disappeared. I had been fascinated to gaze till the end: at last I sank on my knees—I covered my face with my hands: I again looked up; something was floating on the billows towards the shore. It neared and neared. Was that a human form?—It grew more distinct; and at last a mighty wave, lifting the whole freight, lodged it upon a rock. A human being bestriding a sea-chest!—A human being!—Yet was it one? Surely never such had existed before—a misshapen dwarf, with squinting eyes, distorted features, and body deformed, till it became a horror to behold. My blood, lately warming towards a fellow-being so snatched from a watery tomb, froze in my heart. The dwarf got off his chest; he tossed his straight, straggling hair from his odious visage:

"By St Beelzebub!" he exclaimed, "I have been well bested." He looked round and saw me. "Oh, by the fiend! here is another ally of the mighty one. To what saint did you offer prayers, friend—if not to mine? Yet I remember you not on board."

I shrank from the monster and his blasphemy. Again he questioned me, and I muttered some inaudible reply. He continued:—

"Your voice is drowned by this dissonant roar. What a noise the big ocean makes! Schoolboys bursting from their prison are not louder than these waves set free to play. They disturb me. I will no more of their ill-timed brawling.—Silence, hoary One!—Winds, avaunt!—to your homes!—Clouds, fly to the antipodes, and leave our heaven clear!"

As he spoke, he stretched out his two long lank arms, that looked like spider's claws, and seemed to embrace with them the expanse before him. Was it a miracle? The clouds became broken, and fled; the azure sky first peeped out, and then was spread a calm field of blue above us; the stormy gale was exchanged to the softly breathing west; the sea grew calm; the waves dwindled to riplets.

"I like obedience even in these stupid elements," said the dwarf. "How much more in the tameless mind of man! It was a well got up storm, you must allow—and all of my own making."

It was tempting Providence to interchange talk with this magician. But *Power*, in all its shapes, is venerable to man. Awe, curiosity, a clinging fascination, drew me towards him.

"Come, don't be frightened, friend," said the wretch: "I am good-humoured when pleased; and something does please me in your well-proportioned body and handsome face, though you look a little woe-begone. You have suffered a land—I, a sea wreck. Perhaps I can allay the tempest of your fortunes as I did my own. Shall we be friends?"—And he held out his hand; I could not touch it. "Well, then, companions—that will do as well. And now, while I rest after the buffeting I underwent just now, tell me why, young and gallant as you seem, you wander thus alone and downcast on this wild sea-shore."

The voice of the wretch was screeching and horrid, and his contortions as he spoke were frightful to behold. Yet he did gain a kind of influence over me, which I could not master, and I told him my tale. When it was ended, he laughed long and loud: the rocks echoed back the sound: hell seemed yelling around me.

"Oh, thou cousin of Lucifer!" said he; "so thou too hast fallen through thy pride; and, though bright as the son of Morning, thou art ready to give up thy good looks, thy bride, and thy well-being, rather than submit thee to the tyranny of good. I honour thy choice, by my soul!—So thou hast fled, and yield the day; and mean to starve on these rocks, and to let the birds peck out thy dead eyes, while thy enemy and thy betrothed rejoice in thy ruin. Thy pride is strangely akin to humility, methinks."

As he spoke, a thousand fanged thoughts stung me to the heart.

"What would you that I should do?" I cried.

"I!—Oh, nothing, but lie down and say your prayers before you die. But, were I you, I know the deed that should be done."

I drew near him. His supernatural powers made him an oracle in my eyes; yet a strange unearthly thrill quivered through my frame as I said—"Speak!—teach me—what act do you advise?"

"Revenge thyself, man!—humble thy enemies!—set thy foot on the old man's neck, and possess thyself of his daughter!"

"To the east and west I turn," cried I, "and see no means! Had I gold, much could I achieve; but, poor and single, I am powerless."

The dwarf had been seated on his chest as he listened to my story. Now he got off; he touched a spring; it flew open!—What a mine of wealth—of blazing jewels, beaming gold, and pale silver—was displayed therein. A mad desire to possess this treasure was born within me.

"Doubtless," I said, "one so powerful as you could do all things."

"Nay," said the monster, humbly, "I am less omnipotent than I seem. Some things I possess which you may covet; but I would give them all for a small share, or even for a loan of what is yours."

"My possessions are at your service," I replied, bitterly—"my poverty, my exile, my disgrace—I make a free gift of them all."

"Good! I thank you. Add one other thing to your gift, and my treasure is yours."

"As nothing is my sole inheritance, what besides nothing would you have?"

"Your comely face and well-made limbs."

I shivered. Would this all-powerful monster murder me? I had no dagger. I forgot to pray—but I grew pale.

"I ask for a loan, not a gift," said the frightful thing: "lend me your body for three days—you shall have mine to cage your soul the while, and, in payment, my chest. What say you to the bargain?—Three short days."

We are told that it is dangerous to hold unlawful talk; and well do I prove the same. Tamely written down, it may seem incredible that I should lend any ear to this proposition; but, in spite of his unnatural ugliness, there was something fascinating in a being whose voice could govern earth, air, and sea. I felt a keen desire to comply; for with that chest I could command the world. My only hesitation resulted from a fear that he would not be true to his bargain. Then, I thought, I shall soon die here on these lonely sands, and the limbs he covets will be mine no more:—it is worth the chance. And, besides, I knew that, by all the rules of art-magic, there were formula and oaths which none of its practisers dared break. I hesitated to reply; and he went on, now displaying his wealth, now speaking of the petty price he demanded, till it seemed madness to refuse. Thus is it: place our bark in the current of the stream, and down, over fall and cataract it is hurried; give up our conduct to the wild torrent of passion, and we are away, we know not whither.

He swore many an oath, and I adjured him by many a sacred name; till I saw this wonder of power, this ruler of the elements, shiver like an autumn leaf before my words; and as if the spirit spake unwillingly and per force within him, at last, he, with broken voice, revealed the spell whereby he might be obliged, did he wish to play me false, to render up the unlawful spoil. Our warm lifeblood must mingle to make and to mar the charm.

Enough of this unholy theme. I was persuaded—the thing was done. The morrow dawned upon me as I lay upon the shingles, and I knew not my own shadow as it fell from me. I felt myself changed to a shape of horror, and cursed my easy faith and blind credulity. The chest was there—there the gold and precious stones for which I had sold the frame of flesh which nature had given me. The sight a little stilled my emotions: three days would soon be gone.

They did pass. The dwarf had supplied me with a plenteous store of food. At first I could hardly walk, so strange and out of joint were all my limbs; and my voice—it was that of the fiend. But I kept silent, and turned my face to the sun, that I might not see my shadow, and counted the hours, and ruminated on my future conduct. To bring Torella to my feet—to possess my Juliet in spite of him—all this my wealth could easily achieve. During dark night I slept, and dreamt of the accomplishment of my desires. Two suns had set—the third dawned. I was agitated, fearful. Oh expectation, what a frightful thing art thou, when kindled more by fear than hope! How dost thou twist thyself round the heart, torturing its pulsations! How dost thou dart unknown pangs all through our feeble mechanism, now seeming to shiver us like broken glass, to nothingness—now giving us a fresh strength, which can *do* nothing, and so torments us by a sensation, such as the strong man must feel who cannot break his fetters, though they bend in his grasp. Slowly paced the bright, bright orb up the eastern sky; long it lingered in the zenith, and still more slowly wandered down the west: it touched the horizon's verge—it was lost! Its glories were on the summits of the cliff—they grew dun and gray. The evening star shone bright. He will soon be here.

He came not!—By the living heavens, he came not!—and night dragged out its weary length, and, in its decaying age, "day began to grizzle its dark hair;" and the sun rose again on the most miserable wretch that ever upbraided its light. Three days thus I passed. The jewels and the gold—oh, how I abhorred them!

Well, well—I will not blacken these pages with demoniac ravings. All too terrible were the thoughts, the raging tumult of ideas that filled my soul. At the end of that time I slept; I had not before since the third sunset; and I dreamt that I was at Juliet's feet, and she smiled, and then she shrieked—for she saw my transformation—and again she smiled, for still her beautiful lover knelt before her. But it was not I—it was he, the fiend, arrayed in my limbs, speaking with my voice, winning her with my looks of love. I strove to warn her, but my tongue refused its office; I strove to tear him from her, but I was rooted to the ground—I awoke with the agony. There were the solitary hoar precipices—there the plashing sea, the quiet strand, and the blue sky over all. What did it mean? was my dream but a mirror of the truth? was he wooing and winning my betrothed? I would on the instant back to Genoa—but I was banished. I laughed—the dwarf's yell burst from my lips—*I* banished! O, no! they had not exiled the foul limbs I wore; I might with these enter, without fear of incurring the threatened penalty of death, my own, my native city.

I began to walk towards Genoa. I was somewhat accustomed to my distorted limbs; none were ever so ill adapted for a straight-forward movement; it was with infinite difficulty that I proceeded. Then, too, I desired to avoid all the hamlets strewed here and there on the sea-beach, for I was unwilling to make a display of my hideousness. I was not quite sure that, if seen, the mere boys would not stone me to death as I passed, for a monster: some ungentle salutations I did receive from the few peasants or fisherman I chanced to meet. But it was dark night before I approached Genoa. The weather was so balmy and sweet that it struck me that the Marchese and his daughter would very probably have quitted the city for their country retreat. It was from Villa Torella that I had attempted to carry off Juliet; I had spent many an hour reconnoitring the spot, and knew each inch of ground in its vicinity. It was beautifully situated, embosomed in trees, on the margin of a stream. As I drew near, it became evident that my conjecture was right; nay, moreover, that the hours were being then devoted to feasting and merriment. For the house was lighted up; strains of soft and gay music were wafted towards me by the breeze. My heart sank within me. Such was the generous kindness of Torella's heart that I felt sure that he would not have indulged in public manifestations of rejoicing just after my unfortunate banishment, but for a cause I dared not dwell upon.

The country people were all alive and flocking about; it became necessary that I should study to conceal myself; and yet I longed to address some one, or to hear others discourse, or in any way to gain intelligence of what was really going on. At length, entering the walks that were in immediate vicinity to the mansion, I found one dark enough to veil my excessive frightfulness; and yet others as well as I were loitering in its shade. I soon gathered all I wanted to know—all that first made my very heart die with horror, and then boil with indignation. Tomorrow Juliet was to be given to the penitent, reformed, beloved Guido—tomorrow my bride was to pledge her vows to a fiend from hell! And I did this!—my accursed pride—my demoniac violence and wicked self-idolatry had caused this act. For if I had acted as the wretch who had stolen my form had acted—if, with a mien at once yielding and dignified, I had presented myself to Torella, saying, I have done wrong, forgive me; I am unworthy of your angel-child, but permit me to claim her hereafter, when my altered conduct shall manifest that I abjure my vices, and endeavour to become in some sort worthy of her. I go to serve against the infidels; and when my zeal for religion and my true penitence for the past shall appear to you to cancel my crimes, permit me again to call myself your son. Thus had he spoken; and the penitent was welcomed even as the prodigal son of scripture: the fatted calf was killed for him; and he, still pursuing the same path, displayed such open-hearted regret for his follies, so humble a concession of all his rights, and so ardent a resolve to reacquire them by a life of contrition and virtue, that he quickly conquered the kind, old man; and full pardon, and the gift of his lovely child, followed in swift succession.

O! had an angel from Paradise whispered to me to act thus! But now, what would be the innocent Juliet's fate? Would God permit the foul union—or, some prodigy destroying it, link the dishonoured name of Carega with the worst of crimes? Tomorrow at dawn they were to be married: there was but one way to prevent this—to meet mine enemy, and to enforce the ratification of our agreement. I felt that this could only be done by a mortal struggle. I had no sword—if indeed my distorted arms could wield a soldier's weapon—but I had a dagger, and in that lay my every hope. There was no time for pondering or balancing nicely the question: I might die in the attempt; but besides the burning jealousy and despair of my own heart, honour, mere humanity, demanded that I should fall rather than not destroy the machinations of the fiend.

The guests departed—the lights began to disappear; it was evident that the inhabitants of the villa were seeking repose. I hid myself among the trees—the garden grew desert—the gates were closed—I wandered round and came under a window—ah! well did I know the same!—a soft twilight glimmered in the room—the curtains were half withdrawn. It was the temple of innocence and beauty. Its magnificence was tempered, as it were, by the slight disarrangements occasioned by its being dwelt in, and all the objects scattered around displayed the taste of her who hallowed it by her presence. I saw her enter with a quick light step—I saw her approach the window—she drew back the curtain yet further, and looked out into the night. Its breezy freshness played among her ringlets, and wafted them from the transparent marble of her brow. She clasped her hands, she raised her eyes to Heaven. I heard her voice. Guido! she softly murmured, Mine own Guido! and then, as if overcome by the fulness of her own heart, she sank on her knees:—her praised eyes—her negligent but graceful attitude—the beaming thankfulness that lighted up her face—oh, these are tame words! Heart of mine thou imagest ever, though thou canst not pourtray, the celestial beauty of that child of light and love.

I heard a step—a quick firm step along the shady avenue. Soon I saw a cavalier, richly dressed, young and, methought, graceful to look on, advance.—I hid myself yet closer.—The youth approached; he paused beneath the window. She arose, and again looking out she saw him and said—I cannot, no, at this distant time I cannot record her terms of soft silver tenderness; to me they were spoken, but they were replied to by him.

"I will not go," he cried: "here where you have been, where your memory glides like some Heaven-visiting ghost, I will pass the long hours till we meet, never, my Juliet, again, day or night, to part. But do thou my love, retire; the cold morn and fitful breeze will make thy cheek pale, and fill with languor thy love-lighted eyes. Ah, sweetest! could I press one kiss upon them, I could, methinks, repose."

And then he approached still nearer, and methought he was about to clamber into her chamber. I had hesitated, not to terrify her; now I was no longer master of myself. I rushed forward—I threw myself on him—I tore him away—I cried, "O loathsome and foul-shaped wretch!"

I need not repeat epithets, all tending, as it appeared, to rail at a person I at present feel some partiality for. A shriek rose from Juliet's lips. I neither heard nor saw—I *felt* only mine enemy, whose throat I grasped, and my dagger's hilt; he struggled, but could not escape: at length hoarsely he breathed these words: "Do!—strike home! destroy this body—you will still live: may your life be long and merry!"

The descending dagger was arrested at the word, and he, feeling my hold relax, extricated himself and drew his sword, while the uproar in the house, and flying of torches from one room to the other, showed that soon we should be separated—and I—oh! far better die: so that he did not survive, I cared not. In the midst of my frenzy there was much calculation:—fall I might, and so that he did not survive, I cared not for the death-blow I might deal against myself. While still, therefore, he thought I paused, and while I saw the villainous resolve to take advantage of my hesitation, in the sudden thrust he made at me, I threw myself on his sword, and at the same moment plunged my dagger, with a true desperate aim, in his side. We fell together, rolling over each other, and the tide of blood that flowed from the gaping wound of each mingled on the grass. More I know not—I fainted.

Again I returned to life: weak almost to death, I found myself stretched upon a bed—Juliet was kneeling beside it. Strange! my first broken request was for a mirror. I was so wan and ghastly, that my poor girl hesitated, as she told me afterwards; but, by the mass! I thought myself a right proper youth when I saw the dear reflection of my own well-known features. I confess it is a weakness, but I avow it, I do entertain a considerable affection for the countenance and limbs I behold, whenever I look at a glass; and have more mirrors in my house, and consult them oftener than any beauty in Venice. Before you too much condemn me, permit me to say that no one better knows than I the value of his own body; no one, probably, except myself, ever having had it stolen from him.

Incoherently I at first talked of the dwarf and his crimes, and reproached Juliet for her too easy admission of his love. She thought me raving, as well she might, and yet it was some time before I could prevail on myself to admit that the Guido whose penitence had won her back for was myself; and while I cursed bitterly the monstrous dwarf, and blest the well-directed blow that had deprived him of life, I suddenly checked myself when I heard her say—Amen! knowing that him whom she reviled was my very self. A little reflection taught me silence—a little practice enabled me to speak of that frightful night without any very excessive blunder. The wound I had given myself was no mockery of one—it was long before I recovered—and as the benevolent and generous Torella sat beside me, talking such wisdom as might win friends to repentance, and mine own dear Juliet hovered near me, administering to my wands, and cheering me by her smiles, the work of my bodily cure and mental reform went on together. I have never, indeed, wholly recovered my strength—my cheek is paler since—my person a little bent. Juliet sometimes ventures to allude bitterly to the malice that caused this change, but I kiss her on the moment, and tell her all is for the best. I am a fonder and more faithful husband—and true is this—but for that wound, never had I called her mine.

I did not revisit the sea-shore, nor seek for the fiend's treasure; yet, while I ponder on the past, I often think, and my confessor was not backward in favouring the idea, that it might be a good rather than an evil spirit, sent by my guardian angel, to show me the folly and misery of pride. So well at least did I learn this lesson, roughly taught as I was, that I am known now by all my friends and fellow-citizens by the name of Guido il Cortese.

1890

A PASTORAL HORROR

Arthur Conan Doyle

Born in Edinburgh, Scotland, Sir Arthur Conan Doyle (1859–1930) is best known for creating consulting detective Sherlock Holmes, one of the most enduring and fascinating fictional characters of all time. Holmes dominates any discussion of his work, though Conan Doyle was, in fact, a prolific author who wrote not only detective stories, but semi-autobiographical novels such as *The Firm of Girdlestone* (1890) and *The Stark Munro Letters* (1895); historical fiction such as *The White Company* (1891) and *Sir Nigel* (1906); military non-fiction such as *The Great Boer War* (1900) and *The Crime of the Congo* (1909), as well as six volumes of *The British Campaign in France and Flanders* (1916–20); and, in later life, books about spiritualism, of which he was a passionate advocate, such as *The New Revelation* (1918), *The Vital Message* (1919), *The Wanderings of a Spiritualist* (1921), *The Coming of the Fairies* (1922) and the two-volume *The History of Spiritualism* (1926).

Additionally, he wrote many fine supernatural tales, including the chilling "The Leather Funnel", and one of the best and creepiest "mummy" stories ever written, "Lot No. 249".

"A Pastoral Horror", which first appeared in *People Magazine* on 21 December 1890, may well have been influenced by Robert Louis Stevenson's *Strange Case of Dr Jekyll and Mr Hyde*, which was published just four years previously. Certainly, the two stories boast many similarities, sharing as they do the common theme of the beast inside the man. The setting for the story was inspired by a journey taken by Conan Doyle through the Tyrolean Alps of Austria, and to all intents and purposes "A Pastoral Horror" is a proto-werewolf tale—though, interestingly, given his forays into the supernatural and spiritualism in some of his other work, his medical background inhibited him from going the whole hog (or wolf) and have his killer undergo a full physical transformation.

Far above the level of the Lake of Constance, nestling in a little corner of the Tyrolese Alps, lies the quiet town of Feldkirch. It is remarkable for nothing save for the presence of a large and well-conducted Jesuit school and for the extreme beauty of its situation. There is no more lovely spot in the whole of the Vorarlberg. From the hills which rise behind the town, the great lake glimmers some fifteen miles off, like a broad son of quicksilver. Down below in the plains the Rhine and the Danube prattle along, flowing swiftly and merrily, with none of the dignity which they assume as they grow from brooks into rivers. Five great countries or principalities,—Switzerland, Austria, Baden, Wurtemberg, and Bavaria—are visible from the plateau of Feldkirch.

Feldkirch is the centre of a large tract of hilly and pastoral country. The main road runs through the centre of the town, and then on as far as Anspach, where it divides into two branches, one of which is larger than the other. This more important one runs through the valleys across Austrias Tyrol into Tyrol proper, going as far, I believe, as the capital of Innsbruck. The lesser road runs for eight or ten miles amid wild and rugged glens to the village of Laden, where it breaks up into a network of sheep-tracks. In this quiet spot, I, John Hudson, spent nearly two years of my life, from the June of '65 to the March of '67, and it was during that time that those events occurred which for some weeks brought the retired hamlet into an unholy prominence, and caused its name for the first, and probably for the last time, to be a familiar word to the European press. The short account of these incidents which appeared in the English papers was, however, inaccurate and misleading, besides which, the rapid advance of the Prussians, culminating in the battle of Sadowa, attracted public attention away from what might have moved it deeply in less troublous times. It seems to me that the facts may be detailed now, and be new to the great majority of readers, especially as I was myself intimately connected with the drama, and am in a position to give many particulars which have never before been made public.

And first a few words as to my own presence in this out of the way spot. When the great City firm of Spragge, Wilkinson, and Spragge failed, and offered their creditors rather less than eighteen-pence in the pound, a number of humble individuals were ruined, including myself. There was, however, some legal objection which hold out a chance of my being made an exception to the other creditors, and being paid in full. While the case was being fought out I was left with a very small sum for my subsistence.

I determined, therefore, to take up my residence abroad in the interim, since I could live more economically there, and be spared the mortification of meeting those who had known me in my more prosperous days. A friend of mine had described Laden to me some years before as being the most isolated place which he had ever come across in all his experience, and as isolation and cheap living are usually synonymous, I bethought me of his words. Besides, I was in a cynical humour with my fellow-man, and desired to see as little of him as possible for some time to come. Obeying, then, the guidances of poverty and of misanthropy, I made my way to Laden, where my arrival created the utmost excitement among the simple inhabitants. The manners and customs of the red-bearded Englander, his long walks, his check suit, and the reasons which had led him to abandon his fatherland, were all fruitful sources of gossip to the topers who frequented the Gruner Mann and the Schwartzer Bar—the two alehouses of the village.

I found myself very happy at Laden. The surroundings were magnificent, and twenty years of Brixton had sharpened my admiration for nature as an olive improves the flavour of wine. In my youth I had been a fair German scholar, and I found myself able, before I had been many months abroad, to converse even on scientific and abstruse subjects with the now curé of the parish.

This priest was a great godsend to me, for he was a most learned man and a brilliant conversationalist. Father Verhagen—for that was his name—though little more than forty years of age, had made his reputation as an author by a brilliant monograph upon the early Popes—a work which eminent critics have compared favourably with Von Ranke's. I shrewdly suspect that it was owing to some rather unorthodox views advanced in this book that Verhagen was relegated to the obscurity of Laden. His opinions upon every subject were ultra-Liberal, and in his fiery youth he had been ready to vindicate them, as was proved by a deep scar across his chin, received from a dragoon's sabre in the abortive insurrection at Berlin. Altogether the man was an interesting one, and though he was by nature somewhat cold and reserved, we soon established an acquaintanceship.

The atmosphere of morality in Laden was a very rarefied one. The position of Intendant Wurm and his satellites had for many years been a sinecure. Non-attendance at church upon a Sunday or feast-day was about the deepest and darkest crime which the most advanced of the villagers had attained to. Occasionally some hulking Fritz or Andreas would come lurching home at ten o'clock at night, slightly under the influence of Bavarian beer, and might even abuse the wife of his bosom if she ventured to remonstrate, but such cases were rare, and when they occurred the Ladeners looked at the culprit for some time in a half admiring, half horrified manner, as one who had committed a gaudy sin and so asserted his individuality.

It was in this peaceful village that a series of crimes suddenly broke out which astonished all Europe, and for atrocity and for the mystery which surrounded them surpassed anything of which I have ever heard or read. I shall endeavour to give a succinct account of these events in the order of their sequence, in which I am much helped by the fact that it has been my custom all my life to keep a journal—to the pages of which I now refer.

It was, then, I find upon the 19th of May in the spring of 1866, that my old landlady, Frau Zimmer, rushed wildly into the room as I was sipping my morning cup of chocolate and informed me that a murder had been committed in the village. At first I could hardly believe the news, but as she persisted in her statement, and was evidently terribly frightened, I put on my hat and went out to find out the truth. When I came into the main street of the village I saw several men hurrying along in front of me, and following them I came upon an excited group in front of the little stadhouse or town hall—a barnlike edifice which was used for all manner of public gatherings. They were collected round the body of one Maul, who had formerly been a steward upon one of the steamers running between Lindau and Fredericshaven, on the Lake of Constance. He was a harmless, inoffensive little man, generally popular in the village, and, as far as was known, without an enemy in the world. Maul lay upon his face, with his fingers dug into the earth, no doubt in his last convulsive struggles, and his hair all matted together with blood, which had streamed down over the collar of his coat. The body had been discovered nearly two hours, but no one appeared to know what to do or whither to convey it. My arrival, however, together with that of the curé, who came almost simultaneously, infused some vigour into the crowd. Under our direction the corpse was carried up the steps, and laid on the floor of the town hall, where, having made sure that life was extinct, we proceeded to examine the injuries, in conjunction with Lieutenant Wurms, of the police. Maul's face was perfectly placid, showing that he had had no thought of danger until the fatal blow was struck. His watch and purse had not been taken. Upon washing the clotted blood from the back of his head a singular triangular wound was found, which had smashed the bone and penetrated deeply into the brain. It had evidently been inflicted by a heavy blow from a sharp-pointed pyramidal instrument. I believe that it was Father Verhagen, the curé, who suggested the probability of the weapon in question having been a short mattock or small pickaxe, such as are to be found in every Alpine cottage. The Intendant, with praiseworthy promptness, at once obtained one and striking a turnip, produced just such a curious gap as was to be seen in poor Maul's head. We felt that we had come upon the first link of a chain which might guide us to the assassin. It was not long before we seemed to grasp the whole clue.

A sort of inquest was held upon the body that same afternoon, at which Pfiffer, the maire, presided, the curé, the Intendant, Freckler, of the post office, and myself forming ourselves into a sort of committee of investigation. Any villager who could throw a light upon the case or give an account of the movements of the murdered man upon the previous evening was invited to attend. There was a fair muster of witnesses, and we soon gathered a connected series of facts. At half-past eight o'clock Maul had entered the Grüner Mann public-house, and had called for a flagon of beer. At that time there were sitting in the tap-room Waghorn, the butcher of the village, and an Italian pedlar named Cellini, who used to come three times a year to Laden with cheap jewellery and other wares. Immediately after his entrance the landlord had seated himself with his customers, and the four had spent the evening together, the common villagers not being admitted beyond the bar. It seemed from the evidence of the landlord and of Waghorn, both of whom were most respectable and trustworthy men, that shortly after nine o'clock a dispute arose between the deceased and the pedlar. Hot words had been exchanged, and the Italian had eventually left the room, saying that he would not stay any longer to hear his country decried. Maul remained for nearly an hour, and being somewhat elated at having caused his adversary's retreat, he drank rather more than was usual with him. One witness had met him walking towards his home, about ten o'clock, and deposed to his having been slightly the worse for drink. Another had met him just a minute or so before he reached the spot in front of the stadthaus where the deed was done. This man's evidence was most important. He swore confidently that while passing the town hall, and before meeting Maul, he had seen a figure standing in the shadow of the building, adding that the person appeared to him, as far as he could make him out, to be not unlike the Italian.

Up to this point we had then established two facts—that the Italian had left the Grüner Mann before Maul, with words of anger on his lips; the second, that some unknown individual had been seen lying in wait on the road which the ex-steward would have to traverse. A third, and most important, was reached when the woman with whom the Italian lodged deposed that he had not returned the night before until half-past ten, an unusually late hour for Laden. How had he employed the time, then, from shortly after nine, when he left the public-house, until half-past ten, when he returned to his rooms? Things were beginning to look very black, indeed, against the pedlar.

It could not be denied, however, that there were points in the man's favour, and that the case against him consisted entirely of circumstantial evidence. In the first place, there was no sign of a mattock or any other instrument which could have been used for such a purpose among the Italian's goods: nor was it easy to understand how he could come by any such a weapon, since he did not go home between the time of the quarrel and his final return. Again, as the curé pointed out, since Cellini was a comparative stranger in the village, it was very unlikely that he would know which road Maul would take in order to reach his home. This objection was weakened, however, by the evidence of the dead man's servant, who deposed that the pedlar had been hawking his wares in front of their house the day before, and might very possibly have seen the owner at one of the windows. As to the prisoner himself, his attitude at first had been one of defiance, and even of amusement: but when he began to realize the weight of evidence against him, his manner became cringing, and he wrung his hands piteously, loudly proclaiming his innocence. His defence was that after leaving the inn, he had taken a long walk down the Anspach-road in order to cool down his excitement, and that this was the cause of his late return. As to the murder of Maul, he knew no more about it than the babe unborn.

I have dwelt at some length upon the circumstances of this case, because there are points in connection with it which makes it peculiarly interesting. I intend now to fall back upon my diary, which was very fully kept during this period, and indeed during my whole residence abroad. It will save me trouble to quote from it, and it will be a voucher for the accuracy of facts.

May 20th.—Nothing thought of and nothing talked of but the recent tragedy. A hunt has been made among the woods and along the brook in the hope of finding the weapon of the assassin. The more I think of it, the more convinced I am that Cellini is the man. The fact of the money being untouched proves that the crime was committed from motives of revenge, and who would bear such spite towards poor innocent Maul except the vindictive hot-blooded Italian whom he had just offended. I dined with Pfiffer in the evening, and he entirely agreed with me in my view of the case.

May 21st.—Still no word as far as I can hear which throws any light upon the murder. Poor Maul was buried at twelve o'clock in the quiet little village churchyard. The curé read the service with great feeling, and his audience, consisting of the whole population of the village, were much moved, interrupting him frequently by sobs and ejaculations of grief. After the painful ceremony was over I had a short walk with our good priest. His naturally excitable nature has been considerably stirred by recent events. His hand shakes and his face is pale.

"My friend," said he, taking me by the arm as we walked together, "you know something of medicine." (I had been two years at Guy's.) "I have been far from well of late."

"It is this sad affair which has upset you," I said.

"No," he answered, "I have felt it coming on for some time, but it has been worse of late. I have a pain which shoots from here to here," he put his hand to his temples. "If I were struck by lightning, the sudden shock it causes me could not be more great. At times when I close my eyes flashes of light pass before them, and my ears are for ever singing. Often I know not what I do. My fear is lest I faint some time when performing my holy offices."

"You are everworking yourself," I said; "you must have rest and strengthening tonics. Are you writing just now? And how much do you do each day?"

"Eight hours," he answered. "Sometimes ten, sometimes even twelve, when the pains in my head do not interrupt me."

"You must reduce it to four," I said authoritatively. "You must also take regular exercise. I shall send you some quinine which I have in my trunk, and you can take as much as would cover a gulden in a glass of milk every morning and night."

He departed, vowing that he would follow my directions.

I hear from the maire that four policemen are to be sent from Anspach to remove Cellini to a safer goal.

May 22nd.—To say that I was startled would give but a faint idea of my mental state. I am confounded, amazed, horrified beyond all expression. Another and a more dreadful crime has been committed during the night. Freckler has been found dead in his house—the very Freckler who had sat with me on the committee of investigation the day before. I write these notes after a long and anxious day's work, during which I have been endeavouring to assist the officers of the law. The villagers are so paralysed with fear at this fresh evidence of an assassin in their midst that there would be a general panic but for our exertions. It appears that Freckler, who was a man of peculiar habits, lived alone in an isolated dwelling. Some curiosity was aroused this morning by the fact that he had not gone to his work, and that there was no sign of movement about the house. A crowd assembled, and the doors were eventually forced open. The unfortunate Freckler was found in the bedroom upstairs, lying with his head in the fireplace. He had met his death by an exactly similar wound to that which had proved fatal to Maul, save that in this instance the injury was in front. His hands were clenched, and there was an indescribable look of horror, and, as it seemed to me, of surprise upon his features. There were marks of muddy footsteps upon the stairs, which must have been caused by the murderer in his ascent, as his victim had put on his slippers before retiring to his bedroom. These prints, however, were too much blurred to enable us to get a trustworthy outline of the foot. They were only to be found upon every third step, showing with what fiendish swiftness this human tiger had rushed upstairs in search of his victim. There was a considerable sum of money in the house, but not one farthing had been touched, nor had any of the drawers in the bedroom been opened.

As the dismal news became known the whole population of the village assembled in a great crowd in front of the house—rather, I think, from the gregariousness of terror than from mere curiosity. Every man looked with suspicion upon his neighbour. Most were silent, and when they spoke it was in whispers, as if they feared to raise their voices. None of these people were allowed to enter the house, and we, the more enlightened members of the community, made a strict examination of the premises. There was absolutely nothing, however, to give the slightest clue as to the assassin. Beyond the fact that he must be an active man, judging from the manner in which he ascended the stairs, we have gained nothing from this second tragedy. Intendant Wurms pointed out, indeed, that the dead man's rigid right arm was stretched out as if in greeting, and that, therefore, it was probable that this late visitor was some one with whom Freckler was well acquainted. This, however, was, to a large extent, conjecture. If anything could have added to the horror created by the dreadful occurrence, it was the fact that the crime must have been committed at the early hour of half-past eight in the evening—that being the time registered by a small cuckoo clock, which had been carried away by Freckler in his fall.

No one, apparently, heard any suspicious sounds or saw any one enter or leave the house. It was done rapidly, quietly, and completely, though many people must have been about at the time. Poor Pfiffer and our good curé are terribly cut up by the awful occurrence, and, indeed, I feel very much depressed myself now that all the excitement is over and the reaction set in. There are very few of the villagers about this evening, but from every side is heard the sound of hammering—the peasants fitting bolts and bars upon the doors and windows of their houses. Very many of them have been entirely unprovided with anything of the sort, nor were they ever required until now. Frau Zimmer has manufactured a huge fastening which would be ludicrous if we were in a humour for laughter.

I hear tonight that Collini has been released, as, of course, there is no possible pretext for detaining him now; also that word has been sent to all the villages near for any police that can be spared.

My nerves have been so shaken that I remained awake the greater part of the night, reading Gordon's translation of Tacitus by candle-light. I have got out my navy revolver and cleaned it, so as to be ready for all eventualities.

May 23rd.—The police force has been recruited by three more men from Anspach and two from Thalstadt at the other side of the hills. Intendant Wurms has established an efficient system of patrols, so that we may consider ourselves reasonably safe. Today has cast no light upon the murders. The general opinion in the village seems to be that they have been done by some stranger who lies concealed among the woods. They argue that they have all known each other since childhood, and that there is no one of their number who would be capable of such actions. Some of the more daring of them have made a hunt among the pine forests today, but without success.

May 26th.—Events crowd on space. We seem hardly to have recovered from one horror when something else occurs to excite the popular imagination. Fortunately, this time it is not a fresh tragedy, although the news is serious enough.

The murderer has been seen, and that upon the public road, which proves that his thirst for blood has not been quenched yet, and also that our reinforcements of police are not enough to guarantee security. I have just come back from hearing Andreas Murch narrate his experience, though he is still in such a state of trepidation that his story is somewhat incoherent. He was belated among the hills, it seems, owing to mist. It was nearly eleven o'clock before he struck the main road about a couple of miles from the village. He confesses that he felt by no means comfortable at finding himself out so late after the recent occurrences. However, as the fog had cleared away and the moon was shining brightly, he trudged sturdily along. Just about a quarter of a mile from the village the road takes a very sharp bend. Andreas had got as far as this when he suddenly heard in the still night the sound of footsteps approaching rapidly round this curve. Overcome with fear, he threw himself into the ditch which skirts the road, and lay there motionless in the shadow, peering over the side. The steps came nearer and nearer, and then a tall dark figure came round the corner at a swinging pace, and passing the spot where the moon glimmered upon the white face of the frightened peasant, halted in the road about twenty yards further on, and began probing about among the reeds on the roadside with an instrument which Andreas Murch recognized with horror as being a long mattock. After searching about in this way for a minute or so, as if he suspected that some one was concealed there, for he must have heard the sound of the footsteps, he stood still leaning upon his weapon. Murch describes him as a tall, thin man, dressed in clothes of a darkish colour. The lower part of his face was swathed in a wrapper of some sort, and the little which was visible appeared to be of a ghastly pallor. Murch could not see enough of his features to identify him, but thinks that it was no one whom he had ever seen in his life before. After standing for some little time, the man with the mattock had walked swiftly away into the darkness, in the direction in which he imagined the fugitive had gone. Andreas, as may be supposed, lost little time in getting safely into the village, where he alarmed the police. Three of them, armed with carbines, started down the road, but saw no signs of the miscreant. There is, of course, a possibility that Murch's story is exaggerated and that his imagination has been sharpened by fear. Still, the whole incident cannot be trumped up, and this awful demon who haunts us is evidently still active.

There is an ill-conditioned fellow named Hiedler, who lives in a hut on the side of the Spiegelberg, and supports himself by chamois hunting and by acting as guide to the few tourists who find their way here. Popular suspicion has fastened on this man, for no better reason than that he is tall, thin, and known to be rough and brutal. His chalet has been searched today, but nothing of importance found. He has, however, been arrested and confined in the same room which Cellini used to occupy.

*

At this point there is a gap of a week in my diary, during which time there was an entire cessation of the constant alarms which have harassed us lately. Some explained it by supposing that the terrible unknown had moved on to some fresh and less guarded scene of operations. Others imagine that we have secured the right man in the shape of the vagabond Hiedler. Be the cause what it may, peace and contentment reign once more in the village, and a short seven days have sufficed to clear away the cloud of care from men's brows, though the police are still on the alert. The season for rifle shooting is beginning, and as Laden has, like every other Tyrolese village, butts of its own, there is a continual pop, pop, all day. These peasants are dead shots up to about four hundred yards. No troops in the world could subdue them among their native mountains.

My friend Verhagen, the curé, and Pfiffer, the maire, used to go down in the afternoon to see the shooting with me. The former says that the quinine has done him much good and that his appetite is improved. We all agree that it is good policy to encourage the amusements of the people so that they may forget all about this wretched business. Waghorn, the butcher, won the prize offered by the maire. He made five bulls, and what we should call a magpie out of six shots at 230 yards. This is English prize-medal form.

June 2nd.—Who could have imagined that a day which opened so fairly could have so dark an ending? The early carrier brought me a letter by which I learned that Spragge and Co. have agreed to pay my claim in full, although it may be some months before the money is forthcoming. This will make a difference of nearly £400 a year to me—a matter of moment when a man is in his seven-and-fortieth year.

And now for the grand events of the hour. My interview with the vampire who haunts us, and his attempt upon Frau Bischoff, the landlady of the Grüner Mann—to say nothing of the narrow escape of our good curé. There seems to be something almost supernatural in the malignity of this unknown fiend, and the impunity with which he continues his murderous course. The real reason of it lies in the badly lit state of the place—or rather the entire absence of light—and also in the fact that thick woods stretch right down to the houses on every side, so that escape is made easy. In spite of this, however, he had two very narrow escapes tonight—one from my pistol, and one from the officers of the law. I shall not sleep much, so I may spend half an hour in jotting down these strange doings in my diary. I am no coward, but life in Laden is becoming too much for my nerves. I believe the matter will end in the emigration of the whole population.

To come to my story, then. I felt lonely and depressed this evening, in spite of the good news of the morning. About nine o'clock, just as night began to fall, I determined to stroll over and call upon the curé, thinking that a little intellectual chat might cheer me up. I slipped my revolver into my pocket, therefore—a precaution which I never neglected—and went out, very much against the advice of good Frau Zimmer. I think I mentioned some months ago in my diary that the curé's house is some little way out of the village upon the brow of a small hill. When I arrived there I found that he had gone out—which, indeed, I might have anticipated, for he had complained lately of restlessness at night, and I had recommended him to take a little exercise in the evening. His housekeeper made me very welcome, however, and having lit the lamp, left me in the study with some books to amuse me until her master's return.

I suppose I must have sat for nearly half an hour glancing over an odd volume of Klopstock's poems, when some sudden instinct caused me to raise my head and look up. I have been in some strange situations in my life, but never have I felt anything to be compared to the thrill which shot through me at that moment. The recollection of it now, hours after the event, makes me shudder. There, framed in one of the panes of the window, was a human face glaring in, from the darkness, into the lighted room—the face of a man so concealed by a cravat and slouch hat that the only impression I retain of it was a pair of wild-beast eyes and a nose which was whitened by being pressed against the glass. It did not need Andreas Murch's description to tell me that at last I was face to face with the man with the mattock. There was murder in those wild eyes. For a second I was so unstrung as to be powerless; the next I cocked my revolver and fired straight at the sinister face. I was a moment too late. As I pressed the trigger I saw it vanish, but the pane through which it had looked was shattered to pieces. I rushed to the window, and then out through the front door, but everything was silent. There was no trace of my visitor. His intention, no doubt, was to attack the curé, for there was nothing to prevent his coming through the folding window had he not found an armed man inside.

As I stood in the cool night air with the curé's frightened housekeeper beside me, I suddenly heard a great hubbub down in the village. By this time, alas! such sounds were so common in Laden that there was no doubting what it foreboded. Some fresh misfortune had occurred there. Tonight seemed destined to be a night of horror. My presence might be of use in the village, so I set off there, taking with me the trembling woman, who positively refused to remain behind. There was a crowd round the Gruner Mann public-house, and a doxen excited voices were explaining the circumstances to the curé, who had arrived just before us. It was as I had thought, though happily without the result which I had feared. Frau Bischoff, the wife of the proprietor of the inn, had, it seems, gone some twenty minutes before a few yards from her door to draw some water, and had been at once attacked by a tall disguised man, who had cut at her with some weapon. Fortunately he had slipped, so that she was able to seize him by the wrist and prevent his repeating his attempt, while she screamed for help. There were several people about at the time, who came running towards them, on which the stranger wrested himself free, and dashed off into the woods, with two of our police after him. There is little hope of their overtaking or tracing him, however, in such a dark labyrinth. Frau Bischoff had made a bold attempt to hold the assassin, and declares that her nails made deep furrows in his right wrist. This, however, must be mere conjecture, as there was very little light at the time. She knows no more of the man's features than I do. Fortunately she is entirely unhurt. The curé was horrified when I informed him of the incident at his own house. He was returning from his walk, it appears, when hearing cries in the village, he had hurried down to it. I have not told any one else of my own adventure, for the people are quite excited enough already.

As I said before, unless this mysterious and bloodthirsty villain is captured, the place will become deserted. Flesh and blood cannot stand such a strain. He is either some murderous misanthrope who has declared a vendetta against the whole human race, or else he is an escaped maniac. Clearly after the unsuccessful attempt upon Frau Bischoff he had made at once for the curé's house, bent upon slaking his thirst for blood, and thinking that its lonely situation gave hopes of success. I wish I had fired at him through the pocket of my coat. The moment he saw the glitter of the weapon he was off.

June 3rd.—Everybody in the village this morning has learned about the attempt upon the curé last night. There was quite a crowd at his house to congratulate him on his escape, and when I appeared they raised a cheer and hailed me as the "tapferer Englander." It seems that his narrow shave must have given the ruffian a great start, for a thick woollen muffler was found lying on the pathway leading down to the village, and later in the day the fatal mattock was discovered close to the same place. The scoundrel evidently threw these things down and then took to his heels. It is possible that he may prove to have been frightened away from the neighbourhood altogether. Let us trust so!

June 4th.—A quiet day, which is as remarkable a thing in our annals as an exciting one elsewhere. Wurms has made strict inquiry, but cannot trace the muffler and mattock to any inhabitant. A description of them has been printed, and copies sent to Anspach and neighbouring villages for circulation among the peasants, who may be able to throw some light upon the matter. A thanksgiving service is to be held in the church on Sunday for the double escape of the pastor and of Martha Bischoff. Pfiffer tells me that Herr von Weissendorff, one of the most energetic detectives in Vienna, is on his way to Laden. I see, too, by the English papers sent me, that people at home are interested in the tragedies here, although the accounts which have reached them are garbled and untrustworthy.

How well I can recall the Sunday morning following upon the events which I have described, such a morning as it is hard to find outside the Tyrol! The sky was blue and cloudless, the gentle breeze wafted the balsamic odour of the pine woods through the open windows, and away up on the hills the distant tinkling of the cow bells fell pleasantly upon the ear, until the musical rise and fall which summoned the villagers to prayer drowned their feebler melody. It was hard to believe, looking down that peaceful little street with its quaint topheavy wooden houses and old-fashioned church, that a cloud of crime hung over it which had horrified Europe. I sat at my window watching the peasants passing with their picturesquely dressed wives and daughters on their way to church. With the kindly reverence of Catholic countries, I saw them cross themselves as they went by the house of Freckler and the spot where Maul had met his fate. When the bell had ceased to toll and the whole population had assembled in the church, I walked up there also, for it has always been my custom to join in the religious exercises of any people among whom I may find myself.

When I arrived at the church I found that the service had already begun. I took my place in the gallery which contained the village organ, from which I had a good view of the congregation. In the front seat of all was stationed Frau Bischoff, whose miraculous escape the service was intended to celebrate, and beside her on one side was her worthy spouse, while the maire occupied the other. There was a hush through the church as the curé turned from the altar and ascended the pulpit. I have seldom heard a more magnificent sermon. Father Verhagen was always an eloquent preacher, but on that occasion he surpassed himself. He chose for his text:—"In the midst of life we are in death," and impressed so vividly upon our minds the thin veil which divides us from eternity, and how unexpectedly it may be rent, that he held his audience spell-bound and horrified. He spoke next with tender pathos of the friends who had been snatched so suddenly and so dreadfully from among us, until his words were almost drowned by the sobs of the women, and suddenly turning, he compared their peaceful existence in a happier land to the dark fate of the gloomy-minded criminal, steeped in blood and with nothing to hope for either in this world or the next—a man solitary among his follows, with no woman to love him, no child to prattle at his knee, and an endless torture in his own thoughts. So skilfully and so powerfully did he speak that as he finished I am sure that pity for this merciless demon was the prevailing emotion in every heart.

The service was over, and the priest, with his two acolytes before him, was leaving the altar, when he turned, as was his custom, to give his blessing to the congregation. I shall never forget his appearance. The summer sunshine shining slantwise through the single small stained glass window which adorned the little church threw a yellow lustre upon his sharp intellectual features with their dark haggard lines, while a vivid crimson spot reflected from a ruby-coloured mantle in the window quivered over his uplifted right hand. There was a hush as the villagers bent their head to receive their pastor's blessing—a hush broken by a wild exclamation of surprise from a woman who staggered to her feet in the front pew and gesticulated frantically as she pointed at Father Verhagen's uplifted arm. No need for Frau Bischoff to explain the cause of that sudden cry, for there—there in full sight of his parishioners, were lines of livid scars upon the curé's white wrist—scare which could be left by nothing on earth but a desperate woman's nails. And what woman save her who had clung so fiercely to the murderer two days before!

That in all this terrible business poor Verhagen was the man most to be pitied I have no manner of doubt. In a town in which there was good medical advice to be had, the approach of the homicidal mania, which had undoubtedly proceeded from overwork and brain worry, and which assumed such a terrible form, would have been detected in time and he would have been spared the awful compunction with which he must have been seized in the lucid intervals between his fits—if, indeed, he had any lucid intervals. How could I diagnose with my smattering of science the existence of such a terrible and insidious form of insanity, especially from the vague symptoms of which he informed me. It is easy now, looking back, to think of many little circumstances which might have put us on the right scent; but what a simple thing is retrospective wisdom! I should be sad indeed if I thought that I had anything with which to reproach myself.

We were never able to discover where he had obtained the weapon with which he had committed his crime, nor how he managed to secrete it in the interval. My experience proved that it had been his custom to go and come through his study window without disturbing his housekeeper. On the occasion of the attempt on Frau Bischoff he had made a dash for home, and then, finding to his astonishment that his room was occupied, his only resource was to fling away his weapon and muffler, and to mix with the crowd in the village. Being both a strong and an active man, with a good knowledge of the footpaths through the woods, he had never found any difficulty in escaping all observation.

Immediately after his apprehension, Verhagen's disease took an acute form, and he was carried off to the lunatic asylum at Feldkirch. I have heard that some months afterwards he made a determined attempt upon the life of one of his keepers, and afterwards committed suicide. I cannot be positive of this, however, for I heard it quite accidentally during a conversation in a railway carriage.

As for myself, I left Laden within a few months, having received a pleasing intimation from my solicitors that my claim had been paid in full. In spite of my tragic experience there, I had many a pleasing recollection of the little Tyrolese village, and in two subsequent visits I renewed my acquaintance with the maire, the Intendant, and all my old friends, on which occasion, over long pipes and flagons of beer, we have taken a grim pleasure in talking with bated breath of that terrible month in the quiet Vorarlberg hamlet.

1931

MR MELDRUM'S MANIA

John Metcalfe

Born in Heacham, Norfolk, England on 6 October 1891, William John Metcalfe studied philosophy at the University of London, before working as a teacher in Paris until the outbreak of the First World War in 1914. During the war, he served in the Royal Naval Division, the Royal Naval Air Service and the Royal Air Force. When the war ended, he taught for five years at Highgate Junior School in London, and it was here where he wrote his first book, *The Smoking Leg and Other Stories*, which was published in 1925.

Metcalfe's first novel, *Spring Darkness*, was published in 1928, and after emigrating to the USA that same year, he was working as a barge captain on the East River when he wrote his second published novel, *Arm's Length* (1930). He would go on to write several more novels, among which are *Foster-Girl* (1936), *All Friends Are Strangers* (1948) and *My Cousin Geoffrey* (1956), but it was as a writer of macabre short stories that he was best known.

His second collection, *Judas and Other Stories*, was published in 1931, and in 1954 Arkham House published his most renowned work, the novella *The Feasting Dead*, as a limited-edition hardcover. He returned to England in 1964, where he died the following year.

"Mr Meldrum's Mania", which comes from Metcalfe's second collection, is a heady concoction of comedy, psychology, Egyptology and horror. In essence, it is a "possession" story, albeit one where the possessed man ultimately undergoes a horrifying physical transformation.

Elevators (which Mr Meldrum, English, would call "lifts") are properly considered unromantic and mundane, yet the crowd gathered on the first floor (Meldrum "ground") of the Forensic Arts Building at six-thirty on a July morning to stare at this particular elevator seemed to imply a possible exception.

It was neither "accident" nor hold-up. The elevator itself appeared normal—a semi-local stopping at every floor above the twelfth—and it supplied no clue of violence. Indeed, no one affirmed that there *had* been a scene of violence—or otherwise. Three or four hard-bitten newspaper men were now, although reduced to a pathetic state of impotent and dangerous anguish, adopting a transparent pose of sour grapes, protesting that the whole affair was hooey, nothing but a false alarm.

Yet they continued angrily to hang about. The air of the hall held a bleak, mute suggestion of the unsavoury and sinister, as if, some hours ago, it had experienced a large-scale concussion—due to the explosion of an unspeakably tremendous but entirely odourless and silent firework—and was still coldly retrospective, shocked and strained. Yes, something *had* occurred. The elevator had descended from the sixteenth floor around 11.45 last night, and, on that journey, something very curious had taken place. Within the elevator, rumour asserted blandly, had been, besides the operator, a man who had come out of Dr Fazo's office (Dr Fazo himself was not available, had vanished, shortly afterwards, leaving no trace) and one other rather intoxicated individual, wearing a brown Fedora, who had entered at the twelfth. When the elevator reached the bottom, the operator was unstrung, presently raving. He had been packed off (rumour again) to the psychopathic ward at Bellevue, where he had subsequently expired. What had become of his two passengers remained a matter for excited argument.

The crowd increased. Nervous proprietors of a cigar store and an Exchange buffet which opened out into the marble-paved main hall had got wind of the commotion and turned up two hours before their usual time to peer, on tiptoe, at the new operator. Yes, a new operator had already been installed, a huge man, grinning embarrassedly and reaping a week's wages in importunately proffered tips by constantly transporting people to the sixteenth floor. Those temporarily deprived of his society had to content themselves with gazing, in a fixity which later news might prove to have been morbid, at the great gilt-framed, alphabetical director whereon, under the heading "North", they could pick out the name of Dr Fazo and his room number, sixteen fifty-four.

It was now seven o'clock. The little throng grew noisier. Curious accretions from the outer commerce of Sixth Avenue and Twenty-third Street momently poured in. The hall was packed. Where were the police? Someone—a woman—fainted. Mr Whalen's bluecoats were strangely in abeyance, but—Ah! Talk of angels...!

Hubbub declined, then waxed again in a resentful murmuring. "All out! Get outta here!" Curtly commanding voices cut across conflicting cries of vain expostulation. The police had come at last. Die-hards attempting to engage them in obstructive argument were dealt with summarily. Within three minutes more the place was cleared.

Outside, however, until the tide of early morning traffic gradually effected their disintegration, several excited knots of the ejected lingered for discussion. Some of them clustered on the opposite sidewalk, gazed up at the Forensic Arts Building reprehendingly. What had occurred in there they might not know. Even the newspaper men, whose noses (tuned to supernatural keenness for the scenting of unlikely mysteries from afar) had brought them hurrying to the scene an hour ago—even these sleuths had come up unaccountably against a stubborn series of blank walls. "Murder will out"—but here apparently was something worse, something which all authorities concerned were ominously bent on hushing up. There were such things as Public Morals and the "Public Interest"... Well, it was useless to attempt to speculate. Doubtless, the only persons really in the secret were the absconding Dr Fazo (who as everybody knew was that same Dr Fazo who was tried for poisoning his sister—elderly, a masseuse—with a home-made lipstick); the Man in the Fedora (who as everybody knew was that identical Fedora-wearing man who, though he lived out somewhere in the Bronx, bought all his underclothes at Stern's and used to run a gambling joint upon East Fifty-third Street); and, finally, the Other Passenger, that Other Guy, called Meldrum. Was that the Meldrum who, after having been a freak at Coney, had ended up by getting fabulously rich, buying estate at Montauk, and marrying the daughter of an English nobleman? Yes, naturally, it was the very same... Little by little, as their interest flagged or duties pressed, the chagrined groups of resolute mythologists broke up and scattered. By seven-fifteen at latest none of them remained.

Meldrum! Strangely enough, quite inexplicably, they *had* got that bit straight. That *was* his name. And "freak"—they were actually getting warm. Meldrum, however, if he had been at hand to overhear, would certainly have laughed at their preposterous conjectures, would have been tickled to observe how their exiguous fund of information had been ingeniously supplemented by invention, how very wide their guesses always were of the real dreadful mark.

Or no—probably, after all, he would not have laughed. The nuclear components of Mr Meldrum's humour had been long ago disastrously dissolved. It was exactly seven months and eighteen days since he had been amused at anything at all.

On that occasion (so ferociously intact was his appreciation of the comic then) he had recalled, while sitting in a dentist's chair, one of the gorgeous inconsequences of Mr Frank R. Sullivan—and chuckled.

Novocaine had been injected. It was the grisly time of waiting for the pull, yet Mr Meldrum chuckled. He had read Mr Sullivan's extravaganza the previous evening, and now, for some reason, its unabashed and flagrant funniness was more than he could bear. The dentist was a little shocked, vaguely offended too. One's victims did not usually laugh. One's manner became cold and threatening. "Now—wider, please!"

Meldrum's unseasonable merriment was quenched. The tooth ground and cracked numbly in his jaw, and its extraction hurt a trifle more than he had bargained for. He went off chastened.

This was not in New York, but in Toronto. Mr Meldrum, not generally sentimental, had been visiting a town in Ontario where he had spent four years as a boy. Indeed, he had passed several days in his old home, which still belonged to him. Before his new tenants arrived he had rooted pleasantly about in the loft, where books, toys, pictures, other souvenirs of childhood had been stored.

From Toronto he went on to Montreal and Halifax, then sailed for England. The tooth—or rather its now vacant site—still gave him trouble. It did not hurt particularly, yet the disagreeable sensation of numbness persisted. Also—this being the first time he had ever had an adult tooth extracted—the fact that his full complement of thirty-two had been at last reduced to thirty-one rankled absurdly in his mind as quite a serious grievance. Aboard the *Empress of Scotland* he had a birthday—coincidentally enough his thirty-second—and consumed a vast quantity of John Collins, but the liquor only made him more depressed. He would never see thirty-two again and he would never boast thirty-two natural teeth again. All the way over he slept badly, and when the vessel docked at Liverpool he was feeling actually seedy.

At Euston his friend Ronald Spilman met him. London was obscured by a November fog, and, till they reached the flat in St John's Wood, Spilman remained unable to see Mr Meldrum's face distinctly. Then, however, as the electric lights flashed up, Spilman exclaimed: "Why, you look quite knocked up! Had a bad passage, I suppose? Really, you look quite ill!"

"No," said Mr Meldrum querulously. "I'm not ill at all. We did have rather a rough crossing. But it's not that. I think it's this damned tooth that I had pulled when I was staying in Toronto. It still feels sort of swollen."

For another month this was all that happened. Mr Meldrum—whose given name was Amos—continued peevish, and, notwithstanding several contemptuous London dentists, was still inclined to blame the absent tooth. However, his jaw did gradually get better, and he was forced to cast about for other explanations.

Was it his business that was bothering him again? Mr Meldrum, ungrateful for prosperity, had always felt demeaned and fettered by his business, and when he thought, in contrast, of persons like John Masefield, Hegel, Heliogabalus and Edison and the substantial contributions they had made to human progress his sense of stark inferiority became acute. His own trade seemed altogether too much of a "racket", consisting in supplying the entire downtown region of Manhattan with "rare Spanish delicacies". For some years he had owned a couple of stores near Fourteenth Street and Eighth Avenue and two others by the Battery, and it was with an eye to the replenishing of these emporia with Ibanez, olives, espadrillas and Pio Baroja that he now found himself on European soil. Presently he must journey on to Spain.

Yet it was not his scruples in respect of good old Pio that were worrying him now. He was the prey of a peculiar depression which remained obstinately entrenched within his brain. Mr Spilman, to cheer him, brought a number of his boon-companions to the flat—without avail. Ronald's acquaintance could, roughly, be divided into two partially overlapping sections—the candidates for Bright's disease and the aspirants to cirrhosis—but not even from the impressive individuals who belonged to both could Mr Meldrum now derive a shred of consolation. Once, towards the end of a rather hectic evening, they had pretended that he was a corpse and had fanned at him with hands and handkerchiefs. Mr Meldrum, resuscitated, had bounded angrily from his chair. "Don't do that!" he cried. "It hurts. It's not funny!" Ronald gazed at him amazed. "'Hurts'? Why, we didn't come inside a foot of your old face!"

Mr Meldrum grunted. They were drunk and it was no use arguing. But they *had* hurt his face. He had felt their fingers and their handkerchiefs distinctly.

Next day (about a week before he had to go to Spain) he had, out of pure spite, spent an hour in the British Museum, staring morosely at the mummies. A dark cloud of foreboding was overshadowing him. The skin round and above his nose was "creepy", and a little itchy. Absently, and without any real interest, he approached his face towards the glass front of a case in order to make out the hieroglyphs upon a cartouche more exactly.

Suddenly he had a shock. He couldn't get nearer to the glass! His face was still a foot or more away from it, yet he "felt" something—"felt" the glass! His heart bounded, sickly. Yes, he *was* able to get a bit nearer now—about six inches—but only by defying a sensation of increasing pressure. Not pain, merely resistance and a sort of weird discomfort.

He tried again. Ah, it was better. Trembling, he continued to experiment... Not till a footfall sounded close to him did he desist.

One of the Museum attendants was regarding him very curiously. Mr Meldrum turned and left the building.

But, on returning to the flat, he remained nervous, and indeed, dismayed. If that sensation came again he must certainly see a doctor.

"Hi!" Ronald called. "What the hell! What do you think you're doing?"

"Oh—nothing," said Mr Meldrum. Seated in an armchair, and forgetting Mr Spilman's presence, he had been tentatively making passes with his fingers, round his nose.

The trip to Spain had failed to repair Mr Meldrum's spirits, or his temper. It was, in fact, upon the evening of his home-coming to St John's Wood that he at last felt driven to confide in the shocked Mr Spilman. From this point—his first definite avowal of the symptoms that distressed him—were to date both the growing apprehension and concern of all his friends and the progressive, steadily accelerating march of his own mania.

That it *was* mania Mr Spilman never doubted. His crony, upon arrival, had collapsed on a divan. Ronald, bringing whisky, had noticed a queer, "hatchy" expression about his eyes. "Well, Amos, I'm dashed sorry you're not better. Was business bad, or what?"

"Oh, business—business was as good as usual. Madrid was not too bad, and Barcelona; but down south—the flies! You know, even at Christmas, it wasn't cold enough down there to kill them..."

"Oh..." said Ronald uncomfortably. "Yes, how annoying. They kept you awake at night?"

"Yes, they did... But I didn't mind that till it got light and I could—Ronald!" he broke off, "I must tell you. I could feel them on my face when I could *see* that they weren't there!"

"Oh, come now! Really...!" Mr Spilman essayed a smile, but his hand refilling Mr Meldrum's glass was trembling. Amos's face gave one the creeps. It looked shrivelled, empty like a baby's, and, at the same time, haunted. Ronald, though inwardly repelled, put a hand on his shoulder. "Of course, it's simply *nerves*—still, go on, get it off your chest."

Mr Meldrum did. Horror-stricken, he had lain in bed and watched the flies walking, as it were, on nothing—felt them as well, as their perambulations had defined, in space, a contour which did not exist. And in brushing them away at last he had also felt, though less precisely, his own fingers.

"How far away were those flies?" Mr Spilman fearfully inquired.

"About six inches usually. It depended... Straight in front of my nose and forehead they were always farther out. It's the same when I try with my fingers. But I haven't got the feeling now—not since I left Spain."

For a long time they sat talking and drinking. Mr Spilman, though affecting to think lightly of thc matter, was perturbed. People with "delusions" always made his flesh crawl. Upon retiring he was careful to lock his bedroom door.

Mr Meldrum, on the other hand, was relieved at having unloaded his anxieties on his friend. He enjoyed, for a wonder, a fairly good night's rest, and it was only when he got out of bed next morning that his alarm returned.

He was about to go into the bathroom for his customary ablutions when his glance chanced to halt upon the pillow which until very recently had been beneath his head. The impress still remained obscurely, but—was it merely his imagination?—seemed unusual. He had been lying on his right side and now, towards the left of the pillow as one looked at it, in a place corresponding with the then position of his nose, was a long, hook-shaped groove.

He emitted a low, moaning cry. Mr Spilman came running. "What is it? What's the matter?"

"Oh..." Mr Meldrum faltered. This time he had better keep his own counsel. "Oh, it's—it's nothing..."

But his face was ashy and his teeth chattering.

From the nerve-specialist he came away a few days later, discouraged and resentful. True that he had stopped short of telling the neurologist quite *all* his symptoms. For the same reason which restrained him from mentioning the pillow incident to Ronald, he had suppressed the most bizarre. Puzzled, the nerve-specialist had spoken of hyperaesthesia and neuroses, and then, after a pause, proceeded to make ominously casual inquiries concerning Mr Meldrum's family tree and the friends or relatives with whom he might be staying at the moment. Mr Meldrum, shutting up like an oyster, had gone off in something near to panic.

As it happened, however, he was, this very evening, destined to meet Bertram Spoade and in him to discover unexpectedly a friend in need. Mr Spoade was an acquaintance of Ronald's, an eccentric young man who studied geology at the Imperial College of Science and was pretty safely on the cirrhosis list, but for whom Mr Meldrum none the less had always entertained a sneaking tolerance. He was, at any rate, quite easily the least insufferable of Ronald's gang, and when—after the others had uproariously departed with their host to "make a night of it"—Bertie continued hiccupping on the divan, Amos felt almost glad of his society.

Up to this point the evening had, for Mr Meldrum, not been gay. He had not mentioned his consultation with the neurologist, but sensed a strange constraint in Ronald's manner. Once, with sinister irrelevance, Mr Spilman had asked him, suddenly, about his maiden aunt (Amos's sole surviving relative) and, upon being told that the good lady lived in France, tactlessly grew more evidently anxious than before. To Mr Meldrum's other trials now was added the necessity of seeming more than ordinarily sane, a feat which, when attempted too deliberately, is very difficult.

But now Bertie Spoade and Amos were alone. For a while the hiccups from the divan were the only sounds that broke the silence.

Abruptly, Mr Spoade sat up and spoke. "Ronald thinks you've gone batty, and I can see—*hic*—you're pretending not to be. I'm—*hic*—interested. I wish—*hic*—you'd tell me all about it."

Mr Meldrum wondered whether he ought to feel offended, and, on deliberation, decided in the negative. After Ronald and the nerve-specialist he badly needed a sympathetic listener.

"It's my face..." he prefaced awkwardly. "I know it sounds preposterous, but—well, I can feel things in the air in front of it." He narrated his experiences in the British Museum and with the flies in Spain.

Mr Spoade, intrigued, no longer hiccupped. He plied Mr Meldrum eagerly with questions.

"Can you feel it now, like that?"

Mr Meldrum considered. "Yes, in a way... I mean, it's not necessary now for anything to touch it. I—"

"You mean," said Bertie, interrupting, "that you can feel a sort of boundary line in space—a kind of extra surface where the 'you' ends and the 'not-you' begins. Rather like those chappies who've had their legs amputated and still have pains in their toes, eh?"

"Yes," agreed Mr Meldrum, whom this analogy had struck as apt, "it *is* like that, I suppose..." In the excitement of discussing his peculiar symptoms he almost forgot, momentarily, to feel afraid.

"Of course," Mr Spoade continued, "it's probably the brain. I'm not being rude, but I was doing medicine before I went in for geology. The brain is a rare and curious organ. For instance, pressure on the uncinate gyrus results in the characteristic uncinate group of fits, accompanied by olfactory sensations—odours—which have nothing to account for them outside. Get me? You smell things when there's nothing there to smell..."

"Oh..." said Mr Meldrum. He somewhat disapproved of this last parallel. His gyrus, he was sure, was quite all right, and certainly he had no fits.

"Or again," Mr Spoade proceeded, warming, "it may be a psycho-analyst's job entirely. Pity you aren't in Vienna—or still in U.S.A. Alienists are more in vogue out there. And if I were you I shouldn't bleat too much. People are sure to think that you've gone bugs. Look at old Ronald. He was telling all of us just now that if you went on having queer ideas he'd have to find your relative's address and get you put away. He—"

"WHAT?" exclaimed Mr Meldrum, in alarm. "He said that?"

"Yes," replied Mr Spoade composedly. "He did. He was very pessimistic, talking about Commissioners in Lunacy, and—"

Mr Meldrum had sprung to his feet. "I won't stay here another hour, not an instant! If he—"

Bertie, too, had risen. "Well, I don't blame you. Look here, I've got a brain-wave—come along o' me! Just bring a tooth-brush and pyjamas, then in the morning you can fetch your other things. Old Ronald wouldn't mind. In fact... Come on!"

But his entreaties were indeed unnecessary. Mr Meldrum was fairly boiling with indignation. He was so angry that all his terror had departed. It was only when, carrying a small suit-case, he was about to follow Bertie from the flat that any qualms returned.

"And then," Mr Spoade was saying, "tomorrow I should like to make a little, well, experiment. It struck me that it might be kind of interesting to find what shape your face was now—your other face..."

"What *shape...?*" Mr Meldrum was staggered.

"Oh, it's all right. I'll explain what I mean tomorrow. Come along!"

Dubiously, Mr Meldrum came.

*

By way of anaesthetic (this was next morning, at about eleven) Mr Meldrum, his neck imprisoned in a vice, found himself confronted by a large geological map of the British Isles hung on the opposite wall.

"Think," Bertie had instructed, "of the Llandilo Flags, or the Ordovician System and Trilobites—anything. Brood on 'em while I'm getting ready, and whatever you do, don't jerk your dear old bean about once I begin."

Built around Mr Meldrum's head was a sort of cardboard scaffolding, like an unfinished box, through two opposite sides of which, when preparations were complete, Bertie had already inserted numerous bonnet-pins. The pins were to be pushed through slowly, perpendicularly, and knob first, and as soon as each knob "touched" his supernumerary face Mr Meldrum was to exclaim "Now!" Mr Spoade, at that instant, would stop pushing, and, leaving that pin in position, would pass on to the next. In this way, as he delightedly explained, the pin-knobs would ultimately form a variety of three-dimensional graph, from which the shape of Mr Meldrum's phantom countenance could profitably be deduced.

"Just," Bertie went on fanatically to point out, "as if you were a crystal—what?—and I were plotting its indicatrix. Only then it would come out sort of egg-shaped, and I don't expect yours will." Mr Spoade proceeded to talk of birefringence, of ordinates, and of something to do with lightwaves, called "Mu-mu" in a manner that made Mr Meldrum's brain reel. Mr Meldrum now regretted his position. He felt very undignified and, besides that, began to fear that Mr Spoade was not—not *absolutely* normal. No one, to start with, who was thoroughly, unquestionably sane would have been in possession of so many bonnet-pins.

"Ready!" said Bertie. "Now, for the Lord's sake, sit still! Don't twitch an eyelid!"

The experiment proceeded without hitch, Mr Meldrum, at intervals, exclaiming "Now!" or "Ouch!" and Bertie thereupon desisting instantly from pushing in the pin. Finally Mr Spoade unclamped the vice and set his prisoner free.

"Now we can have a squint. But make it snappy. I've a lecture on at twelve."

Bertie had taken an oblong of what seemed to be damp blotting-paper or papier mâché, patting and pressing it delicately against the heads of the bonnet-pins, so that the pliant material, following their varying distances from the cardboard wall, formed a sufficiently close "average" approximation to the ideal surface which the pins had point by point delimited. Having repeated this operation with the other "wall", Mr Spoade brought the two together, peered into the resulting mould, and burst into hysterical laughter. "Good Lord... he, he!... It's—it's a *snout*—or else a bill... the Human Tapir, what?... If you—Hello!"

Mr Meldrum, too, had looked into the mould, turned pale. Bertie deposited him upon a sofa, brought him whisky. "Well, I suppose I *oughtn't* to have laughed. Bit of a shock, no doubt. But really...! Just fancy you among the old Proboscidae... He, he...! Good Lord...!"

Despite perfunctory contrition, Mr Spoade's callous merriment continued. Finally, however, after a startled glance at the clock, he struggled into his coat and swept up a large pile of notebooks. "I've got to scoot... Leave those two moulds to dry. We'll use 'em as a matrix later on... So long!"

Mr Meldrum lay inert. Bertie had been gone twenty minutes when at length he rose unsteadily from the sofa. Shivering, he took a long pull at the whisky, staggered into the bedroom, packed his suit-case. Then, returning to the front room, he placed the two moulds on the floor and passionately trod upon them. It was twelve-twenty-five. He still had the key of Ronald's flat, and Ronald, at this hour, would not be home.

Emerging on to the Cromwell Road, Mr Meldrum took a taxi to the Spilman flat—deserted save for a negligible maid—and hastily collected his belongings. In another taxi he drove to Cowcross Street and there handed over all his luggage to the storage department of Messrs Cook. This done, he wandered vaguely down by Ludgate Hill, along the Strand.

Dazed and light-headed, he strolled for half an hour or more indecisively northwards and westwards and then halted. An imposing grey pediment, supported on fat cylindrical grey columns, confronted him. Euston? No, there were pigeons. It was the British Museum again.

Trembling, and after several seconds' hesitation, he turned in.

Once more he was looking at the mummies. Not at the mummies merely. He gazed unseeingly at scarabs, papyri, colossal heads, representations, yet more terrifying, of grotesque, semi-human deities—Horus, Anubis, Set. Perhaps the whisky had made him slightly drunk, keeping his horror at his own condition in abeyance. He was not thinking specifically about the result of Mr Spoade's experiment. Even, after an hour, he began to feel a little hungry. Only when he was about to leave the building for a meal did anything extraordinary occur.

He was turning away from a large case of pottery when someone jostled him. Mr Meldrum, nerves on edge, swung round wrathfully. An ill-favoured individual, smelling of garlic, returned his angry stare. "Nah then, clumsy...!"

Suddenly, Mr Meldrum's pent emotions were canalized, and liberated in the form of rage. He was seething with indignation. "Clumsy yourself! What do you mean by—"

The garlicky gentleman's features, too, were distorted with passion. "Look 'ere, you shut it, see? 'Cos if yer don't I'll push yer fice in, see? I'll push yer silly fice in...!"

What happened next Mr Meldrum could never recollect distinctly. "I'll push yer fice in, see?"... At these words something snapped in his brain. His face! There was something appallingly wrong with his face. Everyone could see it! He was mad! He heard himself shouting: "I'm mad, I'm mad!" Then his voice changed. His own voice. With his own ears he could hear it change, dropping, in an instant from a delirious scream to a low, senseless chirr, like a bird's, a kind of twittering. He saw the man in front of him fall back, regarding him in horror. Yes, he was mad. He could feel his jaw working, chattering rapidly up and down, making those curious sounds—knew that his eyes were brailing... Attendants were running up, surrounding him. His arms were pinioned. The room swam. He must have fainted.

How had he escaped? He remembered nothing. This was the Strand, and he was walking eastwards, past the Law Courts. His head ached, and his clothes were soiled, his collar torn. Up to a point his memory held good, then stopped. He had had a seizure in the Museum, shouted out that he was mad—but he was not mad now. Not in that way.

By degrees, however, something of his terror returned. How *had* he got away? It was four o'clock and growing dark. There must, he imagined, be some sort of search for him, some sort of hue and cry. He struck northwards, up an alley, avoiding lights.

In a square, a newsboy was running. "Evenin" Stan*dard*...!" Mr Meldrum, signalling, bought a copy.

For some seconds he saw nothing, but presently his glance snapped down, appalled, upon a headline: "*Extraordinary Scene in British Museum. Madman escapes.*" He read on in bewilderment. This was all wrong, ridiculous. No, he could not believe it. *That* was not his name. His name was Meldrum, *Meldrum*...

The paper dropped. He leaned against a railing. Meldrum... It was clever of him to have given the wrong name, though he had no recollection of having done so. Now it might be easier to evade inquiries and detection. But the name he apparently *had* given was so peculiar; he couldn't make it out. The entire history was incredible. If *he* were mad, the Museum authorities were at least equally insane. He must get off, give all of them the slip, Ronald and Bertie, everyone who knew... He must go back at once—back to the States, if he could manage it, on the next boat that sailed.

Retrieving the paper, he glanced round him cautiously. No one was following him. He had been marvellously lucky. He would get something to eat and drink, then think how he might best shake off pursuit. That story in the *Standard* was all bunkum. Also his face was better. It felt almost normal. If he could but return in safety to America he could convince himself that this was nothing but a frightful dream.

On the boat going over, however, an obstinate suspicion clung to him that there was more in it than that. For one thing, his torn collar and soiled clothes proved definitely that he *had* been involved in some quite overt and undignified affray, and, for another, the peculiar sensations round his nose returned. It is necessary to explain that Mr Meldrum had thought it wiser, instead of sailing direct from England, to lose himself for a month upon the Continent, not even risking the removal of his luggage from the warehouse. Drawing funds through Morgan's in the Place Vendôme at Paris, he had gone on to Switzerland and Italy, leaving for New York in a Fabre Line boat from Naples late in February. Now, with his morale somewhat seriously decayed, he spent most of his time in brooding on that mystifying item in the *Evening Standard*.

This account, from which it may be here as well to quote, had run, in part, as follows:

> The stately peace of the British Museum was shattered, early this afternoon, by an unusual incident. A man who had been standing before a case of pottery of the period of the Shepherd Kings and whose actions for some time had seemed suspicious, became suddenly involved in a violent fracas with another man stationed close behind him... Seized and taken for examination to the Assistant Curator's room he protested that this was the thirty-second occasion on which his opponent, James Buggins, had insulted him, that he was a manufacturer of bonnet-pins, and that his own name was Thote (or Thoash?)... What is peculiar about the episode is that the policeman and two attendants in whose custody he was temporarily placed appear unable or unwilling to account for his escape. One of the attendants, in particular, was in such a condition of nervous collapse that he was subsequently removed to a hospital for treatment... It is thought, however, that Thote may have been under the influence of liquor... The affair is being thoroughly investigated and a search made for him.

Mr Meldrum had refrained from looking at any English papers leaving London. He now refused passionately to believe that he could ever have been able to think of nothing better than such a foolish and unlikely name as "Thote", or that he had said what he was reported to have said about the thirty-second insult and the bonnet-pins. Still, he wanted to hear no more of it. He was probably very lucky indeed to have escaped, and even now did not feel absolutely safe. Ronald and the curiously imbecile B. Spoade might long ago have "squealed". Perhaps at this instant, he was shadowed. Perhaps, upon arrival at New York, he would be summarily arrested...

Happily, he was mistaken. It was, for March, a really glorious day, and he was met, outside the Customs shed, by someone who had had advance word of his coming and who, so far from promptly clapping him in irons for the raging maniac he was, laid an affectionate hand of greeting on his shoulder. "Why, hello, Amos... Why, you're looking *swell...!*"

Mr Meldrum's eyes filled gratefully. He knew that he was looking like a fly-blown oleograph of last Saturday's leg-of-mutton, but it was tactful of his friend to say the contrary.

"Why, hello—hello—Smith!"

The real name of the man who welcomed Mr Meldrum was not Smith, still, we propose to call him that—just Smith. He had not yet invested in the brown Fedora.

But of this person, for the present, the less said the better.

Spring had arrived. There was a lamb or two in Central Park and a conspicuous goat or two in Greenwich Village. Weary, steel-jawed executives were returning with last season's wives and niblicks from Florida and setting out with fresh ones for Europe. The rent of penthouses had soared.

Despising, however, the vernal excitements of Manhattan, Mr Meldrum had been living morosely in Linoleumville, S.I., in Jeannette, Pa., and in Emporia, Kan. Save for occasional week-end contacts with the person Smith he had been leading the existence of a hermit.

Under the circumstances he cannot be blamed. Although the curious extension of his face was usually no more than "sentient", so to speak, and only sometimes vaguely "tangible" to his own fingertips, he could not but believe that it was visible as well—and that to everyone who passed him in the street. He rarely ventured out except at night and, through the day, sat brooding in his room. Two letters, sent to his business address, had reached him from Ronald, but, having apprehensively perused the first, he threw the second in the fire unopened. Mr Spilman, making no reference to Bertie or the British Museum, had implored his friend to see a good neurologist immediately. If Amos would but realize that his malady possessed no basis in objective fact, all, Ronald vigorously declared, would yet be well. With this opinion Mr Meldrum violently disagreed. To call his trouble "psychological" was just an insult.

We are now, of course, approaching Dr Fazo and the elevator. Mr Smith—to whom Amos had confided the whole terrible affair—had frequently advised a consultation with an alienist, without success. Ronald's letter, he could see, had had a very bad effect and greatly stiffened Amos's resistance. Still, though discouraged, he was persevering. Upon a sunny Friday morning late in May he donned, for the first time, the brown Fedora, set out from the Grand Central terminal aboard the 10.15, and stubbornly returned to the attack.

Amos (it was now Sunday and lunch-time at Emporia) was expecting him and was standing, with the front-door open, on the veranda. The sun was dazzling in his eyes and the expression on the face of the approaching Mr Smith was indistinct. Mr Meldrum, however, noticed that, when a few yards distant, his friend halted suddenly. Amos moved forward, from the open door, to meet him.

"Well, baby, how's—Why, what the hell...!"

Mr Smith, his gaze stony, was trembling, and it was some time before he recovered sufficiently to explain that he was subject to heart-attacks. Even then it was with obvious reluctance that he suffered Mr Meldrum to lead him into the house and to pour him out a glass of fusel oil, slightly impaired by alcohol.

"'Heart-attacks'? You never spoke of *them* before..."

Mr Meldrum was in turn alarmed. He by no means credited the "heart-attack". To break a painful silence, he inquired presently: "I suppose you've come to have another go at me about this psycho-analyst of yours, this Dr Fazo? Well, I've been thinking over it again, and p'r'aps... p'r'aps I *might* try him after all. It seems the only hope..."

Mr Smith's hollow eyes held no consciousness of victory. He was shivering slightly, displaying a tendency to retch. "I—I don't know that it would do a scrap of good. These alienists..."

"What!..." Mr Meldrum gazed incredulously. "Why, you've been trying all along to—"

"No, it'd be no good..."

"But I shall go!"

"It's not a scrap of good."

"I tell you I *shall* go!"

Mr Smith rose. "I—I'm afraid I've got to hurry. I—I just looked in..."

In vain the astonished Amos sought to detain him. Mr Smith was moving forlornly to the door. "I'll—I'll see you again soon—Sorry I couldn't stop... So long!"

"But, Ferdinand...!"

It was no use. Mr Ferdinand Smith was now well out of the house and walking rapidly towards thc station. Just before turning a corner of the road he was observed by Mr Meldrum to break into a run.

Not until seated in the train and safely on his way back to New York did Mr Smith allow himself to think too concentratedly about what he had seen as, half an hour ago, he had ascended Mr Meldrum's steps, glanced forward, for an instant, past his friend, to the front door.

But then, and in an awful rush, the thing came over him. He understood now, too well, how Mr Meldrum's wonderful "escape" had been effected. He could guess shrewdly at the reason why that policeman and those two attendants let him go. They, he suspected, must have seen what he himself had seen so recently...

What had he seen? With the sun behind him, and casting Mr Meldrum's silhouette upon the lower portion of the open door, he had observed, at first incredulously, a curious shadow. But he could not remain incredulous for long. Mr Meldrum had moved his head slightly, and the shadow had moved too. It was the shadow of something with a strange, beakish prolongation, a little like a crane's head, only the "bill" had been considerably more curved—and sharper.

Dr Fazo, a bland gentleman of fifty, took at the first encounter an instant fancy to poor Mr Meldrum. Observing a pipe in Mr Meldrum's hand, he had rapped out: "What mixture do you smoke?... Ah, Dunhill's 'Royal Yacht'. Bit of a sybarite, eh?" Already prepossessed in his new patient's favour, he had immediately resolved to multiply his fees by 1.5.

Of this our hero had suspected nothing. For a month he had been following Dr Fazo's instructions conscientiously, and now his features wore a peculiar expression, at once debauched, propitiatory and coy, like those of a supremely diffident yet amorous bloodhound. Mr Smith, after his inexplicable *volte-face*, had held himself aloof, but became less standoffish by degrees, and had eventually even formed the habit of accompanying Amos to the alienist's door, frequently meeting him again when he came out. Today—a bright June afternoon—was scheduled to see Mr Meldrum's nineteenth session. "Well, so long, baby. I'll be back at quarter to. Good luck!" Mr Smith departed. Amos rang sharply twice, then entered.

The psycho-analyst received him cordially. Dr Fazo had formed his own opinion concerning Mr Meldrum, which was that he was horribly insane, but he did not allow this melancholy conviction to betray itself. Moreover, he had just got hold of an idea, requiring Mr Meldrum's goodwill, money and cooperation. Before, however, proceeding to its discussion, he subjected his patient to the customary examination.

"Good," he remarked at last. "Progress *most* satisfactory. Persevere with that tatting exercise—only think of it as drizzling or gallooning, not as tatting. It releases the nodal whorls. And I suggest that the expression 'snout' or 'pecker' may do harm. Think of it as a 'nozzle' instead of a 'muzzle' or a 'pecker'..."

"Yes," said Mr Meldrum docilely. "I will. And—could I look at those wax moulds again?"

"Certainly... Here they are..."

For Amos's greater reassurance Dr Fazo had taken several impressions of his face in wax. The resulting simulacra Mr Meldrum now surveyed with resignation if not actual enthusiasm.

"You see—they're perfectly normal... Your notion of a muz—a nozzle, is merely a too-vivid projection and exaggeration of the—ahem—the normal nose-awareness. Like a line divided 'externally' in Euclid, don't you see?"

"I see," said Mr Meldrum, again docilely, though the comparison struck him as inept and puerile. "Shall I talk now?"

"By all means..."

For half an hour Amos "talked" while Dr Fazo listened, taking notes. Mr Meldrum was exhorted, upon these occasions, to "let himself go", speaking without apparent rhyme or reason of anything that came into his head—and these requirements he amazingly fulfilled. Dr Fazo had by this time such an acquaintance with the less creditable idiosyncrasies of Amos's subconscious ego as would have caused a weaker man to blench, but from long practice he was blasé and inured. Always, whilst Mr Meldrum raved complacently of kites and cricket bats or prattled evilly of pacifiers and didies, Dr Fazo would be eagerly pawing over these inanities, dredging and delving in the fond expectation of discovering some childhood trauma which might account (too high a plausibility was not essential) for the perverse delusion of a "snout". Up to the present he had been disappointed. Amos's subconscious was indeed simply hag-ridden by complexes, but these were seldom of the proper kind. However, Dr Fazo persevered. If only—as he was tireless in explaining—if only he could light on the deep-buried origin of hidden conflict, expose its overwhelming triviality to the derisive upper storey of his patient's mind, the thing would end. Once Amos could be brought to realize that his entire nozzle mania was the result of, say, his finding seven ears upon his rocking-horse when he intelligently expected three, he was as good as cured. All the energy which his subconscious had been fatuously expending on this banal if rather puzzling incident since he was four years old would be released. His libido, now choked and damned and in a ghastly state of suppuration, would flow on tranquilly again. He would be well.

At the conclusion of the present recital Dr Fazo ran his eye with apparent satisfaction over his notes. To the lay mind these jottings—representing all his worth-while garnerings from Mr Meldrum's mental detritus over a period of five weeks—might have suggested little or have been misleading. They were:

A. NOSE. Nosy P. Nosey Parker. Central Park. Nozzle. Hose-pipe episode at age six.
B. THIRTY-TWO. His age last birthday. Had thirty-two teeth until quite recently. Plays piquet and bezique. Thirty-two cards in pack. (Other instances in support on p. 13.)
C. EGYPT. Wrote articles on scarabs for school magazine. Father was in Egyptian Civil Service. British Museum.
D. SCRIBE. Is peculiarly sensitive to this and to related words.

Dr Fazo snapped his notebook. He would now broach his big idea.

"Listen," he said. "I want you to agree to something. Your talking is still too inhibited to be much use and my material is insufficient and conflicting. I want you to let me go up to Canada and look over your toys."

"'Toys'?" queried Mr Meldrum weakly.

"Toys and other things. Books and games—everything. It needn't really cost you more than, say, six hundred berries. Do you agree?"

Mr Meldrum looked sheepish. "Oh, I say... Do you really mean that—berries?"

"Dollars, dollars. Don't be absurd. Six hundred dollars."

"Oh, dollars..." said Mr Meldrum. "My nose feels so itchy. Yes, all right. Six hundred dollars."

During Dr Fazo's absence Mr Meldrum, who had given him the keys to his again untenanted Ontario home, stayed at a little place up the Hudson, anxiously awaiting his return.

Occasionally, however, he forgot to be anxious, and then he was just plainly mad—harmlessly and happily, but still mad. Mr Smith, realizing this, was terribly depressed. Amos had a large framed photograph of Dr Fazo hung in his bedroom, and he would often stand in front of it and bark. His landlady, and her husband, too, thought it was all very sad, and had put up the rent and board money to quite a formidable figure.

Nevertheless, this period was probably the most peaceful that poor Amos had enjoyed from the first onset of his mania. By fits and starts he would begin worrying about his neglected business and about his nose, but in the main his condition was one of pleasurable lunacy. His nozzle now had ceased to trouble him save in a mental sense. He knew its contours so exactly that he avoided automatically those painful contacts and collisions which had annoyed him previously. He no longer, for instance, banged it or stubbed it accidentally or burnt it in the soup. To all intents and purposes it was just as if he had been born that way—with a snout or proboscis fifteen inches long—and as if this proboscis then had suddenly become invisible—really a matter for congratulation. Since the commencement of the alienist's ministrations he had grown plainly madder, yet if he now were happier as a result who could regret the fact? He had talked so incessantly to Dr Fazo of his childhood that a state akin to infantilism had, perhaps mercifully, supervened. He would call horses "gee-gees" and his watch a "tick-tick". Frequently Mr

Smith could hardly restrain him, when they were both retiring, from calling out to Mrs Schultzenheimer, his landlady, with a request that she should "tuck him in" and give the two of them a goodnight kiss.

Mr Smith's own feelings towards Amos now were mixed. Although he had managed to persuade himself that the affrighting shadow on the door had been delusion—possibly telepathic—he was far from forgetting that perturbing incident, and his present attitude to Mr Meldrum might be described as one of very gingerly affection. In spite of reason and of common sense he could not always avoid looking at his poor friend's face with something of a horrible expectancy...

But, on the whole, these days passed placidly, and it was really surprising how intelligently Amos would often talk about the absent Dr Fazo. Thanks to the alienist's repeated explanations, he had grasped the root ideas of expressive psycho-therapy with thoroughness, and he was never tired of expounding them, in turn, to Mr Smith. "It's sumsing dat happn when I was little, oo... ever so teeny, called a t'auma. An' de t'auma make me nozzly, Ferdy, only I fordet what it was. Good Dr Fazo's finding it in Tanada, an' when he tum back he tell Amos all 'bout naughty t'auma, an' den Amos laugh an' say 'Oo... *Silly*...!' An' den I give Dr Fazo six hund'ed be'wies—an' no more t'auma, no more nozzle. Nozzle *all* gone 'way...!" It was when, during lucid intervals like these, the mind of Amos would regain, too briefly, all its old familiar power and clarity, that Mr Smith most keenly could appreciate the tragedy of its decay.

Finally, after Dr Fazo had been gone three weeks, the crisis came. Amos and Ferdinand had been strolling after supper by the river, talking little. Exhausted by the heat, they turned in at their lodgings around nine o'clock.

Amos, preceding his companion by a few yards, reappeared at the front door, waving a pale yellow slip of paper, as Mr Smith was entering after him.

The wire from Montreal. They read it together, "GOOD NEWS GREAT DISCOVERY ARRIVING GRAND CENTRAL EIGHT THIRTY P.M. STANDARD TOMORROW CONGRATULATIONS FAZO."

A whole chapter of accidents delayed the momentous interview next day. Owing to the derailment of another train near Troy the Montreal express had been held up. It was past ten when Dr Fazo arrived, and then Mr Meldrum missed him at Grand Central. The alienist made it a strict rule to withhold his private address from all his patients, and Mr Smith and Amos spent an hour 'phoning desperately to his office. Finally they got him. Dr Fazo, realizing their anxiety, and himself ignorant of their present whereabouts, had merely dumped his luggage at his home and gone straight on to the Forensic Arts, waiting for them to ring him. Amos was to come to him there at once.

The building was open all night for people known to the night watchman. A certain sedulously bibulous merchant, intimate with Dr Fazo and whose work often necessitated his sitting up very late, had established, on the twelfth floor, a kind of ultra-private and select speakeasy, never closed. Mr Smith, indeed, had made the acquaintance of a rather nice girl in there, and on previous occasions, while he had been escorting Mr Meldrum to the psycho-analyst, he had often filled in an odd moment talking to her about his home town in Ohio which happened also to be hers. He proposed to do this now.

First, however, he saw Amos to Dr Fazo's door. Mr Meldrum, though greatly excited and upon tiptoe with anticipation, had an obscure something in his manner which Mr Smith could not pretend to like. Amos had snapped back, for some reason, from baby language into ordinary speech, and yet his friend was vaguely conscious that this change had not been for the better. Exactly how he realized this or what precisely he was now afraid of in poor Amos Mr Smith could not say, but that he *was* afraid of him was certain—and very glad to have got rid of him if only for a while when, from inside his sanctum, Dr Fazo called on him to enter.

It was arranged that Mr Smith should come back to the office within half an hour's time.

As Amos walked into the dim outer fringe of light thrown by a reading-lamp upon a desk, Dr Fazo experienced an instant faint uneasiness, a twinge as of alarm. It was so slight that he ignored it at the time, but it did strike him that perhaps his patient was not looking quite so well as when he saw him last. Clasping Mr Meldrum's hand, he smiled, however, and motioned him urbanely to a chair.

"Well, I've good news. I think I've run what we were looking for to earth at last. A long chase—but well worth it, for us both."

Mr Meldrum had sat down. "Tell me," he said. "I—" He stopped. His eyes were glittering. Dr Fazo, searching his face, again had an uncomfortable sensation. Something prompted him, instead of proceeding to an account of his discovery, to veer off, as with an idea of gaining time, upon a trivial topic.

He laughed. "I was a fool to take that day-train down from Montreal. Properly punished, too. Ninety-five minutes late..."

There was a pause. Through a window opening on the airshaft the dull rumble from Sixth Avenue rose faintly. The night was hot. Dr Fazo passed a handkerchief across his forehead, made a humorous gesture as of wringing it out, and emitted a wry "Whew!" Mr Meldrum's intent silence disconcerted him, but he could no longer put off telling him what he had found. He cleared his throat, shot out his cuffs, altered the position of the light a little, and began:

"I want to impress upon you again that the most obstinate, inveterate neuroses have frequently been traced to something so apparently irrelevant, even ridiculous, that the patient may, at first, experience a certain—ahem—difficulty... difficulty in accepting these unrealized traumas as a sufficient explanation of his state. Nevertheless, the trauma *is* the explanation. Once the thing has been disinterred from the subconscious, brought out into the open and, so to speak, projected, the whole trouble goes. I—I've told you all this before, but I want to be sure of your own sympathy, cooperation..."

Dr Fazo passed two fingers round the inside of his neck band. It was really very hot, and, he could not deny it, he felt anxious. He had, he considered, put in a very good job of work for Mr Meldrum up in Canada, but he had some misgivings as to its success. Now came the test. Would the elaborate explanation seem too flimsy and preposterous? Dr Fazo, whilst loyal in the main to his professional ideals, permitted himself a degree of cynicism. He was inclined, on nearing the *experimentum crucis*, to glimpse discouraging resemblances between psycho-analysis and certain allied though less generally established cults. However, he must pull himself together, make the plunge.

"Listen," he said, then cleared his throat once more. He could not understand his own increasing trepidation. Not only had he an unpleasant consciousness that he had somehow chosen his previous words poorly and (the idea even came to him) *dangerously*, but he was actually at a loss how to proceed. Finally, with Mr Meldrum's dancing eyes upon him, he spoke again.

"Listen—and tell me if you understand—SCRIBE OF THE GODS!"

Had Mr Meldrum moved? Had his face twitched? His expression in the dim lamplight, was peculiar, like that of a somnambulist unwillingly aroused, blindly and pitifully clinging to his sleep. So far, that might be good. Dr Fazo had seen that look before, thought himself, momentarily, on surer ground. He had touched something deep, something significant.

"'Scribe of the Gods,'" he repeated slowly. "Does that mean anything to you? Yes, I can see it does."

Amos shuddered slightly. His lips parted. "Yes... it does... I—"

"Think back. I want you to think back. You have always been sensitive to that word 'scribe', to 'Scripture', to the name of the French playwright, Scribe, even to 'Scriabin'. You never knew why. But I shall tell you. 'Scribe of the Gods.' Of the Egyptian Gods?"

The silent form confronting Dr Fazo did not stir.

"Think back. And I shall add another word, a name. The name you gave them as your own in the Museum. Because you were thirty-two years old. Not 'Thote'. They didn't get it right. Not quite, but nearly. It was—THOTH!"

Thoth! It was out at last, and Dr Fazo's bolt was neatly shot. What would he see? But for some reason he did not wish to look too closely at the figure in the chair. Instead, he took up a small parcel which had been lying on his desk. "I have the proof beside me here. A book. A book you glanced at—when you were a little boy. And, on a certain page, are pencil marks, thumb-stains and childish scribblings. Upon a certain page—the thirty-second..."

Again he stopped. What was he going to see? He was aware, and too acutely, of this moment's drama. Yet he refused to glance at Mr Meldrum. Still seated, with his head averted, he busied himself with the untying of the parcel. It was now, as he was pushing back the crackling paper wrappings, that he imagined he could catch a curious noise behind him, a faint sound like a sigh. But even then he did not turn. He opened the book, proceeded, "Here is the page. The figure 32 is very large. And just below it is the illustration—Thoth. Thoth with moon-disk and crescent, ibis-headed, the amanuensis of the Gods. You thought that, when that number had been reached—when you were thirty-two—you would..."

"Yes!" It was Mr Meldrum who had spoken, loudly and electrically. At last the psycho-analyst wheeled round. Mr Meldrum had risen from his chair, was staring—at that beak-faced spectre in the book. Dr Fazo, too, got up. He was more than nervous now. His whole body was bathed in sweat. Something was going wrong. Something was very much amiss. He did not know what it was...

"Yes!" Again Mr Meldrum had spoken, more loudly than before. It was the last word Dr Fazo was to hear him utter. And what was he *doing*! He was going—going away, striding immensely towards the door. Dr Fazo wanted to scream. In the next room, which he knew to be untenanted he thought he heard a rustle, then a bump.

"But—but..." Gathering his courage, the alienist had spurred himself to those twin syllables of vain remonstrance. The next instant he knew better, no longer wished to detain Mr Meldrum. His blood congealed, his mouth grew square in a tense rictus of extravagant dismay. A waft of cold and as it were aloof, bland and remote horror filled the room.

Mr Meldrum had by this time reached the door and opened it. His passage to it across the office floor had taken only a few seconds, yet those short moments had been long enough for Dr Fazo to feel a chill grue of terror travel up his spine. Mr Meldrum, whose back alone was now visible, was in no separable, individual particular transformed, but from his whole appearance—from his gait, his carriage—had been giving off the threat of a tremendous and an imminent alteration. In his departing presence there had been indicated not indeed the fact, but the incipience, of some appalling change. It was most fortunate that Dr Fazo could not see his face.

The door was closed. The sound of footsteps grew fainter down the corridor. Dr Fazo sank back in his chair. His eyes, wildly staring, did not so much as glance at the six-hundred dollar cheque which had been left upon his desk. Instead, and quite unluckily for him, they fastened upon one of the wax moulds of Mr Meldrum's face.

It was as he stared repelled at this wax mould that Dr Fazo fainted.

*

What followed has perhaps in part been guessed. In any case a hint or two may indicate a scene best left to the imagination. Mr Smith himself, who was the only person besides the operator to accompany Mr Meldrum in the elevator, was afterwards unable to give any clear account of what he saw. Not that he gave accounts—there were abundant reasons why his lips should remain sealed. Even if he had not got rather tipsy talking to his little twelfth-floor cutie from Ohio he might have hesitated to accept that sight within the lift as actual fact.

As it was, he fancied (mercifully) at the time that he was merely "seeing things"—as, naturally, he was, though not alone in the strict, technical intention of that phrase. To begin with, he was not then expecting to see Mr Meldrum, and, in a somewhat gruesome sense, it may be doubted that he ever did.

A certain amount of confidence presided over this shortlived encounter. Mr Smith, by 11.30, had become very sozzled and for no reason at all decided to go down to the Western Union and send someone—anyone—a telegram. A few seconds previous to this, Mr Meldrum (if whatever it was that had left Dr Fazo's office can still be narrowly described as "Mr Meldrum") had got into the elevator on the sixteenth floor. About three seconds later Mr Smith also entered, boisterously, at the twelfth. The thing which for convenience we call "Mr Meldrum", would not immediately have attracted his attention if it had not continued wearing Mr Meldrum's clothes.

It had taken, at most, three seconds for the elevator to pass downwards from the sixteenth to the twelfth, and it took considerably less than a proportionate time to reach the first—say seven seconds—Mr Meldrum ceased to be, and something hideously different took his place.

Briefly, as soon as Mr Smith had got into the lift his gaze, bent downwards, chanced to fasten on a pair of shoes. He seemed to recognize those shoes, *did* recognize, with qualms, the pants above. Still, there was something strange about them, too. The limbs which they presumably encased had—there was actually no other word—a curious quality of being *neuter*. Although invisible, their character somehow revealed itself. They were each as blankly, as shockingly neuter as an umbrella handle or the turned leg of a sofa. At the same instant that Mr Smith's glance, travelling upwards, fixed itself in a glassy stare of horror on a changing head, came, from the operator, an appalling shriek.

Past the remaining floors (say six or seven) the lift shot swiftly on its downward way. None of the three stirred. At the bottom the cage bumped to a standstill. The grille rattled open, allowing Mr Smith and the now idiot operator to spill themselves upon the marble floor. The third occupant of the elevator got out the last.

Nobody much was about. Mr Smith remained sitting on the floor. The operator had just begun to gibber. Neither of them, however, took his eyes off the back of a retreating figure, moving slowly towards the door on to Sixth Avenue.

Mr Smith, watching it go, felt no remorse, save for his recent ill-advised potations. This kind of thing might be exciting, but it did not pay—brought back, instead, old nightmares, old hallucinations which he had hoped were long ago dismissed as mere delusions. Yes, that was it. What he had seen a moment or two previously was a bad dream made real—or so it seemed. It was that fearful shadow on the doorway in Emporia come to life.

To this point unmolested, unremarked, a beak-faced monster, wearing Mr Meldrum's clothes, stalked out into the night.

To make a long story somewhat longer it is still necessary to tidy up a few loose ends.

Dr Fazo, left fainting in his chair, came to after a minute, regarded the life-mask of Mr Meldrum in imbecile relief. No, there was *nothing* wrong! The extraordinary sympathetic phenomenon which he believed himself to have witnessed (consisting in the gradual emergence from the mould of a peculiar beak-like process over a foot long) had been imagination, a grotesque mistake. Yes, it was a mistake all right, but Dr Fazo wasn't taking any chances. Pausing only to snatch up the cheque, he bolted. The elevator not working, he had to run down fifteen flights of stairs.

In the main hall he came upon the beginnings of a commotion, and the fag-end of Mr Smith, still squatting on the floor. Mr Smith, however, presumed a casual drunk, was not receiving much attention. The gibbering operator held the centre of the stage. Only a short time had elapsed since the elevator had descended, and the Ohio flapper (as well as a man who had noticed someone get into the cage at the sixteenth and had subsequently seen Dr Fazo start off running down the stairs) had yet to offer testimony.

Dr Fazo assisted Mr Smith to his feet. "Quick! Let's get out of this!"

Get out they did, and only just in time. With one regrettable exception they have not, *in propria persona*, been seen or heard of since.

And what of Mr Meldrum? What of that Thoth incarnate, that grisly hidden fear too aptly disinterred, personified—and stalking, as has been narrated, through the night?

The change of which the onset was foreshadowed dimly in the alienist's office would seem to have been finally accomplished in the lift itself between the twelfth floor and the first. And, after that, the stalking did not last for very long, apparently. At the corner of Seventh Avenue and Twenty-sixth Street—just a few blocks away—a building had come down, another was beginning to shoot upwards in its place. Into the twelve-foot chasm of an excavation *something* fell—fell down and broke its neck. An hour later the "corpse" was discovered, and collected trepidantly. The Medical Inspector was available, and summoned, losing his sleep for several nights in consequence. He was a good Elk, a Rotarian, a K. of C. and a Kiwani, and his responsibilities weighed heavily. Finally, with soul-searching, he decided that the matter should be, if possible, hushed up. Those very odd-looking remains, after a deal of discussion *in camera*, were accorded Christian burial. Nobody knew of it except a haunted few.

It is, perhaps, surprising that this should be so. That this extraordinary history did not "get about" (only by chance, indeed, and after several weeks arriving at the ears of Dr Fazo) is testimony to something—I am not quite sure what. Possibly to the hurrying, hard-headed and neglectful *tempo* of New York. In London such a story would have had the time to seed itself and propagate, have thriven better.

As regards Mr Smith, he never knew quite what to think about it all. Though he had lost a long-loved friend in Mr Meldrum, it appeared foolish to repine. The thing which had walked out of the Forensic Arts Building was not truly Mr Meldrum. It seemed, by the time its transformation was completed, to have been just a sinister emptiness, something without sensations, motives, or affections. When it fell down and broke its neck it had ceased to have a mind—in any sense that "mind" had ordinarily conveyed to human beings. From that point Mr Smith could hardly have desired the course of fate reversed...

How to explain it all? He does not try. "*Omnia exeunt in mysterium*," as his former landlady, Mrs Schultzenheimer, playfully reminded him one day last fall when he encountered her quite accidentally at Long Beach and, to his chagrin, was immediately recognized.

Yet how could *she* have known? This unexpected meeting was, of course, the "regrettable exception" alluded to above and brooding upon Mrs Schultzenheimer has made Mr Smith extremely nervous. Although the complete story never became public and that small early-July-morning hubbub round the elevator was soon entirely forgotten, he still has an exaggerated fear of waking echoes. In spite of this, again, he feels a little like the Ancient Mariner, or like the seedy, weedy fellow of the *Nancy Belle*. He must tell somebody. At Dr Fazo's instigation, and to avoid "repressions", he has himself been psycho'd and has written an account of the whole painful history—but it is most essential that he remain incognito.

It would, I feel, be quite intolerable otherwise. My name, as I have pointed out before, was at the very worst not really Smith, nor is it any name which may be printed over, under, or around this narrative. Nevertheless, I have a morbid dread of something's leaking out, and I have now elaborated and perfected my disguise.

From the date of Mr Meldrum's unfortunate apotheosis I have never worn Ohio flappers or been on nodding terms with brown Fedora hats.

1933

THE BLACK HARE

Flavia Richardson

Flavia Richardson was a pseudonym used by author, editor, literary agent and occultist Christine Campbell Thomson (1897–1985). Under the Flavia Richardson name she wrote a handful of short supernatural stories, many of which appeared in her own *Not at Night* anthology series, which she edited under her real name.

The *Not at Night* series ran to eleven volumes between 1925 and 1936, and was both influential and acclaimed, despite reprinting almost two-thirds of its stories from the US magazine *Weird Tales*. Interestingly, the series was published by Selwyn & Blount Ltd, a publishing company part-owned by Thomson's husband, Oscar Cook, who himself was an author of supernatural tales, and who met Thomson when she became his literary agent after his return from Borneo in the early 1920s.

Even more interestingly, between 2022 and 2025 another contributor to this volume, the esteemed writer, editor and archivist Johnny Mains, tracked down twenty-eight "lost" stories by Oscar Cook, which were published along with his already-known stories in the collection *His Beautiful Hands* (1925).

Aside from her short fiction under a pseudonym and her edited anthologies, Thomson also wrote a number of novels, among which are *The Incredible Island* (1924), *His Excellency* (1927), *Port of Call: Love and Murder in Algeria* (1936) and *Hawk of the Sahara* (1939), and several volumes of non-fiction, including *I Am a Literary Agent* (1951), *The Western Mystery Tradition: The Esoteric Heritage of the West* (1968) and *A Case for Reincarnation* (1972).

"The Black Hare", first published in *Keep on the Light* (1933), the ninth volume of the *Not at Night* series, is a short, simple, but satisfyingly grisly tale, and one of two in this book that can perhaps be said to fall within the "folk horror" subgenre.

When the village fly drew up at the gate of Wisteria Cottage, neither Elizabeth nor Susan could refrain from exclamations of delight. The cottage was compact, yet not unduly square. It had an ivy-covered front with casement windows. The first floor where the bedrooms were was wreathed in pink roses, now in blossom. Above this upper row of windows were two little dormers, giving light to one of the old-fashioned roomy attics that serve as loft and box-room to cottages of this description.

The coachman got down from the box and opened the door of the fly. His round, red face was puckered and worried.

"You be going to stay here alone, misses?" he asked.

Elizabeth nodded. Susan was busy, unpacking herself from the welter of golf-clubs, tennis-racquets, and odds and ends of rugs and suit-cases that seemed to have fallen all over the place.

"Why not?" she asked, a moment later.

The coachman twisted his mouth in a strange grimace. "It's nothing, miss. Only they do say as how... strange things have happened here afore now."

Both girls laughed as they handed out some of the parcels.

"That won't worry us," declared Susan cheerfully. "After all, you must remember that it is our own cottage now."

The man stared at her. "Yours, miss?" he said anxiously.

"Yes, of course." Elizabeth was getting a little impatient. She got out herself and stood at the door of the cab. "Mr Roylance was our uncle, though we didn't know him. But the lawyers advertised for his next-of-kin, and we were it—they. So we got the cottage, and here we are."

She turned as she spoke, and did not see the look of horror that came over the man's face.

Susan got out. Just as she set foot to the ground she saw a shadow on the road—curiously long; it startled her for a second.

"What was it?" Elizabeth noticed her quick movement.

"Nothing—just a shadow. The light plays strange tricks. I thought it was a huge black rabbit that leapt over the road."

At her words the coachman suddenly made the Sign of the Cross.

"What on earth's the matter?" demanded Susan.

"Nothing, miss, nothing. There's no harm in rabbits. But if you had said you'd seen a black hare, now..."

"Well, what if I had?"

"They do say as how they mean terrible bad luck, miss. There be one about here, and none of us will go on the road it's been seen to cross. It's glad I am that what you saw was ahead of you and not behind, for it's a long way back to the stable by the bridge."

"Let's get some of this luggage in," interrupted Elizabeth. She had taken a definite dislike to the gloomy coachman.

But the subject seemed to interest Susan.

"What's wrong with black hares?" she asked, as she picked up a set of golf-clubs and slung them across her shoulder.

The coachman looked to right and left before he replied.

"They're not right animals, as you might say, miss," he said very softly. "There's some as has seen a woman in her cottage one minute and a black hare on the road the next—and where the hare was, there wasn't no woman. A young lad round about here shot one once, so my father told me, and when he got home he found his own mother lying on the bed with a shot-wound in her head..."

"Old-wives' tales," snorted Elizabeth, and her contempt was so manifest that both Susan and the coachman let the matter drop.

Wisteria Cottage had a built-out porch glassed in from the elements. Here the coachman helped to dump the luggage and here he left the girls. He made no offer to help carry anything into the house, and they had a feeling that it would be wiser not to ask. A refusal would have been embarrassing for all parties.

"Now for the keys," said Susan, as she began to fumble in her bag. "Isn't it marvellous to think we are here at last?"

Before Elizabeth could reply, the door of the cottage was opened from the inside and a woman stood on the threshold. Slim and dark-haired, she had a peculiarly lovely pair of eyes. She wore a cotton frock and a large-check apron.

"Oh..." began Susan, a little at a loss.

"I beg your pardon, miss. I was Mr Roylance's housekeeper, as you might say. I came to see if I could be of use to you. I got in the stores you asked for and I've lit a fire."

"Thank you." Susan stepped over the threshold. As she did so she felt a little cold draught touching her face. She shivered for a moment, then went on into the hall.

Bit by bit the luggage was brought in and deposited in the downstair rooms, where the girls decided to unpack. It would have been almost impossible for them to get the heavy trunks up the narrow, winding staircase to the bedrooms.

They had tea and afterwards both went over the ground floor with Mrs Verity. She had been as good as her word. A bright fire was burning in the sitting-room, and in addition to that she had lit the old-fashioned heater by which hot water was supplied to the bathroom upstairs—the only modern part of the house.

"If you don't need me, I should like to be getting back," she suggested, a few moments later.

"Of course. Will you come up tomorrow?" asked Susan. "We'd like to talk to you and get some advice about a woman to come in and clean and that sort of thing. We shall have to do most of it ourselves, but we shall need someone for the rough work."

"Certainly, miss." Mrs Verity turned to leave the kitchen.

"Oh, Mrs Verity!" Elizabeth was speaking. "What's this marvellous story about a black hare being unlucky?"

A strange gleam came into Mrs Verity's eyes. They seemed to grow larger and unusually bright. But her voice was, if anything, still more soft, as she replied: "There are some folks around here, miss, as have more time than sense. They do say as how a black hare crossing your path is unlucky. Some of them—men, mostly—will go miles out of their way to avoid the place where a black hare has crossed the road. For myself, I never saw one in these parts."

Elizabeth laughed. "I thought as much," she said. "The coachman who drove us here seemed all hot and bothered about them."

"Oh, him..." there was a world of contempt in Mrs Verity's voice. "Well, yes, but he... his wife comes from the other side of the border, and in Scotland I believe they set great store by those outlandish superstitions. I never saw a black hare down here."

"Then you have seen one somewhere else?" interposed Susan.

A gleam of annoyance came into Mrs Verity's eyes. "I may have," was all she vouchsafed, but there was that in her manner that made the girls feel it would be wiser to change the subject.

"Then we shall see you in the morning," said Susan, neatly closing the conversation. "By the way, where do you live?"

"At the end of your garden, miss." Mrs Verity drew aside from the window and pointed to where at the bottom of the small lawn a red cottage reared its roof. "That's our bedroom window facing you—the only one on this side—so if by any chance you were wanting something in the night, a good call would fetch me or my husband out o' bed and we could come across."

"Splendid," said Susan. "It's good to know someone is near."

When Mrs Verity had gone, Elizabeth looked round the kitchen.

"I suppose we'd better finish unpacking," she said, "otherwise we shall never get this adorable place straight. Aren't you glad we found it was left to us?"

Susan nodded. "Rather. And enough to live on, too, if we don't want to splash. Marvellous. I'm loving it already."

They unpacked, and lit the lamps, and then made a light supper of eggs and milk and cocoa which Mrs Verity had supplied. As they were washing-up afterwards, Susan said: "I can't make out what is behind Mrs Verity. She seems queer, don't you think so?"

Elizabeth shrugged her shoulders. "Maybe. This whole place seems queer, if you ask me. Did you ever hear so much rot in your life as all that stuff about black hares? Why, the next thing will be that they will accuse us of wandering about in some sort of disguise, got up as pigs or calves."

Susan laughed. "They may. But, anyway, they all believe in this black hare business. So if you see one, turn round and go another way. We don't want any bad luck, just after coming into this lovely cottage. But Mrs Verity is queer. She knows more than she wants to say."

Elizabeth snorted again. "Probably turns into a hare herself, or else knows someone else who does," she suggested. "I don't suppose you'd be particularly keen on talking about it if you had someone with that sort of trait in the family."

Half an hour later, the cottage tidied and doors and windows closed for the night, Elizabeth said:

"I'm going to get a bath. The water's hot, and I'm tired."

"Right," responded Susan. "I'll have the bathroom after you." She paused a second. "Tell you what. While you have a bath, I'm going to explore the attic. We haven't been up there yet."

"Good. I'll see it tomorrow. It's sure to be dusty, and if I've had a bath there's no sense in getting dirty again. Call out if you find an old trunk stuffed with Uncle Roylance's golden hoard or anything really thrilling like that..."

Elizabeth shut the bathroom door. She heard Susan climb the ladder-like steps to the attic, and heard her footsteps overhead. The floor of the attic was not too well built evidently, for the sound came through clearly. Elizabeth got into her bath and lay back in the hot water. She had closed her eyes and was in the pleasant half-dreamy state that often comes at such moments, when her attention was aroused by a tiny plop. For a moment she did not take heed. She thought she had forgotten to turn off the tap. Subconsciously, however, she remembered that she had been especially careful to do this, and she opened her eyes in curiosity.

They remained open in amazement and horror. There was a little red patch on the surface over the bath-water. She lifted her eyes to the ceiling, and there she saw an ominous stain. Then came another plop, and another drop of red joined its fellows in the bath. At the same moment she realized with full awareness that there was no sound from Susan in the attic.

In one minute Elizabeth was out of the bath and in her dressing-gown. She felt so frightened that she hardly dared to open the bathroom door. Yet she must go up to the attic and see what had happened. Susan must have met with a bad accident.

Up the steep little flight of stairs Elizabeth padded, her dressing-gown clutched round her.

"Susan, Susan!" she called, but there was no reply.

Only a strange coldness seemed to fill the house, and a new and terrible stillness that did not belong to this world.

The attic was full of old furniture and boxes, hoarded by Mr Roylance. Elizabeth threaded her way through them till she came to the part of the attic over the bathroom, hidden from the door by a large sideboard. There, on the floor, lay Susan. Her arms were extended, and her head was slightly turned to one side. From her throat welled an ominous red stream, and as Elizabeth, sick with horror, bent over her, she saw that the jugular had been bitten in half by something very sharp and small.

Turning away to control her nausea, she looked out of one of the attic windows. It was at the back of the cottage. Before her were the walls of Mrs Verity's abode. In the bright moonlight the place stood out almost as clear as in the daytime.

Elizabeth was about to scream for help when her heart stood still and the sound died in her throat. As she looked out she saw running across their own garden a large black hare. Even as she watched it, fascinated, it leapt from the wall to the lighted window of the cottage and went inside.

A moment later Mrs Verity pulled the curtains.

1952

THE BEAUTIFUL PEOPLE

Charles Beaumont

Born Charles Leroy Nutt on 2 January 1929, American author Charles Beaumont accumulated a huge number of writing credits during his tragically short life and career. His first story, "The Devil, You Say?", appeared in *Amazing Stories* in January 1951, and by the time of his death in 1967, around sixty of his tales had been published in various science-fiction and men's magazines, such as *F&SF*, *If*, *Orbit*, *Infinity*, *Playboy* and *Esquire*, and in the story collections *The Hunger and Other Stories* (1957), *Yonder* (1958) and *Night Ride and Other Journeys* (1960). In the years since then, around twenty-five further, previously unpublished, stories have seen the light of day, most notably in the collection *A Touch of the Creature* (2000).

In 1962 Beaumont adapted his novel *The Intruder* into a movie script, which was directed by his good friend Roger Corman. Other movies that he scripted or co-scripted include *Queen of Outer Space* (1958), *Night of the Eagle* (1962), *Premature Burial* (1962), *The Haunted Palace* (1963), *7 Faces of Dr Lao* (1964) and *The Masque of the Red Death* (1964).

Today, Beaumont is perhaps best-known for his work on Rod Serling's seminal TV series *The Twilight Zone*, to which he contributed scripts for over twenty episodes, including a 1963 adaptation of his very first published story, which was retitled "The Printer's Devil".

"The Beautiful People" is another of Beaumont's early stories, which he later adapted into an episode of *The Twilight Zone* (this one was retitled "Number Twelve Looks Just Like You"). Published in 1952 in the speculative fiction magazine *If*, "The Beautiful People" is a science-fiction story with a definite undercurrent of body-horror, dealing as it does with transformation via surgical/genetic manipulation. A social comment on beauty and conformity, "The Beautiful People" seems just as relevant today as it undoubtedly did when it was first published over seventy years ago.

Mary sat quietly and watched the handsome man's legs blown off; watched further as the great ship began to crumple and break into small pieces in the middle of the blazing night. She fidgeted slightly as the men and the parts of the men came floating dreamily through the wreckage out into the awful silence. And when the meteorite shower came upon the men, gouging holes through everything, tearing flesh and ripping bones, Mary closed her eyes.

"Mother."

Mrs Cuberle glanced up from her magazine.

"Hmm?"

"Do we have to wait much longer?"

"I don't think so. Why?"

Mary said nothing but looked at the moving wall.

"Oh, that." Mrs Cuberle laughed and shook her head. "That tired old thing. Read a magazine, Mary, like I'm doing. We've all seen *that* a million times."

"Does it have to be on, Mother?"

"Well, nobody seems to be watching. I don't think the doctor would mind if I switched it off."

Mrs Cuberle rose from the couch and walked to the wall. She depressed a little button and the life went from the wall, flickering and glowing.

Mary opened her eyes.

"Honestly," Mrs Cuberle said to a woman sitting beside her,

"you'd think they'd try to get something else. We might as well go to the museum and watch the first landing on Mars. The Mayoraka Disaster—really!"

The woman replied without distracting her eyes from the magazine page. "It's the doctor's idea. Psychological."

Mrs Cuberle opened her mouth and moved her head up and down knowingly.

"Ohhh. I should have known there was *some* reason. Still, who watches it?"

"The children do. Makes them think, makes them grateful or something."

"Ohhh."

"Psychological."

Mary picked up a magazine and leafed through the pages. All photographs, of women and men. Women like Mother and like the others in the room; slender, tanned, shapely, beautiful women; and men with large muscles and shiny hair. Women and men, all looking alike, all perfect and beautiful. She folded the magazine and wondered how to answer the questions that would be asked.

"Mother—"

"Gracious, what is it now! Can't you sit still for a minute?"

"But we've been here three hours."

Mrs Cuberle sniffed.

"Do—do I really have to?"

"Now don't be silly, Mary. After those terrible things you told me, of *course* you do."

An olive-skinned woman in a transparent white uniform came into the reception room.

"Cuberle. Mrs Zena Cuberle?"

"Yes."

"Doctor will see you now."

Mrs Cuberle took Mary's hand and they walked behind the nurse down a long corridor.

A man who seemed in his middle twenties looked up from a desk. He smiled and gestured toward two adjoining chairs.

"Well—well."

"Doctor Hortel, I—"

The doctor snapped his fingers.

"Of course, I know. Your daughter. Ha ha, I certainly do know your trouble. Get so many of them nowadays—takes up most of my time."

"You do?" asked Mrs Cuberle. "Frankly, it had begun to upset me."

"Upset? Hmm. Not good. Not good at all. Ah, but then—if people did not get upset, we psychiatrists would be out of a job, eh? Go the way of the early M.D. But, I assure you, I need hear no more." He turned his handsome face to Mary. "Little girl, how old are you?"

"Eighteen, sir."

"Oh, a real bit of impatience. It's just about time, of course. What might your name be?"

"Mary."

"Charming! And so unusual. Well now, Mary, may I say that I understand your problem—understand it thoroughly?"

Mrs Cuberle smiled and smoothed the sequins on her blouse.

"Madam, you have no idea how many there are these days. Sometimes it preys on their minds so that it affects them physically, even mentally. Makes them act strange, say peculiar, unexpected things. One little girl I recall was so distraught she did nothing but brood all day long. Can you imagine!"

"That's what Mary does. When she finally told me, doctor, I thought she had gone—*you* know."

"That bad, eh? Afraid we'll have to start a re-education program. very soon, or they'll all be like this. I believe I'll suggest it to the senator day after tomorrow."

"I don't quite understand, doctor."

"Simply, Mrs Cuberle, that the children have got to be thoroughly instructed. Thoroughly. Too much is taken for granted and childish minds somehow refuse to accept things without definite reason. Children have become far too intellectual, which, as I trust I needn't remind you, is a dangerous thing."

"Yes, but what has this to do with—"

"With Mary? Everything, of course. Mary, like half the sixteen, seventeen and eighteen year olds today, has begun to feel acutely self-conscious. She feels that her body has developed sufficiently for the Transformation—which of course it has not, not quite yet—and she cannot understand the complex reasons that compel her to wait until some future date. Mary looks at you, at the women all about her, at the pictures, and then she looks into a mirror. From pure perfection of body, face, limbs, pigmentation, carriage, stance, from simon-pure perfection, if I may be allowed the expression, she sees herself and is horrified. Isn't that so, my dear child? Of course—of course. She asks herself, why must I be hideous, unbalanced, oversize, undersize, full of revolting skin eruptions, badly schemed organically? In short, Mary is tired of being a monster and is overly anxious to achieve what almost everyone else has already achieved."

"But—" said Mrs Cuberle.

"This much you understand, doubtless. Now, Mary, what you object to is that our society offers you, and the others like you, no convincing logic on the side of waiting until age nineteen. It is all taken for granted, and you want to know why! It is that simple. A non-technical explanation will not suffice—mercy no! The modern child wants facts, solid technical data, to satisfy her every question. And that, as you can both see, will take a good deal of reorganizing."

"But—" said Mary.

"The child is upset, nervous, tense; she acts strange, peculiar, odd, worries you and makes herself ill because it is beyond our meagre powers to put it across. I tell you, what we need is a whole new basis for learning. And, that will take doing. It will take *doing*, Mrs Cuberle. Now, don't you worry about Mary, and don't *you* worry, child. I'll prescribe some pills and—"

"No, no, doctor! You're all mixed up," cried Mrs Cuberle.

"I beg your pardon, Madam?"

"What I mean is, you've got it wrong. Tell him, Mary, tell the doctor what you told me."

Mary shifted uneasily in the chair.

"It's that—I don't want it."

The doctor's well-proportioned jaw dropped.

"Would you please repeat that?"

"I said, I don't want the Transformation."

"D—Don't want it?"

"You see? She told me. That's why I came to you."

The doctor looked at Mary suspiciously.

"But that's impossible! I have never heard of such a thing. Little girl, you are playing a joke!"

Mary nodded negatively.

"See, doctor. What can it be?" Mrs Cuberle rose and began to pace.

The doctor clucked his tongue and took from a small cupboard a black box covered with buttons and dials and wire.

"Oh no, you don't think—I mean, could it?"

"We shall soon see." The doctor revolved a number of dials and studied the single bulb in the center of the box. It did not flicker. He removed handles from Mary's head.

"Dear me," the doctor said, "dear me. Your daughter is perfectly sane, Mrs Cuberle."

"Well, then what is it?"

"Perhaps she is lying. We haven't completely eliminated that factor as yet; it slips into certain organisms."

More tests. More machines and more negative results.

Mary pushed her foot in a circle on the floor. When the doctor put his hands to her shoulders, she looked up pleasantly.

"Little girl," said the handsome man, "do you actually mean to tell us that you *prefer* that body?"

"Yes, sir."

"May I ask why."

"I like it. It's—hard to explain, but it's me and that's what I like. Not the looks, maybe, but the *me*."

"You can look in the mirror and see yourself, then look at—well, at your mother and be content?"

"Yes, sir." Mary thought of her reasons; fuzzy, vague, but very definitely there. Maybe shc had said the reason. No. Only a part of it.

"Mrs Cuberle," the doctor said, "I suggest that your husband have a long talk with Mary."

"My husband is dead. That affair near Ganymede, I believe. Something like that."

"Oh, splendid. Rocket man, eh? Very interesting organisms. Something always seems to happen to rocket men, in one way or another. But—I suppose we should do something." The doctor scratched his jaw. "When did she first start talking this way," he asked.

"Oh, for quite some time. I used to think it was because she was such a baby. But lately, the time getting so close and all, I thought I'd better see you."

"Of course, yes, very wise. Er—does she also do odd things?"

"Well, I found her on the second level one night. She was lying on the floor and when I asked her what she was doing, she said she was trying to sleep."

Mary flinched. She was sorry, in a way, that Mother had found that out.

"To—did you say 'sleep'?"

"That's right."

"Now where could she have picked that up?"

"No idea."

"Mary, don't you know that nobody sleeps anymore? That we have an infinitely greater life-span than our poor ancestors now that the wasteful state of unconsciousness has been conquered? Child, have you actually *slept?* No one knows how anymore."

"No, sir, but I almost did."

The doctor sighed. "But, it's unheard of! How could you begin to try to do something people have forgotten entirely about?"

"The way it was described in the book, it sounded nice, that's all." Mary was feeling very uncomfortable now. Home and no talking man in a foolish white gown...

"Book, book? Are there *books* at your Unit, Madam?"

"There could be—I haven't cleaned up in a while."

"That is certainly peculiar. I haven't seen a book for years. Not since '17."

Mary began to fidget and stare nervously about.

"But with the tapes, why should you try and read books—where did you get them?"

"Daddy did. He got them from his father and so did Grandpa. He said they're better than the tapes and he was right."

Mrs Cuberle flushed.

"My husband was a little strange, Doctor Hortel. He kept those things despite everything I said."

"Dear me, I—excuse me."

The muscular, black-haired doctor walked to another cabinet and selected from the shelf a bottle. From the bottle he took two large pills and swallowed them.

"Sleep—books—doesn't want the Transformation—Mrs Cuberle, my *dear* good woman, this is grave. Doesn't want the Transformation. I would appreciate it if you would change psychiatrists: I am very busy and, uh, this is somewhat specialized. I suggest Centraldome. Many fine doctors there. Goodbye."

The doctor turned and sat down in a large chair and folded his hands. Mary watched him and wondered why the simple statements should have so changed things. But the doctor did not move from the chair.

"Well!" said Mrs Cuberle and walked quickly from the room.

The man's legs were being blown off again as they left the reception room.

Mary considered the reflection in the mirrored wall. She sat on the floor and looked at different angles of herself: profile, full-face, full length, naked, clothed. Then she took up the magazine and studied it. She sighed.

"Mirror, mirror on the wall—" The words came haltingly to her mind and from her lips. She hadn't read them, she recalled. Daddy had said them, quoted them as he put it. But they too were lines from a book—"who is the fairest of—"

A picture of Mother sat upon the dresser and Mary considered this now. Looked for a long time at the slender, feminine neck. The golden skin, smooth and without blemish, without wrinkles and without age. The dark brown eyes and the thin tapers of eyebrows, the long black lashes, set evenly, so that each half of the face corresponded precisely. The half-parted mouth, a violet tint against the gold, the white, white teeth, even, sparkling.

Mother. Beautiful, Transformed Mother. And back again to the mirror.

"—of them all..."

The image of a rather chubby girl, without lines of rhythm or grace, without perfection. Splotchy skin full of little holes, puffs in the cheeks, red eruptions on the forehead. Perspiration, shapeless hair flowing onto shapeless shoulders down a shapeless body. Like all of them, before the Transformation.

Did they *all* look like this, before? Did Mother, even?

Mary thought hard, trying to remember exactly what Daddy and Grandpa had said, why they said the Transformation was a bad thing, and why she believed and agreed with them so strongly. It made little sense, but they were right. They *were* right! And one day, she would understand completely.

Mrs Cuberle slammed the door angrily and Mary jumped to her feet. She hadn't forgotten about it. "The way you upset Dr Hortel. He won't even see me anymore, and these traumas are getting horrible. I'll have to get that awful Dr Wagoner."

"Sorry—"

Mrs Cuberle sat on the couch and crossed her legs carefully.

"What in the world were you doing on the floor?"

"Trying to sleep."

"Now, I won't hear of it! You've got to stop it! You *know* you're not insane. Why should you want to do such a silly thing?"

"The books. And Daddy told me about it."

"And you mustn't read those terrible things."

"Why—is there a law against them?"

"Well, no, but people tired of books when the tapes came in. You know that. The house is full of tapes; anything you want."

Mary stuck out her lower lip.

"They're no fun. All about the Wars and the colonizations."

"And I suppose books are fun?"

"Yes. They are."

"And that's where you got this idiotic notion that you don't want the Transformation, isn't it? Of course it is. Well, we'll see to that!"

Mrs Cuberle rose quickly and took the books from the corner and from the closet and filled her arms with them. She looked everywhere in the room and gathered the old rotten volumes.

These she carried from the room and threw into the elevator. A button guided the doors shut.

"I thought you'd do that," Mary said. "That's why I hid most of the good ones. Where you'll never find them."

Mrs Cuberle put a satin handkerchief to her eyes and began to weep.

"Just look at you. Look. I don't know what I ever did to deserve this!"

"Deserve what, Mother? What am I doing that's so wrong?" Mary's mind rippled in a confused stream.

"What!" Mrs Cuberle screamed, "*What!* Do you think I want people to point to you and say I'm the mother of an idiot? That's what they'll say, you'll see. Or," she looked up hopefully, "have you changed your mind?"

"No." The vague reasons, longing to be put into words.

"It doesn't hurt. They just take off a little skin and put some on and give you pills and electronic treatments and things like that. It doesn't take more than a week."

"No." The reason.

"Don't you want to be beautiful, like other people—like me? Look at your friend Shala, she's getting her Transformation next month. And *she's* almost pretty now."

"Mother, I don't care—"

"If it's the bones you're worried about, well, that doesn't hurt. They give you a shot and when you wake up, everything's moulded right. Everything, to suit the personality."

"I don't care, I don't care."

"But *why?*"

"I like me the way I am." Almost—almost exactly. But not quite. Part of it, however. Part of what Daddy and Grandpa meant.

"But you're so ugly, dear! Like Dr Hortel said. And Mr Willmes, at the factory. He told some people he thought you were the ugliest girl he'd ever seen. Says he'll be thankful when you have your Transformation. And what if he hears of all this, what'll happen then?"

"Daddy said I was beautiful."

"Well really, dear. You *do* have eyes."

"Daddy said that real beauty is only skin deep. He said a lot of things like that and when I read the books I felt the same way. I guess I don't want to look like everybody else, that's all." No, that's not it. Not at all it.

"That man had too much to do with you. You'll notice that he had *his* Transformation, though!"

"But he was sorry. He told me that if he had it to do over again, he'd never do it. He said for me to be stronger than he was."

"Well, I won't have it. You're not going to get away with this, young lady. After all, I *am* your mother."

A bulb flickered in the bathroom and Mrs Cuberle walked uncertainly to the cabinet. She took out a little cardboard box.

"Time for lunch."

Mary nodded. That was another thing the books talked about, which the tapes did not. Lunch seemed to be something special long ago, or at least different. The books talked of strange ways of putting a load of things into the mouth and chewing these things. Enjoying them. Strange and somehow wonderful.

"And you'd better get ready for work."

"Yes, Mother."

The office was quiet and without shadows. The walls gave off a steady luminescence, distributed the light evenly upon all the desks and tables. And it was neither hot nor cold.

Mary held the ruler firmly and allowed the pen to travel down the metal edge effortlessly. The new black lines were small and accurate. She tipped her head, compared the notes beside her to the plan she was working on. She noticed the beautiful people looking at her more furtively than before, and she wondered about this as she made her lines.

A tall man rose from his desk in the rear of the office and walked down the aisle to Mary's table. He surveyed her work, allowing his eyes to travel cautiously from her face to the draft.

Mary looked around.

"Nice job," said the man.

"Thank you, Mr Willmes."

"Dralich shouldn't have anything to complain about. That crane should hold the whole damn city."

"It's very good alloy, sir."

"Yeah. Say, kid, you got a minute?"

"Yes sir."

"Let's go into Mullinson's office."

The big handsome man led the way into a small cubby-hole of a room. He motioned to a chair and sat on the edge of one desk.

"Kid, I never was one to beat around the bush. Somebody called in little while ago, gave me some crazy story about you not wanting the Transformation."

Mary said "Oh." Daddy had said it would have to happen, some day. This must be what he meant.

"I would've told them they were way off the beam, but I wanted to talk to you first, get it straight."

"Well, sir, it's true. I don't. I want to stay this way."

The man looked at Mary and then coughed, embarrassedly.

"What the hell—excuse me, kid, but—I don't exactly get it. You, uh, you saw the psychiatrist?"

"Yes sir. I'm not insane. Dr Hortel can tell you."

"I didn't mean anything like that. Well—" the man laughed nervously. "I don't know what to say. You're still a cub, but you do swell work. Lot of good results, lots of comments from the stations. But, Mr Poole won't like it."

"I know. I know what you mean, Mr Willmes. But nothing can change my mind. I want to stay this way and that's all there is to it."

"But—you'll get old before you're half through life."

Yes, she would. Old, like the Elders, wrinkled and brittle, unable to move right. Old. "It's hard to make you understand. But I don't see why it should make any difference."

"Don't go getting me wrong, now. It's not me, but, you know, I don't own Interplan. I just work here. Mr Poole likes things running smooth and it's my job to carry it out. And soon as everybody finds out, things wouldn't run smooth. There'll be a big stink. The dames will start asking questions and talk."

"Will you accept my resignation, then, Mr Willmes?"

"Sure you won't change your mind?"

"No, sir. I decided that a long time ago. And I'm sorry now that I told Mother or anyone else. No, sir, I won't change my mind."

"Well, I'm sorry, Mary. You been doing awful swell work. Couple of years you could be centralled on one of the asteroids, the way you been working. But if you should change your mind, there'll always be a job for you here."

"Thank you, sir."

"No hard feelings?"

"No hard feelings."

"Okay then. You've got till March. And between you and me, I hope by then you've decided the other way."

Mary walked back down the aisle, past the rows of desks. Past the men and women. The handsome, model men and the beautiful, perfect women, perfect, all perfect, all looking alike. Looking exactly alike.

She sat down again and took up her ruler and pen.

Mary stepped into the elevator and descended several hundred feet. At the Second Level she pressed a button and the elevator stopped. The doors opened with another button and the doors to her Unit with still another.

Mrs Cuberle sat on the floor by the T-V, disconsolate and red-eyed. Her blond hair had come slightly askew and a few strands hung over her forehead. "You don't need to tell me. No one will hire you."

Mary sat beside her mother. "If you only hadn't told Mr Willmes in the first place—"

"Well, I thought *he* could beat a little sense into you."

The sounds from the T-V grew louder. Mrs Cuberle changed channels and finally turned it off.

"What did you do today, Mother?" Mary smiled.

"Do? What can I do, now? Nobody will even come over! I told you what would happen."

"Mother!"

"They say you should be in the Circuses."

Mary went into another room. Mrs Cuberle followed. "How are we going to live? Where does the money come from now? Just because you're stubborn on this crazy idea. Crazy crazy crazy! Can I support both of us? They'll be firing *me*, next!"

"Why is this happening?"

"Because of you, that's why. Nobody else on this planet has ever refused the Transformation. But you turn it down. You *want* to be ugly!"

Mary put her arms about her mother's shoulders. "I wish I could explain, I've tried so hard to. It isn't that I want to bother anyone, or that Daddy wanted me to. I just don't want the Transformation."

Mrs Cuberle reached into the pockets of her blouse and got a purple pill. She swallowed the pill. When the letter dropped from the chute, Mrs Cuberle ran to snatch it up. She read it once, silently, then smiled.

"Oh, I was afraid they wouldn't answer. But we'll see about this *now!*"

She gave the letter to Mary.

Mrs Zena Cuberle
Unit 451 D
Levels II & III
City

Dear Madam:

In re your letter of Dec 3 36. We have carefully examined your complaint and consider that it requires stringent measures. Quite frankly, the possibility of such a complaint has never occurred to this Dept. and we therefore cannot make positive directives at the moment.

However, due to the unusual qualities of the matter, we have arranged an audience at Centraldome, Eighth Level, Sixteenth Unit, Jan 3 37, 23 sharp. Dr Elph Hortel has been instructed to attend. You will bring the subject in question.

Yrs

DEPT F

Mary let the paper flutter to the floor. She walked quietly to the elevator and set it for Level III. When the elevator stopped, she ran from it, crying, into her room.

She thought and remembered and tried to sort out and put together. Daddy had said it, Grandpa had, the books did. Yes, the books did.

She read until her eyes burned and her eyes burned until she could read no more. Then Mary went to sleep, softly and without realizing it, for the first time.

But the sleep was not peaceful.

"Ladies and gentlemen," said the young-looking, well groomed man, "this problem does not resolve easily. Dr Hortel here, testifies that Mary Cuberle is definitely not insane. Drs. Monagh, Prinn and Fedders all verify this judgment. Dr Prinn asserts that the human organism is no longer so constructed as to create and sustain such an attitude through deliberate falsehood. Further, there is positively nothing in the structure of Mary Cuberle which might suggest difficulties in Transformation. There is evidence for all these statements. And yet we are faced with this refusal. What, may I ask, is to be done?"

Mary looked at a metal table.

"We have been in session far too long, holding up far too many other pressing contingencies. The trouble on Mercury, for example. We'll *have* to straighten that out, somehow."

Throughout the rows of beautiful people, the mumbling increased. Mrs Cuberle sat nervously, tapping her shoe and running a comb through her hair.

"Mary Cuberle, you have been given innumerable chances to reconsider, you know."

Mary said, "I know. But I don't want to."

The beautiful people looked at Mary and laughed. Some shook their heads.

The man threw up his hands. "Little girl, can you realize what an issue you have caused? The unrest, the wasted time? Do you fully understand what you have done? Intergalactic questions hang fire while you sit there saying the same thing over and over. Doesn't the happiness of your Mother mean anything to you?"

A slender, supple woman in a back row cried, "We want action. *Do* something!"

The man in the high stool raised his hand. "None of that, now. We must conform, even though the question is out of the ordinary." He leafed through a number of papers on his desk, leaned down and whispered into the ear of a strong blond man. Then he turned to Mary again. "Child, for the last time. Do you reconsider? Will you accept the Transformation?"

"No."

The man shrugged his shoulders. "Very well, then. I have here a petition, signed by two thousand individuals and representing all the Stations of Earth. They have been made aware of all the facts and have submitted the petition voluntarily. It's all so unusual and I'd hoped we wouldn't have to—but the petition urges drastic measures."

The mumbling rose.

"The petition urges that you shall, upon final refusal, be forced by law to accept the Transformation. And that an act of legislature shall make this universal and binding in the future."

Mary's eyes were open, wide. She stood and paused before speaking.

"Why?" she asked, loudly.

The man passed a hand through his hair.

Another voice from the crowd, "Seems to be a lot of questions unanswered here."

And another, "Sign the petition, Senator!"

All the voices, "Sign it, sign it!"

"But why?" Mary began to cry. The voices stilled for a moment.

"Because—Because—"

"If you'd only tell me that. Tell me!"

"Why, it simply isn't being done, that's all. The greatest gift of all, and what if others should get the same idea? What would happen to us then, little girl? We'd be right back to the ugly, thin, fat, unhealthy-looking race we were ages ago! There can't be any exceptions."

"Maybe they didn't consider themselves so ugly."

The mumbling began anew.

"That isn't the point," cried the man. "You *must* conform!"

And the voices cried "Yes" loudly until the man took up a pen and signed the papers on his desk.

Cheers, applause, shouts.

Mrs Cuberle patted Mary on the top of her head.

"There, now!" she said, happily, "Everything will be all right now. You'll see, Mary."

The Transformation Parlor covered the entire Level, sprawling with its departments. It was always filled and there was nothing to sign and no money to pay and people were always waiting in line.

But today the people stood aside. And there were still more, looking in through doors, TV cameras placed throughout the tape machines in every corner. It was filled, but not bustling as usual.

Mary walked past the people, Mother and the men in back of her, following. She looked at the people. The people were beautiful, perfect, without a single flaw.

All the beautiful people. All the ugly people, staring out from bodies that were not theirs. Walking on legs that had been made for them, laughing with manufactured voices, gesturing with shaped and fashioned arms.

Mary walked slowly, despite the prodding. In her eyes, in *her* eyes, was a mounting confusion; a wide, wide wonderment.

The reason was becoming less vague; the fuzzed edges were falling away now. Through all the horrible months and all the horrible moments, the edges fell away. Now it was almost clear.

She looked down at her own body, then at the walls which reflected it. Flesh of her flesh, bone of her bone, all hers, made by no one, built by herself or someone she did not know. Uneven kneecaps, making two grinning cherubs when they bent, and the old familiar rubbing together of fat inner thighs. Fat, unshapely, unsystematic Mary. But *Mary*.

Of course. Of course! This *was* what Daddy meant, what Grandpa and the books meant. What *they* would know if they would read the books or hear the words, the good, reasonable words, the words that signified more, much more, than any of this.

The understanding heaped up with each step.

"Where *are* these people?" Mary asked half to herself. "What has happened to *them* and don't they miss *themselves*, these manufactured things?"

She stopped, suddenly.

"Yes! That *is* the reason. They have all forgotten themselves!"

A curvaceous woman stepped forward and took Mary's hand. The woman's skin was tinted dark. Chipped and sculptured bone into slender rhythmic lines, electrically created carriage, stance, made, turned out.

"All right, young lady. We will begin."

They guided Mary to a large, curved leather seat.

From the top of a long silver pole a machine lowered itself. Tiny bulbs glowed to life and cells began to click. The people stared. Slowly a picture formed upon the screen in the machine. Bulbs directed at Mary, then redirected into the machine. Wheels turning, buttons ticking.

The picture was completed.

"Would you like to see it?"

Mary closed her eyes, tight.

"It's really very nice." The woman turned to the crowd. "Oh yes, there's a great deal to be salvaged; you'd be surprised. A great deal. We'll keep the nose and I don't believe the elbows will have to be altered at all."

Mrs Cuberle looked at Mary and smiled. "Now, it isn't so bad as you thought, is it?" she said.

The beautiful people looked. Cameras turned, tapes wound.

"You'll have to excuse us now. Only the machines allowed."

Only the machines.

The people filed out.

Mary saw the rooms in the mirror. Saw things in the rooms, the faces and bodies that had been left; the woman and the machines and the old young men standing about, adjusting, readying.

Then she looked at the picture in the screen.

And screamed.

A woman of medium height stared back at her. A woman with a curved body and thin legs; silver hair, pompadoured, cut short; full sensuous lips, small breasts, flat stomach, unblemished skin.

A strange, strange woman no one had ever seen before.

The nurse began to take Mary's clothes off.

"Geoff," the woman said, "come look at this, will you. Not one so bad in years. Amazing that we can keep anything at all."

The handsome man put his hands in his pockets.

"Pretty bad, all right."

"Be still, child, stop making those noises. You know perfectly well nothing is going to hurt."

"But—what will you do with me?"

"That was all explained to you."

"No, no, with *me, me!*"

"Oh, you mean the castoffs. The usual. I don't know exactly. Somebody takes care of it."

"I want me!" Mary cried. "Not that!" She pointed at the screen.

Her chair was wheeled into a semi-dark room. She was naked now, and the men lifted her to a table. The surface was like glass, black, filmed. A big machine hung above.

Straps. Clamps pulling, stretching limbs apart. The screen with the picture brought in. The men and the woman, more women now. Dr Hortel in a corner, sitting with his legs crossed, shaking his head.

Mary began to cry above the hum of the mechanical things.

"Shhh. My gracious, such a racket! Just think about your job waiting for you, and all the friends you'll have and how nice everything will be. No more trouble now."

The big machine hurtling downward.

"Where will I find *me?*" Mary screamed, "when it's all over?"

A long needle slid into rough flesh and the beautiful people gathered around the table.

They turned on the big machine.

1958

FURRY NIGHT

Joan Aiken

An incredible storyteller who wrote close to a hundred books, for all ages, and in a variety of genres, Joan Delano Aiken was born on 4 September 1924. Her father was the American poet Conrad Aiken, but after her parents divorced and her mother remarried, it was her stepfather, the English novelist Martin Armstrong, who was to have the greatest influence on her career. Although Armstrong's work was primarily aimed at adults, he wrote one children's book, for the BBC's Children's Hour, which inspired 16-year-old Joan to write her own story. She submitted it to Children's Hour, and it was immediately accepted.

In 1945 Joan married the journalist Ronald George Brown and they had two children. When Brown died in 1955, she joined the editorial staff of the fiction magazine *Argosy*, which, over the next few years, became one of many magazines to publish her short fiction.

Her 1962 novel, *The Wolves of Willoughby Chase*, set in an alternate nineteenth-century England, is now rightly regarded as a children's classic, and was the first of a twelve-volume series. Her other celebrated series include the *Arabel and Mortimer* books, her Felix trilogy, and her novels that continue or complement works by Jane Austen, such as *Mansfield Revisited* (1984), *Eliza's Daughter* (1994) and *Lady Catherine's Necklace* (2000).

Other books written by Aiken include *The Silence of Herondale* (1968), *A Cluster of Separate Sparks* (1972), *Dark Interval* (1974), *Midnight is a Place* (1976), *The Shadow Guests* (1980), *The Cockatrice Boys* (1996) and *The Scream* (2002).

Her short fiction is collected in *The Windscreen Weepers and Other Tales of Horror and Suspense* (1969), *The Kingdom Under the Sea and Other Stories* (1971), *A Bundle of Nerves* (1976), *A Touch of Chill* (1979), *A Whisper in the Night* (1984), *A Goose on Your Grave* (1987) and many others, including several collections published after her death in 2004.

"Furry Night" was first published in *Argosy* in November 1958, and imagines a world where lycanthropy is a known and treatable condition. This story concerns a temperamental Shakespearean actor who suffers from the condition and his young assistant's constant struggle to keep him calm, as it is not the full moon that provokes the change in this instance, but the man's short temper.

Full of wit, verve and even romance, "Furry Night" presents us with a werewolf story that veers away from established werewolf lore, and is a hugely enjoyable concoction.

The deserted aisles of the National Museum of Dramatic Art lay very, very still in the blue autumn twilight. Not a whisper of wind stirred the folds of Irving's purple cloak; Ellen Terry's ostrich fan was smooth and unruffled; the blue-black gleaming breastplate that Sir Murdoch Meredith, founder of the Museum, had worn as Macbeth, held its reflections as quietly as a cottage kettle.

And yet, despite this hush, there was an air of strain, of expectancy, along the narrow coconut-matted galleries between the glass cases; a tension suggesting that some crisis had taken or was about to take place.

In the total stillness a listener might have imagined that he heard, ever so faintly, the patter of stealthy feet far away among the exhibits.

Two men, standing in the shadow of the Garrick showcase, were talking in low voices.

"This is where it happened," said the elder, white-haired man.

He picked up a splinter of broken glass, frowned at it, and dropped it into a litter-bin. The glass had been removed from the front of the case, and some black tights and gilt medals hung exposed to the evening air.

"We managed to hush it up. The hospital and ambulance men will be discreet, of course. Nobody else was there, luckily. Only the Bishop was worried."

"I should think so," the younger man said. "It's enough to make anybody anxious."

"No, I mean he was *worried*. Hush," the white-haired man whispered. "Here comes Sir Murdoch."

The distant susurration had intensified into soft, pacing footsteps. The two men, without a word, stepped farther back in the shadow until they were out of sight. A figure appeared at the end of the aisle and moved forward until it stood beneath the portrait of Edmund Kean as Shylock. The picture, in its deep frame, was nothing but a square of dark against the wall.

Although they were expecting it, both men jumped when the haunted voice began to speak.

You may as well use question with the wolf
Why he hath made the ewe bleat for the lamb—

A sleeve of one of the watchers brushed against the wall, the lightest possible touch, but Sir Murdoch swung round sharply, his head outthrust, teeth bared. They held their breath, and after a moment he turned back to the picture.

The currish spirit
Governed a wolf, who, hang'd for human slaughter
Even from his gallows did his fell soul fleet...

He paused, with a hand pressed to his forehead, and then leaned forward and hissed,

Thy desires
Are wolvish, bloody, starv'd, and ravenous!

His head sank on his chest. His voice ceased. He brooded for a moment, and then resumed his pacing and soon passed out of sight. They heard the steps go lightly down the stairs, and presently the whine of the revolving door.

After a prudent interval the two others emerged from their hiding-place, left the gallery, and went out to a car which was waiting for them in Great Smith Street.

"I wanted you to see that, Peachtree," said the elder man, "to give you some idea of what you are taking on. Candidly, as far as experience goes, I hardly feel you are qualified for the job, but you are young and tough, and have presence of mind; most important of all, Sir Murdoch seems to have taken a fancy to you. You will have to keep an unobtrusive eye on him every minute of the day; your job is a combination of secretary, companion, and resident psychiatrist. I have written to Dr Defoe, the local G.P. at Polgrue. He is old, but you will find him full of practical sense. Take his advice... I think you said you were brought up in Australia?"

"Yes," Ian Peachtree said. "I only came to this country six months ago."

"Ah, so you missed seeing Sir Murdoch act."

"Was he so very wonderful?"

"He made the comedies too macabre," said Lord Hawick, considering, "but in the tragedies there was no one to touch him. His Macbeth was something to make you shudder. When he said,

> *Alarum'd by his sentinel, the wolf,*
> *Whose howl's his watch, thus with his stealthy pace*
> *With Tarquin's ravishing strides, towards his design*
> *Moves like a ghost—*

he used to take two or three stealthy steps across the stage, and you could literally see the grey fur rise on his hackles, the lips draw back from the fangs, the yellow eyes begin to gleam. It made a cold chill run down your spine. As Shylock and Caesar and Timon he was unrivalled. Othello and Antony he never touched, but his Iago was a masterpiece of villainy."

"Why did he give it up? He can't be much over fifty."

"As with other sufferers from lycanthropy," said Lord Hawick, "Sir Murdoch has an ungovernable temper. Whenever he flew into a rage it brought on an attack. They grew more and more frequent. A clumsy stage-hand, a missed cue, might set him off; he'd begin to shake with rage and the terrifying change would take place.

"On stage it wasn't so bad; he had his audiences completely hypnotized and they easily accepted a grey-furred Iago padding across the stage with the handkerchief in his mouth. But off stage it was less easy; the claims for mauling and worrying were beginning to mount up; Equity objected. So he retired and, for some time, founding the Museum absorbed him. But now it's finished, his temper is becoming uncertain again. This afternoon, as you know, he pounced on the Bishop for innocently remarking that Garrick's Hamlet was the world's greatest piece of acting."

"How do you deal with the attacks? What's the treatment?"

"Wolf's-bane. Two or three drops given in a powerful sedative will restore him for the time. Of course, administering it is the problem, as you can imagine. I only hope the surroundings in Cornwall will be sufficiently peaceful so that he is not provoked. It's a pity he never married; a woman's influence would be beneficial."

"Why didn't he?"

"Jilted when he was thirty. Never looked at another woman. Some girl down at Polgrue, near his home. It was a real slap in the face; she wrote two days before the wedding saying she couldn't stand his temper. That began it all. This will be the first time he's been back there. Well, here we are," said Lord Hawick, glancing out at his Harley Street doorstep. "Come in and I'll give you the wolf's-bane prescription."

The eminent consultant courteously held the door for his young colleague.

*

The journey to Cornwall was uneventful. Dr Peachtree drove his distinguished patient, glancing at him from time to time with mingled awe and affection. Would the harassing crawl down the A.30, the jam in Exeter, the flat tyre on Dartmoor, bring on an attack? Would he be able to cope if they did? But the handsome profile remained unchanged, the golden eyes in their deep sockets stayed the eyes of a man, not those of a wolf, and Sir Murdoch talked entertainingly, not at all discomposed by the delays. Ian was fascinated by his tales of the theatre.

There was only one anxious moment, when they reached the borders of Polgrue Chase. Sir Murdoch glanced angrily at his neglected coverts, where the brambles grew long and wild.

"Wait till I see that agent," he muttered, and then, half to himself, "O, thou wilt be a wilderness again, peopled with wolves."

Ian devoutly hoped that the agent would have a good excuse.

But the Hall, hideous Victorian-Gothic barrack though it was, they found gay with lights and warm with welcome. The old housekeeper wept over Sir Murdoch, bottles were uncorked, the table shone with ancestral silver. Ian began to feel less apprehensive.

After dinner they moved outside with their nuts and wine to sit in the light that streamed over the terrace from the dining-room french windows. A great walnut tree hung shadowy above them; its golden, aromatic leaves littered the flagstones at their feet.

"This place has a healing air," Sir Murdoch said. "I should have come here sooner." Suddenly he stiffened. "Hudson! Who are those?"

Far across the park, almost out of sight in the dusk, figures were flitting among the trees.

"Eh," said the housekeeper comfortably, "they're none but the lads, Sir Murdoch, practising for the Furry Race. Don't you worrit about them. They won't do no harm."

"On my land?" Sir Murdoch said. "Running across my land?"

Ian saw with a sinking heart that his eyes were turning to gleaming yellow slits, his hands were stiffening and curling. Would the housekeeper mind? Did she know her master was subject to these attacks? He felt in his pocket for the little ampoules of wolf's-bane, the hypodermic syringe.

There came an interruption. A girl's clear voice was heard singing:

Now the hungry lion roars,
And the wolf behowls the moon—

"It's Miss Clarissa," said the housekeeper with relief.

A slender figure swung round the corner of the terrace and came towards them.

"Sir Murdoch? How do you do? I'm Clarissa Defoe. My father sent me up to pay his respects. He would have come himself, but he was called out on a case. Isn't it a gorgeous night?"

Sitting down beside them she chatted amusingly and easily, while Ian observed with astonished delight that his employer's hands were unclenching and his eyes were becoming their normal shape again. If this girl was able to soothe Sir Murdoch without recourse to wolf's-bane they must see a lot of her.

But when Sir Murdoch remarked that the evening was becoming chilly and proposed that they go indoors, Ian's embryonic plan received a jolt. He was a tough and friendly young man who had never taken a great deal of interest in girls; the first sight, in lamplight, of Clarissa Defoe's wild beauty came on him with a shattering impact. Could he expose her to danger without warning her?

More and more enslaved he sat gazing as Clarissa played and sang Ariel's songs. Sir Murdoch seemed completely charmed and relaxed.

When Clarissa left, he let Ian persuade him up to bed without the topic of the Furry Race coming up again.

Next morning, however, when Ian went down to the village for a consultation with cheerful, shrewd-eyed old Dr Defoe, he asked about it.

"Heh," said the Doctor. "The Furry Race? My daughter revived it five years ago. There's two villages, ye see, Polgrue, and Lostmid, and there's this ball, what they call the Furry Ball. It's not furry; it's made of applewood with a silver band round the middle, and on the band is written,

Fro Lostmid Parish iffe I goe
Heddes will be broke and bloode will flowe.

"The ball is kept in Lostmid and on the day of the race one of the Polgrue lads has to sneak in and take it and get it over the parish boundary before anybody stops him. Nobody's succeeded in doing it yet. But why do you ask?"

Ian explained about the scene the night before.

"Eh, I see; that's awkward. You're afraid it may bring on an attack if he sees them crossing his land? Trouble is, that's the quickest short cut over the parish boundary."

"If your daughter withdrew her support, would the race be abandoned?"

"My dear feller, she'd never do that. She's mad about it. She's a bit of a tomboy, Clarissa, and the rough-housing amuses her—always is plenty of horseplay, even though they don't get the ball over the boundary. If her mother were still alive now... Bless my soul!" the old doctor burst out, looking troubled, "I wish Meredith had never come back to these parts, that I do. You can speak with Clarissa about it, but I doubt you'll not persuade her. She's out looking over the course now."

The two villages of Lostmid and Polgrue lay in deep adjacent glens, and Polgrue Chase ended on the stretch of high moorland that ran between them. There was a crossroads and a telephone box, used by both villages. A spinney of wind-bitten beeches stood in one angle of the cross, and Clarissa was thoughtfully surveying this terrain. Ian joined her, turning to look back towards the Hall, and noticing with relief that Sir Murdoch was still, as he had been left, placidly knocking a ball round his private golf-course.

It was a stormy, shining day. Ian saw that Clarissa's hair was exactly the colour of the sea-browned beech leaves and that the strange angles of her face were emphasized by the wild shafts of sunlight glancing through the trees.

He put his difficulties to her.

"Oh, dear," she said, wrinkling her brow. "How unfortunate. The boys are so keen on the race. I don't think they'd ever give it up."

"Couldn't they go some other way?"

"But this is the only possible way, don't you see? In the old days, of course, all this used to be common land."

"Do you know who the runner is going to be—the boy with the ball?" Ian asked, wondering if a sufficiently heavy bribe would persuade him to take a longer way round.

But Clarissa smiled with innocent topaz eyes. "My dear, that's never decided until the very *last* minute. So that the Lostmidians don't know who's going to dash in and snatch the ball. But I'll tell you what we *can* do—we can arrange for the race to take place at night, so that Sir Murdoch won't be worried by the spectacle. Yes, that's an excellent idea; in fact it will make it far more exciting. It's next Thursday, you know."

Ian was not at all sure that he approved of this idea, but just then he noticed Sir Murdoch having difficulties in a bunker. A good deal of sand was flying about, and his employer's face was becoming a dangerous dusky red. "Here, in the sands, Thee I'll rake up," he was muttering angrily, and something about murderous lechers.

Ian ran down to him and suggested that it was time for a glass of beer, waving to Clarissa as he did so. Sir Murdoch noticed her and was instantly mollified. He invited her to join them.

Ian, by now head over heels in love, was torn between his professional duty, which could not help pointing out to him how beneficial Clarissa's company was for his patient, and a strong personal feeling that the elderly wolfish baronet was not at all suitable company for Clarissa. Worse, he suspected that she guessed his anxiety and was laughing at it.

The week passed peacefully enough. Sir Murdoch summoned the chairmen of the two parish councils and told them that any trespass over his land on the day of the Furry Race would be punished with the utmost rigour. They listened with blank faces. He also ordered mantraps and spring-guns from the Dominion and Colonial Stores, but to Ian's relief it seemed highly unlikely that these would arrive in time.

Clarissa dropped in frequently. Her playing and singing seemed to have as soothing an effect on Sir Murdoch as the songs of the harpist David on touchy old Saul, but Ian had the persistent feeling that some peril threatened from her presence.

On Furry Day she did not appear. Sir Murdoch spent most of the day pacing—loping was really the word for it, Ian thought—distrustfully among his far spinneys, but no trespasser moved in the bracken and dying leaves. Towards evening a fidgety scuffling wind sprang up, and Ian persuaded his employer indoors.

"No one will come, Sir Murdoch, I'm sure. Your notices have scared them off. They'll have gone another way." He wished he really did feel sure of it. He found a performance of *Caesar and Cleopatra* on TV and switched it on, but Shaw seemed to make Sir Murdoch impatient. Presently he got up, began to pace about, and turned it off, muttering:

And why should Caesar be a tyrant, then?
Poor man! I know he would not be a wolf!

He swung round on Ian. "Did I do wrong to shut them off my land?"

"Well," Ian was temporizing, when there came an outburst of explosions from Lostmid, hidden in the valley, and a dozen rockets soared into the sky beyond the windows.

"That means someone's taken the Furry Ball," said Hudson, coming in with the decanter of sherry. "Been long enough about it, seemingly."

Sir Murdoch's expression changed completely. One stride took him to the french window. He opened it, and went streaking across the park. Ian bolted after him.

"Stop! Sir Murdoch, stop!"

Sir Murdoch turned an almost unrecognizable face and hissed, "Wake not a sleeping wolf!" He kept on his way, with Ian stubbornly in pursuit. They came out by the crossroads and, looking down to Lostmid, saw that it was a circus of wandering lights, clustering, darting this way and that.

"They've lost him," Ian muttered. "No, there he goes!"

One of the lights broke off at a tangent and moved away down the valley, then turned and came straight for them diagonally across the hillside.

"I'll have to go and warn him off," Ian thought. "Can't let him run straight into trouble." He ran downhill towards the approaching light. Sir Murdoch stole back into the shade of the spinney. Nothing of him was visible but two golden, glowing eyepoints.

It was at this moment that Clarissa, having established her red-herring diversion by sending a boy with a torch across the hillside, ran swiftly and silently up the steep road towards the signpost. She wore trousers and a dark sweater, and was clutching the Furry Ball in her hand.

Sir Murdoch heard the pit-pat of approaching footsteps, waited for his moment, and sprang.

It was the thick fisherman's-knit jersey with its roll collar that saved her. They rolled over and over, girl and wolf entangled, and then she caught him a blow on the jaw with the heavy applewood ball, dropped it, scrambled free, and was away. She did not dare look back. She had a remarkable turn of speed, but the wolf was overtaking her. She hurled herself into the telephone box and let the door clang to behind her.

The wolf arrived a second later; she heard the impact as the grey, sinewy body struck the door, saw the gleam of teeth through the glass. Methodically, though with shaking hands, she turned to dial.

Meanwhile Ian had met the red-herring boy just as his triumphant pursuers caught up with him.

"You mustn't go that way!" Ian gasped. "Sir Murdoch's waiting up there and he's out for blood."

"Give over that thurr ball," yelled the Lostmidians.

"'Tisn't on me," the boy yelled back, regardless of the fact that he was being pulled limb from limb. "Caught ye properly, me fine fules. 'Tis Miss Clarissa's got it, and she'm gone backaway."

"*What?*"

Ian waited for no more. He left them to their battle, in which some Polgrue reinforcements were now joining, and bounded back up the murderous ascent to where he had left Sir Murdoch.

The scene at the telephone box was brilliantly lit by the overhead light. Clarissa had finished her call, and was watching with detached interest as the infuriated wolf threw himself repeatedly against the door.

It is not easy to address your employer in such circumstances.

Ian chose a low, controlled, but vibrant tone.

"Down, Sir Murdoch," he said. "Down, sir! Heel!"

Sir Murdoch turned on him a look of golden, thunderous wrath. He was really a fine spectacle, with his eyes flashing, and great ruff raised in rage. He must have weighed all of a hundred and thirty pounds. Ian thought he might be a timber-wolf, but was not certain. He pulled the ampoule from his pocket, charged the syringe, and made a cautious approach. Instantly Sir Murdoch flew at him. With a feint like a bullfighter's, Ian lodged round the callbox.

"Olé," Clarissa shouted approvingly, opening the door a crack. Sir Murdoch instantly turned and battered it again.

"Avaunt, thou damned doorkeeper!" shouted Ian. The result was electrifying. The wolf dropped to the ground as if stunned. Ian seized advantage of the moment to give him his injection, and immediately the wolf-shape vanished, dropping off Sir Murdoch like a label off a wet bottle. He gasped, shivered, and shut his eyes.

"Where am I?" he said presently, opening them again. Ian took his arm, gently led him away from the door, and made him sit on a grassy bank.

"You'll feel better in a minute or two, sir," he said, and, since Shakespeare seemed so efficacious, added, "The cure whereof, my lord, 'Tis time must do." Sir Murdoch weakly nodded.

Clarissa came out of her refuge. "Are you all right now, Sir Murdoch?" she asked kindly. "Shall I sing you a song?"

"All right, thank you, my dear," he murmured. "What are you doing here?" and he added to himself, "I really must not fly into these rages. I feel quite dizzy."

Ian stepped aside and picked up something that glinted on the ground.

"What's that?" asked Sir Murdoch with awakening interest. "It reminds me—May I see it?"

"Oh, it's my medallion," said Clarissa at the same moment. "It must have come off..." Her voice trailed away. They both watched Sir Murdoch. Deep, fearful shudders were running through him.

"Where did you get this?" he demanded, turning his cavernous eyes on Clarissa. His fingers were rigid, clenched on the tiny silver St Francis.

"It was my mother's," she said faintly. For the first time she seemed frightened.

"Was her name Louisa?" She nodded. "Then your father—?"

"Here comes my father now," said Clarissa with relief. The gnarled figure of the doctor was approaching them through the spinney. Sir Murdoch turned on him like a javelin.

"O thou foul thief!" he hissed. "My lost Louisa! Stol'n from me and corrupted by spells and medicines."

"Oh, come, come, come," said the doctor equably, never slowing his approach, though he kept a wary eye on Sir Murdoch. "I wouldn't put it quite like that. She came to me. *I* was looking forward to bachelorhood."

"For the which I may go the finer, I will live a bachelor," murmured Ian calmingly.

"And I'll tell ye this, Sir Murdoch," Dr Defoe went on, tucking his arm through that of Sir Murdoch like an old friend, "You were well rid of her." He started strolling at a gentle but purposeful pace back towards the Hall, and the baronet went with him doubtfully.

"Why is that?" Already Sir Murdoch sounded half convinced, quiescent.

"Firstly, my dear sir, Temper. Out of this world! Secondly, Macaroni Cheese. Every night till one begged for mercy. Thirdly, Unpunctuality. Fourthly, long, horrifying Dreams, which she insisted on telling at breakfast..."

Pursuing this soothing, therapeutic vein, the doctor's voice moved farther away, and the two men were lost in the shadows.

"So that's all right," said Clarissa on a deep breath of relief. "Why, Ian!"

Pent-up agitation was too much for him. He had grabbed her in his arms like a drowning man. "I was sick with fright for you," he muttered, into her hair, her ear, the back of her neck. "I was afraid—oh well, never mind."

"Never mind," she agreed. "Are we going to get married?"

"Of course."

"I ought to find my Furry Ball," she said presently. "They seem to be having a pitched battle down below; there's a good chance of getting it over the boundary while everyone's busy."

"But Sir Murdoch—"

"Father will look after him."

She moved a few steps away and soon found the ball. "Come on; through the wood is quickest. We have to put it on the Polgrue churchyard wall."

No one accosted them as they ran through the wood. Fireworks and shouting in the valley suggested that Lostmid and Polgrue had sunk their differences in happy saturnalia.

"Full surgery tomorrow," remarked Clarissa, tucking the Furry Ball into its niche. "Won't someone be surprised to see this."

When Ian and Clarissa strolled up to the terrace, they found Sir Murdoch and the doctor amiably drinking port. Sir Murdoch looked like a man who had had a festering grief removed from his mind.

"Well," the doctor said cheerfully, "we've cleared up some misunderstandings."

But Sir Murdoch had stood up and gone to meet Clarissa.

"As I am a man," he said gravely, "I do think this lady to be my child."

The two pairs of golden eyes met and acknowledged each other.

"That'll be the end of his little trouble, I shouldn't wonder," murmured the doctor. "Specially if she'll live at the Hall and keep an eye on him."

"But she's going to marry me."

"All the better, my dear boy. All the better. And glad I shall be to get rid of her, bless her heart."

Ian looked doubtfully across the terrace at his future father-in-law, but he recalled that wolves are among the most devoted fathers of the animal kingdom. Sir Murdoch was stroking Clarissa's hair with an expression of complete peace and happiness.

Then a thought struck Ian. "If *he's* her father—"

But Dr Defoe was yawning. "I'm off to bed. Busy day tomorrow." He vanished among the dark trees.

So they were married, and lived happily at the Hall. Clarissa's slightest wish was law. She was cherished equally by both father and husband, and if they went out of their way not to cross her in any particular, this was due quite as much to the love they bore her as to their knowledge that they had dangerous material on their hands.

1960

ROYAL JELLY

Roald Dahl

One of the most eminent and celebrated children's writers of the late twentieth century, Roald Dahl was born in Llandaff, Wales, on 13 September 1916, son of a wealthy Norwegian shipbroker. Despite his success, Dahl's life was blighted by more than its fair share of tragedy, the psychological effect of which influenced much of his work. When he was three, his beloved elder sister Astri died of an infection following a burst appendix, and a few weeks later, his father, overcome by grief, died of pneumonia. Astri's death was echoed years later when Dahl's own daughter, Olivia, died of measles at the same age as his sister. Additionally, a car accident caused his two-year-old son Theo to have brain damage, and in 1967, after fourteen years of marriage, his wife, the Hollywood actress, Patricia Neal, had three massive strokes, which left her unable to speak.

Graduating from the public school Repton in 1934, Dahl joined the eastern staff of Shell, and worked for three years in Dar es Salaam, Tanganyika. When the Second World War broke out, he enlisted in the Royal Air Force, where, after flying Hurricanes in campaigns in Greece and Syria, he received serious head and neck injuries in a crash landing in Libya.

His writing career began in 1942 when the novelist C. S. Forester asked him to make notes on his most exciting flying experience, which Forester aimed to write up for the *Saturday Evening Post*. But after receiving Dahl's article, Forester wrote him a letter, stating: "Did you know you were a writer? I haven't changed a word." Also enclosed was a cheque for $900.

For the first fifteen years of his career, Dahl wrote short stories aimed at adults, which were collected in *Over to You* (1946), *Someone Like You* (1953) and *Kiss Kiss* (1960). *James and the Giant Peach*, published in 1961, was the first of his classic novels for children, and over the next three decades was followed by a string of others, including *Charlie and the Chocolate Factory* (1964), *Fantastic Mr Fox* (1970), *Charlie and the Great Glass Elevator* (1972), *Danny, the Champion of the World* (1975), *The Twits* (1980), *The BFG* (1982), *The Witches* (1983) and *Matilda* (1988), published just two years before his death in 1990.

As a scriptwriter, Dahl was responsible for the James Bond film *You Only Live Twice* (1967), the family classic *Chitty Chitty Bang Bang* (1968), the horror movie *The Night Digger* (1971) and *Willy Wonka & the Chocolate Factory* (1971), an adaptation of his own novel *Charlie and the Chocolate Factory*, which was directed by Mel Stuart and starred Gene Wilder as Willy Wonka.

First published in his collection *Kiss Kiss* (1960), "Royal Jelly" is a body-horror story about obsession, scientific experimentation and that old Nature versus Nurture debate. Although laced with a plentiful supply of Dahl's notoriously dark humour, it is nevertheless a deeply disturbing tale.

"It worries me to death, Albert, it really does," Mrs Taylor said.

She kept her eyes fixed on the baby who was now lying absolutely motionless in the crook of her left arm.

"I just know there's something wrong."

The skin on the baby's face had a pearly translucent quality, and was stretched very tightly over the bones.

"Try again," Albert Taylor said.

"It won't do any good."

"You have to keep trying, Mabel," he said.

She lifted the bottle out of the saucepan of hot water and shook a few drops of milk onto the inside of her wrist, testing for temperature.

"Come on," she whispered. "Come on, my baby. Wake up and take a bit more of this."

There was a small lamp on the table close by that made a soft yellow glow all around her.

"Please," she said. "Take just a weeny bit more."

The husband watched her over the top of his magazine. She was half dead with exhaustion, he could see that, and the pale oval face, usually so grave and serene, had taken on a kind of pinched and desperate look. But even so, the drop of her head as she gazed down at the child was curiously beautiful.

"You see," she murmured. "It's no good. She won't have it."

She held the bottle up to the light, squinting at the calibrations.

"One ounce again. That's all she's taken. No—it isn't even that. It's only three quarters. It's not enough to keep body and soul together, Albert, it really isn't. It worries me to death."

"I know," he said.

"If only they could *find out* what was wrong."

"There's nothing wrong, Mabel. It's just a matter of time."

"Of course there's something wrong."

"Dr Robinson says no."

"Look," she said, standing up. "You can't tell me it's natural for a six-weeks-old child to weigh less, less by more than *two whole pounds* than she did when she was born! Just look at those legs! They're nothing but skin and bone!"

The tiny baby lay limply on her arm, not moving.

"Dr Robinson said you were to stop worrying, Mabel. So did that other one."

"Ha!" she said. "Isn't that wonderful! I'm to stop worrying!"

"Now, Mabel."

"What does he want me to do? Treat it as some sort of a joke?"

"He didn't say that."

"I hate doctors! I hate them all!" she cried, and she swung away from him and walked quickly out of the room toward the stairs, carrying the baby with her.

Albert Taylor stayed where he was and let her go.

In a little while he heard her moving about in the bedroom directly over his head, quick nervous footsteps going tap tap tap on the linoleum above. Soon the footsteps would stop, and then he would have to get up and follow her, and when he went into the bedroom he would find her sitting beside the cot as usual, staring at the child and crying softly to herself and refusing to move.

"She's starving, Albert," she would say.

"Of course she's not starving."

"She *is* starving I know she is. And Albert?"

"Yes?"

"I believe you know it too, but you won't admit it. Isn't that right?"

Every night now it was like this.

Last week they had taken the child back to the hospital, and the doctor had examined it carefully and told them that there was nothing the matter.

"It took us nine years to get this baby, Doctor," Mabel had said. "I think it would kill me if anything should happen to her."

That was six days ago and since then it had lost another five ounces.

But worrying about it wasn't going to help anybody, Albert Taylor told himself. One simply had to trust the doctor on a thing like this. He picked up the magazine that was still lying on his lap and glanced idly down the list of contents to see what it had to offer this week:

AMONG THE BEES IN MAY
HONEY COOKERY
THE BEE FARMER AND THE B. PHARM.
EXPERIENCES IN THE CONTROL OF NOSEMA
THE LATEST ON ROYAL JELLY
THIS WEEK IN THE APIARY
THE HEALING POWER OF PROPOLIS
REGURGITATIONS
BRITISH BEEKEEPERS ANNUAL DINNER
ASSOCIATION NEWS

All his life Albert Taylor had been fascinated by anything that had to do with bees. As a small boy he used often to catch them in his bare hands and go running with them into the house to show to his mother, and sometimes he would put them on his face and let them crawl about over his cheeks and neck, and the astonishing thing about it all was that he never got stung. On the contrary, the bees seemed to enjoy being with him. They never tried to fly away, and to get rid of them he would have to brush them off gently with his fingers. Even then they would frequently return and settle again on his arm or hand or knee, any place where the skin was bare.

His father, who was a bricklayer, said there must be some witch's stench about the boy, something noxious that came oozing out through the pores of the skin, and that no good would ever come of it, hypnotizing insects like that. But the mother said it was a gift given him by God, and even went so far as to compare him with St Francis and the birds.

As he grew older, Albert Taylor's fascination with bees developed into an obsession, and by the time he was twelve he had built his first hive. The following summer he had captured his first swarm. Two years later, at the age of fourteen, he had no less than five hives standing neatly in a row against the fence of his father's small back yard, and already—apart from the normal task of producing honey—he was practising the delicate and complicated business of rearing his own queens, grafting larvae into artificial cell cups, and all the rest of it.

He never had to use smoke when there was work to do inside a hive, and he never wore gloves on his hands or a net over his head. Clearly there was some strange sympathy between this boy and the bees, and down in the village, in the shops and pubs, they began to speak about him with a certain kind of respect, and people started coming up to the house to buy his honey.

When he was eighteen, he had rented one acre of rough pasture alongside a cherry orchard down the valley about a mile from the village, and there he had set out to establish his own business. Now, eleven years later, he was still in the same spot, but he had six acres of ground instead of one, two hundred and forty well-stocked hives, and a small house that he'd built mainly with his own hands. He had married at the age of twenty and that, apart from the fact that it had taken them over nine years to get a child, had also been a success. In fact, everything had gone pretty well for Albert until this strange little baby girl came along and started frightening them out of their wits by refusing to eat properly and losing weight every day.

He looked up from the magazine and began thinking about his daughter.

This evening, for instance, when she had opened her eyes at the beginning of the feed, he had gazed into them and seen something that frightened him to death—a kind of misty vacant stare, as though the eyes themselves were not connected to the brain at all but were just lying loose in their sockets like a couple of small grey marbles.

Did those doctors really know what they were talking about?

He reached for an ashtray and started slowly picking the ashes out from the bowl of his pipe with a matchstick.

One could always take her along to another hospital, somewhere in Oxford perhaps. He might suggest that to Mabel when he went upstairs.

He could still hear her moving around in the bedroom, but she must have taken off her shoes now and put on slippers because the noise was very faint.

He switched his attention back to the magazine and went on with his reading. He finished an article called "Experiences in the Control of Nosema," then turned over the page and began reading the next one, "The Latest on Royal Jelly." He doubted very much whether there would be anything in this that he didn't know already:

> *What is this wonderful substance called royal jelly?*

He reached for the tin of tobacco on the table beside him and began filling his pipe, still reading.

> *Royal jelly is a glandular secretion produced by the nurse bees to feed the larvae immediately they have hatched from the egg. The pharingeal*

glands of bees produce this substance in much the same way as the mammary glands of vertebrates produce milk. The fact is of great biological interest because no other insects in the world are known to have evolved such a process.

All old stuff, he told himself, but for want of anything better to do, he continued to read.

Royal jelly is fed in concentrated form to all bee larvae for the first three days after hatching from the egg; but beyond that point, for all those who are destined to become drones or workers, this precious food is greatly diluted with honey and pollen. On the other hand, the larvae which are destined to become queens are fed throughout the whole of their larval period on a concentrated diet of pure royal jelly. Hence the name.

Above him, up in the bedroom, the noise of the footsteps had stopped altogether. The house was quiet. He struck a match and put it to his pipe.

Royal jelly must be a substance of tremendous nourishing power, for on this diet alone, the honey-bee larva increases in weight fifteen hundred times in five days.

That was probably about right, he thought, although for some reason it had never occurred to him to consider larval growth in terms of weight before.

This is as if a seven-and-a-half-pound baby should increase in that time to five tons.

Albert Taylor stopped and read that sentence again.

He read it a third time.

This is as if a seven-and-a-half-pound baby...

"Mabel!" he cried, jumping up from his chair. "Mabel! Come here!"

He went out into the hall and stood at the foot of the stairs calling for her to come down.

There was no answer.

He ran up the stairs and switched on the light on the landing. The bedroom door was closed. He crossed the landing and opened it and stood in the doorway looking into the dark room. "Mabel," he said. "Come downstairs a moment, will you please? I've just had a bit of an idea. It's about the baby."

The light from the landing behind him cast a faint glow over the bed and he could see her dimly now, lying on her stomach with her face buried in the pillow and her arms up over her head. She was crying again.

"Mabel," he said, going over to her, touching her shoulder. "Please come down a moment. This may be important."

"Go away," she said. "Leave me alone."

"Don't you want to hear about my idea?"

"Oh, Albert, I'm *tired*," she sobbed. "I'm so tired I don't know what I'm doing any more. I don't think I can go on. I don't think I can stand it."

There was a pause. Albert Taylor turned away from her and walked slowly over to the cradle where the baby was lying, and peered in. It was too dark for him to see the child's face, but when he bent down close he could hear the sound of breathing, very faint and quick. "What time is the next feed?" he asked.

"Two o'clock, I suppose."

"And the one after that?"

"Six in the morning."

"I'll do them both," he said. "You go to sleep."

She didn't answer.

"You get properly into bed, Mabel, and go straight to sleep, you understand? And stop worrying. I'm taking over completely for the next twelve hours. You'll give yourself a nervous breakdown going on like this."

"Yes," she said. "I know."

"I'm taking the nipper and myself *and* the alarm clock into the spare room this very moment, so you just lie down and relax and forget all about us. Right?" Already he was pushing the cradle out through the door.

"Oh, Albert," she sobbed.

"Don't you worry about a thing. Leave it to me."

"Albert..."

"Yes?"

"I love you, Albert."

"I love you too, Mabel. Now go to sleep."

Albert Taylor didn't see his wife again until nearly eleven o'clock the next morning.

"Good *gracious* me!" she cried, rushing down the stairs in dressing-gown and slippers. "Albert! Just look at the time! I must have slept twelve hours at least! Is everything all right? What happened?"

He was sitting quietly in his armchair, smoking a pipe and reading the morning paper. The baby was in a sort of carrier cot on the floor at his feet, sleeping.

"Hullo, dear," he said, smiling.

She ran over to the cot and looked in. "Did she take anything, Albert? How many times have you fed her? She was due for another one at ten o'clock, did you know that?"

Albert Taylor folded the newspaper neatly into a square and put it away on the side table. "I fed her at two in the morning," he said, "and she took about half an ounce, no more. I fed her again at six and she did a bit better that time, two ounces..."

"*Two ounces!* Oh, Albert, that's marvellous!"

"And we just finished the last feed ten minutes ago. There's the bottle on the mantelpiece. Only one ounce left. She drank three. How's that?" He was grinning proudly, delighted with his achievement.

The woman quickly got down on her knees and peered at the baby.

"Don't she look better?" he asked eagerly. "Don't she look fatter in the face?"

"It may sound silly," the wife said, "but I actually think she does. Oh, Albert, you're a marvel! How did you do it?"

She's turning the corner," he said. "That's all it is. Just like the doctor prophesied, she's turning the corner."

"I pray to God you're right, Albert."

"Of course I'm right. From now on, you watch her go."

The woman was gazing lovingly at the baby.

"You look a lot better yourself too, Mabel."

"I feel wonderful. I'm sorry about last night."

"Let's keep it this way," he said. "I'll do all the night feeds in future. You do the day ones."

She looked up at him across the cot, frowning. "No," she said. "Oh no, I wouldn't allow you to do that."

"I don't want you to have a breakdown, Mabel."

"I won't, not now I've had some sleep."

"Much better we share it."

"No, Albert. This is my job and I intend to do it. Last night won't happen again."

There was a pause. Albert Taylor took the pipe out of his mouth and examined the grain on the bowl. "All right," he said. "In that case

I'll just relieve you of the donkey work, I'll do all the sterilizing and the mixing of the food and getting everything ready. That'll help you a bit, anyway."

She looked at him carefully, wondering what could have come over him all of a sudden.

"You see, Mabel, I've been thinking..."

"Yes, dear."

"I've been thinking that up until last night I've never even raised a finger to help you with this baby."

"That isn't true."

"Oh yes it is. So I've decided that from now on I'm going to do *my* share of the work. I'm going to be the feed-mixer and the bottle-sterilizer. Right?"

"It's very sweet of you, dear, but I really don't think it's necessary..."

"Come on!" he cried. "Don't change the luck! I done it the last three times and just *look* what happened! When's the next one? Two o'clock, isn't it?"

"Yes."

"It's all mixed," he said. "Everything's all mixed and ready and all you've got to do when the time comes is to go out there to the larder and take it off the shelf and warm it up. That's *some* help, isn't it?"

The woman got up off her knees and went over to him and kissed him on the cheek. "You're such a nice man," she said. "I love you more and more every day I know you."

Later, in the middle of the afternoon, when Albert was outside in the sunshine working among the hives, he heard her calling to him from the house.

"Albert!" she shouted. "Albert, come here!" She was running through the buttercups toward him.

He started forward to meet her, wondering what was wrong.

"Oh, Albert! Guess what!"

"What?"

"I've just finished giving her the two-o'clock feed and she's taken the whole lot!"

"No!"

"Every drop of it! Oh, Albert, I'm so happy! She's going to be all right! She's turned the corner just like you said!" She came up to him and threw her arms around his neck and hugged him, and he clapped her on the back and laughed and said what a marvellous little mother she was.

"Will you come in and watch the next one and see if she does it again, Albert?"

He told her he wouldn't miss it for anything, and she hugged him again, then turned and ran back to the house, skipping over the grass and singing all the way.

Naturally, there was a certain amount of suspense in the air as the time approached for the six-o'clock feed. By five thirty both parents were already seated in the living-room waiting for the moment to arrive. The bottle with the milk formula in it was standing in a saucepan of warm water on the mantelpiece. The baby was asleep in its carrier cot on the sofa.

At twenty minutes to six it woke up and started screaming its head off.

"There you are!" Mrs Taylor cried. "She's asking for the bottle. Pick her up quick, Albert, and hand her to me here. Give me the bottle first."

He gave her the bottle, then placed the baby on the woman's lap. Cautiously, she touched the baby's lips with the end of the nipple. The baby seized the nipple between its gums and began to suck ravenously with a rapid powerful action.

"Oh, Albert, isn't it wonderful?" she said, laughing.

"It's terrific, Mabel."

In seven or eight minutes, the entire contents of the bottle had disappeared down the baby's throat.

"You clever girl," Mrs Taylor said. "Four ounces again."

Albert Taylor was leaning forward in his chair, peering intently into the baby's face. "You know what?" he said. "She even seems as though she's put on a touch of weight already. What do you think?"

The mother looked down at the child.

"Don't she seem bigger and fatter to you, Mabel, than she was yesterday?"

"Maybe she does, Albert. I'm not sure. Although actually there couldn't be any *real* gain in such a short time as this. The important thing is that she's eating normally."

"She's turned the corner," Albert said. "I don't think you need worry about her any more."

"I certainly won't."

"You want me to go up and fetch the cradle back into our own bedroom, Mabel?"

"Yes, please," she said.

Albert went upstairs and moved the cradle. The woman followed with the baby, and after changing its nappy, she laid it gently down on its bed. Then she covered it with sheet and blanket.

"Doesn't she look lovely, Albert?" she whispered. "Isn't that the most beautiful baby you've ever seen in your *entire* life?"

"Leave her be now, Mabel," he said. "Come on downstairs and cook us a bit of supper. We both deserve it."

After they had finished eating, the parents settled themselves in armchairs in the living-room, Albert with his magazine and his pipe, Mrs Taylor with her knitting. But this was a very different scene from the one of the night before. Suddenly, all tensions had vanished. Mrs Taylor's handsome oval face was glowing with pleasure, her cheeks were pink, her eyes were sparkling bright, and her mouth was fixed in a little dreamy smile of pure content. Every now and again she would glance up from her knitting and gaze affectionately at her husband. Occasionally, she would stop the clicking of her needles altogether for a few seconds and sit quite still, looking at the ceiling, listening for a cry or a whimper from upstairs. But all was quiet.

"Albert," she said after a while.

"Yes, dear?"

"What was it you were going to tell me last night when you came rushing up to the bedroom? You said you had an idea for the baby."

Albert Taylor lowered the magazine onto his lap and gave her a long sly look.

"Did I?" he said.

"Yes." She waited for him to go on, but he didn't.

"What's the big joke?" she asked. "Why are you grinning like that?"

"It's a joke all right," he said.

"Tell it to me, dear."

"I'm not sure I ought to," he said. "You might call me a liar."

She had seldom seen him looking so pleased with himself as he was now, and she smiled back at him, egging him on.

"I'd just like to see your face when you hear it, Mabel, that's all."

"Albert, what *is* all this?"

He paused, refusing to be hurried.

"You do think the baby's better, don't you?" he asked.

"Of course I do."

"You agree with me that all of a sudden she's feeding marvellously and looking one-hundred-per-cent different?"

"I do, Albert, yes."

"That's good," he said, the grin widening. "You see, it's me that did it."

"Did what?"

"I cured the baby."

"Yes, dear, I'm sure you did." Mrs Taylor went right on with her knitting.

"You don't believe me, do you?"

"Of course I believe you, Albert. I give you all the credit, every bit of it."

"Then how did I do it?"

"Well," she said, pausing a moment to think. "I suppose it's simply that you're a brilliant feed-mixer. Ever since you started mixing the feeds she's got better and better."

"You mean there's some sort of an art in mixing the feeds?"

"Apparently there is." She was knitting away and smiling quietly to herself, thinking how funny men were.

"I'll tell you a secret," he said. "You're absolutely right. Although, mind you, it isn't so much *how* you mix it that counts. It's what you put in. You realize that, don't you, Mabel?"

Mrs Taylor stopped knitting and looked up sharply at her husband. "Albert," she said, "don't tell me you've been putting things into the child's milk?"

He sat there grinning.

"Well, have you or haven't you?"

"It's possible," he said.

"I don't believe it."

He had a strange fierce way of grinning that showed his teeth.

"Albert," she said. "Stop playing with me like this."

"Yes, dear, all right."

"You haven't *really* put anything into her milk, have you? Answer me properly, Albert. This could be serious with such a tiny baby."

"The answer is yes, Mabel."

"*Albert Taylor!* How could you?"

"Now don't get excited," he said. "I'll tell you all about it if you really want me to, but for heaven's sake keep your hair on."

"It was beer!" she cried. "I just know it was beer!"

"Don't be so daft, Mabel, please."

"Then what was it?"

Albert laid his pipe down carefully on the table beside him and leaned back in his chair. "Tell me," he said, "did you ever by any chance happen to hear me mentioning something called royal jelly?"

"I did not."

"It's magic," he said. "Pure magic. And last night I suddenly got the idea that if I was to put some of this into the baby's milk..."

"How *dare* you!"

"Now, Mabel, you don't even know what it is yet."

"I don't care what it is," she said. "You can't go putting foreign bodies like that into a tiny baby's milk. You must be mad."

"It's perfectly harmless, Mabel, otherwise I wouldn't have done it. It comes from bees."

"I might have guessed that."

"And it's so precious that practically no one can afford to take it. When they do, it's only one little drop at a time."

"And how much did you give to our baby, might I ask?"

"Ah," he said, "that's the whole point. That's where the difference lies. I reckon that our baby, just in the last four feeds, has already swallowed about fifty times as much royal jelly as anyone else in the world has ever swallowed before. How about that?"

"Albert, stop pulling my leg."

"I swear it," he said proudly.

She sat there staring at him, her brow wrinkled, her mouth slightly open.

"You know what this stuff actually costs, Mabel, if you want to buy it? There's a place in America advertising it for sale this very moment for something like five hundred dollars a pound jar! *Five hundred dollars!* That's more than gold, you know!"

She hadn't the faintest idea what he was talking about.

"I'll prove it," he said, and he jumped up and went across to the large bookcase where he kept all his literature about bees. On the top shelf, the back numbers of *The American Bee Journal* were neatly stacked alongside those of *The British Bee Journal*, *Beecraft*, and other magazines. He took down the last issue of *The American Bee Journal* and turned to a page of small classified advertisements at the back.

"Here you are," he said. "Exactly as I told you. 'We sell royal jelly—$480 per lb. jar wholesale.'"

He handed her the magazine so she could read it herself.

"Now do you believe me? This is an actual shop in New York, Mabel. It says so."

"It doesn't say you can go stirring it into the milk of a practically new-born baby," she said. "I don't know what's come over you, Albert, I really don't."

"It's curing her, isn't it?"

"I'm not so sure about that, now."

"Don't be so damn silly, Mabel. You know it is."

"Then why haven't other people done it with *their* babies?"

"I keep telling you," he said. "It's too expensive. Practically nobody in the world can afford to buy royal jelly just for *eating* except maybe one or two multimillionaires. The people who buy it are the big companies that make women's face creams and things like that. They're using it as a stunt. They mix a tiny pinch of it into a big jar of face cream and it's selling like hot cakes for absolutely enormous prices. They claim it takes out the wrinkles."

"And does it?"

"Now how on earth would I know that, Mabel? Anyway," he said, returning to his chair, "that's not the point. The point is this. It's done so much good to our little baby just in the last few hours that I think we ought to go right on giving it to her. Now don't interrupt, Mabel.

Let me finish. I've got two hundred and forty hives out there and if I turn over maybe a hundred of them to making royal jelly, we ought to be able to supply her with all she wants."

"Albert Taylor," the woman said, stretching her eyes wide and staring at him. "Have you gone out of your mind?"

"Just hear me through, will you please?"

"I forbid it," she said, "absolutely. You're not to give my baby another drop of that horrid jelly, you understand?"

"Now, Mabel..."

"And quite apart from that, we had a shocking honey crop last year, and if you go fooling around with those hives now, there's no telling what might not happen."

"There's nothing wrong with my hives, Mabel."

"You know very well we had only half the normal crop last year."

"Do me a favour, will you?" he said. "Let me explain some of the marvellous things this stuff does."

"You haven't even told me what it is yet."

"All right, Mabel. I'll do that too. Will you listen? Will you give me a chance to explain it?"

She sighed and picked up her knitting once more. "I suppose you might as well get it off your chest, Albert. Go on and tell me."

He paused, a bit uncertain now how to begin. It wasn't going to be easy to explain something like this to a person with no detailed knowledge of apiculture at all.

"You know, don't you," he said, "that each colony has only one queen?"

"Yes."

"And that this queen lays all the eggs?"

"Yes, dear. That much I know."

"All right. Now the queen can actually lay two different kinds of eggs. You didn't know that, but she can. It's what we call one of the miracles of the hive. She can lay eggs that produce drones, and she can lay eggs that produce workers. Now if that isn't a miracle, Mabel, I don't know what is."

"Yes, Albert, all right."

"The drones are the males. We don't have to worry about them. The workers are all females. So is the queen, of course. But the workers are unsexed females, if you see what I mean. Their organs are completely undeveloped, whereas the queen is tremendously sexy. She can actually lay her own weight in eggs in a single day."

He hesitated, marshalling his thoughts.

"Now what happens is this. The queen crawls around on the comb and lays her eggs in what we call cells. You know all those hundreds of little holes you see in a honeycomb? Well, a brood comb is just about the same except the cells don't have honey in them, they have eggs. She lays one egg to each cell, and in three days each of these eggs hatches out into a tiny grub. We call it a larva.

"Now, as soon as this larva appears, the nurse bees—they're young workers—all crowd round and start feeding it like mad. And you know what they feed it on?"

"Royal jelly," Mabel answered patiently.

"Right!" he cried. "That's exactly what they do feed it on. They get this stuff out of a gland in their heads and they start pumping it into the cell to feed the larva. And what happens then?"

He paused dramatically, blinking at her with his small watery-grey eyes. Then he turned slowly in his chair and reached for the magazine that he had been reading the night before.

"You want to know what happens then?" he asked, wetting his lips.

"I can hardly wait."

"'Royal jelly,'" he read aloud, "'must be a substance of tremendous nourishing power, for on this diet alone, the honey-bee larva increases in weight *fifteen hundred times* in five days!'"

"How much?"

"*Fifteen hundred times*, Mabel. And you know what that means if you put it in terms of a human being? It means," he said, lowering his voice, leaning forward, fixing her with those small pale eyes, "it means that in five days a baby weighing seven and a half pounds to start off with would increase in weight to *five tons!*"

For the second time, Mrs Taylor stopped knitting.

"Now you mustn't take that too literally, Mabel."

"Who says I mustn't?"

"It's just a scientific way of putting it, that's all."

"Very well, Albert. Go on."

"But that's only half the story," he said. "There's more to come. The really amazing thing about royal jelly, I haven't told you yet. I'm going to show you now how it can transform a plain dull-looking little worker bee with practically no sex organs at all into a great big beautiful fertile queen."

"Are you saying our baby is dull-looking and plain?" she asked sharply.

"Now don't go putting words into my mouth, Mabel, please. Just listen to this. Did you know that the queen bee and the worker bee, although they are completely different when they grow up, are both hatched out of exactly the same kind of egg?"

"I don't believe that," she said.

"It's true as I'm sitting here, Mabel, honest it is. Any time the bees want a queen to hatch out of the egg instead of a worker, they can do it."

"How?"

"Ah," he said, shaking a thick forefinger in her direction. "That's just what I'm coming to. That's the secret of the whole thing. Now—what do *you* think it is, Mabel, that makes this miracle happen?"

"Royal jelly," she answered. "You already told me."

"Royal jelly it is!" he cried, clapping his hands and bouncing up on his seat. His big round face was glowing with excitement now, and two vivid patches of scarlet had appeared high up on each cheek.

"Here's how it works. I'll put it very simply for you. The bees want a new queen. So they build an extra-large cell, a queen cell we call it, and they get the old queen to lay one of her eggs in there. The other one thousand nine hundred and ninety-nine eggs she lays in ordinary worker cells. Now, as soon as these eggs hatch out into larvae, the nurse bees rally round and start pumping in the royal jelly. All of them get it, workers as well as queen. But here's the vital thing, Mabel, so listen carefully. Here's where the difference comes. The worker larvae only receive this special marvellous food for the *first three days* of their larval life. After that they have a complete change of diet. What really happens is that they get weaned, except that it's not like an ordinary weaning because it's so sudden. After the third day they're put straight away onto more or less routine bees food—a mixture of honey and pollen—and then about two weeks later they emerge from the cells as workers.

"But not so the larva in the queen cell! This one gets royal jelly *all the way through its larval life*. The nurse bees simply pour it into the cell, so much so in fact that the little larva is literally floating in it. And that's what makes it into a queen!"

"You can't prove it," she said.

"Don't talk so damn silly, Mabel, please. Thousands of people have proved it time and again, famous scientists in every country in the world. All you have to do is take a larva out of a worker cell and put it in a queen cell—that's what we call grafting—and just so long as the nurse bees keep it well supplied with royal jelly, then presto!—it'll grow up into a queen! And what makes it more marvellous still is the absolutely enormous difference between a queen and a worker when they grow up. The abdomen is a different shape. The sting is different. The legs are different. The..."

"In what way are the legs different?" she asked, testing him.

"The legs? Well, the workers have little pollen baskets on their legs for carrying the pollen. The queen has none. Now here's another thing. The queen has fully developed sex organs. The workers don't. And most amazing of all, Mabel, the queen lives for an average of four to six years. The worker hardly lives that many months. And all this difference simply because one of them got royal jelly and the other didn't!"

"It's pretty hard to believe," she said, "that a food can do all that."

"Of course it's hard to believe. It's another of the miracles of the hive. In fact it's the biggest ruddy miracle of them all. It's such a hell of a big miracle that it's baffled the greatest men of science for hundreds of years. Wait a moment. Stay there. Don't move."

Again he jumped up and went over to the bookcase and started rummaging among the books and magazines.

"I'm going to find you a few of the reports. Here we are. Here's one of them. Listen to this." He started reading aloud from a copy of the *American Bee Journal*:

"'Living in Toronto at the head of a fine research laboratory given to him by the people of Canada in recognition of his truly great contribution to humanity in the discovery of insulin, Dr Frederick A. Banting became curious about royal jelly. He requested his staff to do a basic fractional analysis...'"

He paused.

"Well, there's no need to read it all, but here's what happened. Dr Banting and his people took some royal jelly from queen cells that contained two-day-old larvae, and then they started analysing it. And what d'you think they found?

"They found," he said, "that royal jelly contained phenols, sterols, glycerils, dextrose, *and*—now here it comes—and eighty to eighty-five per cent *unidentified* acids!"

He stood beside the bookcase with the magazine in his hand, smiling a funny little furtive smile of triumph, and his wife watched him, bewildered.

He was not a tall man; he had a thick plump pulpy-looking body that was built close to the ground on abbreviated legs. The legs were slightly bowed. The head was huge and round, covered with bristly short-cut hair, and the greater part of the face—now that he had given up shaving altogether—was hidden by a brownish yellow fuzz about an inch long. In one way and another, he was rather grotesque to look at, there was no denying that.

"Eighty to eighty-five per cent," he said, "unidentified acids. Isn't that fantastic?" He turned back to the bookshelf and began hunting through the other magazines.

"What does it mean, unidentified acids?"

"That's the whole point! No one knows! Not even Banting could find out. You've heard of Banting?"

"No."

"He just happens to be about the most famous living doctor in the world today, that's all."

Looking at him now as he buzzed around in front of the bookcase with his bristly head and his hairy face and his plump pulpy body, she couldn't help thinking that somehow, in some curious way, there was a touch of the bee about this man. She had often seen women grow to look like the horses that they rode, and she had noticed that people who bred birds or bull terriers or pomeranians frequently resembled in some small but startling manner the creature of their choice. But up until now it had never occurred to her that her husband might look like a bee. It shocked her a bit.

"And did Banting ever try to eat it," she asked, "this royal jelly?"

"Of course he didn't eat it, Mabel. He didn't have enough for that. It's too precious."

"You know something?" she said, staring at him but smiling a little all the time. "You're getting to look just a teeny bit like a bee yourself, did you know that?"

He turned and looked at her.

"I suppose it's the beard mostly," she said. "I do wish you'd stop wearing it. Even the colour is sort of bee-ish, don't you think?"

"What the hell are you talking about, Mabel?"

"Albert," she said. "Your language."

"Do you want to hear any more of this or don't you?"

"Yes, dear, I'm sorry. I was only joking. Do go on."

He turned away again and pulled another magazine out of the bookcase and began leafing through the pages. "Now just listen to this, Mabel. 'In 1939, Heyl experimented with twenty-one-day-old rats, injecting them with royal jelly in varying amounts. As a result, he found a precocious follicular development of the ovaries directly in proportion to the quantity of royal jelly injected.'"

"There!" she cried. "I knew it!"

"Knew what?"

"I knew something terrible would happen."

"Nonsense. There's nothing wrong with that. Now here's another, Mabel. 'Still and Burdett found that a male rat which hitherto had been unable to breed, upon receiving a minute daily dose of royal jelly, became a father many times over.'"

"Albert," she cried, "this stuff is *much* too strong to give to a baby! I don't like it at all."

"Nonsense, Mabel."

"Then why do they only try it on rats, tell me that? Why don't some of these famous scientists take it themselves? They're too clever, that's why. Do you think Dr Banting is going to risk finishing up with precious ovaries? Not him."

"But they *have* given it to people, Mabel. Here's a whole article about it. Listen." He turned the page and again began reading from the magazine. "'In Mexico, in 1953, a group of enlightened physicians began prescribing minute doses of royal jelly for such things as cerebral neuritis, arthritis, diabetes, autointoxication from tobacco, impotence in men, asthma, croup, and gout... There are stacks of signed testimonials... A celebrated stockbroker in Mexico City contracted a particularly stubborn case of psoriasis. He became physically unattractive. His clients began to forsake him. His business began to suffer. In desperation he turned to royal jelly—one drop with every meal—and presto!—he was cured in a fortnight. A waiter in the Café Jena, also in Mexico City, reported that his father, after taking minute doses of this wonder substance in capsule form, sired a healthy boy child at the age of ninety. A bullfight promoter in Acapulco, finding himself landed with a rather lethargic-looking bull, injected it with one gram of royal jelly (an excessive dose) just before it entered the arena. Thereupon, the beast became so swift and savage that it promptly dispatched two picadors, three horses, and a matador, and finally...'"

"Listen!" Mrs Taylor said, interrupting him. "I think the baby's crying."

Albert glanced up from his reading. Sure enough, a lusty yelling noise was coming from the bedroom above.

"She must be hungry," he said.

His wife looked at the clock. "Good gracious me!" she cried, jumping up. "It's past her time again already! You mix the feed, Albert, quickly, while I bring her down! But hurry! I don't want to keep her waiting."

In half a minute, Mrs Taylor was back, carrying the screaming infant in her arms. She was flustered now, still quite unaccustomed to the ghastly nonstop racket that a healthy baby makes when it wants its food. "Do be quick, Albert!" she called, settling herself in the armchair and arranging the child on her lap. "Please hurry!"

Albert entered from the kitchen and handed her the bottle of warm milk. "It's just right," he said. "You don't have to test it."

She hitched the baby's head a little higher in the crook of her arm, then pushed the rubber teat straight into the wide-open yelling mouth. The baby grabbed the teat and began to suck. The yelling stopped. Mrs Taylor relaxed.

"Oh, Albert, isn't she lovely?"

"She's terrific, Mabel—thanks to royal jelly."

"Now, dear, I don't want to hear another word about that nasty stuff. It frightens me to death."

"You're making a big mistake," he said.

"We'll see about that."

The baby went on sucking the bottle.

"I do believe she's going to finish the whole lot again, Albert."

"I'm sure she is," he said.

And a few minutes later, the milk was all gone.

"Oh, what a good girl you are!" Mrs Taylor cried, as very gently she started to withdraw the nipple. The baby sensed what she was doing and sucked harder, trying to hold on. The woman gave a quick little tug, and *plop*, out it came.

"Waa! Waa! Waa! Waa! Waa!" the baby yelled.

"Nasty old wind," Mrs Taylor said, hoisting the child onto her shoulder and patting its back.

It belched twice in quick succession.

"There you are, my darling, you'll be all right now."

For a few seconds, the yelling stopped. Then it started again.

"Keep belching her," Albert said. "She's drunk it too quick."

His wife lifted the baby back onto her shoulder. She rubbed its spine. She changed it from one shoulder to the other. She lay it on its stomach on her lap. She sat it up on her knee. But it didn't belch again, and the yelling became louder and more insistent every minute.

"Good for the lungs," Albert Taylor said, grinning. "That's the way they exercise their lungs, Mabel, did you know that?"

"There, there, there," the wife said, kissing it all over the face. "There, there, there."

They waited another five minutes, but not for one moment did the screaming stop.

"Change the nappy," Albert said. "It's got a wet nappy, that's all it is." He fetched a clean one from the kitchen, and Mrs Taylor took the old one off and put the new one on.

This made no difference at all.

"Waa! Waa! Waa! Waa! Waa!" the baby yelled.

"You didn't stick the safety pin through the skin, did you, Mabel?"

"Of course I didn't," she said, feeling under the nappy with her fingers to make sure.

The parents sat opposite one another in their armchairs, smiling nervously, watching the baby on the mother's lap, waiting for it to tire and stop screaming.

"You know what?" Albert Taylor said at last.

"What?"

"I'll bet she's still hungry. I'll bet all she wants is another swig at that bottle. How about me fetching her an extra lot?"

"I don't think we ought to do that, Albert."

"It'll do her good," he said, getting up from his chair. "I'm going to warm her up a second helping."

He went into the kitchen, and was away several minutes. When he returned he was holding a bottle brimful of milk.

"I made her a double," he announced. "Eight ounces. Just in case."

"Albert! Are you mad! Don't you know it's just as bad to overfeed as it is to underfeed?"

"You don't have to give her the lot, Mabel. You can stop any time you like. Go on," he said, standing over her. "Give her a drink."

Mrs Taylor began to tease the baby's upper lip with the end of the nipple. The tiny mouth closed like a trap over the rubber teat and suddenly there was silence in the room. The baby's whole body relaxed and a look of absolute bliss came over its face as it started to drink.

"There you are, Mabel! What did I tell you?"

The woman didn't answer.

"She's ravenous, that's what she is. Just look at her suck."

Mrs Taylor was watching the level of the milk in the bottle. It was dropping fast, and before long three or four ounces out of eight had disappeared.

"There," she said. "That'll do."

"You can't pull it away now, Mabel."

"Yes, dear. I must."

"Go on, woman. Give her the rest and stop fussing."

"But *Albert*..."

"She's famished, can't you see that? Go on, my beauty," he said. "You finish that bottle."

"I don't like it, Albert," the wife said, but she didn't pull the bottle away.

"She's making up for lost time, Mabel, that's all she's doing."

Five minutes later the bottle was empty. Slowly, Mrs Taylor withdrew the nipple, and this time there was no protest from the baby, no sound at all. It lay peacefully on the mother's lap, the eyes glazed with contentment, the mouth half open, the lips smeared with milk.

"Twelve whole ounces, Mabel!" Albert Taylor said. "Three times the normal amount! Isn't that amazing!"

The woman was staring down at the baby. And now the old anxious tight-lipped look of the frightened mother was slowly returning to her face.

"What's the matter with *you?*" Albert asked. "You're not worried by that, are you? You can't expect her to get back to normal on a lousy four ounces, don't be ridiculous."

"Come here, Albert," she said.

"What?"

"I said come here."

He went over and stood beside her.

"Take a good look and tell me if you see anything different."

He peered closely at the baby. "She seems bigger, Mabel, if that's what you mean. Bigger and fatter."

"Hold her," she ordered. "Go on, pick her up."

He reached out and lifted the baby up off the mother's lap. "Good God!" he cried. "She weighs a ton!"

"Exactly."

"Now isn't that marvellous!" he cried, beaming. "I'll bet she must almost be back to normal already!"

"It frightens me, Albert. It's too quick."

"Nonsense, woman."

"It's that disgusting jelly that's done it," she said. "I hate the stuff."

"There's nothing disgusting about royal jelly," he answered, indignant.

"Don't be a fool, Albert! You think it's *normal* for a child to start putting on weight at this speed?"

"You're never satisfied!" he cried. "You're scared stiff when she's losing and now you're absolutely terrified because she's gaining! What's the matter with you, Mabel?"

The woman got up from her chair with the baby in her arms and started toward the door. "All I can say is," she said, "it's lucky I'm here to see you don't give her any more of it, that's all I can say." She went out, and Albert watched her through the open door as she crossed the hall to the foot of the stairs and started to ascend, and when she reached the third or fourth step she suddenly stopped and stood quite still for several seconds as though remembering something. Then she turned and came down again rather quickly and re-entered the room.

"Albert," she said.

"Yes?"

"I assume there wasn't any royal jelly in this last feed we've just given her?"

"I don't see why you should assume that, Mabel."

"Albert!"

"What's wrong?" he asked, soft and innocent.

"How *dare* you!" she cried.

Albert Taylor's great bearded face took on a pained and puzzled look. "I think you ought to be very glad she's got another big dose of it inside her," he said. "Honest I do. And this *is* a big dose, Mabel, believe you me."

The woman was standing just inside the doorway clasping the sleeping baby in her arms and staring at her husband with huge eyes. She stood very erect, her body absolutely stiff with fury, her face paler, more tight-lipped than ever.

"You mark my words," Albert was saying, "you're going to have a nipper there soon that'll win first prize in any baby show in the *entire* country. Hey, why don't you weigh her now and see what she is? You want me to get the scales, Mabel, so you can weigh her?"

The woman walked straight over to the large table in the centre of the room and laid the baby down and quickly started taking off its clothes. "Yes!" she snapped. "Get the scales!" Off came the little nightgown, then the undervest.

Then she unpinned the nappy and she drew it away and the baby lay naked on the table.

"But Mabel!" Albert cried. "It's a miracle! She's fat as a puppy!"

Indeed, the amount of flesh the child had put on since the day before was astounding. The small sunken chest with the rib-bones showing all over it was now plump and round as a barrel, and the belly was bulging high in the air. Curiously, though, the arms and legs did not seem to have grown in proportion. Still short and skinny, they looked like little sticks protruding from a ball of fat.

"Look!" Albert said. "She's even beginning to get a bit of fuzz on the tummy to keep her warm!" He put out a hand and was about to run the tips of his fingers over the powdering of silky yellow-brown hairs that had suddenly appeared on the baby's stomach.

"*Don't you touch her!*" the woman cried. She turned and faced him, her eyes blazing, and she looked suddenly like some kind of a little fighting bird with her neck arched over toward him as though she were about to fly at his face and peck his eyes out.

"Now wait a minute," he said, retreating.

"You must be mad!" she cried.

"Now wait just one minute, Mabel, will you please, because if you're still thinking this stuff is dangerous... That *is* what you're thinking, isn't it? All right, then. Listen carefully. I shall now proceed to *prove* to you once and for all, Mabel, that royal jelly is absolutely harmless to human beings, even in enormous doses. For example—why do you think we had only half the usual honey crop last summer? Tell me that."

His retreat, walking backwards, had taken him three or four yards away from her, where he seemed to feel more comfortable.

"The reason we had only half the usual crop last summer," he said slowly, lowering his voice, "was because I turned one hundred of my hives over to the production of royal jelly."

"You *what?*"

"Ah," he whispered. "I thought that might surprise you a bit. And I've been making it ever since right under your very nose." His small eyes were glinting at her, and a slow sly smile was creeping around the corners of his mouth.

"You'll never guess the reason, either," he said. "I've been afraid to mention it up to now because I thought it might... well... sort of embarrass you."

There was a slight pause. He had his hands clasped high in front of him, level with his chest, and he was rubbing one palm against the other, making a soft scraping noise.

"You remember that bit I read you out of the magazine? That bit about the rat? Let me see now, how does it go? 'Still and Burdett found that a male rat which hitherto had been unable to breed...'" He hesitated, the grin widening, showing his teeth.

"You get the message, Mabel?"

She stood quite still, facing him.

"The very first time I ever read that sentence, Mabel, I jumped straight out of my chair and I said to myself if it'll work with a lousy rat, I said, then there's no reason on earth why it shouldn't work with Albert Taylor."

He paused again, craning his head forward and turning one ear slightly in his wife's direction, waiting for her to say something. But she didn't.

"And here's another thing," he went on. "It made me feel so absolutely marvellous, Mabel, and so sort of completely different to what I was before that I went right on taking it even after you'd announced the joyful tidings. *Buckets* of it I must have swallowed during the last twelve months."

The big heavy haunted-looking eyes of the woman were moving intently over the man's face and neck. There was no skin showing at all on the neck, not even at the sides below the ears. The whole of it, to a point where it disappeared into the collar of the shirt, was covered all the way around with those shortish silky hairs, yellowy black.

"Mind you," he said, turning away from her, gazing lovingly now at the baby, "it's going to work far better on a tiny infant than on a fully developed man like me. You've only got to look at her to see that, don't you agree?"

The woman's eyes travelled slowly downward and settled on the baby. The baby was lying naked on the table, fat and white and comatose, like some gigantic grub that was approaching the end of its larval life and would soon emerge into the world complete with mandibles and wings.

"Why don't you cover her up. Mabel?" he said. "We don't want our little queen to catch a cold."

1965

TEMPLE OF THE FOX

James Wade

Detailed autobiographical information about James Wade is hard to come by, though I know he was born in the USA on 5 January 1930, and that he loved South Korea so much after visiting the country in 1954, while enlisted in the US Army, that in 1960 he returned to become a permanent resident.

For ten years, from 1964 to 1974, he wrote a column called *Scouting the City* for the *Korea Times*, and in 1967 he published a book entitled *One Man's Korea*.

He wrote around thirty stories of the macabre, many of which were set in the universe of H. P. Lovecraft's Cthulhu Mythos, and which have been published—some posthumously—in such anthologies as *Tales of the Cthulhu Mythos* (1969), *The Disciples of Cthulhu* (1976), *The Hastur Cycle* (1993), *The New Lovecraft Circle* (1996), *The Innsmouth Cycle* (1998) and *A Mountain Walked* (2014).

He also wrote poetry, again much of it inspired by the work of Lovecraft, as well as book and film reviews, articles on music, and more general pieces for a variety of publications.

He died on 1 August 1983, though a comprehensive collection of his work, *Such Things May Be: Collected Writings*, was published in 2018 by Shadow Publishing, edited by Edward P. Berglund and containing a foreword by Fritz Leiber.

First published in the *The Korea Times* on 31 October 1965, "Temple of the Fox" is a ghoulish and claustrophobic tale set in a Buddhist monastery. The remote location and the "fish out of water" aspect make this story particularly creepy and disturbing. It's a hidden gem, which deserves to be rediscovered, and which I'm delighted to present here.

Who sees ghost foxes is not apt ever to see anything else. Dead souls ravenous for life, though always fastidious, they gathered in old temples and wayside shrines, demons attached to the maize goddess. Trouble is the only thing that thaws their icy courtesy.

DAVID STACTON: SEGAKI

I

It had been a hard climb, up the pine-wooded slope where the long slanting rays of afternoon sun washed green thickets with a haze of gold, past the chattering little stream whose steep descent had worn a deep gulley among clumps of enduring rock. The sounds of the small village on the lower shelf of Song-Ni Mountain had long faded; the picnickers and tradesmen shuffling through the dust of the single street beside a widened, placid pooling of the same stream were inaudible, now, even in this dense hush. Martinson knew he must be near the gently domed peak he had glimpsed from the valley road far below, though the thick pine growth still prevented his seeing it. The temple must be near, then; though the villagers, indeed, had only gestured vaguely in this direction to confirm his supposition about its exact location.

Martinson stopped for a moment to try to orient himself. The cessation of his footsteps crackling in the undergrowth crystallized the silence. This was remote, certainly; about as remote as one can get, even in a remote corner of the world like southwest Korea. He mentally retraced his pilgrimage from its beginning: the crowded, noisy Victorian train station in Seoul; all night on the antique sleeper, alighting in the deserted early morning of a market town way-station, the long dusty bus ride ever higher into the mountains, then the broken-down jitney that staggered up winding, steeply sloped roads overlooking dizzy drops and a miniature landscape that seemed unrolled from some ancient oriental scroll. Finally he had gotten as far as modern conveniences could take him, and the all-afternoon hike up from the little village by the pond was nearing its end.

Far as the heat and dust of the journey, Martinson wasn't sorry about his decision to spend a week's vacation at a Buddhist temple. A Fulbright lecturer in Seoul couldn't say he had seen Korea properly without travelling to outlying districts and actually living there for a time. When his colleague Thorwald came back the month before with stories of this Song-Ni district and its dozens of tiny cloud-scraping temples set on the mountainsides far above the immense Popju-Sa Monastery, Martinson had resolved to spend time in the area, and to live at the particular hermitage glimpsed by Thorwald, the location of which he had sketched so painstakingly. After almost a year in Korea, Martinson was sure his knowledge of the spoken language, shaky though it was, would get him through everyday situations. And temples were traditionally ready to accept guests, especially paying guests who were willing and even eager to follow the temple regulations: vegetarian meals and early prayers at 3 A.M., announced by the clatter of wooden clappers and ringing of bells.

As Martinson glanced about, he was unaccountably startled to realize that he was not alone on the mountainside. Off to the left, near the concealed foaming of the stream, he glimpsed a patch of grey that moved; soon he made out a figure in monk's robe, bald brown head bowed over a staff with whose aid its owner was ascending slowly, laboriously. The American altered his course, plunging through the light undergrowth at right angles to his previous direction.

Martinson hailed the man politely, realizing as he did so that the monk was not as old as his shambling gait had suggested. If the man was surprised to hear his language spoken by a foreigner, he gave no evidence of it. On the other hand, his own responses were difficult for Martinson to grasp; his Korean must be very scholarly or very old-fashioned, perhaps both.

Yes, there was a temple at the head of this slope; he himself was a *bonze* attached to it, and was returning there now. Yes, they could entertain guests who might deign to accept their humble fare, though very few pilgrims ever got this far.

As he spoke, something about the hoarse, high voice suggested to Martinson what he had read of the eunuchs of the old royal palace. But the man couldn't be that old; almost nobody of that time was still alive. The monk peered at the intruder (Martinson expected to assume the role of intruder, for the first few days at least) less with curiosity than a son of disinterested appraisal. The man's mouth opened in a seemingly permanent, mirthless, canine grin, revealing broken and blackened teeth. The eyes told him nothing, though he had been in the Orient long enough to discard the cliché of inscrutability.

The monk was speaking again: If the young *yang-ban* would just follow him, they could reach the temple well before dusk, before the dinner hour. (They began to climb slowly, Martinson adjusting his strides to the deliberate pace of the other.) The dinner might seem very meager to a hungry traveler, since the monks did not often have meat. (But aren't Buddhist temples always strictly vegetarian? Perhaps he had misunderstood.) How many brothers lived at this temple? Six, ordinarily. They were poor, did their own farming on a few hillside plots, tended to their devotions and studies, had little to do with the outside world, even with the mountain village below. Right now, several of the brothers were off in the remote depths of the mountains, gathering edible mushrooms. The young gentleman must know that this Song-Ni district was famous for the quality of its mushrooms, and this was the time of year, autumn, when they were gathered. It was the one cash crop of the year, which provided money for clothing, upkeep of the temple, and any little amenities for the winter ahead. A very important time of year; everyone worked very hard.

They had continued to climb through the slanting sunset rays that gilded the tall pines. Now a distinct hint of dusk clung to the ground; the valley below was hazy with twilight, picked out by a few, a very few, remote, twinkling cook-fires. A smell of wood smoke drifted in the air; Martinson did not think it came from as far away as the valley. Sure enough, a steeper slope led suddenly to a crude, weathered set of stone steps. Climbing this precarious barrier, they alighted on a sort of broad ledge, whether leveled artificially in whole or part Martinson could not tell. There stood the temple compound, still surrounded on three sides by the encroaching pines, the trees flowing up behind it on a steep rocky slope that must have led to the summit of the mountain itself.

The temple was very small and quite ordinary from an architectural viewpoint, as he had expected. It consisted of four buildings, the unpretentious main temple and two tiny side-shrines devoted to propitiating the mountain gods from whom this land had been wrested; further up the slope a primitive straw-roofed farm house indicated the living quarters of the monks, the source of the wood-smoke smell. Framing the temple buildings on three sides was a breast-high wall of mud bricks surmounted by clay roof-tiles. The main temple buildings, of weathered, painted wood, with high peaked roofs, also tile-covered, could be any age: they were probably late Yi-Dynasty, but might have been older if fire and warfare had spared them, as might well be the case in such a remote spot. Here, Martinson thought, was what he had been looking for; a chance to blend into the Korean countryside, to sit passively, not even trying to study or absorb, but letting the spirit of the place come to him. A chance for the aroma of ancient Korea to fill him in a way that could never happen in a less isolated, undisturbed spot.

They were walking now toward the temple. Perhaps, his companion inquired, he would like to glance at the buildings while there was still enough light? (Dusk had begun rapidly to fill the small courtyard, with its struggling, unkempt flower beds.) Yes, he would very much like to see them.

Peering through the elaborate and much-damaged carved wooden doors into the shallow sanctuary, Martinson could just see the solemn shape of the seated Buddha. Though he knew little of Buddhist art, this statue seemed to him rather untypical, and he wondered vaguely if it might be an artistic find of some interest. The pose of the figure was strange, less placid and serene than most. The hands were held differently, too. He could not see the face clearly.

They walked to one of the side chapels devoted to the mountain gods. Here the last rays of the setting sun fell upon a carved figure perhaps no more grotesque than most to be found in this strange blending of sophisticated religion and primitive animism. But he noticed in the tangled, gaudy paintings on the back wall one anomaly. The laughing, white-bearded old man, a nature-spirit carried over from Chinese tradition, was usually pictured astride a tiger. Here he was seated upon a fox, whose strange grin matched his own, and somehow reminded Martinson of the smile of his grey-clad guide.

"What is the name of this temple?" asked Martinson suddenly.

"The Temple of the Fox," replied his companion.

Odd! Shouldn't a temple have a more religious name? And weren't foxes in Korean folklore rather sinister, devilish creatures? How could this be called the Temple of the Fox?

The old man looked at him disinterestedly, still smiling his gap-toothed, broken grin. No, no, truly, this was the Temple of the Fox—.

II

It was deep night; the darkness matched the dense texture of the silence. Martinson lay on a straw mat, shivering under the thin blanket from his knapsack, the one luxury he had permitted himself to pack. Not much of a luxury at that, he reflected grimly. He had known that even October nights in the mountains could be cold, and suspected that frugal monks would not light the fires that ran through flues under the clay sleeping-floors until the first snowfall. Well, he had been determined to live as the monks lived, and he certainly wasn't going to begin by asking for extra heat.

He felt he had made a good initial impression. The four monks who gathered for the evening meal had smiled at him, darting quick appraising glances when they didn't think he was looking. He had answered their polite questions politely: he was from Seoul, he was a teacher, a *pak-sa*; he wished to live for a short while at the temple to share the wisdom and peace of those devoted to the Great Eightfold Way. They had smiled and nodded. In days to come he would try to speak to them in some detail, however lamely, about their temple and its peculiar name. He thought vaguely that here might be some hitherto unrecorded intrusion of pure animism into the Buddhist religion, perhaps worth a tentative initial monograph for the *Transactions* of the Royal Asiatic Society's Korea branch, though religion was not his field. He had made out all right with the meal, too, eating his thin bean-sprout soup noisily enough to indicate approval, managing the rough wooden chopsticks with aplomb as he picked up bits of peppery pickled vegetables, lotus root, and mushrooms in vinegar (this was mushroom country, he remembered). Some meat would have been welcome, but at least there was rice, and that was filling.

Soon after the meal his initial guide, whose name was Chae, showed him to a small, stuffy private room that had been cleared for him, handed him a pile of old but clean straw mats and bade him goodnight.

His room, like all the rooms in the L-shaped house, opened onto a narrow, elevated porch of polished wood. Before he retired he glanced outside and noticed that the monks were still wakeful. Candle lights flickered behind the rice paper panes of the sliding door panels leading into their main room, used for sleeping and eating. He could hear their voices; all of them seemed to speak in the same high, sibilant tone and antique locutions that old Chae employed. He found their voices vaguely disquieting, and wondered if this were some kind of ritualized religious intonation. From this distance he couldn't make out any words, but they seemed to be laughing, and he caught inflections that sounded sarcastic and mocking. He wondered if they were talking about him.

Later he lay shivering under the light blanket and waiting for time to pass. Despite his tired muscles, he did not seem to be able to relax. Sounds had ceased in the other wing of the house around nine o'clock. He must have dozed intermittently, for when he next looked at his watch, the luminous dial registered close to two A.M. Since he did not seem able really to sleep, he thought he might get up for the prayer-service at three. But this was his first day here, and it might be resented as an intrusion. He would ask about attending services tomorrow, for tonight he would content himself with listening, seeing only as much as he might glimpse from his own doorway.

He may have partially dozed again, for he started violently when a clatter arose close at hand. The monks were evidently leaving their quarters in procession, beating on the hollow, round wooden *mok-t'ak*, winch he had often seen and heard used for daytime prayer services at other temples. The dinning of a gong seemed added to the racket as well.

Gradually the noise passed by and Martinson stretched stiffly, stood up, and quietly slid his door aside. His room commanded an oblique view of the main sanctuary where the anomalous Buddha squatted in darkness. But to his surprise the procession had moved out of sight, around to the far side of this structure. He could see the flicker of torchlight and a steadier glow which might be a small bonfire. There was no question about it; the devotees had gathered around the little shrine to the mountain spirit, where he had seen the painted god astride a fox.

Voices were now raised in chant: a feeble, puling whine that was particularly unpleasant. Martinson even thought he heard furtive snorts and yelps of glee, degraded laughter and bestial mumbling under the flowing chanted line. It was certainly unlike any Buddhist service he had ever heard—but then was it directed at all toward the Lord Gautama? Apparently not. Suddenly the gongs and rattles sounded again, overwhelming a concerted human yell of surprise or triumph. The flickering glow visible above the peaked temple roof writhed and shifted, flaring momentarily enough for Martinson to spot a small moving shape that darted around the front of the building toward him. The animal froze for a second as if undecided which way to run. Martinson saw, with an unthinking reflex of chill, that it was a large fox. The fox suddenly turned and scurried across the courtyard, disappearing into the black pine woods.

A few moments later the procession of monks paraded sedately around the corner of the temple. They were silent now. The leader carried a torch. Martinson noted that there were only three of them. One monk must be ill; or perhaps three were sufficient to carry out this distinctly unorthodox service. Before they got too near, Martinson stepped back discreetly into his room and slid the door panel shut. As they passed, he heard muttered words in that high-pitched bantering tone; he thought he caught the words for "change" and "surprise".

His thoughts and reactions were confused when night and silence had closed in on him again. Were these heretic monks, worshipping a fox spirit under the guise of Buddhism? He had never heard of such a thing in Korea, but he knew that primitive nature-religions died hard, even in advanced civilizations. Did the monks keep a tame fox or foxes at the temple as part of their wayward beliefs? For that matter, can a wild fox ever be tamed? He wasn't sure.

He wanted a cigarette badly, but had brought none along on what he had considered an ascetic as well as aesthetic retreat. That wasn't how it was turning out, was it? But why, no matter how unorthodox these religions might be, should he feel a strong misgiving, a sense of peril and repugnance mixed?

He settled back to wait for daylight.

III

While the monks were rousing and dressing themselves in the clear, white light of dawn, Martinson slipped out of his room and down the gentle slope to the temple compound. The harsh early rays of the sun made the center sanctuary look even older and more decrepit than it had the previous evening. Its wooden panels and door frames were mostly grey and weather-beaten; only a few flakes of faded paint in once-gaudy hues stuck to the wood, faintly outlining where the conventional pictures and rococo decorative patterns had been. When he glanced inside, he was shocked: the hard morning light fell full on the face of the seated image, and it was truly like no Buddha he had ever seen before. The face was grimacing and cruel: the carved aureole behind the figure seemed to represent writhing flames. Where had he seen that pose and expression before? Perhaps in prints of the Buddhist hell and its grim master. Later decadent Buddhism had spawned a hell as ingenious and depraved as medieval Europe's, ignoring completely the doctrines of Buddha himself. Yes, this image must be the terrible KANG-HEE, Lord of Hell and scourge of accursed souls.

But Martinson wanted especially to see the side temple where the ceremony had been held last night. Passing the main temple, he turned the corner and approached the small, closet-size structure, almost like a medieval European wayside shrine. Here was where they had gathered and chanted, where the fox had suddenly, terrifyingly dashed away into the forest. He would see the sodden ashes of a small bonfire, but no other sign of disturbance. He approached the building, glancing first at the malevolently painted figure on the back wall, the cruelly grinning old man astride a fox. Yes, he had been right about that, it was surely a fox, its grin as depraved as that of its rider. But then his eye fell on the carved idol enshrined on the central pedestal. Again he experienced shock. Why hadn't he noticed last evening? Though the statue now seemed more than customarily grotesque, its stylized distortions tended in one direction. The elongated jaw that was almost a muzzle, the cruel, tiny eyes, the tawny tint to the skin of the face: this figure, too, was the symbolic human, but unmistakably bestial, representation of a fox.

IV

Martinson felt an inexplicable repugnance at the thought of joining the monks for their morning meal. Besides, the drowsiness that had eluded him last night was now descending upon him. He went back to his room unnoticed, closed the door, and almost immediately fell asleep.

When he woke, his watch told him it was well after noon. Stepping outside, he saw that the entire temple area was deserted. The monks were probably at their fields, wherever these might be. Although he wasn't hungry, he unwrapped and ate several chocolate bars from his knapsack, which he had packed for emergencies. He decided, more from restlessness than any other reason, to take a hike around the area. Perhaps he would come upon the cleared patches of hillside that the monks farmed. Shouldering the knapsack, he struck off at an angle downhill, not retracing the route by which he had ascended.

The forest was as quiet as it had been the day before, but the silence did not seem as peaceful and secure as then. This was probably because the outlandish discoveries he had made at the temple had unaccountably unnerved him. Certainly the sun-striped glades of pines that shifted past him as he walked held no undertone of menace. Neither did the temple, really, if one thought about it logically. The full light of day was fast dispelling the unsettling fancies of darkness.

Then he became aware, just as on the previous afternoon, that he was not alone.

The man was standing still beneath a tall, somber pine, looking at him. This man was no monk, he wore the rough, dark work clothes of a peasant. His smile was uncertain and questioning, and his voice when he answered Martinson's hail was harsh and deep, not like the monks' feminine whine.

He carried a shapeless sack over one shoulder, and in response to questions explained that he was a gatherer of mushrooms and lived in the little village down at the foot of the mountain.

Martinson introduced himself and said that he was staying at a temple on this mountain.

The man glanced at him oddly. "Surely you mean a temple on the other mountain, down the slope and around the other side. There is no temple on this mountain."

Martinson, puzzled, checked his reply and rapidly substituted, "Yes, but there is a temple on this mountain, too. I caught a glimpse of it over there." He gestured in the direction from which he had come.

"No", insisted the man; "there is no temple there now, just some deserted buildings. Once it had been a temple, but no monks had lived there for a hundred years. No one lived there now."

"But it looked well cared for. There were no trees or plants grown up around the buildings," insisted Martinson.

"It is cared for, yes, but not by people. It is the home of—." The man used an unfamiliar phrase which seemed to contain the Korean word for fox.

"Foxes?" questioned Martinson, feeling a breath of chill, angry at himself for admitting it.

"Yes, the fox-spirits dwell there." In his earnestness the man spat out the harsh Korean consonants explosively. "No one comes near here, especially at night, because the fox-spirits are very dangerous and sometimes kill men. Everybody in the valley knows this and stays away. Sometimes at night one can see lights shining up here, and echoes of strange noises reach the valley. When that happens, the monks of the great Popju-Sa Temple burn incense and chant sutras to avert the evil. But no one comes up here at night, ever."

"What do these fox-spirits do?"

"In our old stories we have many accounts of foxes who assume human form. Sometimes the fox is a beautiful girl who will entice a young man to her house. After they make love she becomes again a thousand year-old fox and devours him. Sometimes the foxes keep an inn and kill travellers who stop there. It is the way of fox-spirits, very dangerous and cunning, very ancient."

Martinson had heard stories like this before; the Koreans, like the Chinese, have many legends of tigers, foxes, even bears who assume human form, a reversal of western werewolf myths.

After he had left the mushroom-gatherer, who stared after him in some trepidation, as if he might be a fox-spirit himself instead of just another blundering "big-nose" foreigner, Martinson felt some of the cobwebs clear away. A natural thing, really, for renegade monks to take possession of an abandoned temple site and keep superstitious fears alive to protect their usurpation from exposure! Such persons might actually be rough customers indeed, highly desirable to avoid. He would certainly not spend the full week with them as he had planned. Tomorrow he would take off for that temple on the other mountain which the man had spoken of. But since the fox-worshipping monks had not molested him in any way last night, surely one more evening at their temple would be small risk. He wanted badly to see and take notes on the heretical ritual they were performing in the night. This might be an important anthropological find.

V

And yet when he returned to the temple for the evening meal it was hard to fight down the old repugnance. All six monks had assembled this time, and their jovially whining voices seemed latently sinister as they sat on the wooden porch awaiting the meal. One man especially had a high, yelping laugh that was not seemly. Another, stripped in the courtyard to bathe from a wooden bucket, revealed a mat of thick red-brown hair covering his body—Martinson had never seen an Oriental man with so much body hair.

Finally the meal was served. It was the same as last night's and the old man Chae once again apologized sententiously that there was no meat today. One of the younger monks glanced at Martinson in mischievous glee as the American deflected the apology with gracious words. Why was he amused?

When the meal ended, Martinson addressed Chae, who seemed the eldest, though he had never ascertained what rank or authority existed in this place. He would very much like, if it were permitted, to attend the early morning prayer service here, part of which he had heard last night. Might this be possible?

Yes, replied Chae, widening his blackened smile, certainly. They would wake the young *yang-ban* some little time before the service. They would be honored by his participation.

The other monks seemed to glance carefully away from Martinson and each other. Conversation was silenced, and a tenuous feeling of tension, of anticipation, descended with the gathering darkness.

VI

He had thought that sleep would elude him again, but nervous tension can be as exhausting as physical exertion, and despite the unreasoning foreboding he felt, drowsiness overtook him as soon as he lay down in the little cubicle. He must have dozed intermittently a long time, for the warning rap on his door a little before three startled him as much as last night's musical outburst had done. He leaped to his feet and sprang through the sliding door almost too quickly to indicate a meditative frame of mind.

The six priests, in their grey outer robes and baggy knickerbockers, were assembling outside their quarters. As they formed a line for the procession, Chae, the one who had summoned Martinson, indicated that the American would come last in the line. He himself hobbled over rapidly to head it, carrying a stubby torch.

And now the procession paced slowly forward in the darkness, to the rattle of *mok-t'aks* and blurred whirring of gongs. Martinson couldn't help feeling that the idea of marching about so solemnly under the stars with none to witness was a bit ridiculous; but he thought of the pathos and dignity of the clergy in English backwaters who maintained the ritual of service with or without a congregation.

They were passing the central sanctuary; torchlight fell malevolently upon the crouched god—devil?—inside; the painted eyes seemed to glare, the carved flames to flicker. Now they were approaching the Fox-Shrine, forming a little semi-circle around the front of it. Martinson stood a bit to one side.

Old Chae touched his torch to a pile of brushwood that must have been prepared in advance, then placed the torch in an iron ring fastened to the shrine. The other monks put their musical implements aside.

The monk Chae addressed the others in a high, ritual tone. He was not speaking Korean, Martinson was sure; whether it was Chinese or another, perhaps older, language he could not guess. The monks whined a response in the same tongue, apparently. Then Chae let his eyes and gestures turn toward the stranger who stood almost outside the circle of firelight. He smiled with that black, gaping grimace that mirrored the unseen images in the shrine at his back. The monks turned toward Martinson, and they were smiling, too.

Suddenly the fire seemed to flare of its own accord, and a curious milling or stirring swept over the group of monks. They were bowing—genuflecting; no, they were actually prostrating themselves. They resembled—they had actually become—only heaps of garments scattered on the ground around the fire!

These heaps of garments stirred, shook. Martinson was rooted to the spot, bewildered, too uncomprehending to feel fear.

From each pile of discarded robes emerged a large, tawny fox eyeing him slyly, slowly advancing, jaws gaped in the shared grin of the shrine figures, of the monks.

Martinson tried to scream.

There was meat, the first in a long time, on the menu of the Temple of the Fox the next day.

(NOTE: The author knows of no recent or historical diabolist sect in Korean Buddhism; nor of any surviving belief in the were-fox legends of antiquity. But it is the privilege of the fantasiste to invent and aside from these matters, the customs and locales are rendered as accurately as possible. A real temple is described, with all apology to the worthy and no doubt thoroughly prosaic inmates.)

1971

DAVID'S WORM

Brian Lumley

Like the previous contributor, James Wade, Brian Lumley was heavily influenced by the work of H. P. Lovecraft, and he has likewise written many stories set in the universe of Lovecraft's Cthulhu Mythos. Born in County Durham on 2 December 1937, Lumley became obsessed with Lovecraft in his early twenties, when, while serving with the Corps of Royal Military Police in Germany, he happened upon a collection of Lovecraft's stories, and was so taken with it that he made it his mission to track down everything Lovecraft had written. This led to Lumley sending some of his Lovecraft-inspired fiction to Lovecraft's publisher, August Derleth, at Arkham House, which culminated in Lumley's first two stories, "The Sister City" and "Cement Surroundings", appearing in the Derleth-edited anthology *Tales of the Cthulhu Mythos* (1969).

Arkham House went on to publish three of Lumley's books, the novel *Beneath the Moors* (1974) and two collections of his short fiction, *The Caller of the Black* (1971) and *The Horror at Oakdeene and Others* (1977).

Although Lumley had had over a dozen books published by the mid-1980s, his breakthrough novel came in 1986 with the publication of *Necroscope*, the first in his multimillion-selling series featuring hero Harry Keogh. *Necroscope*'s many sequels and spin-offs include *Necroscope II: Wamphyri!* (1988), *Necroscope III: The Source* (1989), *Necroscope IV: Deadspeak* (1990), *Necroscope V: Deadspawn* (1991), *Vampire World I: Blood Brothers* (1992), *Vampire World II: The Last Aerie* (1993) and *Vampire World III: Bloodwars* (1994).

Over the course of his long career, Lumley wrote well over a hundred stories, many of which were collected in over a dozen collections. These include *The Compleat Crow* (1987), *Iced on Aran and Other Dream Quests* (1990), *Fruiting Bodies and Other Fungi* (1993), *Dagon's Bell and Other Discords* (1994), *The Whisperer and Other Voices* (2001) and *The Taint and Other Novellas* (2007). His last published short story, "A Dreamer's Tale", appeared in *Phantasmagoria: Special Edition Series* magazine in December 2022, just over a year before his death in January 2024.

First published in *Pulp* magazine in 1971, "David's Worm" is one of hundreds, perhaps even thousands, of cautionary tales about humankind's tendency to dabble in areas of science that are best left alone. Like much of Lumley's work, it is deliciously nasty and pulls no punches.

Professor Lees—chief radio-biologist at the Kendall nuclear research and power station—was showing his son some slides he had prepared weeks earlier from pond and sea water irradiated test tubes. David was only seven, but already he could understand much of what his famous father said.

"Look," the professor explained as the boy peered eagerly into the microscope. "That's an *amoeba*, quite dead, killed off by radiation. Just like a little jelly-fish, isn't it? And this..." he swapped slides, "... is a tiny-wee plant called a *diatom*. It's dead too—they all are—that's what hard radiation does to living things..."

"What's this one?" David asked, changing the slides himself.

"That's a young flatworm, David. It's a tiny fresh-water animal. Lives in pools and streams. Funny little thing. That one's a type with very strange abilities. D'you know, when one *planarian* (that's what they're called) eats another—" David looked up sharply at his father, who smiled at the boy's expression "Oh, no! They're not cannibals—at least I don't think so—but if a dead worm is chopped up and fed to another, why! The live worm 'inherits' the knowledge of the one it's eaten!"

"Knowledge?" David looked puzzled. "Are they clever, then?"

"Noooo—not strictly *clever*, but they can be taught simple things: like how a drop in temperature means it's feeding time; stuff like that, as I've said, when one of them is dead and chopped up, whatever he knew before he died is passed on to the planarian who eats him."

"And they're not cannibals?" David still looked puzzled.

"Why, no," the professor patiently explained. "I don't suppose for one minute they'd eat each other if they *knew* what they were eating—we do chop them up first!" He frowned. "I'm not absolutely sure though... you could, I suppose, call them *unwilling* cannibals if you wished. Is it important?"

But David was not listening. Suddenly his attention seemed riveted on the tiny creature beneath the microscope.

"He moved—!"

"No he didn't, David—that's just your imagination. He *couldn't* move, he's dead." Nonetheless the scientist pulled his son gently to one side to have a look himself. It wasn't possible—no, of course not. He had been studying the specimens for three weeks, since the experiment, watching them all die off; and since then there had not been a sign of returning life in any of them. Certainly there could be none now. Even if the sustained blast of hard radiation had not killed them off proper (which of course it had), then colouring them and fixing them to the slides certainly must have. No, they were dead, all of them, merely tiny lumps of useless gelatin...

The next day was Saturday and David was not at school. He quit the house early saying he was going fishing at the pool. Shortly after he left, his father cleaned off his many slides, hardly missing the one with the tiny planarian worm—the one in David's pocket!

David *knew* he had seen the worm move under the microscope; a stiff, jerky movement, rather like the slug he had pinned to the garden with a twig through its middle one evening a few weeks earlier...

David's pool was his own. It lay in the grounds of the house, set far back from the road, in the copse that marked the boundary of his father's land. In fact it was a run-off from the river, filled nine months of the year by high waters flooding the creek running to it. There were fish, but David had never caught any of the big ones, not with his bent pin. He had seen them often enough in the reeds—even a great pike—but his catches were never any bigger than the occasional newt or minnow. That Saturday it was not even his intention to fish; that had only been an excuse to his mother to allow him to get down to the pool.

The truth was that David was a very humane boy really and the idea that the flatworm had been *alive* on that slide, no matter how, was abhorrent to him. His father had said the creature was a fresh-water dweller; well, if it *was* alive, David believed it should be given another chance. Immersion in water, its natural habitat, might just do the trick!

He put the slide down on a stone in a part of the pool not quite so shaded by the surrounding trees, so that the creature upon it might benefit from what was left of the late summer sun. There he could see it just beneath the surface of the water. He kept up a watch on the tiny speck on the slide for almost an hour before growing tired of the game. Then he went home to spend the rest of the day in the library—boning up on planarian worms...

In defiance of everything the books said, "Planny" (as David christened the creature the day after he saw it detach itself from the slide and swim almost aimlessly away) grew up very strangely indeed. Instead of adopting a worm-shape as it developed, with a lobey, spade-shaped head, it took on one more like an amoeba. It was simply a shapeless blob—or, at best, a roundish blob.

Now one might ask: "Just how did David manage, in such a large pool, to follow the comings and goings of such a small animal?" And the answer would be that Planny did not stay small for very long. Indeed no, for even on that morning when he got loose from the slide he trebled his size: that is, be *converted* many times his own weight in less wily, even smaller denizens of David's pool. In just a day or two he was as big as a Ping-Pong ball; and David had taken to getting up very early, before school, so that he could go down to the copse to check the creature's rate of growth.

Two weeks later there was not a single minnow left in the pool, nor a stickleback, and even the numbers of the youngest of the larger fish were on a rapid decline.

David never discovered just how Planny swam. He could see that there were no fins or anything, no legs, yet somehow the animal managed quite nimbly in the water without such extensions—and especially after dining on the first of the larger fish. It had been noticeable, certainly, how much the freakish flatworm "learned" from the minnows: how to hunt and hide in the reeds, how to sink slowly to the bottom if ever anything big came near, things like that. Not that Planny really *needed* to hide, but he was not aware of that yet; he only had the experience ("inherited" of course) of the minnows and other fish he had eaten. Minnows, being small, have got to be careful... so David's worm was careful too! Nor did he get much from the bigger fish; though they did help his self-assurance somewhat and his speed in the water; for naturally, they had the bustling attitude of most aquatic adults.

Then, when Planny was quite a bit bigger, something truly memorable happened!

He was all of five weeks reborn when he took the pike. David was lucky enough to see the whole bit. That old pike had been stalking Planny for a week, but the radiation-transformed worm had successfully managed to avoid him right until the best possible moment: that is, until their sizes were more or less equal... in mass if not in shape.

David was standing at the pool-side, admiring Planny as he gently undulated through the water, when the ugly fish came sliding out of the reed-patch; its wicked eyes fixed firmly on the vaguely globular, greyish-white thing in the water. David's worm had eyes too, two of them, and they were fixed equally firmly on the pike.

The boy gawked at the way it happened. The fish circled once, making a tight turn about his revolving "prey," then flashed in to the attack at a speed which left David breathless. The boy knew all about this vicious species of fish, especially about the powerful jaws and great teeth; but the pike in question might never have had any teeth at all—might well have been a caviar sandwich—for all Planny worried! He simply *opened up*, seeming to split down the middle and around his circumference until David, still watching from the pool-side, thought he must tear himself in two. But he did not. David saw a flash of rapidly sawing rows of rasp-like teeth marching in columns along Planny's insides—and then the creature's two almost-halves ground shut on the amazed pike.

Planny seemed to go mad then, almost lifting himself (or being lifted) out of the water as the fish inside him thrashed about. But not for long. In a few seconds his now somewhat *elongated* shape became very still, then wobbled tiredly out of sight into deeper water to sleep it off...

For a full four days after this awesome display David's worm was absent from its rebirth-place. There had been some rain and the creek was again swollen; which was as well for the oddly mutated flatworm, for there were no fish left in the pool. In fact, there was not much of *anything* left in the pool—at least, not until the afternoon of the pike's vanquishment, when heavy rain brought the river waters to restock the Planny-depleted place. For that ugly, sadly vulnerable fish had been the pool's last natural inhabitant, and until the rain came it would have been perfectly true to say of David's pool that it was the most sterile stretch of open water in the whole world!

Now it is probably just as well that the majority of tales told by fishermen are usually recognized for what they usually are, for certainly a few strange stories wafted up from the riverside during that four-day period, and not *all* of them from rod-and-liners. Who can say what the result might have been had anyone really tried to check those stories out?

For Planny was coming along nicely, thank you, and in no time at all he had accumulated all the nastiness of quite a large number of easily devoured pike of all sizes. He had developed a taste for them. Also, he had picked up something of the unreasonable antagonism of a particularly unfriendly, yappy little dog whose master called for him in vain from the river bank until late into the fourth night.

On the fifth morning, having almost given up hope of ever seeing the curious creature again, David went down to the pool as usual. Planny was back, and much bigger! Not only had he put on a lot of weight but his capacity for learning had picked up too. The little dog had gone down (or rather *in*!) almost without a burp, and Planny's very efficient digestive system had proved only slightly superior to his "natural" talent for, well, *picking* brains...

But while the animal's hidden abilities were not so obvious, his growth assuredly was!

David gaped at the creature's size—almost two feet in diameter now—as it came sliding out of the reed-patch with the top three inches of its spongy, greyish-white bulk sticking up out of the water. The eyes were just below the surface, peering out liquidly at the boy on the bank. It is not difficult to guess what was going on in Planny's composite knowledge-cells... or brain... or ganglia... or whatever! The way he had been hiding in the reeds and the way he carefully came out of them undoubtedly highlighted a left-over characteristic from his earlier, minnow period; the gleam in his peculiar eyes (of which David was innocently unaware) was suspiciously like that glassiness, intense and snide, seen in the eyes of doggies as they creep up on the backsides of postmen; and there was also something of a very real and greedy *intent* in there somewhere. Need we mention the pike?

Up into the shallows Planny came, flattening a little as his body edged up out of the water, losing something of its buoyancy; and David—innocent David—mistakenly saw the creature's approach as nothing if not natural. After all, had he not saved the poor thing's life?—and might he not therefore expect Planny to display friendship and even loyalty and gratitude? Instinctively he reached our his hand...

Now dogs are usually loyal only to their rightful masters—and minnows are rarely loyal at all, except perhaps to other minnows. But pike? Why the pike is a notoriously unfriendly fish, showing never a trace of gratitude or loyalty to anyone...

Approximately one hundred and thirty yards away and half an hour later. Professor Lees and his wife rose up from their bed and proceeded to the kitchen where they always had breakfast. A rather pungent, stale-water smell had seemingly invaded the house; so that the scientist's wife, preceding her husband, sniffed suspiciously at the air, dabbing at her nose with the hem of her dressing gown as she opened the kitchen door and went in.

Her throbbing scream of horror and disbelief brought her husband in at the run through the open kitchen door a few seconds later. There was his wife, crouched defensively in a corner, fending off a hideously wobbly *something* with her bleeding, oddly dissolved and pulpy hands.

David's father did not stop to ponder what or why, fortunately he was a man of action. Having seen at a glance the destructive properties of Planny's weird acid make-up, he jumped forward, snatching the patterned cloth from the table as he went. Flinging the table-cloth over the bobbing, roughly globular thing on the floor, he hoisted it bodily into the air. Fortunately for the professor, Planny had lost much of his bulk in moisture-seepage during his journey from the pool, but even so the creature was heavy. Three quick steps took the scientist to the kitchen's great, old-fashioned all-night fire. Already feeling the acid's sting through the thin linen, he kicked open the heavy iron fire-door and bundled his wobbly, madly pulsating armful—table-cloth and all—straight in atop the glowing coals, slamming the door shut on it. Behind him his wife screamed out something ridiculous and fainted, and almost immediately—even though he had put his slippered foot against it—the door burst open and an awfully wounded Planny leapt forth in a hissing cloud of poisonous steam. Slimy and dripping, shrunken and mephitic, the creature wobbled drunkenly, dementedly about the floor; only to be bundled up again in the space of a few seconds, this time in the scientist's sacrificed dressing gown, and hurled once more to the fire. And this time, so as to be absolutely sure. David's father put his hands to the hot iron door, holding it firmly shut. He threw all his weight into the job, staying his ground until his fingers and palms, already blistered through contact with Planny's singular juices, blackened and cracked. Only then, and when the pressures from within ceased, did he snatch his steaming, monstrously damaged hands away...

It was only in some kind of blurred daze that Professor Lees managed to set the wheels of action in motion from that time onwards. Once the immediate panic had subsided a sort of shocked lethargy crept over him; but in spite of this he cleaned up his unconscious wife's bubbly hands as best he could, and his own—though that proved so painful he almost fainted himself—and then, somehow, he phoned for the doctor and the police.

Then, after a further minute or so, still dazed but remembering something of the strange things his wife had screamed before she fainted, David's father went upstairs to look for his son. When he found the boy's room empty he became once more galvanized into frantic activity. He began rushing about the house calling David's name before remembering his son's odd habit of the last month or so—how he would get up early in the morning and go off down to the pool before school.

As he left the house a police car was just polling up on the drive outside. He shouted out to the two constables, telling them they would find his wife in the house... would they look after her? Then, despite the fact that they called out after him for an explanation, he hurried off towards the copse.

At first the policemen were appalled by the loathsome stench issuing undiluted from the house; then, fighting back their nausea, they went in and began doing what they could to improve Mrs Lees' lot. The doctor arrived only a moment later. He could see instantly what was wrong—there had been some sort of accident with acid. Relieved at the arrival of this sure-handed professional, the bewildered policemen followed the scientist's tracks to the pool.

There they found him sitting at the pool-side with his head in his tattily bandaged hands. He had seen the slide on the stone in the pool; and, in a dazed sort of fashion, he had noted the peculiar, flattened *track* in the grass between the house and the copse. And then, being clever, totalling up these fragile facts, he had finally arrived at the impossible solution...

It all hinged, of course, on those mad things his wife had screamed before fainting. Now, thinking back on those things, David's father could see the connections. He *remembered* now that there had been a slide missing from his set. He recalled the way in which David had declared the flatworm—the *planarian* worm—on a certain slide to be alive.

Quite suddenly he took one hand from his face and shoved it into his mouth right up to the bandaged knuckles. Just for a moment his eyes opened up very wide; and then he let both his hands fall and turned his face up to the patient policemen.

"God... God... *God-oh-God!*" he said then. "My wife! She said... she said..."

"Yes, sir—" one of the officers prompted him, "what did she say?"

Aimlessly the professor got to his feet. "She said that—that it was sitting at the breakfast table—sitting there in David's chair—*and she said it called her Mummy!*"

1971

STRANGE ROOTS

David Case

No anthology featuring stories about transformation can be complete without a werewolf story by David Case (1937–2018). In the first half of the 1970s he produced a string of superb stories about lycanthropes, all of which appeared consecutively in instalments of *The Pan Book of Horror Stories*. Starting with "The Cell" in volume eleven and ending with "Among the Wolves" in volume fifteen, each story can justifiably claim to be a classic of the genre, and have today been gathered ("formed into a pack", one might say) in the excellent collection *The Cell and Other Transmorphic Tales* (2015). "Strange Roots" appeared in *The 14th Pan Book of Horror Stories* in 1973, having first been published in *Fengriffen and Other Stories* (1971).

David Francis Case was born in upstate New York in 1937, but moved to London in the early 1960s, where he spent the majority of his life until his passing in 2018. He wrote three short horror novels—*Fengriffen: A Chilling Tale* (1970), which was adapted into the Amicus film *And Now the Screaming Starts!* (1973), directed by Roy Ward Baker and starring Peter Cushing and Herbert Lom; *Wolf Tracks* (1980), another werewolf tale; and *The Third Grave* (1981). He also wrote a trio of Westerns—*Plumb Drillin'* (1976) (later reissued under the title *Gold Fever*); *Black Hats* (1981); and *The Fighting Breed* (1990).

The majority of his twenty-five or so short stories are collected in *Brotherly Love & Other Tales of Faith and Knowledge* (1990); *Pelican Cay & Other Disquieting Tales* (2010), the title story of which, having first appeared in the anthology *Dark Terrors 5* (2000), was nominated for a

World Fantasy Award in 2001; and an omnibus volume in the Masters of the Weird Tales series from Centipede Press (2015).

Like the previous story, "David's Worm", "Strange Roots" is a tale about the horrific results of scientific misconduct. Often described as "psycho-sexual horror", this is a dark, visceral story with a deeply unsettling atmosphere and a pay-off that hits you like a truck.

Anton Plotnikov was interested in werewolves.

He had been born of peasant stock in the Balkans, which undoubtedly stimulated this interest, but he had become a psychologist and therefore his interest took a scientific and rational turn, although traces of the ancient superstitions still lurked somewhere in his most primitive cells. Mainly, however, he sought scientific truth. Anton had left his unfortunate homeland after the last war and emigrated to England; took a well-paid job in research and married a passionate girl named Beta. They were reasonably happy. He bought, in due course, a fine house in the country and, with company funds, installed a small but efficient laboratory in the basement. It was understood that this laboratory would be used for the company's profit, of course, but since Anton was a valuable and brilliant scientist he was allowed a measure of freedom. This suited Anton very well, for he was a man who saw that research must not be limited, and in his spare time (and a great deal of the company's time, if truth be told) he began a comprehensive study of lycanthropy. This did not seem dishonest to Anton. His well-paid work involved investigation into the effects of chemical and glandular imbalance in mental disorders and Anton was convinced that the phenomenon of the werewolf was based on just that—that there were scientific and medical grounds behind the legend. From time to time he reported on his work, being careful not to use the word *werewolf* but to mention only the chemical-psychological aspects in learned but vague terms. Since he was far more intelligent than the company men who read his reports, this worked out well enough. His work progressed. He began to spend more and more time in the laboratory and his wife, who was truly passionate, began to take a series of lovers. This suited her splendidly. Anton worked on a labour of love, Beta loved laboriously and even the company, due to recent research, prospered.

There followed a series of important breakthroughs in the study of how bodily chemistry affects the behaviour of mankind. Gradually old prejudices broke down. Freud turned over ponderously in his grave. The psycho-analysts tore their hair out by the roots and moaned that Armageddon was come. Psychiatrists carried banners of protest through the streets. Shaggy students cheerfully joined the march, passionately defending the creaking knowledge that they were creatures driven by the traumas of adolescence, warped by society, inexorably motivated by events of the past. Because they had seen their mothers naked when they were three, they threw rocks at the police. Because the police had all dreamed of being marched upon by immoral women wearing boots, they arrested the students. Because the judge had once placed his penis in his sister's shoe, he fined them heavily. But through it all the research progressed. It became documented and understood that all forms of mental malfunction, save the minor fetishes, were caused by chemical imbalance. The students, no fools these, began to be converted, to throw stones at psychiatrists and plead in court that they were not guilty because their hormone secretions had ruled their behaviour. The judges took a tolerant view except when they had hangovers. Truth was beginning to conquer. But it was a long and difficult struggle. In the United States the psychiatrists lobbied in Congress, pressing for laws against this blasphemous research and finding direct relationships between glandular secretions and marihuana. The Congressmen seldom smoked marihuana but were well aware of the sluggish chemistry of their bodies and the lobby was defeated.

But only in America did the people actually believe in psychiatry and analysis, for there it had become a social thing, a status symbol. Once analysis was proven about as valid as astrology it became even more snobbish. After all, what could be more pretentious than squandering money on a myth? The analysts found a new prosperity for a time, until reverse snobbery followed and the wealthy types began to consult with their dustmen. They called them garbage collectors. The dustmen called themselves sanitary engineers, and were quite ready to lower their trash cans and take the woes of the world unto themselves. For, after all, what is it but garbage? So the dustmen became honoured and the analysts became a luxury of the middle-class. But that was America, where such things happen. The rest of the world had never believed in psychiatry anyway, and could not afford it.

Through it all, Anton Plotnikov worked on.

He was a physiological psychologist and understood that the functions of the mind were inseparable from those of the body. He had no desire to get wealthy clients on a couch. But eventually his work reached an impasse. He had gathered all possible data, his theories were formed, and it became necessary to advance along different lines—to observe rather than theorize, to experiment rather than gather information. For this experimentation he needed money. He needed supplies. Specifically, he needed a wolf...

Or rather, he required the secretions from the glands and blood of wolves. He put in a request to the company. He had not produced anything of value for some time and the company demanded further details. Anton supplied them. The company could see no possible profit motive in this line of research and turned his request down. Anton was annoyed and unhappy. He brooded. Eventually, unknown to the company and against their principles, he applied for a government grant. Complicated forms were sent to him by the appropriate agencies. He was asked to outline his work and did so. The government agencies requested further details and results and assured him his application was being considered. It was filed and forgotten. Anton waited impatiently. He continued to work as best he could and submitted, from time to time, further reports. Nothing happened. Finally Anton decided he could wait no longer. He took his own savings and determined to carry on unaided. He contacted a team of Canadian ecologists and arranged to receive the necessary secretions from wolves. They were willing to help. Their work involved knocking *canis lupis* out with tranquillizer pellets and clamping bands on the creatures' ears and it was not difficult to take samples of blood and hormone secretions in the process. Anton met a sinister fellow named Chowder who agreed to kidnap dogs for him. This was expensive, since he felt it necessary to use the oldest breeds of dog such as greyhounds and Afghans. But, once decided, Anton gritted his teeth and paid out his hard-earned money and in due course found his laboratory stocked with caged canines. The samples arrived from Canada. He was ready to continue his work. He spent more and more time in his laboratory. The company sent him curt reminders that his work was falling behind and Beta, extremely displeased to find their savings gone, took more lovers. Anton noticed nothing, concentrating on his work. Or chose to ignore it, it was all the same to his wife. And still, from time to time, Anton sent progress reports to the various government agencies and hoped and worked and worked...

Anton's reports did not go entirely unnoticed. There was a bright lad named Smith in the government agency who took a certain interest and a definite amusement in the reports which trickled in. Smith had no Balkan ancestry, but was a devoted fan of Peter Cushing. He actually read the reports before filing them. Rather more improbably, he actually understood them. And, incredibly, he even took a few notes. These are a few examples:

Lycanthropy: The supposed power of a human being to transform into a wolf. Belief in werewolves.

Lycorexia: A morbid pathological condition in which one has a fixation that he is actually a wolf. He has a raging hunger for raw flesh, he mimics the movements of the animal, he howls and snarls. For practical purposes, he is the wolf. There is glandular disturbance and symptoms sometimes diagnosed as possession.

Virilism: Technically, the appearance in a female of male physical and sexual characteristics. Hirsuteness. Plotnikov believes that this term is applied only to the female because it is obviously more noticeable in them, but that a male may suffer from the same disease without attracting attention, being merely considered as exceptionally virile and masculine. There is reason to believe that this glandular disturbance may be directly related to the so-called criminal type theory. This, however, is not Plotnikov's field, and is mentioned only in passing.

Pathology: Investigation of structural and functional changes in tissue, caused by disease.

Pathomorphism: Abnormality of bodily structure.

Pathomimesis: Simulation of disease found in hysteria.

To sum up: It is Plotnikov's belief that certain chemical imbalances (substantiated by recent research into psychological disorders) were responsible for a glandular malfunction which caused the symptoms of virilism and lycorexia to appear simultaneously. This combination gave rise to the werewolf legend. Plotnikov seems to have kept an open mind here, and mentions other possible causes. For example, the last of the Neanderthal men must have seemed monstrous creatures to emerging Homo Sapiens. However, he feels that the legend is rooted in more recent times and takes the view that, due to various conditions and factors, the above mentioned glandular malfunctions were commonplace.

My viewpoint: It seems to me that his theory is valid. However, I can find no practical application for his work. His later reports indicate that he is actually doing laboratory work on certain substances derived from living wolves and hopes to isolate, or even create, the chemical which caused the disease. This is rather fascinating. However, it still seems to have no practical value, even if he succeeds.

Unless he wants to create a werewolf, ha ha.

Anton's research, at first, proved negative.

He injected dog after dog with the various derivatives and serums he had created and found them unaffected. He was desolate. He could not see where he was blundering. But he pressed on. He could not use the same dog more than once, for that would destroy the experimental control, and was forced to employ Chowder once again. His funds sank to a new low. The dogs thrived with healthy (but normal) appetites. His wife thrived with healthy sexual appetites. Anton, who had always slumped, slumped more and found that his hair was rapidly departing. Chowder demanded more money. The company sent him an ultimatum which he tore up in a rare rage. He worked on doggedly with test tube and hypodermic, despairing but never quite losing hope. He was haggard and gaunt and, indeed, resembled a mad scientist in a bad film, holding a bubbling test tube up and regarding it with a red-rimmed eye; leering as he approached a dog with a dripping needle; talking to himself as he stirred and mixed his various brews.

And then, quite by accident, as often proves the case in scientific advance, a startling factor came to light...

Anton had just received a new greyhound from Chowder and was leading it to a cage. His mind was preoccupied and he inadvertently passed close by one of the other occupied cages, containing a vague sort of terrier which had been injected several days before and shown no effects, ill or otherwise. As he led the greyhound past, the terrier suddenly thrust his muzzle through the bars and nipped the greyhound on the flank. The greyhound spun, snarling, but Anton managed to restrain it and haul it away from the aggressor. He examined the wound and found it superficial; cleansed it and applied a disinfectant and left the greyhound in a cage. He thought little of this, at the time. He was busily at work on a new serum. This serum would not be ready for a few days and, in the meanwhile, the greyhound was not injected. It stood behind its bars and regarded Anton with a solemn and baleful eye. Then it lay down and slept. Anton worked into the night until at last, exhausted, he left the laboratory and went to bed. Beta was already asleep, smiling in her dreams. Anton crawled in carefully, so as not to disturb her. This was not because he was solicitous for her slumber as much as selfish for his own. He was well aware that his wife had rather over-developed sexual urges and knew that, if she should awaken, she would undoubtedly demand servicing. Now, Anton loved his wife, no doubt of that, but his love was not inclined towards the physical. He loved scientifically or rationally and could not stand up to the rigours of sexual relations as frequently as Beta required them. Therefore, he slipped carefully in beside her and rested his weary head on the pillow. He thought he was too exhausted to sleep, but after a while he drifted off. He tossed restlessly as his tired muscles began to relax. And then he began to dream. His dreams, as his waking thoughts, invariably centred on lycanthropy. He stood in the land of Morpheus and listened to the howlings of tormented werewolves. He trembled in delight and fear. The howling grew louder, closer. He trembled more. His delight faded and his fear increased. It occurred to the sleeping scientist that the werewolves were hungry and that he was alone. It was a dark world of twisted barren trees and deep shadows and a full white moon. Anton ran through his dreams. He fled madly, with gnarled limbs snapping at his face and tangled roots gripping his ankles. He was panting and sweating. He could not run very fast. The howling was behind him, following him and drawing ever closer. He came to a shattered ridge surmounted by a solitary, mangled tree. It was an oak tree, hideously malformed. Anton decided he must climb that tree and seek sanctuary in the high branches while the werewolves raged below. He began to climb. The rough bark scraped his hands, his feet slipped seeking purchase, gravity hauled him back. He elevated himself by scant inches. The wolves were in full cry. Dark forms shot through the shadows, he saw the gleam of a yellow eye, a flash of fangs. He screamed and drew himself upwards, knowing he was too late, too slow.

And then the werewolves were upon him...

Anton cried out in the grip of fang and talon.

The wolves dragged him down from the tree. He rolled in the earth, screaming, as ravenous jaws tore him asunder and savage throats gulped down his flesh. He beat with feeble arms and drew his knees up to his chest, and wondered how long it would take him to die.

Then his wife said, "Wake up!"

Anton opened his eyes.

Anton stared, unbelievingly, at the metamorphosis.

Beta was leaning over him, shaking him.

Gradually the transformation registered in his mind. Fang and claw became well-manicured fingernails, fiendish haunches were well-turned soft flanks, hairy chests were exquisite mounds capped with delightful nipples, slavering jaws were ripe red lips. And blood lust was... well, just lust, he thought, with a groan.

"Wake up," she demanded.

"Not tonight, darling," Anton whimpered.

"What?"

"I'm really frightfully tired, dearest."

Beta stared at him with a pretty frown and suddenly, shockingly, the howling came again, transcending the realm of nightmare to register in his waking mind. Anton's eyes leaped wide, bewildered.

"What is it?" he asked.

Beta waited a moment, peering at him; ascertaining that he was fully awake now.

"One of those damned brutes in the laboratory, obviously," she said. "What else? You'll have to do something, Anton. I can't sleep with that horrid howling."

Anton sighed with relief.

"Of course, dearest," he said, thankful that she had awakened him for something less than carnal needs. It was far easier to descend to the laboratory and administer a sedative than to ascend his wife and administer the orgastic tranquillizer. He got up and tied his dressing-gown around himself; slid his feet into well-worn slippers. He felt a chill as the perspiration of his nightmare evaporated. Beta curled up under the covers and Anton moved from the room. He was fully awake now. As he reached the top of the stairs, the howling sounded once again, and quite suddenly Anton felt another chill—a chill which had nothing to do with evaporation as it clambered up the segments of his spine.

He stood, gripping the banister, and looked down into the darkness below.

Once again the howling sounded.

It was not the howling of a dog.

Anton knew.

Anton had never heard that sound before, but somewhere deep in his primary cells he knew.

It was the cry of the wolf...

*

The savage cry faded away, seeping into the fabric of the house and running out into the night, but the fierce echo still reverberated in Anton's heart. His scientist's mind was able to baffle and channel the sound, directing it along the course of reason, but in his Balkan heart the drums of fear were beating. He stood very still. His hand gripped the railing. He was aware of a clock ticking in a recess down the hall and the slight creaking of the bed as his wife shifted her position. Then he began to tremble. This reaction was symptomatic of two emotions, far different and yet inextricably linked. There was the fear and there was also surging joy. He became a man divided, his sentience separated by the flat, calm plane of reason, dissected cleanly and sharply so that his two halves were linked only by the connecting chain between those two emotions, breaking through the calm surface of the rational division exactly as the chain of an anchor runs down from the ship to the dark anchor at the depths. Joy was the ship, riding above the deep, light and bouyant. Fear was the anchor, heavy and cold, slowly turning far below. The sails of the ship billowed and strained as joy sought to run gaily before the wind of success but that solid anchor restrained it on the groaning chain. And Anton was restrained as these antagonistic elements waged their tug of war within the corporal shell. He stood trembling for long moments. He was well aware of the conflict but could not join in, could not take sides in the struggle. He was an objective observer, no more, and his observation was hampered, the bathysphere of reason could not descend to the depths of the anchor. The pressures were too great, the cold too severe, the amorphous submarine creatures too formidable. No light was reflected at that depth. The clock ticked on, the bed was silent now. Anton told himself that he was about to realize the fruits of his labours, the truth of his theory, the verification of his predictions, and these thoughts sent the wind at gale force behind the anchored vessel. But then the cry sounded yet again, wild and piercing, and the anchor plummeted down. The chain, fully extended, creaked and strained. The anchor was rebounding, threatening to drag the ship beneath the surface and send Anton in mad thoughtless flight.

Then the chain snapped.

Fear settled slowly into the mire and Anton was free.

Anton went very calmly down to the laboratory...

He opened the door very slowly, just a crack, without fear now, but with great caution. It was dark inside. The door scraped slightly and the sounds of carnage increased for a moment, horrible growlings and violent snarls. Anton waited, holding the door firmly, until the noise subsided a bit and then slipped his hand in to fumble for the light switch. The flesh crawled up his forearm, he half expected powerful jaws to close on his hand and his fingers felt like icicles in the process of melting, the drips running back down his arm. Then he pressed the switch and bright, overhead lights burst on. There was an abrupt and profound silence in the sudden glare. The silence was somehow more menacing than the sounds, with the sinister and minatory implications of soundlessness—the silent stalk, the controlled savagery awaiting prey. Anton risked an eye around the corner of the door. Then he sighed with relief.

The cages were all intact.

He opened the door further and looked about the laboratory. The dogs were cringing, every aspect of their bearing implying terror, backed in the corner of their cages, tails curled between their legs, necks bristling, all facing towards the back of the room. Anton looked along the line of their fearful vision. There was one dog which was not cringing, and Anton cringed when he looked upon it.

It was the greyhound.

And it was terrible.

The brute, frozen in sudden illumination, stared back at him. It had been fixed in the instant of a snarl, lips drawn back in a rictus. It was hideous and it was, somehow, changed. Its coat was shaggier and coarser, its eyes were wild, its fangs yellow and dripping. It poised on coiled haunches. Anton felt shelves of horror slough down his back. And then the beast sprang. It crashed against the bars and fell back. The bars were stout. They shook but held. The brute sprang again. The cage quivered. Again it fell back, snarling now, and the other dogs began to whine and whimper pitifully. Anton went into the room and closed the door behind him and for a long time he stood there looking at the thing which was no longer quite a dog...

Anton was not thinking logically.

He thought only that he must somehow stop that terrible howling. He moved to the work bench and prepared a powerful sedative. His hands were remarkably calm. The beast continued to throw itself against the bars, slobbering with bloodlust. Anton did not dare approach the cage. He considered, thinking carefully, and finally fastened the hypodermic to the end of a measuring stick, the needle extending beyond the end. Then he advanced, holding this makeshift weapon like a spear. The hound howled in a frenzy as he drew near, obviously seeing Anton as raw meat. Froth flew in heavy shards from its jaws. Anton approached as near as he could and extended the stick. The dog ignored it, straining its terrible muzzle through the bars, attempting to reach Anton. The needle slipped into the brute's shoulder and Anton pressed in, injecting the sedative, as the dog spun, snapping at the wound. The powerful jaws splintered the stick and the hypodermic hung for a moment from the shaggy shoulder. Then it dropped out as the beast renewed its attack on the bars. Its violence reached a new peak of fury before gradually subsiding. The drug took effect. The dog's motions became uncertain, its legs splayed. Presently it sat down, curling in a circle, and laid its head on its forepaws. Those glowing yellow eyes began to close. And all the while, even as the lids came down, it looked with hatred and hunger at Anton.

It took great courage to open that cage.

The dog was unconscious, no doubt of that, but it took great courage nonetheless for a man of Balkan peasant ancestry to enter that cage. But he did it. It was necessary, he knew, to take samples of blood and glandular secretions, and his hands were still incredibly calm and quiet as he did so. Then he locked the cage again and took his samples back to the work bench. And only then did the fact—the startling fact—strike him. He stared at the test tubes and then he turned to stare at the dog. He realized that the greyhound had not been injected with any form of serum. For an instant he was stricken with regret, thinking that the creature had gone mad with rabies or some other canine disease and then he remembered that the dog had been bitten by the terrier. His mind very precisely followed the steps of scientific reasoning. The terrier had been injected with the serum but had not reacted as predicted. The terrier had bitten the greyhound. The greyhound had reacted exactly as predicted for the terrier. Then precise reasoning shattered and the truth struck him like an axe between the eyes.

He had discovered a chemical imbalance which was infectious.

Contagious madness...

And horror...

From that point, all further investigation fell in place exactly as Anton had predicted. He was delighted; saw himself unravelling the dark secrets through which his ancestors trembled in the Transylvanian nights. There had been a solitary oversight in his former work and, now that aleatory circumstances had bridged that gap his work followed a logical and evident trail. The aggressive whim of a dog had founded knowledge. Anton's error was in overlooking the necessary intermediate state; in failing to see that the substance might need to mature in the living tissue of a host, combining with saliva and blood and hormones which acted as a catalyst and changed the substance from dormant to malignant. Now that problem was resolved, Anton knew, his work could continue quickly, results would be rapid, perhaps even financial aid would be forthcoming. He decided to submit a new report as soon as the next stage of investigation was completed.

In the morning, the greyhound was awake and placid. No traces of the madness were visible and the other dogs no longer regarded it with fear. Anton rubbed his hands together at this discovery, this proof that the disease waxed and ebbed in accordance with a cycle. It was predictable by inductive reasoning and explained the old legends of werewolves undergoing metamorphosis when the moon was full but, more important, it seemed to prove that his experiment was valid—that no unidentified virus had caused the madness but that it had been purely chemical. He continued with his work. He spent a great deal of time analysing the substances drawn from the greyhound and in due course discovered that it was the saliva which acted as the catalyst. He experimented with the saliva and found, further, that he was unable to create a serum which was effective in the initial injection stage—that it could only be transferred from one living organism to another in a blood–saliva–blood cycle. This complicated his work somewhat, in that he had to persuade the dogs to bite one another. But he managed. The laboratory became a bedlam, a howling house of horrors, as, from time to time, several dogs went mad simultaneously. Anton grew accustomed to it. His wife did not, but after a few days of objection seized upon the noise as an excellent excuse for spending nights away from home. Her love life prospered. And, unhindered by her protests, Anton's work advanced. He placed two infected dogs in the same cage and waited for the madness to come upon them. However, the smaller dog went mad first and tore the larger asunder. In a very short time only a few scraps of hide, shattered bones and evil, dark stains remained to testify to the larger beast's existence. Anton saw that the cycle was affected by the animal's weight and metabolism. He constructed a double cage, separated by a sliding door which he could operate from a distance and put an infected dog in each side. One was an Alsatian, the other a Staffordshire terrier. The terrier went berserk first and the Alsatian cringed and quivered. But several hours later the Alsatian, too, went mad. Anton drew the separation from between the cages. The two savage brutes were at one another instantly, with a ferocity both fascinating and appalling. The terrier, bred to fight, retained its inherited ability despite the madness; went low and slashed across and the Alsatian was down. The terrier tore at his opponent, ripping great mouthfuls of flesh from it while it still lived—and, while it still lived, the Alsatian continued to tear at his killer's belly. Anton winced and felt his stomach churn as he realized this was more than a fight to the death; realized that the fight was incidental to the fact; realized that the two dogs were eating each other alive!

He had to hurry from the room and vomit.

When he returned the Alsatian was dead.

The terrier was eating the body. The terrier's belly had been torn out and his entrails hung down in slippery coils and, from time to time, he mistakenly tore a mouthful from his own intestines as he fiendishly satisfied the mad hunger.

Anton went right back out and vomited again.

Two weeks after the first attack, the greyhound again underwent metamorphosis. The other infected beasts followed similar patterns, although the time cycle varied. Anton calculated and observed and made a fairly accurate chart and drew a graph correlating weight to frequency of madness. When this was done he projected the figures to include the normal weight of a man, and saw that the cycle would complete itself approximately once every month in an average-sized human being. This projection pleased him. It was in accord with the full moon cycle of the legend. He carried this line of prediction further, into unsubstantiated theory, and saw the possibility that the moon was more than a coincidence. Lunatics are a fact. A man often feels strange urges, looking at the full moon. The glandular secretions can be stimulated in many ways and, just as the adrenal glands release hormones when a creature is angry or frightened, so might the substance of madness be released by the mood of the moon. As soon as this theory had taken form, Anton was excited. He was also frustrated, for obviously he would be unable to prove it—could not deliberately inject madness into a human. But he felt it to be true and, taking it as the initial premise, he logically pursued possibilities and concluded that, in a human, the metamorphosis would be even more startling than in a dog. A man can reason and a mind can be caused to reason in twisted patterns and the process, in man, would be psychological as well as physical. In the ability to reason lies the capacity for insanity. In the dogs the disease was purely chemical but in the mind of a man...

Anton shivered.

He had a distinct image, behind closed eyelids, of a peasant walking the rolling hills in the light of a full moon—a peasant who had been bitten, some time before, by a wild dog. He saw this unfortunate man pause; saw him stir restlessly, a captive of urges beyond and below his comprehension; saw him tilt his head back and gaze up at the moon. The white light washed his upthrust face. He shuddered. He frowned, wondering what illness was upon him. He was unable to take his eyes from the moon. It hung above him like a slender disc of silver, compelling, demanding... inexorable. The peasant sank to the ground, on all fours. His face was still thrust back. Strange sounds emanated from his tightening vocal chords, he felt his teeth, they seemed too large for his mouth; felt his fingers, crooked, the nails too long. But his mind was that of a man, and slowly he realized what was happening to him—understood the unspeakable curse upon him. And in that moment he was no longer a peasant. He was not a wolf, but he was something other than a man. And through it all his tortured mind continued to work, his reason forced into alien channels, his thoughts misshapen, mangled beyond evil, beyond human comprehension.

And then he would howl...

And presently another peasant would come along—a peasant who had not been savaged by a wild dog—with hurried steps through the night. And the one who was no longer quite a man would be waiting.

And a legend would be born anew.

Anton shook his head violently to clear these hideous images from his mind.

It was a thing he would never see, he told himself.

After all, he could not experiment on a man.

Could he?

Anton completed a long and detailed report and sent it off to the government agency where, eventually, it came into the hands of the bright, young lad named Smith. Smith was certainly no fool. In fact, he was even more intelligent than the shaggy students who carry banners in protests. Smith realized instantly that this was an incredible discovery. He lowered the report and stared into space for a while. His lips moved. He mumbled, "Contagious glandular malfunction," several times, letting it sink in. And then he drew up a brief report of his own and sent it to the head of his department. This gentleman knew that Smith was bright and had nothing else to do anyway, and he actually read the report. He nodded and hummed and smoked his pipe, but he read it. He read it over a second time and then a third. Presently he understood what it meant. His mind was ponderous but large. It turned slowly but remorselessly and, like a millstone, ground concepts into a fine powder of their separate parts. And when his grist-mill of a mind had finished, he applied himself to the all-important problem of rearranging the parts into a whole which would be profitable.

Well, men being what they are, and departmental heads of government agencies more so, he came to his decision. One assumes he was guided by patriotism. He sent Anton's report and Smith's report and an explanatory (although totally incomprehensible) covering note of his own, along to a certain unnamed research building. This building, and the agency it housed, was unnamed because the general public, not wise and patriotic like the heads of departments, is less tolerant and even inclined to stage protest marches against such agencies.

He sent it, in other words, to the biological warfare department...

Alvin Johnstone, who was a secret agent or spy of sorts, left his motorcar in his private parking-place and entered the unnamed agency building which housed the central office. The laboratories were located elsewhere but within this edifice the decisions were taken, the judgements made, the results coordinated. Johnstone passed through the system of clearance and identification and went on up to the Chief's office. The Chief had summoned him. Johnstone did not mind working for this particular agency and knew how to calm the troubled waters of the conscience with the soothing oils of patriotism; how to rationalize that, if he did not do the job, someone else would. The Chief, on the other hand, had never felt the need for justifying his offices and knew, without really thinking about it, that expediency outweighed ethical and humanitarian ideals. He was an organizer, a practical man of the type necessary to direct scientists, whom everyone knows are impractical. He did not look practical. He looked more like an auctioneer, a jolly fellow who took snuff and wore handpainted ties. He chuckled a great deal. But beneath this façade he was pragmatic and efficient and knew the value of biological warfare—believed it superior to more conventional methods of destruction because it did not destroy the wealth of the enemy country, left the cities standing and the treasures intact and killed only living things which, after all, are only of evanescent value.

The Chief was glancing at a report when Johnstone entered. He was wearing one of his favourite ties. It had a woodpecker on it. He had a pencil in one hand and was making his own notes to add to the file. He made methodical notes. He glanced up from under a shaggy brow.

"Ah, Johnstone," he said.

"Morning, Chief."

Johnstone took a seat.

"We seem to have an interesting thing here," said the Chief. "Don't know if it will prove feasible for us or not. Not really our field. Not virology, actually. But it's a new concept and there appears to be no other agency to deal with it. We might have to set up a special branch if it proves worth while. In the meanwhile I think we'd better look into it thoroughly."

Johnstone waited, watching the woodpecker.

The Chief gathered the reports together and turned them; shoved them across to Johnstone. Johnstone winced at the thickness of the pile.

"Shall I read in depth?" he asked.

"Skip the technical stuff for now. Probably wouldn't understand that anyway. Just get the main idea. Rather amusing, really. Don't know if this Plotnikov fellow knows what he has here. Not sure I do, myself. But, not to put too fine a point on it, the man seems to have discovered a method of creating, well, yes, ah, werewolves..."

Johnstone looked at the Chief.

The Chief looked right back at him.

"Well, yes, really," he said.

Johnstone read the reports.

After a few pages he found his interest growing to the extent that he read more than he skimmed. The Chief took some snuff and continued to jot down ideas on his pad. He did not sneeze when he took snuff. Had he sneezed he would have used handpainted handkerchiefs. Presently Johnstone stacked the papers neatly and looked up.

"I see," said Johnstone.

"I thought you might."

"It seems truly horrible."

"But will it be effective? That's the point. No sense in horror just for the hell of it, eh?"

Johnstone had no reply to that.

"However, if the information in these reports is correct, and if it can be adapted for use against human beings... well, I've been jotting down a few of the advantages which come to mind. Have a look."

He turned his pad towards Johnstone. Johnstone looked at the neat outline.

This was the list of advantages:

One: The disease can only be transferred by contact, so it eliminates the danger of feedback or blowback inherent in germ warfare. One would have to merely isolate the enemy and wait for results.

Two: Chemicals would be far safer to handle than virus. Even our laboratory boys are worried about the possibility of one of their pet germs escaping, but a chemical can't very well escape.

Three: There is likelihood that biological warfare may be outlawed by international agreement. This weapon, being chemical (like tear-gas) would not fall under the outlawed definitions.

Four: There is no way to immunize a population against glandular imbalance. For every virus we create the enemy is working on antidotes and vice versa. But there can be no preventive defence against this weapon. Treatment and cure will undoubtedly be developed but can only be that—a cure, not a prophylactic.

Five: This weapon can be justified as humanitarian because it is not lethal. The enemy will kill themselves, of course, but that's hardly our fault, eh? And at first it won't even be recognized as a weapon.

Six: Perhaps the greatest advantage of all will be a side effect in the minds of the enemy. The panic, the fear, the disintegration of their culture as a legend comes alive in their streets. Especially when dealing with our Balkan friends, eh? All those superstitious Slavs...

Johnstone passed the notepad back.

He made no comment.

The Chief said, "You know, of course, that we've long toyed with similar ideas. LSD in the water supplies, that sort of stuff. But that's cumbersome and impractical, almost impossible to manage. This is different. If this disease proves contagious all the difficulties are removed. We would only have to inject a few prisoners of war and send them back across the lines. Or even inject a few of our own men—volunteers, one supposes—and send them in. They wouldn't develop the symptoms, but they'd carry the disease. And the fear."

"I can't imagine many men volunteering for that."

"Hum. Well, perhaps it wouldn't be necessary to let them know all the details, eh?"

Johnstone, patriotic rather than expedient, winced.

"Of course, we might use animals as carriers..."

Johnstone nodded.

"But an animal might well wander back across the lines, you know. I wouldn't fancy that."

Johnstone stared at the woodpecker and said, "I don't much like this idea, Chief."

The Chief chose to ignore that.

"Anyway," he said, "I want you to call on this Plotnikov. Get a general impression. I'm having a thorough check-up done on the man. He's a foreigner, you know. Have a look at some of these dogs. Find out if the serum can be taken orally. Things like that."

"Right," said Johnstone.

He stood up.

"Oh, Johnstone..."

Johnstone turned back.

"Better eat some garlic and carry a crucifix, eh? Ho ho ho. I can just imagine all those communist Slavs sitting in the wine cellars while a plague of werewolves howls through the streets. Scare hell out of 'em, eh?"

The Chief was chuckling. Johnstone left. The Chief took some snuff.

Anton, who would have been troubled had he known where his report had been directed was, at the moment, troubled instead by his wife's absence. Anton had laboured through the night and, by morning, completed analysis of a skin sample taken from an infected animal. The results had been enlightening. He had discovered a great amount of porphyrias in the infected cells, a substance which, in excess, caused human skin to be particularly sensitive to sunlight. In the extreme form of this condition, Gunther's disease, the victim has flesh hideously corrugated from sunburn, sprouts unnaturally coarse hair, and his teeth are discoloured to a reddish hue. The relation between such unfortunate sufferers and the appearance legend attributes to werewolves was obvious, and Anton was well pleased with his discovery. He was so pleased, in fact, that he decided to relax for the rest of the day. He left the laboratory in a fine mood. He felt like talking. He felt so fine he was not even loath to perform his marital duties, and went up to the bedroom. But Beta was not there and the bed had not been slept in. Anton stood in the doorway for a moment, disappointed and confused. It occurred to him that his wife had not been home very much at all during the last few weeks; that she had stayed out many nights without even mentioning where she had been. He frowned as he realized this, and regretted that he'd been so engrossed in his work that he hadn't fully appreciated the fact before. Anton, in his way, loved his wife. It had never occurred to him that there was any danger of losing her, and certainly he had not questioned the state of her fidelity, but now terrible doubts assailed him. He sank down on the bed and passed a hand across his brow. He fancied he could remember little danger signals, small changes in Beta which had registered and been stored below the level of actual comprehension but which came clustering to awareness now. He remembered seeing her come home several times, smiling and satisfied, her movement gracefully tired, exactly as she had appeared in the early days of their marriage, before Anton's sexual prowess had ebbed. And Beta had not even made demands on his services during the last weeks, which had seemed a relief at the time but now seemed minatory. Anton began to brood. He felt helpless. He had no idea of how to behave in such circumstances. He was a polite man and hated unpleasant scenes and accusations—feared to let on that he knew, let alone to issue an ultimatum. Beta might scorn an ultimatum, might leave him if he attempted to disrupt her affairs. It was very frustrating. Anton sat there on the unused bed and he brooded and he brooded. He was still brooding when Alvin Johnstone arrived...

Beta Plotnikov turned over languidly and kissed her current lover. He was, she thought, the best of her long line of lovers, although she always thought that about the latest one. It was a satisfying way to think. Her lover's name was Hancock and he was a robust and virile gentleman, a physical education instructor and ex-paratrooper. He was well-built and strong. He was not very intelligent. In fact, truth be known, he was slightly moronic. But that suited Beta admirably. It provided a complete contrast with her husband, who was slight and slumping but highly intelligent. It provided the best of both worlds, as far as Beta, passionate but none too bright herself, could see. Hancock grunted when she kissed him.

"I'll have to be off now, darling," she said.

"Uh," said Hancock.

"Miss me?"

"Uh."

"Love me?"

"Uh."

"Think I'm beautiful?"

"Not exactly an eyesore."

Compliments came seldom from Hancock. Beta kissed him gratefully. Then she swung her long legs over the edge of the bed and sat up. Hancock scratched his geometrically muscled belly. He watched her dress. He seemed slightly confused by the whole thing. He had never, despite his sinews and muscle, had much success with women. But Beta had responded instantly to his very first grunt and he was still, vaguely, trying to figure out why; whether he had mysteriously become irresistible or whether there were nymphomaniac factors involved. He wondered, also, about the husband.

"Listen," he said.

Beta listened, perhaps expecting another compliment.

"What about your husband?"

"What?"

"Doesn't he wonder where you sleep?"

"Oh, he only thinks about his work."

"That's funny," said Hancock, who never thought about his own work, even while working.

"He's not suspicious, don't worry."

"Not worried. Just wondered."

"Anton doesn't even notice that I'm gone," said Beta.

But he had, he had...

"Then I understand," said Alvin Johnstone, as they came up from the laboratory, "that the initial attack follows within hours of being bitten and a cycle develops subsequently, but the disease is continuously infectious. Is that right?"

"Yes, that's correct," Anton said.

They moved into the library-study. Anton looked about vaguely, not accustomed to visitors and uncertain as to the etiquette involved. He shifted his meagre weight about. Johnstone leaned against a bookcase. Johnstone had been very subtle, even after discovering that Plotnikov was hardly versed enough in social intercourse to recognize the difference, and now he debated the advisability of several diverse approaches. They were silent for some time.

At last Anton said, "If I'd known you were coming, sir, I could have arranged for a demonstration. As it is, I have no uninfected canines at present..."

"Oh, we don't doubt the truth of your reports."

"I'm pleased that interest has been aroused in my work. I... I wonder... just which government department are you representing?"

"Oh, research. General research. We haven't actually assigned your work yet. Haven't decided in which branch it should be included. Not a common field, as you may well imagine."

Anton smiled. Then, immediately, he looked worried.

"But you do think I'll get a grant?"

"Oh, yes. Yes, I should think so. A great deal depends on my report which, I might say, will be favourable."

"Oh, thank you."

"Perhaps a grant from..." Johnstone paused, smiled. "Perhaps medical research. In the stricter sense. But tell me... how would your serum affect a human being?"

Anton, unsuspecting, said, "Well, in theory, that is just what I am seeking to prove. That the legend of the lycanthrope has pathological roots, and that, in the past, this disease was not uncommon. Now, of course, it is very rare indeed. I can't honestly claim my studies will be of medical value, you know. Oh, there are—one hears of—isolated instances from time to time. But they are seldom investigated. Prejudice and scientific incredulity and fashionable scepticism combine against truth in this case..."

Anton paused and peered at Johnstone. Johnstone looked very interested, tilting his head in concentration, and Anton began to lose his nervousness as he spoke of a topic close to his heart and mind.

"There are many, oh so many, cases recorded in history, of course. And in what is now thought of as mythology. Lycaon, transformed into a wolf by Zeus—that is possibly the first known example. Odysseus' men transmuted into swine. Even in the Bible we have Nebuchadnezzar thinking himself an ox and eating grass—although that is more properly termed boanthropy, it is simply a variant symptom of the disease. Oh yes, there are many instances one might quote. However, as I say, the disease is no longer common, if it exists at all. It can hardly be a medical study..."

"Oh, it exists," said Johnstone.

"Oh?" said Anton.

"You have created it," said Johnstone.

And he smiled politely.

In due course Anton's limited social sense sent a message to his mind. He offered his guest a seat. Johnstone took it, pulling his sharply creased trousers up, smiling all the while. Anton sat opposite. He fidgeted. He alternately smiled and frowned. It occurred to him to offer a drink, but he did not know where, or even if, his wife kept alcohol in the house. But Johnstone seemed perfectly at ease, perfectly satisfied with the situation and the development of the interview, and eventually his attitude caused Anton to relax a bit. Johnstone smoked. Anton hastened to fetch an ashtray; could not find one and dashed back to the laboratory to return with a culture tray. Johnstone deposited ash with self-confidence, like a Roman casting salt over the ruins of Carthage.

"But if your serum, as it stands, were administered to a human? Would the effect be the same, or similar, to that with the dogs?"

Anton nodded slowly.

"In theory, yes. The adreno-salivary effect would cause hormone secretions which, in turn, would cause the victim to undergo mental and physical symptoms. His metabolism, growth, behaviour would all be affected and he would, I believe, think himself a wolf... or a wolf man. I must confess that I shudder at the thought. Some inherited fear passed down chemically through the genes, perhaps." Anton looked slightly sheepish. "And yet, despite this revulsion, I have always felt myself drawn to study such morbid pathogenic conditions. Man has strange, perverse motivations, I fear."

Johnstone nodded knowledgeably.

"Of course, we can't know for certain. I mean, we can't actually experiment with a man."

"Um. I wonder."

Anton raised his brows.

"In the name of science..."

Anton's brows went higher and higher.

"A volunteer, of course."

"Good heavens, I couldn't do that. Why... why, it would be monstrous!"

Johnstone looked placid.

"You do understand that it must be transferred via living saliva. Surely no man would volunteer to savage another? Or, worse, to submit to the infected bite, knowing the expected results? Surely not..."

"Oh, it might be arranged. For the good of science." Johnstone looted sharply at Anton. "And for the good of the country," he added. "You have not, perhaps, realized the potential value of your discovery as a weapon..."

Anton was appalled.

"I... I don't know... I don't think I could allow myself to work on a morbific in a practical sense..."

"Um. It was just a thought, you understand."

Anton nodded.

"Just a casual thought. Quite natural, really. I mean, one always does think first of one's country, does one not?"

Johnstone's glance pinned Anton like a butterfly on a display board. Anton squirmed. He had never thought much of his country, or any country. But he had thought often of a government grant. Very slowly and uncertainly and tentatively, he nodded.

"What I mean," said Johnstone, softly, "in war, things are sometimes justified which normally... you do understand? Against an enemy, a threat to our happiness and freedom and way of life... You do see what I mean?"

Anton, in the grip of doubts, not fully understanding, still fixed on the pinpoints of Johnstone's gaze, continued to move his head up and down.

Then Johnstone broke the spell.

"However, we needn't discuss that for the moment. It was just an idle thought that occurred to me. Continue with your good work and I'll submit my report and we'll try to get you some money."

He stood up. Anton jumped up, relieved to be freed from the pins. He walked to the door with Johnstone and they shook hands. Johnstone left smiling. Anton looked after him. Anton was not smiling. Anton had never before known that it was acceptable to treat one's enemies outside one's moral code. It was a novel and intriguing concept. Of course, Anton had never had an enemy. He stood there in the open doorway while Johnstone got in his car and drove off. Then he stepped back and started to close the door; paused as his wife's car came down the road and turned into the drive. Anton leaned against the door. His wife was smiling behind the wheel. She looked very satisfied and happy. Anton had never had an enemy before...

Beta came up to the door with that leisurely long-legged stride, kissed her husband *en passant*, and walked down the hallway. Anton turned, watching the swing of her hips with an interest unusual for him and turmoil in his mind. Beta went up the stairs. Anton started to close the door, then paused once again as that sinister character named Chowder emerged from the trees fringing the drive. Chowder had orange hair and, for a moment, Anton believed that a gigantic sunflower had appeared on the scene. Chowder was facing in the other direction, rubbing his corrugated neck and staring after Johnstone's car. Then he turned with a heavy scowl and came clumping up to the door. Anton, who was never quite comfortable with Chowder in the house and who had, indeed, noted the way the man sized up the silverware, waited nervously. Chowder stopped on the steps.

"That feller a copper?" he asked.

"Who?"

Chowder jerked a thumb over his shoulder.

"Feller wot just left."

"Good heavens, no."

Chowder squinted suspiciously.

"That so? Looked like a copper to me. I can smell coppers a mile away. You sure he weren't no copper?"

"Not at all. The gentleman was from a government agency."

"Oh. Oh, that explains it. Same smell, you know. I thought maybe they were on to us."

"On to us?"

"'Bout them nicked dogs."

Anton, who had never considered the illegal aspects of purchasing stolen dogs, and perhaps had not even realized they were stolen, looked puzzled.

Chowder said, "Huh. Well, I come to see if you were ready for another delivery. Got a new scheme worked out. Real complicated and clever. Reckon to make a raid on White City just after the dog races, get the lot. Bit expensive, but they'll be better than your run o' the mill hound."

"Actually, it appears that any sort of dog will do," Anton said, and Chowder's face fell. Anton glanced back into the house. He looked to ascertain if any valuables were in the hall before inviting Chowder in, but as he did so his gaze fell on the stairway where Beta had ascended and instantly a plan sprang upon his mind. He blinked. He turned back to Chowder. He didn't hesitate.

"I may have another job for you," Anton whispered.

"Yeah? What's that then?"

"Shhh."

Chowder looked about.

Anton bit his fingernails.

"Well?"

"My wife..."

"Yeah? You want her kidnapped too, huh?"

"No, no. But I... I wonder... do you think you might follow her?"

"Might. Why?"

"I fear she is... well, perhaps... being untrue to me."

"Huh?"

That perhaps she loves another."

"Like that, is it, mate?"

"I fear so."

"Sure, I'll follow her for you. I know how it is. My own wife ran off with an Armenian. I didn't follow her, though."

Chowder nodded in sympathy. Anton nodded nervously. After they had finished nodding they made their plans.

The Chief snapped his snuffbox shut and tilted his chair back. Johnstone had just finished his verbal report. The Chief was wearing a different tie. It had a naked woman painted on it and when the Chief, as he sometimes did, pressed a bulb attached behind the tie, the naked woman's breasts ballooned. It was very clever. But he didn't press the bulb now, he shuffled through some papers.

"Initial check-up on this fellow Plotnikov. Seems a genuine type. Background okay. Company he works for did a thorough inquiry on him. Industrial secrets and such. Much more careful than our counter-intelligence boys, actually. More important, one assumes. His wife runs around with other men. But she's English, so that's all right. But you say he didn't seem keen on the idea, eh?"

"Not very."

"Pressures?"

"Well, he needs the money. Then there are the dogs, of course. Obviously stolen. Not mongrels, good-looking dogs. Could blackmail him with that."

"Anyway, we'll think of something. This is too good to miss. Werewolves! Why, this could be the start of a new Empire."

Johnstone smiled politely.

The Chief pressed the button.

Hancock sat up abruptly.

Beta slid down from his neck.

"Thought I saw something peculiar at the window," he said.

"What, darling?"

"Well, it looked like a bloody great sunflower."

"Nonsense, dearest."

"I guess you must be right."

"But it was romantic of you to think of flowers, dear."

"Huh," said Hancock.

In the cages, the dogs watched with baleful eyes and, at the table, Anton and Chowder leaned close together like Russian anarchists. Anton was pale. Chowder, whose own wife had left him for an Armenian, was gleeful.

"She's got a man, all right," he said.

"Oh dear."

"I followed her, see. Real careful. Professional. She never twigged a thing. Well, she went to this 'ere flat and used her own key to open it. It was a basement flat, so I nipped round to the side to have a dekko through the window. And let me tell you, they didn't waste no time. I'm nippy on my feet, you know. Got to be in my trade, ducking and diving. But quick as I was, they were hard at it by the time I got to the window. Hard at it, they were. I'll say. Really going to town. Not just a casual poke, like what one gets in an alley, either. Real lovey-dovey stuff. All that kissing and love-biting..."

"Love-biting?" asked Anton, in his grief.

"Sure. You know. Like when a bird nibbles your neck so that the blood comes oozing through the skin and then later your old lady spots the mark and gets so annoyed that she runs off with Armenians. That sorta stuff."

Anton, vaguely, had heard of such things. He even thought he recalled Beta trying to do it to him, on their honeymoon, although he couldn't be sure. Chowder was proceeding to reveal the sordid details, but Anton's mind had stuck at the words "love-biting". They played over and over again on a jammed track in his mind. Love-biting. Love-biting. Love-biting. Love-biting. And then, somehow, the words became detached from one another. They registered separately. Love. Biting. Love. Biting. His wife loved another man. His wife bit another man. The other man was Beta's lover. Therefore the other man was Anton's enemy. It was perfectly all right to bite an enemy. Johnstone had told him so. Sparks flew across gaps in Anton's mind. Anton thought and thought.

"Oh dear," said Beta. "I do believe I'm going down with a horrid cold."

She blew her nose daintily.

"Perhaps you're run down, dear," Anton said. "You've been out too much. You should relax at home."

"Yes, dear," she said, not hearing him. "I do hope it doesn't get worse. I have an important social engagement this evening."

Anton winced.

"Perhaps I'll phone Doctor Blackshaw. Dreadful nuisance, though. I can never see why, if you're a doctor, you can't give antibiotic shots and things."

"I've explained before, dear. I'm not a medical doctor. It's a different thing."

"More useful if you were."

She blew her nose again.

Anton blinked. Anton looked down at his hands. Anton pursed his lips.

"I suppose I could give you an injection of, ah, penicillin, darling," he said.

"Oh, could you? That would be convenient."

"Yes, of course I could," he said. "I could give you a shot."

And, presently, he did.

"I won't be able to come tomorrow, dear," said Beta Plotnikov.

"Why's that?" asked Hancock.

"My husband."

"Suspicious, is he?"

"Oh no, poor dear. He never suspects a thing. Not a thing. He doesn't even notice those marks you leave on my neck sometimes. That's how easy it is to deceive him. It makes me feel wicked sometimes when I think how innocent the poor dear is. So deliciously wicked."

"Well, come to think of it, you are sort of wicked. Glad you're not my wife."

"Oh, I'd never cheat against you."

"Huh."

She nuzzled him.

"But, anyway, I can't see you tomorrow. Anton has asked me to stay at home with him. Says he's been working hard and is going to take the whole day off and relax. He does work terribly hard, you know. So I guess I owe him one day of my time, after all. And he seemed so... well... almost demanding about it. Sort of worried, too. As if maybe he was afraid I'd refuse."

"Well, that's okay then."

"I won't sleep with him, of course."

"Huh? He's your husband, isn't he?"

"Why, of course. But I simply couldn't be unfaithful to you, dearest."

"Huh," said Hancock, and after a while they began to bill and coo and, because she was not going to see him for a whole day, Beta felt she should make the most of this occasion, and squirmed and moaned and, soon enough, they were gyrating in the horizontal gavotte and, in the towering heights of oestral heat, they kissed and kissed...

Later, while dressing, Hancock paused to look in the mirror. Hancock was vain about his muscles and smiled at the deltoids. Then, abruptly, he scowled.

"What's wrong, my love?" asked Beta, from the bed.

"Huh! I don't know about your husband, but my pupils are no fools. What the hell are they going to say about these marks on my neck, huh?"

Beta giggled.

Later she went home.

Anton, for a time, suffered misgivings and regrets. He tried to convince himself that the man who had cuckolded him deserved to be punished, but found it feeble justification; tried, rather medievally, to believe that it was in the hands of the gods, like trial by combat, for he had no way of knowing whether Beta would actually kiss her lover fiercely enough to transmit the disease, nor even, other than in theory, whether it would prove effective against a human being; tried, even, to believe his actions were motivated by a desire to increase scientific knowledge. But none of these forms of rationalization were strong enough to deceive his doubts. He went through turmoils and upheavals of thought. He even worked, for a time, on the antidote he had been considering—worked desultorily, however, knowing as he turned from aspect to aspect that no antidote would be found without weeks and months of labour, and soon gave up the effort.

Then Beta came home.

She came home radiant and happy, and as he looked at her Anton felt his doubts fade. He felt the justification which he'd been unable to find within his own mind, in his wife's obvious satisfaction. He no longer resented her infidelity, and no longer worried about it—did not know, of course, that Hancock was but one of many, and that her behaviour would not be changed by Hancock's elimination. The peace of accomplishment stilled his troubled thoughts and he came to regret but one thing—that he would not be able to take credit, in his next report, for having created—well, whatever it was that he had created. He was not absolutely sure what that would be. He waited, with interest, for the next day to pass, certain that the evening newspapers, perhaps even special editions, would bring him the results of his experiment.

That night, he made love to his wife.

He did not, however, allow her to kiss him.

There was a full moon.

Anton had not planned it that way—had not even realized that such would be the case—but when he became aware of the fact he felt a tingle. It seemed so very appropriate. It seemed to place the stamp of fate's approval upon his act. He had only to wait. He waited. The day passed slowly. Anton did not know the relevant data about Hancock's weight and metabolism, and therefore could not predict with any certainty when the madness would strike the man, but he knew it would be within twenty-four hours. The only thing necessary was to keep his wife safely at home during that period. Beta, however, had showed signs of restlessness during the day. It was the first day she had spent at home for some weeks. As the afternoon wore on Anton began to fear she might make some excuse to slip away, and he could think of no way to convince her, short of the impossible truth, that she must not be with her lover that day. Doing her best to be a dutiful wife, temporarily, Beta was determined to remain with Anton, but she was surprised by her own nervous energy, her own restless wanderings from room to room. She wondered whether her feelings for Hancock—for what else could cause her dysphoria other than the enforced separation?—were deeper than she had imagined them to be. And yet Hancock did not seem connected with her restlessness. She merely felt an overwhelming urge to leave the house—to divagate without any particular goal, even to take a long and uncharacteristic walk through the darkening countryside. This confused her. She could not understand the impulse. Presently she forced herself to take a seat by the window in the library-study, determined to fight down her restlessness.

Anton, at his desk, glanced towards his wife from time to time. He could just see the angle of her profile from behind, but it was sufficient to note the internal struggle reflected in her expression. She wants to go to him, he thought. He was worried. What if she simply got up and left? Anton did not know how to prevent this, short of physically restraining her, and even that was doubtful. Anton was not strong. Truth be known, he was exceptionally weak. Beta was a big, healthy woman. Anton felt sure she was stronger than he, and certainly fitter. He watched her hand open and close upon the arm of the chair and he worried. He thought of how it would be if she went to her lover—if she were in his arms when the disease came upon him in all its horrible fury. After a while he rose and moved very quietly to the door. He turned the key in the lock and then returned to his desk and placed the key at the very back of the drawer; locked the drawer as well. It would be very embarrassing, he knew, if she demanded the key, but any degree of unpleasantness was far better than letting her go. He felt better with that precaution taken; went over to stand behind her chair and place his hand on her shoulder. Together they looked out at the moon. It was very bright, a silver disc behind shredding clouds.

There were a few stars. Anton stood quietly for a time. Beta seemed tense beneath his hand. Usually, at the slightest touch, she took it as encouragement and began to squirm. But now she was still and taut. He wondered what occupied her thoughts—told himself, with a twinge of sadness, that she must be thinking of her lover. Then anger replaced the anguish. She would think of him, perhaps, but she would never again rest in his arms. She would never again come home flushed and weary with love, her pure throat blemished with those marks of passion...

Anton stiffened.

Those marks of love...

His mouth dropped open, his heart stopped for a moment and then thundered. His terrible oversight came cascading into his mind. If Beta had infected her lover and he, in turn, had kissed her in that manner... afterwards... when his glands were already secreting the hormones...

Anton looked down at his wife.

She sat very still. He saw only the side of her face. But he saw her hand, as well, and her hand was hooked over the edge of the arm-rest. Hooked like a claw. The veins stood out in the back of her hand and ran in pronounced ridges up her forearms. Anton stepped back. Beta did not move. Beta was looking at the moon. The moonlight fell over her face. Anton walked backwards to the door, his eyes fixed upon her. She did not move at all. He reached behind his back and grasped the doorknob. But the door was locked. The key was in the desk and the desk was in the centre of the room. Anton stood there for some time, unable to advance. And then, with the fibre of his body blurred by terror, he started to tiptoe towards his desk. He made no sound. But he had not yet reached the desk when his wife stood up. She stood up quickly and stiffly, facing the window. Anton halted. He had not reached the desk. He stood motionless and looked at his wife and she stood motionless and looked at the moon.

And then his wife turned around.

What had once been his wife turned around.

Anton crouched, quivering, against the locked door. His ancestry screamed in his mind. He whimpered, the sound of a small and helpless animal, transfixed by the glowing eyes of the predator.

Then Beta moved towards him.

She moved slowly. Anton looked at her burning eyes and he looked at her crooked hands and he looked at her ravenous mouth...

Anton was totally insane before she reached him...

Which was probably just as well for him...

1984

ARBOR DAY

Mary Danby

Mary Danby is a truly remarkable woman. Writer, editor, TV producer, inventor, designer of board games, and great-great-granddaughter of Charles Dickens, she has excelled at everything she has turned her hand to.

Born Mary Heather Danby in Dorking, Surrey, on 26 May 1941, Danby left school at sixteen and worked as a secretary, before spending almost a decade as a producer for ABC Television in Teddington. When ABC merged with Rediffusion in 1968 and became Thames Television, she was offered redundancy, and went to work in the USA. Upon her return she was offered a job at Collins Publishers (now Harper Collins) as a fiction editor for their Fontana paperback imprint. Although she had never worked in publishing before, she took over the editorship of both the *Fontana Book of Great Horror Stories* series, which was primarily aimed at adults, and the *Armada Ghost Book* series, which was aimed at children. She ultimately edited the final thirteen volumes in each series—volumes five to seventeen of the Fontana series, and volumes three to fifteen of the Armada series.

During this time, she also started writing her own excellent stories, which became a mainstay of both series. All twenty-six of these stories, plus the three she wrote for her three-volume series *Nightmares* (1983–1985), and a brand new story called "Red Shoes", were collected in the volume *Party Pieces* (2012), published by another contributor to this volume, Johnny Mains, under his occasional publishing imprint, Noose & Gibbet.

As Danby's writing and editing career ended, so her new career as a toy and game inventor began. In the past four decades she has licensed around 150 products, including many board games, among which are such perennial favourites as *The Dickens Game* for MB Games (now Hasbro), *Mysteries of Old Peking* (known as *Junior Detective* in the US), which has sold over three and a half million units worldwide, *Pooh's Hide and Seek Game* and *Yo Ho Ho*. These endeavours culminated in her being presented with a prestigious I.D.I.O.T. (International Designer and Inventor of Toys) Award.

"Arbor Day", which is taken from *Nightmares 2* (1984), is a creepy slice of folk horror about the perils of tampering with tradition. As with all of Danby's short fiction, her directness and her clarity of style make the tale a joy to read.

The village of Oakholme in June was so green and leafy that from the air one could barely distinguish it from the wooded hills that surrounded it, though a keen observer might have spotted the silver spire of St Stephen's Church, or the bell tower on the old primary school. Every garden was lush with foliage, every road edged with greenery.

Early in the month, the Arbor Day Committee met to choose from the younger members of the village those who would lead their celebration of all this greenness. On the morning of their meeting, Sid Aythorpe, the secretary, pinned a sheet of paper to the village notice board.

Oakholme Arbor Day, it said.

Saturday, June 21st

Assemble outside school at 11.15 a.m.

Procession to start at 11.30 a.m.

Green Man: Raymond Sturgess

Green Lady: Stephanie Pendleton

Leaf Maidens: Jennifer Smith, Lisa Murray

Lisa, cycling past, stopped to have a look. Leaf Maiden again. Second year running. Wasn't that just typical! And that podgy Stephanie Pendleton with her wide-eyed, babydoll face, getting to be Green Lady to swoony Raymond Sturgess. The unfairness of it. She pedalled away, hunched and scowling, to break the news to her friend Jennifer.

*

People came from all over to Oakholme on Arbor Day. It always took place on the third Saturday in June, around the time of the Summer solstice—the longest day—in commemoration of the Greening of the Year. Its origins were in the distant, pagan past, but the tradition remained strong. The village lay in a hollow, surrounded by trees, and many of its people worked at the nearby timber mills. In centuries gone by, the villagers of Oakholme had taken a good living from the woods, cutting down strong elms and ash trees for firewood, making oak beams for their cottages, bending hazel twigs into fencing, carving bowls and implements, making solid furniture to sell in the towns. The woods were their wealth and their shelter; the people of Oakholme owed the trees their livelihoods and their lives.

Arbor Day was the recognition of this. To call the ceremonies "tree worship" in these modern times was perhaps a little extreme, but there were some who still felt that certain rites were necessary to preserve the serenity of the village and to keep the woods on their side: "hand in branch," as one of the committee members whimsically put it. What would happen if the tradition were abandoned no one knew, but it was rumoured that the real Green Man—not Raymond Sturgess dressed in a green outfit and with twigs in his hair—would come down from the woods and bring terror to the village. Who or what the Green Man really was, no one was too sure, but the dictionary described him as the age-old spirit of the trees, and ancient books painted him sometimes as a fool, a capering, foliage-bedecked Jack-in-the-green, sometimes a tall, threatening figure, dark and mean and evil-looking.

There were two weeks to go until June 21st.

Lisa, kicking at the concrete of the Oldworth School playground with the toe of her shoe, said: "I suppose I'd better wear that dreary green skirt again, if I can still get into it." She thought she had grown quite a bit in the last year, but she was still annoyingly smaller than most girls of her age. She wore her dark hair very short, to make her neck seem longer.

Jennifer bounced a ball against the side of the bicycle shed and said her mother would have to dye something for her to wear. This was Jennifer's first year as a Leaf Maiden, and she was excited at the prospect.

"It's terribly important, isn't it," she said, "to wear the right things. Mrs Aythorpe told me in all the years of Oakholme having their Arbor Day nobody can remember anyone spoiling the tradition. But something must have gone wrong once, because everyone is sure that something dreadful can happen if you break the rules."

"Such as?" Lisa's scornful tone was put on for effect. Underneath her careless attitude she believed in the rituals as much as all the rest.

Jennifer elaborated. "Oh, you know... They say that if someone alters anything to do with the ceremonies the Green Man is angry, and the trees come and take them away and they're never heard of again. Something like that."

"You mean the trees grow legs and come shuffling down into the village?" Lisa laughed, but despite herself she looked over towards the hill where the Oakholme woods began. They darkened suddenly as the sun went in, the pale, shimmery treetops becoming a scowling face, and she felt a tap-tap-tap inside her, as if fear were knocking at her heart, come to warn her that she mocked at her peril...

Jennifer was watching Stephanie Pendleton approach them, stepping daintily sideways to avoid a group of first years playing hopscotch.

Stephanie was a well-groomed teenager, who managed to appear fashionable even in her dowdy uniform of navy blue skirt and beige shirt. She had strong features, but her large eyes and wide mouth—both often open in a look of vacant wonder—gave her an aura of glamour.

She pushed her thick, rust-red hair behind one ear. "I've heard you two are going to be Leaf Maidens."

Meaning, thought Lisa, mimicking Stephanie's little-girl tones in her head: *Have you heard* I'm *to be Green Lady?* "'S right," she said out loud, giving Stephanie a defiant stare.

Jennifer, unaware of her friend's feelings, said: "Are you excited at being Green Lady, Stephanie? Lucky old you... I *mean*, Raymond Sturgess... You'll get to dance with him at the Virtue, won't you."

The Virtue was the name given to the party held on the village green on the evening of Arbor Day. Nobody was sure about the name: some said it was after *vert*, the French word for green, or the Latin *vertere*, to turn or change, like the seasons, or perhaps it had something to do with the purity, the supposed virtue, of the young couple chosen to head the celebrations. There would be a floodlit area cleared for dancing, with tables and chairs all around, and a fiddler and accordion-player, and Jennifer's uncle Martin on the drums. All of Oakholme would be there, and often there were visitors from other villages.

"Oh, Raymond and I are old friends," said Stephanie in answer to Jennifer's comment. "He's no big deal."

Raymond Sturgess? No big deal? Who was she kidding? Lisa had shadowed him for years, feeling weak at the knees every time he bestowed a glance in her direction, writing Valentine cards to him and being too shy to send them, scratching "Lisa 4 Raymond" on the wall of the girls' cloakroom, practising a hopeful signature in her exercise books: Lisa Diane Sturgess... Lisa D. Sturgess... Mrs Lisa Sturgess.

"Oh, I think he's quite nice really," she said with a cool smile. "A bit stuck-up for me, though. I don't like his friends."

Stephanie ignored the insult. "What are you going to wear? Your usual green skirt, Lisa? Does it still fit? I expect it does—you haven't grown much, have you. My mother is making me a gorgeous long gown. Silk polyester, in a sort of jade green to go well with my hair." She tossed the flaming mane back over her shoulder.

The Green Lady always wore on her head a glamorous creation of ferns and green branches. The Leaf Maidens had small wreaths and carried baskets of fresh leaves. There were rules about how the headgear was made.

"We have to go to Baxter's Copse before sunset on the day before," Lisa told the others, "to pick all our twigs and leaves and things. Everyone has to make their own head-dress."

"Yes, I know," said Stephanie. "It's like a kind of offering, my mother says. To please the trees. Let's go to Baxter's Copse together after school on Friday, then you could both come home with me to make the head-dresses. Mummy will do tea for us."

Jennifer looked at Lisa. She knew her friend couldn't stand Stephanie's mother, Mrs Pendleton, but she said: "I'd ask you to our place, but Dad's redecorating. It's a bit of a mess."

Before Lisa could offer her own house, Stephanie said with a patronizing smile: "And we'd be a bit cramped at Lisa's, wouldn't we, what with the baby and everything."

She belittles my best boy, my clothes, my height and my home, thought Lisa. And there was no way to get back at her.

"I think we should go to Stephanie's," declared Jennifer, "because her father's got a shed we could put the stuff in overnight."

Lisa eventually agreed, and walked away to avoid the glint of triumph in Stephanie's blue eyes.

The big mower was at work on the Green, making a dance floor out of the rough grass, when the three girls headed for Baxter's Copse on the afternoon of June 20th. Each carried a big plastic sack, and Stephanie twirled and skipped ahead of the others, as if already showing off her Arbor Day gown.

"Aren't I lucky," she said, as they entered the wood. "I only have to make a head-dress. Poor you, having to pick all those leaves." She wafted about, clipping off sprigs of birch and ash, fronds of rowan, willow and larch, while Lisa and Jennifer painstakingly picked enough single leaves to fill the Leaf Maidens' baskets. When they had enough in their sacks, they broke off a few twigs of oak and sycamore for their wreaths, then the three girls left the copse and headed for Stephanie's modern bungalow down Hickory Lane, where her mother offered them sandwiches and cake, and cleared the kitchen table for them.

"What do you need?" she asked them. "Secateurs? Wire? Pliers?" She produced green florists' wire and some snippers. "Have you shown them your dress, Stephie?" she asked her daughter.

"Not yet, Mummy," said Stephanie. "I'm going to give everyone a great big surprise on the day. Now—how am I going to make my head-dress? I want it to be the best there's ever been. I think I'll use my old sunhat as a base. No, no... you mustn't help me, Mummy. It's got to be all my own work, and I'm going to do everything just right. I wouldn't want the trees to come and get me!" She shivered playfully and gave a tinkly laugh. Lisa looked at her, a sly smile beginning to twitch the corners of her mouth.

While the other two bent and wove their twigs into wreaths, Stephanie assembled a dramatic creation that floated and rippled almost with a life of its own. When she eventually lifted it with both hands to place it on her head, waving ferns stuck out far beyond her shoulders, and the crown rose to a high, leafy point, surmounted by a pale green sprig of beech.

"What do you think?" she asked with a confident smile.

"Ooh, it's lovely," replied Jennifer.

Lisa thought it was a real show-off effort, and silly-looking into the bargain, but she was saved from having to comment by Mrs Pendleton, who came into the kitchen with much clapping of hands and exclamations of exultation.

"Such a clever girl, my Stephie," she told the two others. "They were so right to choose her as Green Lady." She looked down at the table. "Oh, are these your little wreaths, girls? How nice. And leaves for your baskets? Well, you have been busy little bees."

After they had cleared the mess from the table, Lisa asked if they might put the head-dresses and leaves in the Pendleton's potting shed overnight. It was cool there, and a spray of cold water would keep everything nice and fresh for the next morning.

Stephanie arranged her creation on the table under the potting shed window. There was no room for the wreaths next to it, so Lisa and Jennifer made a space for them on the shelves, among the mildew sprays and rooting compounds. The sacks of leaves stood on the floor underneath.

Everything was ready now for Arbor Day. Almost.

That night, after the rest of her family had gone to bed, Lisa pulled on a pair of jeans and slipped out of the back door. The moon was bright and she had no need of the torch she was carrying to guide her through the village and out along Hickory Lane. Every house was in darkness; not even the bark of a dog nor the hoot of an owl broke the stillness.

She thought of Stephanie, asleep in her frilly pink bedroom, dreaming dreams of tomorrow's glory, and she smiled to herself as she set about the task she had planned.

As she returned from her errand a slight wind blew up, rustling the trees in the spinney at the side of the road. "Lisa..." they sang accusingly. "Li-s-sa... Li-ss-sa..." They seemed to be pointing their branches at her, whispering and muttering between themselves. The moon ducked suddenly behind a cloud, and she was in blackness. Staring this way and that at the trees, she thought she could see something in them. Faces. Gaunt and bony, their thin eyes peered nastily down at her through the branches, leering, gloating.

The air grew suddenly chilly, and somewhere in the wood a rabbit screamed.

Breaking into a stumbling run, Lisa hurried towards home, not daring to look behind her at those taunting faces. They're not real, she told herself. I've imagined them to punish myself.

Back in the safety of her house she locked the back door behind her and stood in the kitchen recovering her breath. Then she crept out into the hall and soft-footed her way up to bed.

Lisa overslept the next morning, and was woken by her mother calling up the stairs.

"If you're going to be a Leaf Maiden, you'd better stir yourself. Jennifer's here for you already."

She rolled out of bed, still giddy from a nightmare of clutching branches. As consciousness took over, she was aware of a feeling of excitement mingled with unease. She tried to shrug it off, telling herself that last night's escapade had been a joke, nothing more. And it wasn't as if anything would actually *happen*.

Hanging from her wardrobe door was a green blouse of her sister's, and the old green skirt which this year pinched her waist but still covered her knees. She dressed hurriedly and quickly combed her hair.

Jennifer, drinking tea and feeding biscuits to Lisa's baby brother at the kitchen table, wore a pale green sundress. It had been cream-coloured before her mother dyed it.

"Nearly eleven," said Mrs Murray as Lisa hurtled down the stairs.

"Why didn't you wake me?" Lisa demanded, taking a couple of biscuits from the packet for breakfast.

The baby began to wail.

"Here's why." Mrs Murray plucked him from his high chair and jigged him up and down. "Been like this all morning. Teething," she told Jennifer. "Then I've had the cakes and that to finish for the Virtue. I don't have time to run up and down stairs waking people who've got alarm clocks."

"Come on, Jen," said Lisa, wiping biscuit crumbs from her mouth. "We'd best go and get our leaves and stuff."

They walked together down the lane towards the Pendletons' house. As they drew near they heard a man's voice shouting, and a high, bleating noise, together with the sound of someone crying. They walked round the side of the house, and there, just outside the potting shed, they saw Stephanie, tears dripping on to her long green dress, between her angry father and agitated mother.

"It's a matter for the police," Mr Pendleton was saying. "There may be fingerprints."

"Oh, what's the use!" his wife moaned, her arm around Stephanie, comforting. "What's done is done. Poor Stephie. Poor baby."

Stephanie raised her stricken face and saw the other two girls. "In there," she sniffed, motioning them towards the potting shed.

Mr Pendleton stopped them. "I don't suppose you two know anything about this, do you? I mean, whoever did it left *your* stuff well alone."

"Oh, nonsense, Geoffrey," said Mrs Pendleton. "Of course they don't. They're Stephie's friends, aren't you dears?"

When they looked inside the potting shed, they saw what all the fuss was about. Their own wreaths and leaves had survived the night well. They were as fresh and green as if they had just been picked. But Stephanie's flamboyant head-dress was a soggy mess of blackened foliage.

As Lisa and Jennifer stared, open-mouthed, Mr Pendleton showed them a small bottle on one of the shelves. "Brushwood killer. Empty," he said. "An act of deliberate vandalism."

"How awful," said Lisa.

"What a rotten thing to do," agreed Jennifer.

"That's modern youth for you," said Mr Pendleton. "They should lock up these hooligans and throw away the key."

Outside the potting shed, Mrs Pendleton was patting Stephanie's tear-stained cheeks with a paper tissue. "You shall wear the hat I wore to Auntie Pamela's wedding," she said, as if conveying a great favour. "And Daddy will fix some lovely greenery to it."

"You'll look fine, really," Jennifer said kindly to Stephanie. "Your dress is great."

"But the rules," wailed Stephanie. "I have to wear a head-dress. I have to make it myself. You know I do."

She sounded panicky. Lisa began to wish she had left well alone. She had only wanted to frighten Stephanie, not send her into hysterics. "Oh, come on," she said briskly. "You don't really believe in all that superstitious rubbish, do you?"

It was time for the procession to assemble. Lisa and Jennifer fixed on their wreaths and carried their sacks of leaves up the lane to the school, where Mrs Aythorpe ticked off their names on her list and gave them their Leaf Maiden baskets.

A large crowd had assembled to watch the start of the procession, and Sid Aythorpe was dashing about trying to get everyone in line. At the front was Ted Robinson with his accordion, flanked by children from the primary school with tambourines. Then came the Brownies and Guides, the Cubs and Scouts and the darts team from the Royal Oak, who wore dark green T-shirts and carried boughs of yew which they waved like palms. Pupils from the local dancing school were wood nymphs in apple green chiffon and with flowers in their hair, and this year the Oakholme Youth Club were entirely green, in green outfits and with their hands and faces covered in green make-up.

At the end of the procession the Leaf Maidens had to prepare the way for the Green Man and his Lady by strewing leaves on the ground they were to walk on. Raymond Sturgess was there: an impressive Green Man in a twiggy crown and a tunic made from hundreds of leaves. At the last moment, Stephanie ran on to the school playground, clutching to her head her mother's pink straw hat, to which was fixed a spray of ivy from the Pendletons' garden. Her face was red and smouldering—there had obviously been an argument about the hat—and nobody dared ask why she was not wearing the traditional Green Lady's headgear.

Scowling, she held out her hand. Raymond Sturgess offered her his arm, and the procession moved off. The roads were lined with villagers, who cheered the front of the procession and stopped, agape and muttering, when they saw Stephanie in the pink wedding hat.

The group reached the edge of the woods and began to weave their way through the trees. When they reached a clearing the music stopped and the tambourines were still. Raymond Sturgess stepped forward with Stephanie and spoke ancient words of praise and thanksgiving. The air was cold in the clearing. No sun penetrated the branches. Everyone's eyes were on Stephanie, who stood rigid, her eyes flicking nervously to the trees. When Raymond finished speaking the silence was absolute. Not a leaf stirred.

Then the procession moved on, back into the village. When it reached the Royal Oak, where the landlord awaited them with jugs of orange squash, Stephanie tore off her hat, flung it to the ground and rushed away to cry in the Ladies' Room.

By eight o'clock that evening, when the band was set up on the green and the catering committee had assembled their pies and cakes and flagons of cider on long trestle tables, Stephanie had recovered enough to lead off the dancing with Raymond Sturgess. She looked much happier—her ordeal was over and no terrible fate had befallen her. In fact, she had enjoyed basking in everyone's sympathy, once the story of the ruined head-dress had travelled around the village. Arbor Day costumes had now been discarded, and Stephanie wore a pretty, candy-striped dress and flimsy sandals that showed off her well-shaped legs, even though they weren't entirely suitable for dancing on grass. Every time she stumbled, she gave a little giggle and managed to fall forward into Raymond's arms. It seemed she had decided that he *was* quite a big deal, after all.

Lisa and Jennifer, with lemonade and packets of crisps, were assessing the young men. Some of the village boys had got hold of a bottle of cider and were furtively swigging from it behind the cricket pavilion. A crowd of Oldworth boys were strolling around, not yet asking anyone to dance. Perhaps they would get round to that later, when it got darker and some of the older people had gone home. In the meantime, Lisa concentrated on Raymond, hoping to catch his eye, in the hope that he might eventually ask her to dance.

The evening was well under way, and Lisa still hadn't danced, when one of the local boys took Jennifer away for a ring dance, where all the men made a circle on the outside, and the ladies paraded round in the opposite direction on the inside. When the music stopped, each man took the nearest partner and danced with her.

Not wanting to be seen sitting alone, and reluctant to join her parents, Lisa slipped through the ring of men to join Jennifer. At least this way she'd get to dance with *somebody*. The music began. The men circled. The ladies paraded. Stephanie gave a little wiggly wave of her fingers to Raymond each time she passed him.

The music stopped.

Opposite Lisa was someone she hadn't noticed before, which was surprising. He was the man of every girl's dreams: a genuine tall, dark and handsome stranger. He had black curly hair and sparkling brown eyes. With a devastating smile he held out his hand to her and led her into the dance.

"You're Lisa, aren't you?" he said in a low, musical voice.

"How did you know?" Lisa felt so tense it was as if she were holding her breath.

"Your fame goes before you," he said mysteriously, then laughed. "I'm Jack."

Lisa hoped Stephanie was watching them. Compared with this Jack, Raymond was a puny weed.

"Have you come from Oldworth?" she asked, trying to sound casual.

She thought he nodded his head, and then he was sweeping across the grass, turning wildly to the music. When they stopped, they were outside the floodlit area, in the dark shadows along the edge of the green. He put an arm around her shoulders, and together they strolled along, out of breath and laughing, until they reached the end of the green, where a path led deep into Baxter's Copse.

"I think we ought to turn back," Lisa said, looking up at him. "My parents will be wondering where I am."

His dark eyes, staring into hers, made her feel powerless, as if she was under some kind of spell.

"Just a little further," he coaxed. "Have you never been in the woods at night?"

Warning bells jangled in Lisa's head. She avoided his gaze and fought the weakness. "No," she said awkwardly. "And I really don't think... Look, why don't we go back." She stopped, then turned away and began to walk firmly towards the lights and music, but he caught up with her and took her roughly by the arm.

She shrieked, but the band was playing a noisy gallop, and no one heard her. She pulled away from him, but his grip grew harder.

Slowly, she was being dragged along the path into Baxter's Copse.

"Leave me alone!" she shouted, beating at him with her fist, clawing at his face. Was it the shadows of the trees, or was his face becoming darker, craggier?

"Let go, will you!"

Panic spread through her. She struck out wildly, again and again, but it was like hitting solid oak. His body was rough and unyielding. The shining eyes, now cruel slits, never left her, and the curly hair twisted and clung like bindweed across the ridged brow.

She screamed for the last time, and then damp leaves were in her mouth, and her legs and arms were held fast by wormlike tendrils that snaked up around her body. She felt her feet being torn down into the earth, and her skin began to dry up, to darken and crack. Agonizing pain took over her body. Sharp green shoots sprouted viciously from her face, her shoulders, out through her hair. Her sight began to fade. But in her last moments of human existence she could see clearly the true nature of this handsome stranger. This was none other than Jack-in-the-Green. But this was no clownish idiot, no cavorting jester. The man who stood so pitilessly before her was a terrifying figure of power and vengeance. This, then, was the Green Man.

A week later when police enquiries in the village had begun to die down, Raymond took Stephanie for a walk in Baxter's Copse. It was a very hot day, and they stopped for a while beside a young oak tree, its leaves a pale, tender green against the ripeness of its neighbours. Raymond took out his penknife. "Here Steph," he said. "I'll carve our initials. This tree's only small. We can come back when we're ninety and see if our initials have grown huge, eh?"

"Don't cut too deep, will you," said Stephanie.

Raymond laughed. "You are a funny one," he said.

"You won't hurt it, will you." Stephanie gave a little shudder and looked at him with big round eyes.

He opened the penknife. "Honestly, Steph," he said, "to hear you go on, anyone would think trees had feelings."

Grinning, he made the first cut.

1985

THE JAGUAR HUNTER

Lucius Shepard

Although Lucius Shepard claimed to have been born in 1947, both the 1945 census in Florida and the US Public Records Office confirm his birthdate as 21 August 1943. He was born in Lynchburg, Virginia, but raised in Daytona, Florida, where his early life was turbulent, his teacher father William using threats and even violence to force his son to read the classics. Well-read but with a hatred and fear of home life, Shepard literally jumped ship at the age of fifteen, boarding a freighter for Ireland, and subsequently spending several years travelling in Europe, North Africa and Asia.

During this time, according to Shepard, he worked in a cigarette factory in Germany, as a nightclub bouncer in Spain, and was even marginally involved in the international drug trade. Upon returning to the USA, he entered the University of North Carolina, where he met and married Joy Wolf, a fellow student, with whom he had a son, Gullivar. Shepard reports that he dropped out of university on several occasions, during which time he travelled extensively in Spain, Southeast Asia, and South and Central America, with the latter's culture ultimately influencing much of his work. In 1980, with his marriage on the rocks, Shepard attended a Clarion Writers' Workshop at Michigan State University, and finally discovered a profession that he claimed gave his life meaning.

For the next two and a half decades, before his death in 2014, Shepard produced a vast amount of high-quality, award-winning fiction, much of which, due to his very particular imagination, made it both unclassifiable but also highly appealing to readers of horror, fantasy and science-fiction. Liberally laced with elements of magic realism, his novels and novellas include *Green Eyes* (1984), *Life During Wartime* (1987), *The Scalehunter's Beautiful Daughter* (1988), *Kalimantan* (1990), *The Golden* (1993), *A Handbook of American Prayer* (2000), *Floater* (2003), *Softspoken* (2007) and *Beautiful Blood* (2014), published in the year of his death.

His many short stories are collected in *The Jaguar Hunter* (1987), *The End of the Earth* (1991), *Beast of the Heartland* (1999), *Two Trains Running* (2004), *Trujillo* (2004), *Dagger Key* (2007), two volumes of *The Best of Lucius Shepard* (2008/2021) and several other volumes.

From 2000 to 2013, Shepard contributed a regular column on SF cinema and American culture in general to *The Magazine of Fantasy and Science Fiction*, some of which, plus other work, can be found in the non-fiction collection *Weapons of Mass Seduction: Film Reviews and Other Ravings* (2005).

Set in Honduras, a country he had a particular affinity for, *The Jaguar Hunter*, which was first published in the May 1985 issue of *The Magazine of Fantasy and Science Fiction*, is in many ways an archetypal Lucius Shepard story, and an excellent introduction to his work if you haven't read him before. Part fantasy, part horror, part magic realism, it is an evocative, erotic and captivating tale, which expertly treads a fine line between the realistic and the mystical.

It was his wife's debt to Onofrio Esteves, the appliance dealer, that brought Esteban Caax to town for the first time in almost a year. By nature he was a man who enjoyed the sweetness of the countryside above all else; the placid measures of a farmer's day invigorated him, and he took great pleasure in nights spent joking and telling stories around a fire, or lying beside his wife, Incarnación. Puerto Morada, with its fruit company imperatives and sullen dogs and cantinas that blared American music, was a place he avoided like the plague: indeed, from his home atop the mountain whose slopes formed the northernmost enclosure of Bahía Onda, the rusted tin roofs ringing the bay resembled a dried crust of blood such as might appear upon the lips of a dying man.

On this particular morning, however, he had no choice but to visit the town. Incarnación had—without his knowledge—purchased a battery-operated television set on credit from Onofrio, and he was threatening to seize Esteban's three milk cows in lieu of the eight hundred lempiras that was owed; he refused to accept the return of the television, but had sent word that he was willing to discuss an alternate method of payment. Should Esteban lose the cows, his income would drop below a subsistence level, and he would be forced to take up his old occupation, an occupation far more onerous than farming.

As he walked down the mountain, past huts of thatch and brushwood poles identical to his own, following a trail that wound through sun-browned thickets lorded over by banana trees, he was not thinking of Onofrio but of Incarnación. It was in her nature to be frivolous, and he had known this when he had married her; yet the television was emblematic of the differences that had developed between them since their children had reached maturity. She had begun to put on sophisticated airs, to laugh at Esteban's country ways, and she had become the doyenne of a group of older women, mostly widows, all of whom aspired to sophistication. Each night they would huddle around the television and strive to outdo one another in making sagacious comments about the American detective shows they watched; and each night Esteban would sit outside the hut and gloomily ponder the state of his marriage. He believed Incarnación's association with the widows was her manner of telling him that she looked forward to adopting the black skirt and shawl, that—having served his purpose as a father—he was now an impediment to her. Though she was only forty-one, younger by three years than Esteban, she was withdrawing from the life of the senses; they rarely made love anymore, and he was certain that this partially embodied her resentment of the fact that the years had been kind to him. He had the look of one of the Old Patuca—tall, with chiseled features and wide-set eyes; his coppery skin was relatively unlined and his hair jet black. Incarnación's hair was streaked with gray, and the clean beauty of her limbs had dissolved beneath layers of fat. He had not expected her to remain beautiful, and he had tried to assure her that he loved the woman she was and not merely the girl she had been. But that woman was dying, infected by the same disease that had infected Puerto Morada, and perhaps his love for her was dying, too.

The dusty street on which the appliance store was situated ran in back of the movie theater and the Hotel Circo Del Mar, and from the inland side of the street Esteban could see the bell towers of Santa María del Onda rising above the hotel roof like the horns of a great stone snail. As a young man, obeying his mother's wish that he become a priest, he had spent three years cloistered beneath those towers, preparing for the seminary under the tutelage of old Father Gonsalvo. It was the part of his life he most regretted, because the academic disciplines he had mastered seemed to have stranded him between the world of the Indian and that of contemporary society; in his heart he held to his father's teachings—the principles of magic, the history of the tribe, the lore of nature—and yet he could never escape the feeling that such wisdom was either superstitious or simply unimportant. The shadows of the towers lay upon his soul as surely as they did upon the cobbled square in front of the church, and the sight of them caused him to pick up his pace and lower his eyes.

Farther along the street was the Cantina Atomica, a gathering place for the well-to-do youth of the town, and across from it was the appliance store, a one-story building of yellow stucco with corrugated metal doors that were lowered at night. Its façade was decorated by a mural that supposedly represented the merchandise within: sparkling refrigerators and televisions and washing machines, all given the impression of enormity by the tiny men and women painted below them, their hands upflung in awe. The actual merchandise was much less imposing, consisting mainly of radios and used kitchen equipment. Few people in Puerto Morada could afford more, and those who could generally bought elsewhere. The majority of Onofrio's clientele were poor, hard-pressed to meet his schedule of payments, and to a large degree his wealth derived from selling repossessed appliances over and over.

Raimundo Esteves, a pale young man with puffy cheeks and heavily lidded eyes and a petulant mouth, was leaning against the counter when Esteban entered; Raimundo smirked and let out a piercing whistle, and a few seconds later his father emerged from the back room: a huge slug of a man, even paler than Raimundo. Filaments of gray hair were slicked down across his mottled scalp, and his belly stretched the front of a starched *guayabera*. He beamed and extended a hand.

"How good to see you," he said. "Raimundo! Bring us coffee and two chairs."

Much as he disliked Onofrio, Esteban was in no position to be uncivil: he accepted the handshake. Raimundo spilled coffee in the saucers and clattered the chairs and glowered, angry at being forced to serve an Indian.

"Why will you not let me return the television?" asked Esteban after taking a seat; and then, unable to bite back the words, he added, "Is it no longer your policy to swindle my people?"

Onofrio sighed, as if it were exhausting to explain things to a fool such as Esteban. "I do not swindle your people. I go beyond the letter of the contracts in allowing them to make returns rather than pursuing matters through the courts. In your case, however, I have devised a way whereby you can keep the television without any further payments and yet settle the account. Is this a swindle?"

It was pointless to argue with a man whose logic was as facile and self-serving as Onofrio's. "Tell me what you want," said Esteban.

Onofrio wetted his lips, which were the color of raw sausage. "I want you to kill the jaguar of Barrio Carolina."

"I no longer hunt," said Esteban.

"The Indian is afraid," said Raimundo, moving up behind Onofrio's shoulder. "I told you."

Onofrio waved him away and said to Esteban, "That is unreasonable. If I take the cows, you will once again be hunting jaguars. But if you do this, you will have to hunt only one jaguar."

"One that has killed eight hunters." Esteban set down his coffee cup and stood. "It is no ordinary jaguar."

Raimundo laughed disparagingly, and Esteban skewered him with a stare.

"Ah!" said Onofrio, smiling a flatterer's smile. "But none of the eight used your method."

"Your pardon, *don* Onofrio," said Esteban with mock formality. "I have other business to attend."

"I will pay you five hundred lempiras in addition to erasing the debt," said Onofrio.

"Why?" asked Esteban. "Forgive me, but I cannot believe it is due to a concern for the public welfare."

Onofrio's fat throat pulsed, his face darkened.

"Never mind," said Esteban. "It is not enough."

"Very well. A thousand." Onofrio's casual manner could not conceal the anxiety in his voice.

Intrigued, curious to learn the extent of Onofrio's anxiety, Esteban plucked a figure from the air. "Ten thousand," he said. "And in advance."

"Ridiculous! I could hire ten hunters for this much! Twenty!"

Esteban shrugged. "But none with my method."

For a moment Onofrio sat with his hands enlaced, twisting them, as if struggling with some pious conception. "All right," he said, the words squeezed out of him. "Ten thousand!"

The reason for Onofrio's interest in Barrio Carolina suddenly dawned on Esteban, and he understood that the profits involved would make his fee seem pitifully small. But he was possessed by the thought of what ten thousand lempiras could mean: a herd of cows, a small truck to haul produce, or—and as he thought it, he realized this was the happiest possibility—the little stucco house in Barrio Clarín that Incarnación had set her heart on. Perhaps owning it would soften her toward him. He noticed Raimundo staring at him, his expression a knowing smirk; and even Onofrio, though still outraged by the fee, was beginning to show signs of satisfaction, adjusting the fit of his *guayabera*, slicking down his already-slicked-down hair. Esteban felt debased by their capacity to buy him, and to preserve a last shred of dignity, he turned and walked to the door.

"I will consider it," he tossed back over his shoulder. "And I will give you my answer in the morning."

"Murder Squad of New York," starring a bald American actor, was the featured attraction on Incarnación's television that night, and the widows sat cross-legged on the floor, filling the hut so completely that the charcoal stove and the sleeping hammock had been moved outside in order to provide good viewing angles for the latecomers. To Esteban, standing in the doorway, it seemed his home had been invaded by a covey of large black birds with cowled heads, who were receiving evil instruction from the core of a flickering gray jewel. Reluctantly, he pushed between them and made his way to the shelves mounted on the wall behind the set; he reached up to the top shelf and pulled down a long bundle wrapped in oil-stained newspapers. Out of the corner of his eye, he saw Incarnación watching him, her lips thinned, curved in a smile, and that cicatrix of a smile branded its mark on Esteban's heart. She knew what he was about, and she was delighted! Not in the least worried! Perhaps she had known of Onofrio's plan to kill the jaguar, perhaps she had schemed with Onofrio to entrap him. Infuriated, he barged through the widows, setting them to gabbling, and walked out into his banana grove and sat on a stone amidst it. The night was cloudy, and only a handful of stars showed between the tattered dark shapes of the leaves; the wind sent the leaves slithering together, and he heard one of his cows snorting and smelled the ripe odor of the corral. It was as if the solidity of his life had been reduced to this isolated perspective, and he bitterly felt the isolation. Though he would admit to fault in the marriage, he could think of nothing he had done that could have bred Incarnación's hateful smile.

After a while, he unwrapped the bundle of newspapers and drew out a thin-bladed machete of the sort used to chop banana stalks, but which he used to kill jaguars. Just holding it renewed his confidence and gave him a feeling of strength. It had been four years since he had hunted, yet he knew he had not lost the skill. Once he had been proclaimed the greatest hunter in the province of Neuva Esperanza, as had his father before him, and he had not retired from hunting because of age or infirmity, but because the jaguars were beautiful, and their beauty had begun to outweigh the reasons he had for killing them. He had no better reason to kill the jaguar of Barrio Carolina. It menaced no one other than those who hunted it, who sought to invade its territory, and its death would profit only a dishonorable man and a shrewish wife, and would spread the contamination of Puerto Morada. And besides, it was a black jaguar.

"Black jaguars," his father had told him, "are creatures of the moon. They have other forms and magical purposes with which we must not interfere. Never hunt them!"

His father had not said that the black jaguars lived on the moon, simply that they utilized its power; but as a child, Esteban had dreamed about a moon of ivory forests and silver meadows through which the jaguars flowed as swiftly as black water; and when he had told his father of the dreams, his father had said that such dreams were representations of a truth, and that sooner or later he would discover the truth underlying them. Esteban had never stopped believing in the dreams, not even in face of the rocky, airless place depicted by the science programs on Incarnación's television: that moon, its mystery explained, was merely a less enlightening kind of dream, a statement of fact that reduced reality to the knowable.

But as he thought this, Esteban suddenly realized that killing the jaguar might be the solution to his problems, that by going against his father's teaching, that by killing his dreams, his Indian conception of the world, he might be able to find accord with his wife's; he had been standing halfway between the two conceptions for too long, and it was time for him to choose. And there was no real choice. It was this world he inhabited, not that of the jaguars; if it took the death of a magical creature to permit him to embrace as joys the television and trips to the movies and a stucco house in Barrio Clarín, well, he had faith in this method. He swung the machete, slicing the dark air, and laughed. Incarnación's frivolousness, his skill at hunting, Onofrio's greed, the jaguar, the television... all these things were neatly woven together like the elements of a spell, one whose products would be a denial of magic and a furthering of the unmagical doctrines that had corrupted Puerto Morada. He laughed again, but a second later he chided himself: it was exactly this sort of thinking he was preparing to root out.

Esteban waked Incarnación early the next morning and forced her to accompany him to the appliance store. His machete swung by his side in a leather sheath, and he carried a burlap sack containing food and the herbs he would need for the hunt. Incarnación trotted along beside him, silent, her face hidden by a shawl. When they reached the store, Esteban had Onofrio stamp the bill PAID IN FULL, then he handed the bill and the money to Incarnación.

"If I kill the jaguar or if it kills me," he said harshly, "this will be yours. Should I fail to return within a week, you may assume that I will never return."

She retreated a step, her face registering alarm, as if she had seen him in new light and understood the consequences of her actions; but she made no move to stop him as he walked out the door.

Across the street, Raimundo Esteves was leaning against the wall of the Cantina Atomica, talking to two girls wearing jeans and frilly blouses; the girls were fluttering their hands and dancing to the music that issued from the cantina, and to Esteban they seemed more alien than the creature he was to hunt. Raimundo spotted him and whispered to the girls; they peeked over their shoulders and laughed. Already angry at Incarnación, Esteban was washed over by a cold fury. He crossed the street to them, rested his hand on the hilt of the machete, and stared at Raimundo; he had never before noticed how soft he was, how empty of presence. A crop of pimples straggled along his jaw, the flesh beneath his eyes was pocked by tiny indentations like those made by a silversmith's hammer, and, unequal to the stare, his eyes darted back and forth between the two girls.

Esteban's anger dissolved into revulsion. "I am Esteban Caax," he said. "I have built my own house, tilled my soil, and brought four children into the world. This day I am going to hunt the jaguar of Barrio Carolina in order to make you and your father even fatter than you are." He ran his gaze up and down Raimundo's body and, letting his voice fill with disgust, he asked, "Who are you?"

Raimundo's puffy face cinched in a knot of hatred, but he offered no response. The girls tittered and skipped through the door of the cantina; Esteban could hear them describing the incident, laughter, and he continued to stare at Raimundo. Several other girls poked their heads out the door, giggling and whispering. After a moment, Esteban spun on his heel and walked away. Behind him there was a chorus of unrestrained laughter, and a girl's voice called mockingly, "Raimundo! Who are you?" Other voices joined in, and it soon became a chant.

Barrio Carolina was not truly a barrio of Puerto Morada; it lay beyond Punta Manabique, the southernmost enclosure of the bay, and was fronted by a palm hammock and the loveliest stretch of beach in all the province, a curving slice of white sand giving way to jade-green shallows. Forty years before, it had been the headquarters of the fruit company's experimental farm, a project of such vast scope that a small town had been built on the site: rows of white frame houses with shingle roofs and screen porches, the kind you might see in a magazine illustration of rural America. The company had touted the project as being the keystone of the country's future, and had promised to develop high-yield crops that would banish starvation; but in 1947 a cholera epidemic had ravaged the coast and the town had been abandoned. By the time the cholera scare had died down, the company had become well-entrenched in national politics and no longer needed to maintain a benevolent image; the project had been dropped and the property abandoned until—in the same year that Esteban had retired from hunting—developers had bought it, planning to build a major resort. It was then the jaguar had appeared. Though it had not killed any of the workmen, it had terrorized them to the point that they had refused to begin the job. Hunters had been sent, and these the jaguar *had* killed. The last party of hunters had been equipped with automatic rifles, all manner of technological aids; but the jaguar had picked them off one by one, and this project, too, had been abandoned. Rumor had it that the land had recently been resold (now Esteban knew to whom), and that the idea of a resort was once more under consideration.

The walk from Puerto Morada was hot and tiring, and upon arrival Esteban sat beneath a palm and ate a lunch of cold banana fritters. Combers as white as toothpaste broke on the shore, and there was no human litter, just dead fronds and driftwood and coconuts. All but four of the houses had been swallowed by the jungle, and only sections of those four remained visible, embedded like moldering gates in a blackish green wall of vegetation. Even under the bright sunlight, they were haunted-looking: their screens ripped, boards weathered gray, vines cascading over their façades. A mango tree had sprouted from one of the porches, and wild parrots were eating its fruit. He had not visited the barrio since childhood: the ruins had frightened him then, but now he found them appealing, testifying to the dominion of natural law. It distressed him that he would help transform it all into a place where the parrots would be chained to perches and the jaguars would be designs on table-cloths, a place of swimming pools and tourists sipping from coconut shells. Nonetheless, after he had finished lunch, he set out to explore the jungle and soon discovered a trail used by the jaguar: a narrow path that wound between the vine-matted shells of the houses for about a half mile and ended at the Rio Dulce. The river was a murkier green than the sea, curving away through the jungle walls; the jaguar's tracks were everywhere along the bank, especially thick upon a tussocky rise some five or six feet above the water. This baffled Esteban. The jaguar could not drink from the rise, and it certainly would not sleep there. He puzzled over it a while, but eventually shrugged it off, returned to the beach, and, because he planned to keep watch that night, took a nap beneath the palms.

Some hours later, around midafternoon, he was started from his nap by a voice hailing him. A tall, slim, copper-skinned woman was walking toward him, wearing a dress of dark green—almost the exact color of the jungle walls—that exposed the swell of her breasts. As she drew near, he saw that though her features had a Patucan cast, they were of a lapidary fineness uncommon to the tribe; it was as if they had been refined into a lovely mask: cheeks planed into subtle hollows, lips sculpted full, stylized feathers of ebony inlaid for eyebrows, eyes of jet and white onyx, and all this given a human gloss. A sheen of sweat covered her breasts, and a single curl of black hair lay over her collarbone, so artful-seeming it appeared to have been placed there by design. She knelt beside him, gazing at him impassively, and Esteban was flustered by her heated air of sensuality. The sea breeze bore her scent to him, a sweet musk that reminded him of mangoes left ripening in the sun.

"My name is Esteban Caax," he said, painfully aware of his own sweaty odor.

"I have heard of you," she said. "The jaguar hunter. Have you come to kill the jaguar of the barrio?"

"Yes," he said, and felt shame at admitting it.

She picked up a handful of sand and watched it sift through her fingers.

"What is your name?" he asked.

"If we become friends, I will tell you my name," she said. "Why must you kill the jaguar?"

He told her about the television set, and then, to his surprise, he found himself describing his problems with Incarnación, explaining how he intended to adapt to her ways. These were not proper subjects to discuss with a stranger, yet he was lured to intimacy; he thought he sensed an affinity between them, and that prompted him to portray his marriage as more dismal than it was, for though he had never once been unfaithful to Incarnación, he would have welcomed the chance to do so now.

"This is a black jaguar," she said. "Surely you know they are not ordinary animals, that they have purposes with which we must not interfere?"

Esteban was startled to hear his father's words from her mouth, but he dismissed it as coincidence and replied, "Perhaps. But they are not mine."

"Truly, they are," she said. "You have simply chosen to ignore them." She scooped up another handful of sand. "How will you do it? You have no gun. Only a machete."

"I have this as well," he said, and from his sack he pulled out a small parcel of herbs and handed it to her.

She opened it and sniffed the contents. "Herbs? Ah! You plan to drug the jaguar."

"Not the jaguar. Myself." He took back the parcel. "The herbs slow the heart and give the body a semblance of death. They induce a trance, but one that can be thrown off at a moment's notice. After I chew them, I will lie down in a place that the jaguar must pass on its nightly hunt. It will think I am dead, but it will not feed unless it is sure that the spirit has left the flesh, and to determine this, it will sit on the body so it can feel the spirit rise up. As soon as it starts to settle, I will throw off the trance and stab it between the ribs. If my hand is steady, it will die instantly."

"And if your hand is unsteady?"

"I have killed nearly fifty jaguars," he said. "I no longer fear unsteadiness. The method comes down through my family from the Old Patuca, and it has never failed, to my knowledge."

"But a black jaguar..."

"Black or spotted, it makes no difference. Jaguars are creatures of instinct, and one is like another when it comes to feeding."

"Well," she said, "I cannot wish you luck, but neither do I wish you ill." She came to her feet, brushing the sand from her dress.

He wanted to ask her to stay, but pride prevented him, and she laughed as if she knew his mind.

"Perhaps we will talk again, Esteban," she said. "It would be a pity if we did not, for more lies between us than we have spoken of this day."

She walked swiftly down the beach, becoming a diminutive black figure that was rippled away by the heat haze.

That evening, needing a place from which to keep watch, Esteban pried open the screen door of one of the houses facing the beach and went onto the porth. Chameleons skittered into the corners, and an iguana slithered off a rusted lawn chair sheathed in spiderweb and vanished through a gap in the floor. The interior of the house was dark and forbidding, except for the bathroom, the roof of which was missing, webbed over by vines that admitted a gray-green infusion of twilight. The cracked toilet was full of rainwater and dead insects. Uneasy, Esteban returned to the porch, cleaned the lawn chair, and sat.

Out on the horizon the sea and sky were blending in a haze of silver and gray; the wind had died, and the palms were as still as sculpture; a string of pelicans flying low above the waves seemed to be spelling a sentence of cryptic black syllables. But the eerie beauty of the scene was lost on him. He could not stop thinking of the woman. The memory of her hips rolling beneath the fabric of her dress as she walked away was repeated over and over in his thoughts, and whenever he tried to turn his attention to the matter at hand, the memory became more compelling. He imagined her naked, the play of muscles rippling her haunches, and this so enflamed him that he started to pace, unmindful of the fact that the creaking boards were signaling his presence. He could not understand her effect upon him. Perhaps, he thought, it was her defense of the jaguar, her calling to mind of all he was putting behind him... and then a realization settled over him like an icy shroud.

It was commonly held among the Patuca that a man about to suffer a solitary and unexpected death would be visited by an envoy of death, who—standing in for family and friends—would prepare him to face the event; and Esteban was now very sure that the woman had been such an envoy, that her allure had been specifically designed to attract his soul to its imminent fate. He sat back down in the lawn chair, numb with the realization. Her knowledge of his father's words, the odd flavor of her conversation, her intimation that more lay between them: it all accorded perfectly with the traditional wisdom. The moon rose three-quarters full, silvering the sands of the barrio, and still he sat there, rooted to the spot by his fear of death.

He had been watching the jaguar for several seconds before he registered its presence. It seemed at first that a scrap of night sky had fallen onto the sand and was being blown by a fitful breeze; but soon he saw that it was the jaguar, that it was inching along as if stalking some prey. Then it leaped high into the air, twisting and turning, and began to race up and down the beach: a ribbon of black water flowing across the silver sands. He had never before seen a jaguar at play, and this alone was cause for wonder; but most of all, he wondered at the fact that here were his childhood dreams come to life. He might have been peering out onto a silvery meadow of the moon, spying on one of its magical creatures. His fear was eroded by the sight, and like a child he pressed his nose to the screen, trying not to blink, anxious that he might miss a single moment.

At length the jaguar left off its play and came prowling up the beach toward the jungle. By the set of its ears and the purposeful sway of its walk, Esteban recognized that it was hunting. It stopped beneath a palm about twenty feet from the house, lifted its head, and tested the air. Moonlight frayed down through the fronds, applying liquid gleams to its haunches; its eyes, glinting yellow-green, were like peepholes into a lurid dimension of fire. The jaguar's beauty was heart-stopping—the embodiment of a flawless principle—and Esteban, contrasting this beauty with the pallid ugliness of his employer, with the ugly principle that had led to his hiring, doubted that he could ever bring himself to kill it.

All the following day he debated the question. He had hoped the woman would return, because he had rejected the idea that she was death's envoy—that perception, he thought, must have been induced by the mysterious atmosphere of the barrio—and he felt that if she were to argue the jaguar's cause again, he would let himself be persuaded. But she did not put in an appearance, and as he sat upon the beach, watching the evening sun decline through strata of dusky orange and lavender clouds, casting wild glitters over the sea, he understood once more that he had no choice. Whether or not the jaguar was beautiful, whether or not the woman had been on a supernatural errand, he must treat these things as if they had no substance. The point of the hunt had been to deny mysteries of this sort, and he had lost sight of it under the influence of old dreams.

He waited until moonrise to take the herbs, and then lay down beneath the palm tree where the jaguar had paused the previous night. Lizards whispered past in the grasses, sand fleas hopped onto his face: he hardly felt them, sinking deeper into the languor of the herbs. The fronds overhead showed an ashen green in the moonlight, lifting, rustling; and the stars between their feathered edges flickered crazily as if the breeze were fanning their flames. He became immersed in the landscape, savoring the smells of brine and rotting foliage that were blowing across the beach, drifting with them; but when he heard the pad of the jaguar's step, he came alert. Through narrowed eyes he saw it sitting a dozen feet away, a bulky shadow craning its neck toward him, investigating his scent. After a moment it began to circle him, each circle a bit tighter than the one before, and whenever it passed out of view, he had to repress a trickle of fear. Then, as it passed close on the seaward side, he caught a whiff of its odor.

A sweet, musky odor that reminded him of mangoes left ripening in the sun.

Fear welled up in him, and he tried to banish it, to tell himself that the odor could not possibly be what he thought. The jaguar snarled, a razor stroke of sound that slit the peaceful mesh of wind and surf, and realizing it had scented his fear, he sprang to his feet, waving his machete. In a whirl of vision, he saw the jaguar leap back, he shouted at it, waved the machete again, and sprinted for the house where he had kept watch. He slipped through the door and went staggering into the front room. There was a crash behind him, and turning, he had a glimpse of a huge black shape struggling to extricate itself from a moonlit tangle of vines and ripped screen. He darted into the bathroom, sat with his back against the toilet bowl, and braced the door shut with his feet.

The sound of the jaguar's struggles subsided, and for a moment he thought it had given up. Sweat left cold trails down his sides, his heart pounded. He held his breath, listening, and it seemed the whole world was holding its breath as well. The noises of wind and surf and insects were a faint seething; moonlight shed a sickly white radiance through the enlaced vines overhead, and a chameleon was frozen among peels of wallpaper beside the door. He let out a sigh and wiped the sweat from his eyes. He swallowed.

Then the top panel of the door exploded, shattered by a black paw. Splinters of rotten wood flew into his face, and he screamed. The sleek wedge of the jaguar's head thrust through the hole, roaring. A gateway of gleaming fangs guarding a plush red throat. Half-paralyzed, Esteban jabbed weakly with the machete. The jaguar withdrew, reached in with its paw, and clawed at his leg. More by accident than design, he managed to slice the jaguar, and the paw, too, was withdrawn. He heard it rumbling in the front room, and then, seconds later, a heavy thump against the wall behind him. The jaguar's head appeared above the edge of the wall; it was hanging by its forepaws, trying to gain a perch from which to leap down into the room. Esteban scrambled to his feet and slashed wildly, severing vines. The jaguar fell back, yowling. For a while it prowled along the wall, fuming to itself. Finally there was silence.

When sunlight began to filter through the vines, Esteban walked out of the house and headed down the beach to Puerto Morada. He went with his head lowered, desolate, thinking of the grim future that awaited him after he returned the money to Onofrio: a life of trying to please an increasingly shrewish Incarnación, of killing lesser jaguars for much less money. He was so mired in depression that he did not notice the woman until she called to him. She was leaning against a palm about thirty feet away, wearing a filmy white dress through which he could see the dark jut of her nipples. He drew his machete and backed off a pace.

"Why do you fear me, Esteban?" she called, walking toward him.

"You tricked me into revealing my method and tried to kill me," he said. "Is that not reason for fear?"

"I did not know you or your method in that form. I knew only that you were hunting me. But now the hunt has ended, and we can be as man and woman."

He kept his machete at point. "What are you?" he asked.

She smiled. "My name is Miranda. I am Patuca."

"Patucas do not have black fur and fangs."

"I am of the Old Patuca," she said. "We have this power."

"Keep away!" He lifted the machete as if to strike, and she stopped just beyond his reach.

"You can kill me if that is your wish, Esteban." She spread her arms, and her breasts thrust forward against the fabric of her dress. "You are stronger than I, now. But listen to me first."

He did not lower the machete, but his fear and anger were being overridden by a sweeter emotion.

"Long ago," she said, "there was a great healer who foresaw that one day the Patuca would lose their place in the world, and so, with the help of the gods, he opened a door into another world where the tribe could flourish. But many of the tribe were afraid and would not follow him. Since then, the door has been left open for those who would come after." She waved at the ruined houses. "Barrio Carolina is the site of the door, and the jaguar is its guardian. But soon the fevers of this world will sweep over the barrio, and the door will close forever. For though our hunt has ended, there is no end to hunters or to greed." She came a step nearer. "If you listen to the sounding of your heart, you will know this is the truth."

He half-believed her, yet he also believed her words masked a more poignant truth, one that fitted inside the other the way his machete fitted into its sheath.

"What is it?" she asked. "What troubles you?"

"I think you have come to prepare me for death," he said, "and that your door leads only to death."

"Then why do you not run from me?" She pointed toward Puerto Morada. "That is death, Esteban. The cries of the gulls are death, and when the hearts of lovers stop at the moment of greatest pleasure, that, too, is death. This world is no more than a thin covering of life drawn over a foundation of death, like a scum of algae upon a rock. Perhaps you are right, perhaps my world lies beyond death. The two ideas are not opposed. But if I am death to you, Esteban, then it is death you love."

He turned his eyes to the sea, not wanting her to see his face. "I do not love you," he said.

"Love awaits us," she said. "And someday you will join me in my world."

He looked back to her, ready with a denial, but was shocked to silence. Her dress had fallen to the sand, and she was smiling. The litheness and purity of the jaguar were reflected in every line of her body; her secret hair was so absolute a black that it seemed an absence in her flesh. She moved close, pushing aside the machete. The tips of her breasts brushed against him, warm through the coarse cloth of his shirt; her hands cupped his face, and he was drowning in her heated scent, weakened by both fear and desire.

"We are of one soul, you and I," she said. "One blood and one truth. You cannot reject me."

Days passed, though Esteban was unclear as to how many. Night and day were unimportant incidences of his relationship with Miranda, serving only to color their lovemaking with a spectral or a sunny mood; and each time they made love, it was as if a thousand new colors were being added to his senses. He had never been so content. Sometimes, gazing at the haunted façades of the barrio, he believed that they might well conceal shadowy avenues leading to another world; however, whenever Miranda tried to convince him to leave with her, he refused: he could not overcome his fear and would never admit—even to himself—that he loved her. He attempted to fix his thoughts on Incarnación, hoping this would undermine his fixation with Miranda and free him to return to Puerto Morada; but he found that he could not picture his wife except as a black bird hunched before a flickering gray jewel. Miranda, however, seemed equally unreal at times. Once as they sat on the bank of the Rio Dulce, watching the reflection of the moon—almost full—floating upon the water, she pointed to it and said, "My world is that near, Esteban. That touchable. You may think the moon above is real and this is only a reflection, but the thing most real, that most illustrates the real, is the surface that permits the illusion of reflection. Passing through this surface is what you fear, and yet it is so insubstantial, you would scarcely notice the passage."

"You sound like the old priest who taught me philosophy," said Esteban. "His world—his heaven—was also philosophy. Is that what your world is? The idea of a place? Or are there birds and jungles and rivers?"

Her expression was in partial eclipse, half-moonlit, half-shadowed, and her voice revealed nothing of her mood. "No more than there are here," she said.

"What does that mean?" he said angrily. "Why will you not give me a clear answer?"

"If I were to describe my world, you would simply think me a clever liar." She rested her head on his shoulder. "Sooner or later you will understand. We did not find each other merely to have the pain of being parted."

In that moment her beauty—like her words—seemed a kind of evasion, obscuring a dark and frightening beauty beneath; and yet he knew that she was right, that no proof of hers could persuade him contrary to his fear.

One afternoon, an afternoon of such brightness that it was impossible to look at the sea without squinting, they swam out to a sandbar that showed as a thin curving island of white against the green water. Esteban floundered and splashed, but Miranda swam as if born to the element; she darted beneath him, tickling him, pulling at his feet, eeling away before he could catch her. They walked along the sand, turning over starfish with their toes, collecting whelks to boil for their dinner, and then Esteban spotted a dark stain hundreds of yards wide that was moving below the water beyond the bar: a great school of king mackerel.

"It is too bad we have no boat," he said. "Mackerel would taste better than whelks."

"We need no boat," she said. "I will show you an old way of catching fish."

She traced a complicated design in the sand, and when she had done, she led him into the shallows and had him stand facing her a few feet away.

"Look down at the water between us," she said. "Do not look up, and keep perfectly still until I tell you."

She began to sing with a faltering rhythm, a rhythm that put him in mind of the ragged breezes of the season. Most of the words were unfamiliar, but others he recognized as Patuca. After a minute he experienced a wave of dizziness, as if his legs had grown long and spindly, and he was now looking down from a great height, breathing rarefied air. Then a tiny dark stain materialized below the expanse of water between him and Miranda. He remembered his grandfather's stories of the Old Patuca, how—with the help of the gods—they had been able to shrink the world, to bring enemies close and cross vast distances in a matter of moments. But the gods were dead, their powers gone from the world. He wanted to glance back to shore and see if he and Miranda had become coppery giants taller than the palms.

"Now," she said, breaking off her song, "you must put your hand into the water on the seaward side of the school and gently wiggle your fingers. Very gently! Be sure not to disturb the surface."

But when Esteban made to do as he was told, he slipped and caused a splash. Miranda cried out. Looking up, he saw a wall of jade-green water bearing down on them, its face thickly studded with the fleeting dark shapes of the mackerel. Before he could move, the wave swept over the sandbar and carried him under, dragging him along the bottom and finally casting him onto shore. The beach was littered with flopping mackerel; Miranda lay in the shallows, laughing at him. Esteban laughed, too, but only to cover up his rekindled fear of this woman who drew upon the powers of dead gods. He had no wish to hear her explanation; he was certain she would tell him that the gods lived on in her world, and this would only confuse him further.

Later that day as Esteban was cleaning the fish, while Miranda was off picking bananas to cook with them—the sweet little ones that grew along the riverbank—a Land-Rover came jouncing up the beach from Puerto Morada, an orange fire of the setting sun dancing on its windshield. It pulled up beside him, and Onofrio climbed out the passenger side. A hectic flush dappled his cheeks, and he was dabbing his sweaty brow with a handkerchief. Raimundo climbed out the driver's side and leaned against the door, staring hatefully at Esteban.

"Nine days and not a word," said Onofrio gruffly. "We thought you were dead. How goes the hunt?"

Esteban set down the fish he had been scaling and stood. "I have failed," he said. "I will give you back the money."

Raimundo chuckled—a dull, cluttered sound—and Onofrio grunted with amusement. "Impossible," he said. "Incarnación has spent the money on a house in Barrio Clarín. You must kill the jaguar."

"I cannot," said Esteban. "I will repay you, somehow."

"The Indian has lost his nerve, Father." Raimundo spat in the sand. "Let my friends and I hunt the jaguar."

The idea of Raimundo and his loutish friends thrashing through the jungle was so ludicrous that Esteban could not restrain a laugh.

"Be careful, Indian!" Raimundo banged the flat of his hand on the roof of the car.

"It is you who should be careful," said Esteban. "Most likely the jaguar will be hunting you." Esteban picked up his machete. "And whoever hunts this jaguar will answer to me as well."

Raimundo reached for something in the driver's seat and walked around in front of the hood. In his hand was a silvered automatic. "I await your answer," he said.

"Put that away!" Onofrio's tone was that of a man addressing a child whose menace was inconsequential, but the intent surfacing in Raimundo's face was not childish. A tic marred the plump curve of his cheek, the ligature of his neck was cabled, and his lips were drawn back in a joyless grin. It was, thought Esteban—strangely fascinated by the transformation—like watching a demon dissolve its false shape: the true lean features melting up from the illusion of the soft.

"This son of a whore insulted me in front of Julia!" Raimundo's gun hand was shaking.

"Your personal differences can wait," said Onofrio. "This is a business matter." He held out his hand. "Give me the gun."

"If he is not going to kill the jaguar, what use is he?" said Raimundo.

"Perhaps we can convince him to change his mind." Onofrio beamed at Esteban. "What do you say? Shall I let my son collect his debt of honor, or will you fulfill our contract?"

"Father!" complained Raimundo; his eyes flicked sideways. "He..."

Esteban broke for the jungle. The gun roared, a white-hot claw swiped at his side, and he went flying. For an instant he did not know where he was; but then, one by one, his impressions began to sort themselves. He was lying on his injured side, and it was throbbing fiercely. Sand crusted his mouth and eyelids. He was curled up around his machete, which was still clutched in his hand. Voices above him, sand fleas hopping on his face. He resisted the urge to brush them off and lay without moving. The throb of his wound and his hatred had the same red force behind them.

"... carry him to the river," Raimundo was saying, his voice atremble with excitement. "Everyone will think the jaguar killed him!"

"Fool!" said Onofrio. "He might have killed the jaguar, and you could have had a sweeter revenge. His wife..."

"This was sweet enough," said Raimundo.

A shadow fell over Esteban, and he held his breath. He needed no herbs to deceive this pale, flabby jaguar who was bending to him, turning him onto his back.

"Watch out!" cried Onofrio.

Esteban let himself be turned and lashed out with the machete. His contempt for Onofrio and Incarnación, as well as his hatred of Raimundo, was involved in the blow, and the blade lodged deep in Raimundo's side, grating on bone. Raimundo shrieked and would have fallen, but the blade helped to keep him upright; his hands fluttered around the machete as if he wanted to adjust it to a more comfortable position, and his eyes were wide with disbelief. A shudder vibrated the hilt of the machete—it seemed sensual, the spasm of a spent passion—and Raimundo sank to his knees. Blood spilled from his mouth, adding tragic lines to the corners of his lips. He pitched forward, not falling flat but remaining kneeling, his face pressed into the sand: the attitude of an Arab at prayer.

Esteban wrenched the machete free, fearful of an attack by Onofrio, but the appliance dealer was squirming into the Land-Rover. The engine caught, the wheels spun, and the car lurched off, turning through the edge of the surf and heading for Puerto Morada. An orange dazzle flared on the rear window, as if the spirit who had lured it to the barrio was now harrying it away.

Unsteadily, Esteban got to his feet. He peeled his shirt back from the bullet wound. There was a lot of blood, but it was only a crease. He avoided looking at Raimundo and walked down to the water and stood gazing out at the waves; his thoughts rolled in with them, less thoughts than tidal sweeps of emotion.

It was twilight by the time Miranda returned, her arms full of bananas and wild figs. She had not heard the shot. He told her what had happened as she dressed his wounds with a poultice of herbs and banana leaves. "It will mend," she said of the wound. "But this"—she gestured at Raimundo—"this will not. You must come with me, Esteban. The soldiers will kill you."

"No," he said. "They will come, but they are Patuca... except for the captain, who is a drunkard, a shell of a man. I doubt he will even be notified. They will listen to my story, and we will reach an accommodation. No matter what lies Onofrio tells, his word will not stand against theirs."

"And then?"

"I may have to go to jail for a while, or I may have to leave the province. But I will not be killed."

She sat for a minute without speaking, the whites of her eyes glowing in the half-light. Finally she stood and walked off along the beach.

"Where are you going?" he called.

She turned back. "You speak so casually of losing me..." she began.

"It is not casual!"

"No!" She laughed bitterly. "I suppose not. You are so afraid of life, you call it death and would prefer jail or exile to living it. That is hardly casual." She stared at him, her expression a cypher at that distance. "I will not lose you, Esteban," she said. She walked away again, and this time when he called she did not turn.

*

Twilight deepened to dusk, a slow fill of shadow graying the world into negative, and Esteban felt himself graying along with it, his thoughts reduced to echoing the dull wash of the receding tide. The dusk lingered, and he had the idea that night would never fall, that the act of violence had driven a nail through the substance of his irresolute life, pinned him forever to this ashen moment and deserted shore. As a child he had been terrified by the possibility of such magical isolations, but now the prospect seemed a consolation for Miranda's absence, a remembrance of her magic. Despite her parting words, he did not think she would be back—there had been sadness and finality in her voice—and this roused in him feelings of both relief and desolation, feelings that set him to pacing up and down the tidal margin of the shore.

The full moon rose, the sands of the barrio burned silver, and shortly thereafter four soldiers came in a jeep from Puerto Morada. They were gnomish, copper-skinned men, and their uniforms were the dark blue of the night sky, bearing no device or decoration. Though they were not close friends, he knew them each by name. Sebastian, Amador, Carlito, and Ramón. In their headlights Raimundo's corpse—startlingly pale, the blood on his face dried into intricate whorls—looked like an exotic creature cast up by the sea, and their inspection of it smacked more of curiosity than of a search for evidence. Amador unearthed Raimundo's gun, sighted along it toward the jungle, and asked Ramón how much he thought it was worth.

"Perhaps Onofrio will give you a good price," said Ramón, and the others laughed.

They built a fire of driftwood and coconut shells, and sat around it while Esteban told his story; he did not mention either Miranda or her relation to the jaguar, because these men—estranged from the tribe by their government service—had grown conservative in their judgments, and he did not want them to consider him irrational. They listened without comment; the firelight burnished their skins to reddish gold and glinted on their rifle barrels.

"Onofrio will take his charge to the capital if we do nothing," said Amador after Esteban had finished.

"He may in any case," said Carlito. "And then it will go hard with Esteban."

"And," said Sebastian, "if an agent is sent to Puerto Morada and sees how things are with Captain Portales, they will surely replace him and it will go hard with us."

They stared into the flames, mulling over the problem, and Esteban chose the moment to ask Amador, who lived near him on the mountain, if he had seen Incarnación.

"She will be amazed to learn you are alive," said Amador. "I saw her yesterday in the dressmaker's shop. She was admiring the fit of a new black skirt in the mirror."

It was as if a black swath of Incarnación's skirt had folded around Esteban's thoughts. He lowered his head and carved lines in the sand with the point of his machete.

"I have it," said Ramon. "A boycott!"

The others expressed confusion.

"If we do not buy from Onofrio, who will?" said Ramón. "He will lose his business. Threatened with this, he will not dare involve the government. He will allow Esteban to plead self-defense."

"But Raimundo was his only son," said Amador. "It may be that grief will count more than greed in this instance."

Again they fell silent. It mattered little to Esteban what was decided. He was coming to understand that without Miranda, his future held nothing but uninteresting choices; he turned his gaze to the sky and noticed that the stars and the fire were flickering with the same rhythm, and he imagined each of them ringed by a group of gnomish, copper-skinned men, debating the question of his fate.

"Aha!" said Carlito. "I know what to do. We will occupy Barrio Carolina—the entire company—and *we* will kill the jaguar. Onofirio's greed cannot withstand this temptation."

"That you must not do," said Esteban.

"But why?" asked Amador. "We may not kill the jaguar, but with so many men we will certainly drive it away."

Before Esteban could answer, the jaguar roared. It was prowling down the beach toward the fire, like a black flame itself shifting over the glowing sand. Its ears were laid back, and silver drops of moonlight gleamed in its eyes. Amador grabbed his rifle, came to one knee, and fired: the bullet sprayed sand a dozen feet to the left of the jaguar.

"Wait!" cried Esteban, pushing him down.

But the rest had begun to fire, and the jaguar was hit. It leaped high as it had that first night while playing, but this time it landed in a heap, snarling, snapping at its shoulder; it regained its feet and limped toward the jungle, favoring its right foreleg. Excited by their success, the soldiers ran a few paces after it and stopped to fire again. Carlito dropped to one knee, taking careful aim.

"No!" shouted Esteban, and as he hurled his machete at Carlito, desperate to prevent further harm to Miranda, he recognized the trap that had been sprung and the consequences he would face.

The blade sliced across Carlito's thigh, knocking him onto his side. He screamed, and Amador, seeing what had happened, fired wildly at Esteban and called to the others. Esteban ran toward the jungle, making for the jaguar's path. A fusilade of shots rang out behind him, bullets whipped past his ears. Each time his feet slipped in the soft sand, the moonstruck façades of the barrio appeared to lurch sideways as if trying to block his way. And then, as he reached the verge of the jungle, he was hit.

The bullet seemed to throw him forward, to increase his speed, but somehow he managed to keep his feet. He careened along the path, arms waving, breath shrieking in his throat. Palmetto fronds swatted his face, vines tangled his legs. He felt no pain, only a peculiar numbness that pulsed low in his back; he pictured the wound opening and closing like the mouth of an anemone. The soldiers were shouting his name. They would follow, but cautiously, afraid of the jaguar, and he thought he might be able to cross the river before they could catch up. But when he came to the river, he found the jaguar waiting.

It was crouched on the tussocky rise, its neck craned over the water, and below, half a dozen feet from the bank, floated the reflection of the full moon, huge and silvery, an unblemished circle of light. Blood glistened scarlet on the jaguar's shoulder, like a fresh rose pinned in place, and this made it look even more an embodiment of principle: the shape a god might choose, that some universal constant might assume. It gazed calmly at Esteban, growled low in its throat, and dove into the river, cleaving and shattering the moon's reflection, vanishing beneath the surface. The ripples subsided, the image of the moon reformed. And there, silhouetted against it, Esteban saw the figure of a woman swimming, each stroke causing her to grow smaller and smaller until she seemed no more than a character incised upon a silver plate. It was not only Miranda he saw, but all mystery and beauty receding from him, and he realized how blind he had been not to perceive the truth sheathed inside the truth of death that had been sheathed inside her truth of another world. It was clear to him now. It sang to him from his wound, every syllable a heartbeat. It was written by the dying ripples, it swayed in the banana leaves, it sighed on the wind. It was everywhere, and he had always known it: If you deny mystery—even in the guise of death—then you deny life, and you will walk like a ghost through your days, never knowing the secrets of the extremes. The deep sorrows, the absolute joys.

He drew a breath of the rank jungle air, and with it drew a breath of a world no longer his, of the girl Incarnación, of friends and children and country nights... all his lost sweetness. His chest tightened as with the onset of tears, but the sensation quickly abated, and he understood that the sweetness of the past had been subsumed by a scent of mangoes, that nine magical days—a magical number of days, the number it takes to sing the soul to rest—lay between him and tears. Freed of those associations, he felt as if he were undergoing a subtle refinement of form, a winnowing, and he remembered having felt much the same on the day when he had run out the door of Santa María del Onda, putting behind him its dark geometries and cobwebbed catechisms and generations of swallows that had never flown beyond the walls, casting off his acolyte's robe and racing across the square toward the mountain and Incarnación: it had been she who had lured him then, just as his mother had lured him to the church and as Miranda was luring him now, and he laughed at seeing how easily these three women had diverted the flow of his life, how like other men he was in this.

The strange bloom of painlessness in his back was sending out tendrils into his arms and legs, and the cries of the soldiers had grown louder. Miranda was a tiny speck shrinking against a silver immensity. For a moment he hesitated, experiencing a resurgence of fear; then Miranda's face materialized in his mind's eye, and all the emotion he had suppressed for nine days poured through him, washing away the fear. It was a silvery, flawless emotion, and he was giddy with it, light with it; it was like thunder and fire fused into one element and boiling up inside him, and he was overwhelmed by a need to express it, to mold it into a form that would reflect its power and purity. But he was no singer, no poet. There was but a single mode of expression open to him. Hoping he was not too late, that Miranda's door had not shut forever, Esteban dove into the river, cleaving the image of the full moon; and—his eyes still closed from the shock of the splash—with the last of his mortal strength, he swam hard down after her.

2014

THE GIRL ON THE SUICIDE BRIDGE

Johnny Mains

Johnny Mains was born in Galashiels, Roxburghshire, Scotland, on 15 April 1976. He studied at Earlston High School, Berwickshire, and left home at seventeen, after which, in his own words he "experienced a lost decade due to homelessness and drug abuse". He turned his life around in 2006 and his first piece of fiction, "The Spoon", was published in *The Third Black Book of Horror* (2008). His first collection of short stories, *With Deepest Sympathy* (2010), was published by Obverse Books, and 2012 saw the publication of a second short fiction collection, *Frightfully Cosy and Mild Stories for Nervous Types*.

Under his own Noose & Gibbet publishing imprint, he published *Back from the Dead: The Legacy of the Pan Book of Horror Stories* (2010), which would go on to win the British Fantasy Award for Best Anthology in 2011. This led Pan Macmillan to hire Mains as the Project Editor for their reissue of the 1959 volume *The Pan Book of Horror Stories*.

In 2014 Mains created the book series *Dead Funny: Horror Stories by Comedians* (co-edited with Robin Ince) and between 2014 and 2018 he edited three volumes of *Best British Horror*. In 2017 he dipped his toe into rediscovering "lost" works of fiction, and his anthologies for Black Shuck Books, *A Suggestion of Ghosts* (2017), *An Obscurity of Ghosts* (2018) and *Remembering the Dead at Halloween and Christmas* (2019), quickly cemented his position as a genre researcher of some regard.

His first novel, *A Distasteful Horror Story*, was published in 2019, and this was followed by *A Man at War* in 2022. Mains's work with the British Library began with *Celtic Weird: Tales of Wicked Folklore and Dark Mythology* (2022), and has been followed by four other works: *Scotland the Strange: Weird Tales from Storied Lands* (2023), *Halloweird: Classic Stories from the Season of Samhain* (2024), *The Dead of Summer: Strange Tales of May Eve & Midsummer* (2025), and *Illusions of Presence: Lost Christmas Ghost Stories* (2025).

Originally published under the name J. A. Mains in the anthology *Beside the Seaside* (2014), "The Girl on the Suicide Bridge" is a short but deeply affecting tale about suicide, loss, love, redemption and acceptance. It is sombre, but also uplifting, and an excellent way to round off this anthology.

Elsie was awoken by the screams of her mother. Panicked, she fell out of bed, pulling the duvet with her. Her dad came into the bedroom, his face was stretched tight with grief.

"It's your brother," was all he managed to get out before he collapsed onto the floor, the bones in his body succumbing to that invisible onslaught of despair.

"Ben? What's happened to Ben?" Elsie started to scream, her voice rising to such a pitch that the empty glass on the dresser began to vibrate ever so gently.

All three sat on the sofa, silent, destroyed. The police officer was in Dad's favourite chair, a look of practised empathy on her face. Her notebook next to her, closed, on the worn arm—the place where Dad always sat his mug of tea.

"Can Elsie leave the room for a second, please?" The officer wasn't surprised when the mother grasped her daughter as if she was in danger of drowning, and held on for dear life, shaking her head; *no*.

"Very well. The person we believe to be Ben has been taken to the mortuary, and we'll need someone to formally identify him," she said softly. She glanced at Elsie who was staring at her toenails, painted a delicate blue. The young girl's face was puffy, her eyes red and raw.

Mum wailed. Dad looked lost and confused; knowing deep in his heart that he was in some way responsible for his son having hanged himself from the Valley Bridge.

*

It was a notorious spot, and with every death there was more pressure heaped on the council to install barriers. It wasn't just a local problem. People who wanted to end their life from all over the country had heard and had travelled to Scarborough. News of a new death was already circulating, and the residents of Scarborough had reached a tipping point. Ben was only seventeen and had been the first person to have hanged himself from the bridge—everyone before had thrown themselves off. At the moment he had jumped and the rope bit, snapping his neck and nearly taking his head off, a Vauxhall Nova containing a family of five returning to Galashiels in the Scottish Borders had been driving along the Valley Road.

Within the suicide note stuffed into the back pocket of his cords, Ben had written that he didn't want to be remembered like the others who had thrown themselves off—those who had severely injured innocent travellers, in one instance killing the driver of an Audi 100.

Relatives began to visit, filling the day with more pain than the house could possibly bear, weeping aunties and uncles, sullen and confused younger cousins in tow. The phone was constantly ringing; the funeral parlour, the Housemaster of the college who promised a full investigation as to how Ben left the grounds, distant relatives.

Elsie went to her room, numbed by their aggressive sympathy. She wanted to go into Ben's room but was too scared to bring herself to do it; afraid of the silence and the knowledge that the room now belonged to no one. It was his space no longer. It was just a room full of stuff.

She opened the squeaking cupboard door and pulled out her jacket and beaten-up trainers. She folded the jacket and put that and her trainers under the pillow. She looked around her room, at posters on the wall, photos that were above the bed, trophies for gymnastics on top of the bookcase and then, the soft whisper of death called out to her, a seductive void that invited her to join her brother.

*

Elsie, at thirteen, wasn't as naive as her age may have suggested and knew the real reason behind Ben going to Scarborough College, even though they only lived in the semi-detached haven of Ryndle Walk. Ben was different, and because of that difference, was despised (?)—Elsie didn't know if that was the word she would have attributed to her dad's feelings of her older brother—but it was close.

"Ben needs structure," was all Dad would say when she asked why Ben had been sent to college, but she had to continue to go to Scalby. The "boys" as Mum called them (always with a slight edge to her voice) had been butting heads ever since Elsie's tenth birthday party, and it wasn't long after that that Ben was sent to the College. He would come home for the holidays, of course, and that was the time Elsie and Ben would jump on a bus and travel to Whitby, up by the Abbey, playing with holidaying children at the East Cliff hostel.

There was hardly any mention of problems at home, and if there was Ben would brush it off saying that "Dad would come round, one day."

Dinner was stew, brought round by the next-door neighbour but one, Mrs Michaels. Dad was in his shed, drinking whisky. Mum staring into space, her face blank, rubbery.

The Reverend called round later in the evening. Mum was a little more alert, enough to allow her hand to be patted sympathetically. Dad had stumbled upstairs and was snoring off the Grouse.

When death visits, and drapes its cloak over a particular household, all normal noises like the house groaning and settling down for the night are stilled. Nocturnal animals are nowhere to be seen, frightened by the wispy, grey aura of despair that seeps out of the very brick the house is made from.

Elsie put on her scuffed trainers and her jacket, hidden under her pillow earlier on in the day, because if she had tried to get them from the cupboard now, the noise that the door would make, a high-pitched continuous screeching would wake up her parents, no matter the amount of alcohol her dad had put away.

She opened her bedroom door very, very gently and crept out of the room, sticking to the right-hand side of the stairs as she went down; the wood on the left-hand side had some slight warping and would let out what Elsie thought of as a sharp cough of surprise.

Downstairs she tiptoed her way to the kitchen and to the scullery where the back door was. The key was hanging on the nail that had been hammered into the casing that ran up the side of the door. Letting herself out, she locked the door from the outside, so no opportunistic burglars would visit.

Elsie zipped her jacket all the way up to her chin and started walking, her destination the Valley Bridge.

She walked past the Ryndle Court Hotel, crossed the road and nipped through a gap in the hedge and then ran as fast as she could through Peasholm Park, through the trees, just enough light in the sky to navigate by until she was next to the artificial boating lake, staring idly at the inky blackness of the water.

Picking up the pace she walked past the cricket club, hiding behind a parked van as she spied a car coming towards her, fearing that her parents were awake and had phoned the police.

A flap of torn police tape adorned one of the rails. Elsie walked over to it slowly, her galloping heart feeling like it was swelling up in her chest, fit to burst. She could see a solitary bunch of flowers ahead. The spot. Aware of the sea to her left, every step she took made her feel she was adrift, being engulfed by tumultuous waves on all sides. But the paving was sure underfoot, it wasn't going anywhere, the bridge wasn't going anywhere. A milk float drove past her slowly, the driver paying her no notice.

When she arrived at where the flowers were, two things sucked the air from her, threatened to collapse her there and then, have her scream so hard that she'd throw herself off the bridge to stop the agony.

Footprints on the railing. And what seemed like a deep scuff mark.

That's where the rope was something inside her wailed. *He jumped! He didn't climb up and sit, then drop. He jumped. He wanted his...*

Elsie bit down on her bottom lip, hard. The reality of blood stopped her for a second.

She grabbed onto the railing and breathed in deeply, complex organs taking in more air than she ever thought possible. She felt *everything*. And that's when she decided to never let go.

Elsie looked down at her digital watch; the time was eight-thirty A.M. She could feel people staring at her as they walked by. She sometimes met their gaze.

At ten o'clock, one of her school friends, Julianne Crosby, saw Elsie and ran across. She tried to console her, but Elsie said simply, "Don't touch me, it'll stop everything. If you touch me, it'll stop."

"I don't understand," Julianne said, her hand hovering above Elsie's right shoulder, fear creeping into her voice. A part of her wanted to grab her. "What will stop?"

By eleven-thirty a small group of onlookers had surrounded her. The bridge had accepted her and Elsie accepted the bridge. From the moment her hands first grabbed the pale green railing she *was* the bridge, felt the terror, anguish, fear, confusion and freedom of every person who'd met their end here. It thrummed through her body.

She felt Ben, felt his last seconds, knew his final thoughts, heard the squeak of rubber soles on metal; felt the tightening of the rope as it snapped taut…

And the bridge knew that here was someone who could take *its* pain away. Years of sadness had tainted its pale green lattice work. The paint had blistered and split to reveal blood red rust. The damage, not from the heat of the sun, but the pain of the overburdened metal which sagged a little more with each tragedy.

So, the metal crept onto Elsie's skin, sank into her flesh, solidified her finger bones, her hands turning shades of mint green and rust. Elsie's breathing was calm; her heartbeat steady for the first time since she'd first heard the terrible news.

And with each breath the bridge crept a little further up her arms, delicate hairs that had been ruffled in the early morning breeze forever frozen.

All the onlookers were local; one of them knew Elsie, knew her parents and ran as fast as he could to the nearest phone box.

By the time her parents arrived the metal had crept up to her shoulders. The Police, Ambulance and Fire Brigade were in attendance. All had frozen and were looking at her, unsure, scared even.

But as those who watched and wondered remained still, Archie Clarence, *Scarborough News*' Chief Reporter, arrived. He looked a little worse for wear, having been at a wedding reception in York the night before. He'd heard about Ben, someone at work had placed a phone call to him—he was the 'deathbridge' correspondent after all, but a family gathering was a family gathering. There were obligations to be met as a Clarence and so he'd stayed away. Now, he watched with the others as Elsie's Mum collapsed to the ground. Dad swore at his daughter, seemingly drunk, not seeing the way that she was, not seeing what she was *becoming*. Both were led away, and Clarence took his chance to approach her. The police allowed him to, unable to think of what else to do.

"Elsie, it's Archie. You know my daughter Lillias. You've been round a few times."

Elsie turned her head a few inches. It was a laboured movement; she looked to be in considerable pain. When she talked the noise that came from her sounded metallic; a hammer head pulling out a rusted nail from wood that will not give.

"I know you, Mr Clarence. And you'll help me?"

He didn't know how he could. The story to end all stories was there, right in front of him. He wouldn't just win prizes, accolades, notoriety. He'd have a ticket that would open any door he wished to go through. He'd be world famous. He'd be Archie *Fucking* Clarence.

He reached out instinctively, like his job taught him to console those in a bad way. His hand touched the nape of her neck, and he yelped as a bolt of electricity shot through him.

And he saw *his* son.

The vision of Caleb Clarence was older than his current fourteen years and he was standing on the bridge. He was smiling. He yelled "I hate you *all*!" before jumping and cracking his skull wide open on the road a second or two later.

Elsie looked at Clarence and said quietly, "I can stop this."

And Archie Clarence understood.

He understood that if word got out, it would be the end of Scarborough, the end of their part of the world. Or worse. Caleb might not be stopped.

Something was happening that he simply couldn't comprehend—this young girl was being eaten alive by the bridge that had seen her brother end his life.

"What do you need?" he asked.

"To be left alone. For a while."

And those were the last coherent words that Elsie uttered.

The residents of Scarborough became Elsie's bubble. No news escaped the centre of town. There was word put in the newspapers and broadcast on the local news that there would be major works around the Valley Bridge and that it would be a no-go area for at least a week.

No news escaped the town. All of the roads out were closed by the police. All boats were scuppered, with the bill going to a willing but scared Council which promised to pay after the embargo had passed.

Everybody in the town knew that something much bigger was going on, something important. They were happy to let it happen. They didn't know if Elsie was a sacrifice, a willing participant or if she had been struck by lightning.

At this point, all of Elsie was metal. Her eyelids blinked for the last time that morning, a slight flutter, like a dying butterfly's wings. A garbled sound, like steam being released from boiler room pipes came escaped from her.

Every inch that was flesh was flesh no more. But still she was alive, and more alive than she had ever been. She sensed the emotions of every person in Scarborough. When they were low, she felt their pain. And they would come to her. She was the centre of loss, and they would sit by her, this statue of grief and pay thanks to her sacrifice.

Her dad visited each day. Talked to her, shouted at her, even took a rock to her but not a mark was made. Elsie felt everything, not as pain, she had gone way beyond mere sensation of the flesh, but as infinite sorrow. There was no memory, just heat ebbing and flowing through her core every time he struck her.

The town slowly settled, and Elsie was regarded by visitors as a statue that happened to look out to sea. No one remarked on her features, so intricately carved—the way that the fabric of her dress was so expertly made that it looked like it hugged those small legs.

No one noticed the rust that utterly covered both hands but stopped at each wrist. Archie, members of the council and the Police made sure that the spot where Elsie stood was never troubled—that the bridge was repaired as soon as a problem was reported.

The suicides stopped and Valley Bridge saw no more pain.

That's not to say that people who wanted to end their life stopped travelling there. In fact, more people than before visited the town of Scarborough, a sort of pilgrimage to their "Suicide Sister". They would sit with her to cry or scream or despair. Then each one would touch her. Lay hands on her. A natural instinct. An incredible calm would wash over them as they became hardwired to Elsie. They felt the undeniable love that emanated from this figure of forever and beyond. They felt the very *soul* of the bridge and discovered the answers to every question and half question that they had. Every doubt they carried would be given a remedy. It stopped them. Elsie stopped them long enough to find strength to return home and find solace, friends and family. There would be conversation, recriminations, outbursts, tears and laughter.

But still, the suicides stopped. In Scarborough, the suicides stopped.

Elsie Tabster lives and loves for her brother.

Perhaps you've seen her.

ALSO AVAILABLE

"Where grow pines and firs amain,
Under Stars, sans heat or rain,
Chief of Hammand, 'ware thy Bane!"

So goes the ancient rhyme of the Hammands, a family hounded for centuries by a ferocious beast whose visitations wreak death and disorder. Now, in the wake of the First World War, siblings Oliver and Swanhild are the last of the Hammands, safe again at their ancestral home in the South Downs—until Oliver is beset by a creature in the pines by night. Desperate to dispel the curse, the siblings call on the occult detective Luna Bartendale to help unearth the dark origins of the Undying Monster and unshackle them from a savage doom.

First published in 1922, this cult novel is a heady brew of black magic lore, Norse mythology and weird mysteries spilling out of an eldritch 'fifth dimension'—complete with the first female occult detective to appear in an English novel, the 'White Witch' Luna Bartendale.

ALSO AVAILABLE

A headless coachman drives his carriage of lost souls towards a violent fate. A mother's obsession with eugenics spirals into a cruel madness. An adulterous pair are plagued by the suspicion that their dog means to expose their darkest secrets.

In 1911, Violet Hunt published her groundbreaking collection of short stories entitled *Tales of the Uneasy*, which explored a world of psychological and ghostly hauntings, shot through with high tragedy and strange horror. Over time, Hunt's reputation as a literary hostess obscured her important contribution to British weird fiction, and now her uncanny collection—recognised by R. S. Hadji as one of his thirteen "neglected masterpieces of the macabre"—is long overdue its rightful place among the great weird works of the Edwardian era.

At times utterly chilling, startlingly bleak and darkly comic, this new edition also includes Hunt's rare and revised novella version of the beguiling title story, 'The Tiger Skin'.

For more Tales of the Weird titles
visit the British Library Shop (shop.bl.uk)

We welcome any suggestions, corrections or feedback you may have, and will aim to respond to all items addressed to the following:

The Editor (Tales of the Weird), British Library Publishing,
The British Library, 96 Euston Road, London NW1 2DB

We also welcome enquiries through our social media accounts, @BL_Publishing.